A BLESSING OF UNICORNS

David Perks has asserted his rights to be identified as the author of this work under the Copyright, Designs and Patent Act, 1988. All rights reserved.

To those I taught and those who taught me.

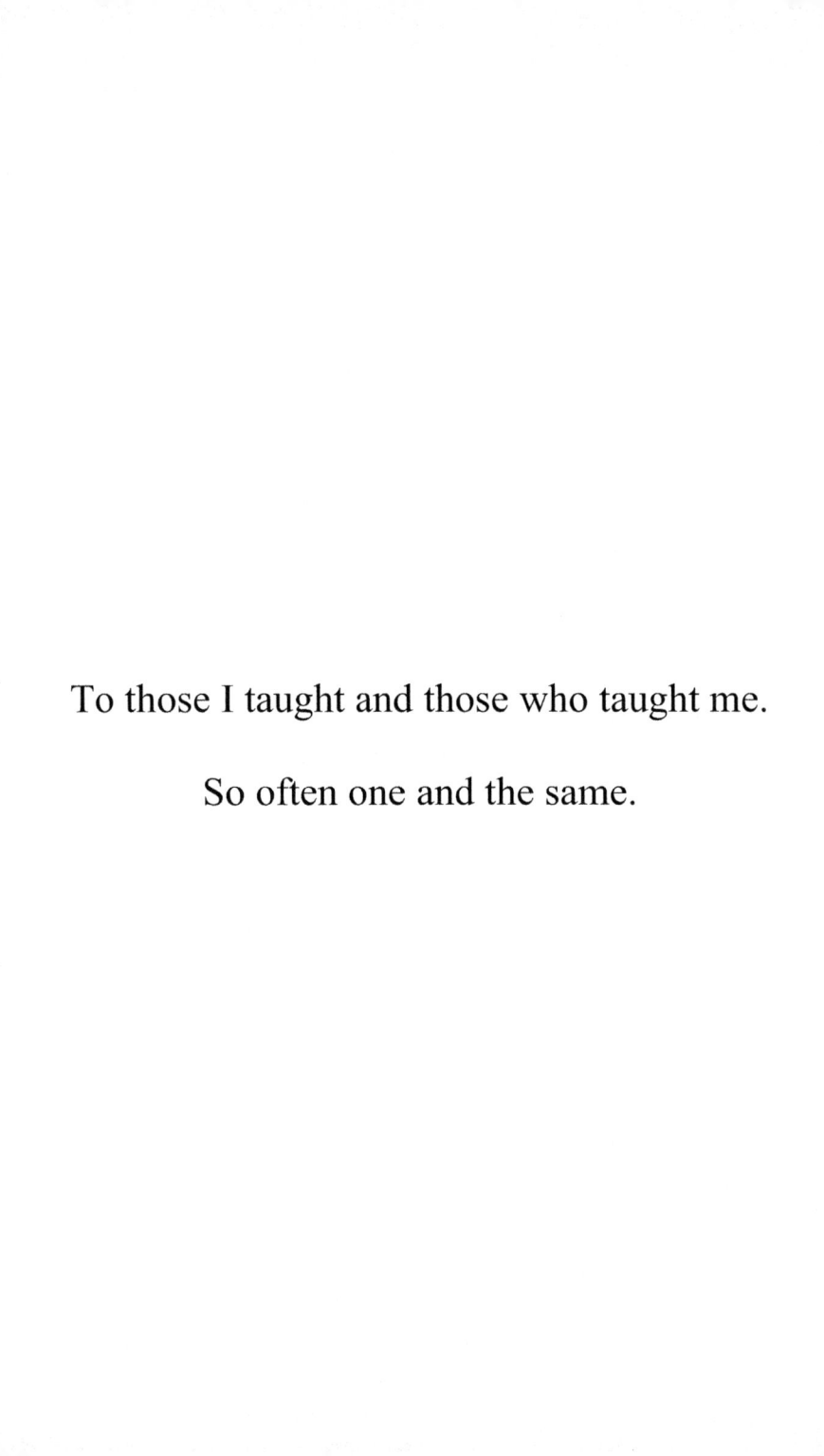

So often one and the same.

CHAPTER 1

AUGUST 2016

This was just so wrong. How on earth had he ever thought that he could do this? If this were a film or a novel, he would be tall, handsome with a wide range of physical and intellectual abilities. He was none of these things. He was an ordinary bloke who was now feeling what most ordinary blokes would feel in this situation – absolutely petrified. When he first had this idea, this moment seemed so far off as to cause him only minor concern. He had been waiting for this moment for nearly seven years. Perhaps, if he were being honest, never believing it would ever happen but now he just had to accept that the time had come at last. Could he really dare to think it was going to work?

    He lowered the window of the van as if to enable him to savour this moment with all his senses. As the early summer warm air entered the van, he inhaled the smells of the countryside that evoked memories of climbing trees and building dens long into the evenings of his childhood, growing up in his South Wales village. The seemingly plaintive hoot of a solitary owl, waiting in hope of a reply that did not come, broke the silence. He put his hand out of the window in what he knew was a ridiculous attempt to feel the tension that seemed too palpable not to actually exist in some physical form. In trying to complete the analogy, it would be stupid he knew, to believe that he could taste the fear that seemed to be continually sending him the message that all of this was a huge mistake and that he was embarking on a process that was way beyond his abilities. But if fear had a taste then this was surely it.

    He had waited with what seemed like an untreatable ache for this day. A day he thought would never come. His life had been ruined once and came very close to being finished completely. Even now, he knew that the chances of success were slim but despite the odds, this was a promise he was determined to keep, whatever the personal cost to himself. Even if that cost was his own life, because the people he had made the promise to had meant more to him than life itself.

As he looked through his night vision binoculars, out of the back window of the van in which he was hidden, he could clearly see that thirty metres from where he was sitting, was a fifteen year old girl. She was standing on the flatbed of a lorry, parked with its rear almost touching a twelve foot brick wall that encircled the mansion and extensive grounds owned by one of the top criminal families in the UK. The girl Galizia, who had been born in Lithuania, was standing motionless against the cab of the truck, steadying herself at the beginning of her shortened run-up, before she would launch the especially modified javelin 35 metres, at exactly the optimum angle to hit the designated target she couldn't see. Just as she had practised under the demanding eye of her PE teacher Miss Harrison, every day for the last month. It didn't matter that she couldn't see the target. She had been positioned in exactly the correct place for a throw that would be guided by muscle memory, so often had she been through this process.

Miss Harrison, who was standing down on the ground, more for reassurance than feeling she could offer any more in the way of coaching advice at this late stage, counted down as the clock approached 2.00am, tapped the bed of the truck and having ensured she had Galizia's attention, simply nodded. Galizia needed no second urging. She lived for any competitive situation where she could prove yet again to herself, something she once would never have believed, that she was a good as anyone and should never accept second best. But this occasion was doubly important as far as she was concerned, as it was an opportunity to pay back these people who had done so much to give her that self belief and stability in her life today, compared to the lost little soul she had been five years ago.

Gripping the javelin in the fingers and palm of her right hand and supporting it just above her head, with the forearm almost touching her ear, Galizia started to jog and then build up pace until she was sprinting towards the end of the lorry. Just before the end she pulled her arm back behind her, turned to the side, took two crossover steps before slamming down her left foot, over which she pivoted to bring her arm through and hurl the matt black, camouflaged javelin into space towards its intended target. While she over rotated off the back of the truck to land safely on the gymnastic crash mat, being held for just that purpose by four men clothed head to toe in black, the javelin left her hand and hurtled through the gap between the top of the wall and the lowest branch of the tree on this side of the wall, to climb into the air before dropping on exactly the parabola that had been calculated would be needed, before diving towards the target which it hit perfectly with a satisfying thunk. Only after having heard the contact, did a grinning Galizia allow Miss Harrison to push a motorcycle helmet down over her head, as she climbed onto the back of the motorcycle that her teacher was already astride and be taken off back to school, having completed her part of the operation, the further details of which she had absolutely no idea. The van driver's realisation that there was now no turning back, gave him cause to think back to when all this had begun. What seemed like a lifetime ago.

CHAPTER 2

SATURDAY 14^(TH) FEBRUARY 2009

At 49 Greenfield Avenue, it had become part of their ritual, whenever the girls went shopping with their mother, that their father Rob Price, would help them get ready, while always asking them the same two questions. What present would they bring him back? To which they would reply 'nothing' and he would look deeply hurt but knowing full well they would return with a packet of Jelly Babies, seemingly to his delighted surprise. They would then spend the evening sneakily taking the jelly babies without him apparently noticing, until he would suddenly act as if he were upset and angry much to their real amusement. The other question was which numbers they would give mummy when she bought that weeks Euro lottery ticket and what would we buy if we won. The reply was always the same. 'The birthdays of themselves and their mum and a castle with two unicorns, one for each of them'. Today however, was also Valentine's Day and he knew that their giggling and sly looks meant that he would be receiving something extra when they returned. Invariably, something that they would also really enjoy sharing.

"What is this castle going to look like then?"

"It will be really, really big with towers and up and down bits on the walls and dungeons where we can put people who are naughty." His eldest daughter Holly was always very clear about what she wanted.

"The 'up and down bits' are called crenellations. And Penny what will the Unicorns be like?" he asked his youngest daughter by eighteen months.

"Mine will be white and Holly's will be silver and they will have curly horns and big wings"

"Some unicorns can't fly you know."

"Well ours will and Holly and me will fly around the castle whenever we want to." Rob chastised himself on the absurdity of trying to debate with his daughter about whether Unicorns could fly or not and as he helped his two daughters on with their coats, the doorbell rang and Holly, who felt as a seven year old that it was her duty and right as the oldest of his two daughters, rushed to answer it. It helped that she knew who was likely to be on the other side of the door and what that person would be likely to have for her and her younger sister Penny. It didn't matter that while she could reach the handle, she was still too short to reach the door lock and that it would be her father who actually opened the door to Matt, his closest friend since they had met on their first day at teacher training college almost twenty years ago. A Cornishman, with a wide grin and in his hand, the object that had elicited the excitement of his arrival from Holly and Penny and their rush to hug him.

"Matt, we spend all week persuading the girls to eat healthily, and then you turn up and ruin it all with packets of Haribo."

"If I can't spoil my favourite nieces it's a pretty poor show," came the usual reply, in an accent that still strongly reflected his South-West origins.

"Thankfully they are not your real nieces as I would fear for their future if they were related to you by blood," Rob retorted quickly, getting into the rhythm of 'put down' and counter that had been their way since that first evening together in the college bar, after which they had become almost inseparable.

They both knew this would continue for the afternoon they would share together, in what had become an annual custom. Every year since they had stopped sharing a house together, when they had both got married ten years ago, they had watched the Wales versus England Six nations rugby encounter together, alternating between whoever's house represented the home fixture. This year the match was to be played in Cardiff and so the Newport born Rob was hosting. But before that could happen, the disruptive whirlwinds that were Holly and Penny had to be removed and as if on cue, a more mature whirlwind appeared from upstairs, greeting and hugging Matt while at the same time sorting out the girls' clothes that Rob had singularly failed to assemble correctly.

Carol was the reason why Rob had got married and given up the life of a bachelor. He thanked his lucky stars and contemplated nearly every day that, not only was she way out of his league, as far as looks and intelligence were concerned but she was also one of the most caring people he had ever met and in terms of their outlook on life, and more importantly how they wanted their children to turn out, they were soul mates, who shared many interests, one of which however, was most definitely not sport. So while Saturday morning was usually the time for taking the girls shopping and the afternoon normally a time when they did things as a family, Carol was more than happy to take the girls out, to leave Rob in the warm embrace of Wales getting one over on England. Of course, if that was not the outcome, then better for the girls not to be present to see their father distraught at the result of some silly sports match. On the other hand, Matt's presence would guarantee that if the result was not in Wales favour, the unmerciful ribbing Rob would receive would ensure that when she and the girls returned it would serve as a welcome release and he would be more delighted than usual to see them.

"I hope you have arranged something special for Ronnie tonight, or didn't you even remember it was Valentines Day?" Carol asked Matt about his wife, who was also Carol's best friend, as she sorted the girls out.

"Actually, we will be going to Cini's for a romantic Italian meal and she has already received the customary card and flowers, which I would have been stupid to forget if I wanted to guarantee being allowed to watch the match this afternoon. Actually, not a lot of people know this but Valentines Day is the second most popular time for sending cards, the first being Christmas."

So used to having to listen to Matt spouting obscure facts, she had no problem ignoring his latest offering and simply warned him, "You will go easy on him if Wales lose won't you?"

"Actually, not a lot of people know this but Wales have won every match against England in the last year of the decade since 1939. But this year it will be different." Carol managed to only partially mute the groan that was normally the response to Matt's penchant for coming out with facts à la Michael Caine, before grabbing her car keys and ushering the girls towards the car as she kissed Rob on the cheek and wished him luck.

Both men waved the car out of the drive and sat in front of the TV, ready to shout down the inane observations of the studio experts, before the game started, fortified with nibbles and cold bottles of beer for the ritual they observed year after year. Carol had never been able to understand why Rob could believe that his incoherent rants at the telly, would actually affect the result but as she and the girls drove away, she smiled and wallowed in the warm feeling she always felt when she recognised how lucky she was to be married to him.

Having parked the car in the municipal car park on the edge of Blaby, their nearest shopping centre, Carol had managed to persuade the girls to suffer the tediousness of some shopping for basic necessities, with the promise of cakes and milkshakes at their favourite café. Having completed the shopping, they were all three laughing and in high spirits as they waited for the light to change to green for them to cross the road, at which point the girls, with café in sight on the other side of the road, began skipping across in anticipation while dragging their mum with them as they both held one of her hands. As they neared the centre of the road there was a squeal of tyres and Carol became aware of a black 4 x 4 rounding the corner and, totally ignoring the red traffic light, ploughed into the only three people on the zebra crossing. Having made contact with the Price family, the car came to a sudden halt but after just a few seconds the car then accelerated through and over the bodies that barred their way on the road.

Where seconds ago there had been the usual hubbub of noise and activity of a Saturday afternoon, there was now an eerie silence and calm, until a few of the shocked and horrified onlookers saw what remained of the horrendous collision and began to wail and scream, while others ran to help the three bodies lying lifeless in the road.

With fifteen minutes of the match remaining, both Rob and Matt were literally on the edge of their seats, as they both willed the score at the top left hand corner of the screen to show in their favour at the end. A close and tense game had seen their earlier bragging 'put downs' replaced by back pedalling of respectful but grudging praise for their opponents, as a precursor to any potential embarrassment and a year of ribbing a loss would bring. Just as Wales were pressing the English tryline there was a ring at the doorbell. "Who on earth can that be?" they both seemed to shout together.

"You go Matt as we are more likely to score here."

"Oh great, some host you are," replied Matt, secretly concerned that Rob could be right, as he moved from the sofa towards the door, all the while turning his head to see the screen. As Wales had drive after drive repelled, Rob was oblivious to the murmurings coming from the front door until Matt walked back into the room with an imposing, dark haired man, dressed in an expensive looking blue suit, pink striped shirt and contrasting tie which was exposed by the similarly blue coloured, open rain coat he was wearing, presenting an image one would expect from a high end car salesman. He was followed in by a petite, short haired female, dressed more subtly in a dark suit and white blouse and with the intelligent eyes of someone who was new to her job but determined to do it well. All this was lost on Rob, who hadn't looked up or even noticed their presence as they entered the room but simply said to Matt, "Typical bloody English, killing the game to stop us winning."

When he didn't receive the expected reply and put down, Rob looked up with a knowing smile on his face, which turned to surprise to see two people he didn't know. But even stranger and more concerning, was to see the look on his best friend's face. It was a look he had never seen before and failed to decipher, as he looked again at the two visitors and asked Matt who they were. "Would you mind just turning off the TV a minute Mr. Price?" The tall man asked as Matt seemed frozen in thought and deed. On the verge of demanding why on earth he should do such a thing in his own house, Rob suddenly realised from their demeanour and Matt's metamorphosis into someone totally alien to everything he knew of him, that something was wrong.

The icy snake of dread started slithering down his spine and as Rob reached for the remote, Matt motioned for the two visitors to sit down and in a voice unrecognisable to any sound he had made previously that day, he managed to say, "Rob, these people are police officers and…….." Before he could say any more Rob had stood up. "Oh my God, this must mean there has been an accident. Don't waste any more time, you can explain to me on the way to the hospital, I'll just grab my…."

"Mr Price would you just sit down a minute please, there is something we need to tell you?" On the verge of telling the woman police officer he didn't want to waste any more time, Rob recognised something in her tone of voice that stopped him in his tracks and he slowly sank back down into his seat, needing, but not wanting to hear what these harbingers of potential doom might have to say. At the same time, he was frantically scrabbling around in his brain for the facts he could give them that would prove that whatever it was they were about to tell him had to be a mistake.

"Mr Price, I am Detective Chief Inspector Damian Grey and this is my colleague, Detective Sergeant Bright. There is no easy way to say this but approximately forty-five minutes ago, your wife and two children were fatally injured in a hit and run incident on the Lutterworth Road in Blaby." As his life was falling apart with every word the man uttered, he just wanted him to shut up but at the same time was also trying to find the flaw in what he was saying to prove they had made a mistake. But deep down he knew that the very worst of things had happened and the initial numbness brought on by this terrible news began to be replaced by an ache that he felt spreading through him and he emitted a loud, keening wail, before breaking down onto the sofa with a heart-rending sob.

Matt, who himself had been seemingly frozen in time, after hearing the words repeated for the second time, after opening the door to the two detectives and receiving the gut wrenching news on the doorstep, dropped onto the sofa next to his friend and hugged him close and tight, until the sobbing relented to a pitiful whimper. It suddenly occurred to Matt, that you wouldn't normally have a Detective Chief Inspector be the one to come and deliver news of a road traffic accident fatality and turning to DCI Grey, asked him about just that.

Although both of the detectives had been carefully observing the reactions of both men from the moment the door was opened, Detective Grey decided that now was the beginning of the formal process for which he was employed. He gave a slight nod to his colleague, who took out a notebook and pen, as he explained to Rob and Matt that the reason they were the bearers of such terrible news as opposed to the usual constable, was because Carol, Holly and Penny had been killed by people as yet unknown, who were in the process of driving away from a bank robbery and so as well as the hit and run aspect of the accident, their deaths would be part of a criminal investigation and maybe even a murder inquiry.

Rob gradually began to compute the information he had just been given, that above and beyond the huge loss he had suffered, it could unbelievably be even worse and in a voice still affected by grief but with added incredulity, turned to the two detectives, "You mean they could have been killed deliberately?"

"You have to understand Mr. Price, that we are right at the beginning of our investigation and as yet we know very little. However, even if the collision was not premeditated, the total lack of concern for human life in ensuring their escape, would result in a manslaughter charge at the very least".

While he knew that he would never feel normal again, Rob tried to push away the dull ache that seemed to consume him and gain some control. "I need to see my three girls," came out as a cry for help, as much as a demand.

"Of course we will arrange that as soon as possible Mr. Price but they are presently being transported to the morgue and as soon as they are in a place where their dignity in death can be guaranteed, we would like to ask you a few questions if that is alright with you, to enable us to help catch whoever did this to your wife and children. Matt stood up and facing the police officers suggested, "Surely this can wait for another day? You can see how distraught he is officers."

"I fully appreciate how difficult this is Mr Carter but it is best if we can sort this out quickly, while events are still fresh and when we have finished here, it should then be OK for us to take Mr. Price to see the bodies and make a formal identification." Matt reluctantly accepted the logic and offered to make everyone a drink but nobody was interested.

For the next forty five minutes Rob, with the support of Matt, was asked all about how the day had been from the moment they had got up that morning, until his family had left the house. Carefully hidden amongst these questions, were other questions aimed at surreptitiously finding out about the relationships in the house and whether or not Rob could have had any hand in what had happened in Blaby, or whether he could think of any reason why someone might wish to harm his wife, perhaps as a means of getting at him.

When the two detectives felt that they had all they needed for now, they suggested to Rob that he should spend a few minutes getting himself ready to accompany them to identify the bodies and perhaps arrange for someone to stay with him that night, or for somewhere to go where he would not be on his own. Matt said that he would ring his wife and they would arrange all that needed to be done to ensure Rob was not alone. DCI Grey said they would wait in their car until Rob and Matt were ready.

As the two detectives walked to their car, DS Bright asked her boss what he thought. "Well I think everything seems as it should be but when we get back to the station you can escort Mr Price and Mr Carter to the morgue, as I'm no good at the compassionate stuff, while I start the process of looking into the financial and relationship situation in the Price family." The Detective Sergeant was used to being given the unpleasant jobs by her boss but she was forced to wonder if she had been a man, whether it would still be assumed that the junior should be the one carrying out this task.

Back in the house while Rob wandered about in a haze of loss and shock, Matt had the horrible task of explaining to his wife Veronica, what had happened. Feeling caught between the impossible situation of wanting to be with her, to be able to comfort her after she received the news of the loss of her closest friend and godchildren, and the need to support Rob, who seemed to be falling apart by the minute. It was fortunate that, while obviously devastated by the news, Ronnie, as she was known to those closest to her, was no shrinking violet and after the initial shock and the reaction of just wanting to curl up and cry for the rest of the day, she did what she always did when needed and took control of everything that would make life slightly more bearable for Rob. Knowing that they would share their moment of deep mourning together later, Matt once again thanked his lucky stars that he had Ronnie as his lifelong partner, told her he loved her, then began the process of getting Rob ready to go through something that no-one should ever have to experience.

In the car nobody spoke and at the mortuary it was simply to explain the procedures they were about to go through, that DI Bright addressed Rob, before leading him into a room with a large window strategically placed, so that the bodies could be observed. Rob knew it was illogical, wishful thinking, to believe that a mistake had been made and that in a few hours time some other poor so and so would be standing here, identifying who these bodies really were. Nonetheless, he felt no guilt in wishing this to be the case. When the covering sheets were pulled back to disclose the three people he had loved most in the world and for whom he would gladly have given his own life to reverse this situation, there was no longer any doubt and he simply nodded. "Mr Price I am so sorry but we do need you to verbally acknowledge that these are the bodies of your wife and two daughters," DS Bright said apologetically. To which Rob managed to mutter a resigned, "Yes," before crumpling to the floor, where he pulled up his knees and sobbed silently into his legs.

Having had the window blinds lowered to hide the three bodies behind the window but knowing that the vision of what he had just seen would remain with Rob for the rest of his life, DS Bright called Matt in to enable him to offer the support and comfort that would never be adequate enough for what Rob was feeling but which would at least provide him with the solace of knowing he wouldn't have to go through this alone.

She explained to Matt, as Rob was obviously in no fit state to take anything in, that a car would take them home but that she would be in regular contact to keep them updated on how the case was progressing and to check how Rob was getting on. She also gave him her card should he feel the need to contact her urgently. Matt gently took Rob by the arm and guided him along the route to the car, following the DS. Rob simply allowed himself be led, with his mind a lifetime away from where he actually was and as they drove away from the mortuary, he took one last look back and wept quietly, as he thought of his three girls lying there alone.

CHAPTER 3

DS Bright arrived back at the station, where DCI Grey called his team together to gather in the incident room, all of them with the knowledge that this would be the start of something that made the normal humdrum nature of the job so exciting and worthwhile and yet always at the expense of some innocent person's happiness.

"OK, what have we got?" Grey's purposeful look had already silenced the general hubbub of exchanged thoughts. DS Bright stood and walked to the front at the beginning of a well practised routine, which would hopefully end with somebody being charged and convicted. But all of those sitting there knew that this was going to be a long and arduous process that would bring more frustration before any hopeful success.

"At two thirty this afternoon, three armed assailants carried out an armed robbery on the Santander Building Society in Blaby. Having grabbed the contents of the safe they had forced the tellers to open, they jumped into a black 4x4 driven by a fourth individual, which then took off down Blaby High Street before turning onto the Lutterworth Road towards Leicester, where a female adult and her two daughters were crossing legally at the lights.

Eyewitnesses report that the 4x4 turned the corner and accelerated across the pedestrian crossing against the lights, where the vehicle ploughed into the three females. The car carried on out of town before it was lost on the town's CCTV cameras and did not appear on any of the cameras on the main roads out of town, implying that the getaway vehicle was exchanged somewhere in the area not covered by cameras. A search is presently on for that car and we are also trawling through all outgoing cameras, to see if we can pick up the car they changed to."

"OK, where are we with witnesses?" the DCI asked unnecessarily, as Bright sat down and made way at the front for her colleague Sandy Wilson, as if in a well choreographed routine.

"This is where we have fallen lucky boss, because despite the professionalism of the actual theft, the getaway was an 'amateur's day trip', firstly, because as the robbers were leaving the premises in a calm and unhurried manner, the getaway driver was loudly revving the engine and then further bringing attention to themselves with squealing tyres cornering into the main street. Add to that the horrendous collision with the Price family, which meant that everyone in the vicinity was staring at the car and its occupants. Their witness statements have been taken and are being cross-checked this very minute with the statements taken from people at the bank. The early suggestion seems to be that this was a professional job, but for some reason with a less-than-competent getaway driver."

"Ok what do we know about the Prices?" Grey asked the room.

DC Tony Grant, a newcomer to the team, rather nervously stood up, "Well we have a bit more to do in terms of looking at their finances but initial research suggests nothing untoward there, with in and outgoings commensurate with a teacher and a non-working mum. Neighbours all agree that they are a happy, loving family who are not only friendly but community spirited and the girls apparently were a real delight and it seems that they will be sorely missed."

"Ok, but let's not jump to conclusions. People aren't always the same as the image they like to project, so let's keep an open mind and complete those checks. As a matter of urgency, we need to find that car and see if there is any forensics from the robbery itself."

The noise of the incident room door being thrown back, as a uniformed officer burst in looking embarrassed but excited all at the same time, stopped DCI Grey in mid sentence. The DCI glared at the object of the interruption, who, nevertheless had the confidence to apologise for the disturbance but continued to say that he had information that the DCI would want to receive immediately.

"Go ahead officer," was Grey's impatient response, "but this had better be good."

"Sir, we have had a number of reports of a helicopter taking off from the vicinity of a sports field near Lutterworth on the edge of town. A response car has been to have a look and they have found the 4X4 presumed to have been involved in today's major incident."

"Thank you officer, you have my forgiveness and just about avoided my boot on your backside for your noisy entrance." The uniformed officer left the room feeling relieved but wondered if it was a pre-requisite of being a detective that you had to also be a pratt.

"This could be the break we need. Johnny, take Naz and get down there to ensure everything is done by the book."

"Boss, could this mean that if the helicopter is related to this incident, then we can immediately narrow down the line of enquiry, because there are only a small number of firms capable of utilising, let alone having the audacity to think of using that level of sophisticated transport? In fact, if they are from this neck of the woods I can think of only one." Bright's comment had all the officers in the room nodding and while nobody said it, if speech bubbles had suddenly appeared above their heads to show what they were thinking, they would all have said the same thing, 'the Duncan family'.

"Let's not get ahead of ourselves DS Bright. When you have done this job as long as I have, you learn not to jump to conclusions. We can't go blaming every crime in the area on the Duncans and let us just remember that they have never actually been found guilty of being a "firm" as you so dramatically put it. I don't want us to take our eye off the ball with Mr. Price. Is he having an affair? Has he got money problems and needs the life insurance? There are all sorts of things that need clearing up until we cross him off our list of suspects."

"No boss, of course you are right," Bright replied, quietly seething at yet another attempted put-down from her boss. But she knew that the others in the room felt the same as her and she couldn't understand why he was still so insistent on looking at Rob Price as the guilty party.

CHAPTER 4

Having returned to No. 49, Rob had gone through the mutual sympathising with Matt's wife Ronnie, who had been Carol's best friend since they had met fifteen years previously, as the partners of Rob and Matt, on what in those days was called a 'double date'. While she was struggling to come to terms with the news of the death of her best friend and her two gorgeous Godchildren, Holly and Penny, Ronnie had recognised that this was no time for her to be the focus. She had tried to start the process of getting Rob to try and not think about the pain and fear his girls would have suffered in their last moments but unsurprisingly with little progress. Now he was slumped in a chair, staring at the blank screen of the TV with a whisky in his hand and refusing to eat, much against the wishes of his friends. He did however, agree to them making the phone calls to those people who would need to know what had happened, before them having the shock of reading it in the papers. Despite their protestations, this also included Carol's parents and sister, Joanna. Ronnie and Matt felt Carol's family would be better off receiving this horrendous news from Rob himself but he begged them not to put him through the pain of that, on top of what he was already feeling.

So it was that Ronnie and Matt spent the next hour making the calls that no one ever wanted to make, simply because they felt that Rob's state of mind would in fact increase the torture of the message to be imparted. The responses to each of the phone calls was as they would have expected but they managed to persuade Carol's parents that it would be better to leave it until tomorrow before coming to comfort their son-in-law, so that they could go through their own grieving process before having to help the man who they saw more as an actual son, than simply the husband of their daughter.

Carol's sister was travelling in India and so Ronnie, who had made the initial call, was at least spared that phone call but pitied the parents who would have to tell Joanna about her sister and nieces. Eventually, feeling unable to continue with the heart-wrenching task they had been given, Matt and Ronnie persuaded a few of their closest friends to spread the terrible news and were in the process of discussing what they could do next to best help him, when the silence of the house was disturbed by a ring at the doorbell. Ronnie rushed to answer it before the visitor rang again and further disturbed the peace that Rob craved. At the door was a delivery man, who explained the purpose of his visit before leaving Ronnie with the small parcel he had brought to the house. Uncertain of the best course of action, she went into the lounge where Rob asked her if it had been the police at the door with more news.

"No Rob it wasn't. It was a special delivery from Shirelings, the jewellers. Apparently Carol and the girls had been in there today to pick up a gift meant for you but because they had made a mistake with the engraving they had promised Carol they would correct it then bring it round. She held out a small gift-wrapped parcel to Rob, who stood and grabbed it in a futile attempt to have some connection to his loved ones.

There was a gift card attached which read,

'To the best Husband and Daddy in the world. Something for you to remember us by, whenever we are apart and as a token of our love on Valentine's day.
With all our love, Mummy and her Unicorns.'

"Rob, I'm so sorry this has happened now. Carol told me that this was meant to be ready yesterday but because of their engraving error, the jewellers had promised it would be ready today but it looks like it wasn't ready when Carol and the girls went to pick it up." Ronnie explained.

Rob hadn't believed his grief could get any worse but looking at Carol's writing on the gift card created a feeling of utter loss that caused him to collapse into his seat. Matt and Ronnie did all they could to comfort Rob over the next couple of hours, knowing all the time that they were failing miserably. It was a guilty relief to them therefore when, despite their desire to support their friend, Rob explained that much as he loved them and would need them in the future, he needed to be on his own at this particular moment. At last he managed to persuade Ronnie and Matt to leave him, so that he could try and compute all that had happened and how he was going to deal with it. Much against their better judgement but also realising that they also needed to have some space to grieve, if they were going to be of any use to Rob over the next few months, his two close friends agreed to leave on the basis that he would ring them at any time during the night should he need them and that they would be back the following morning.

Shutting the door on his reluctant departees, Rob leant his forehead against the door and came to the same conclusion that he had already reached on first hearing of what had happened to his family. There was absolutely no way he could ever deal with this. Returning to his seat in the lounge, he looked again at the gift that had been delivered but could not bring himself to open it. Placing the gift unopened on the floor at the side of his chair, he topped up his whisky and agonised over not just what he would do over the next few weeks but from minute to minute. In his few lucid moments over the next couple of hours, he decided that there was no point in carrying on without the three people who had made his life whole. He would get through the funerals somehow and then he knew he would have nothing to live for. With the last of the whisky finished, Rob fell into a deep but fitful sleep and only woke when the doorbell brought him back from the comfort of partial oblivion, to the reality he had hoped did not exist; that it was the morning after the day his wife and children had died.

    A throbbing headache and the aches of sleeping in an armchair made the journey to the door uncomfortable and he greeted the concerned faces of Ronnie and Matt with little enthusiasm. They were both carrying bags, which were deposited in the kitchen and while Matt started to make some breakfast, Ronnie persuaded Rob he needed to shower and get himself in some sort of condition to deal with what was going to be, the first of many long days. Offering little in the way of a response, Rob moved reluctantly to do as bidden. While he was upstairs, Ronnie and Matt shared their concerns about the state of their friend but had to admit they had no experience of anyone they knew having to cope with something quite so traumatic and agreed that they would have to tread carefully, while at the same time concealing their own pain.

    On his return, Matt and Ronnie noticed that, while he had indeed showered, Rob had not bothered to shave or change his clothes. When Ronnie suggested that he should perhaps open the gift that Carol and the girls had bought for him, he was horrified and told her to put it away, so he wasn't reminded of happier times. Not wanting to antagonise what was already a tense situation, Ronnie placed the gift on the mantelpiece, then Matt sat Rob down to what would be, in normal circumstances, a much anticipated feast of a full English, croissants, orange juice and coffee. He played with, as much as ate, part of a croissant, then took his glass of orange juice back to the chair he had seemingly taken up residence in and poured the whisky remaining in his glass from the night before, into the orange and drank it back in one. Matt started to remonstrate but the look he received from Rob sent a message that made him change tack and try to get him to give some thought to how they were going to navigate their way through the immediate future and more importantly what he wanted to do about the funerals.

"I can't think about anything right now, let alone how I am going to be strong enough to say the final goodbye to my family. I really appreciate what you are trying to do but I would much prefer to be left on my own for a while."

Realising that this was not the time to try and have a logical debate, Matt and Ronnie agreed to go but not before getting Rob to promise them that he would not drink any more whisky and he would eat. They would phone-check him tonight but then tomorrow they would be over to start planning what needed to be done. Rob readily agreed, if only to get them to leave him alone and as they opened the door to leave, there was the sound and flashes of cameras, while microphones and recording devices were shoved in front of their faces.

"Rob, go in and shut the door and I will deal with this." An appalled Matt pushed Rob back inside and as the door was closing, there was a confusion of shouting, amongst which, just as the door clicked shut, Rob heard someone shout, "Mr Price do you think the people who did this should be charged with murder?"

Matt and Ronnie pushed the first few reporters back and reminded them all that they were trespassing and that Matt would be ringing the police. As they retreated, Matt rang the number on the card given to him by DS Bright. She answered on the third ring and after he had explained the situation, she promised to have someone come and keep people away until the interest died down. Seeing that Rob had drawn the downstairs curtains and that the press had in fact respected their demand to get off the property, Matt and Ronnie ran the gauntlet of questions about who they were without reply, all the way to their car, where they sat and waited, until a police car pulled up outside the house and they felt it was safe to drive away.

Back at Leicestershire police head quarters in Enderby, witness statements forensics and trawling of CCTV, were beginning to provide a picture of what had occurred, if not of exactly who did it. However, that was becoming slightly clearer also.

"Johnny, bring us up to date with where you've got to, looking into the Prices."

DC Johnny Hutchinson stood, as all eyes turned to face him. "Well Rob Price was born and brought up in South Wales near Newport. He was an only child but both his parents passed away three years apart when he was in his twenties. Before that, he went to Birmingham University where he studied Sports Science and then stayed on to gain a teacher training qualification. This is also where he met his wife to be,

Carol Williams and also Mr and Mrs Carter, who all became inseparable friends apparently and have remained so ever since. Mr Carter also trained as a teacher of maths and both Mr. Price and Mr. Carter got themselves jobs in Leicester and are now both Heads of their respective departments. Mrs. Price used her degree in English to get a job in recruitment but had not returned to work after the birth of the two daughters Holly and Penelope, while Mrs Carter is a solicitor specialising in banking and corporate finance. Mr. and Mrs Carter do not have children but are Godparents to the Price girls. All the colleagues and friends I have spoken to, have only nice things to say about all four of them and financial records confirm that they are squeaky clean."

"Perhaps too good to be true?" suggested the DCI.

" Well sir, I think because we tend to deal with the problems of society every day we sometimes lose sight of the fact that the vast majority of people are just good and once you ladle off the scum at the top, you find that people like the Prices are more the norm than not."

"Thank you for your expert insight into human behaviour Johnny, but I think that I have managed to gain a more realistic grasp of human nature in my time getting to my rank. You just do the legwork and I will take care of the thinking from now on if you don't mind. Keep looking."

DS Bright was not the only one in the room to mind, not just on behalf of Johnny but for themselves also, as Grey was basically suggesting that he was really the only one in the room capable of solving any case. None of them were stupid enough to voice their thoughts to their boss however. They all believed separately and unanimously, that none of this had anything to do with Mr. Price, unless he happened to be a very poorly rewarded Mr. Big, who had overseen the robbery and therefore the resultant collision. This was looking more and more like a fatal hit and run, carried out in the wake of the getaway from the robbery of the Building society in Blaby.

Having the likely robbers narrowed down to just a few potential candidates, based on the sophistication of the robbery and the use of a helicopter in the getaway, should have helped greatly but the person leading the investigation seemed intent on making their job more difficult than it already was. While witnesses at the bank were unable to give full descriptions, on account of the fact that the robbers wore masks, the bodily descriptions, along with CCTV, helped filter likely candidates further. Also, while anyone sat in the back of the 4x4 could not be seen because of tinted windows, the two people sat in the front had been picked out from photos shown to them by the police. Interestingly, the person in the passenger seat of the car was picked out as Peter Fitzpatrick, the most senior of the lieutenants in one of the country's leading crime families, the Duncans, who had already served time in prison for armed robbery some years back.

Perhaps more interesting was the driver of the car, who was picked out as Bradley Duncan, the youngest of the Duncan clan and who, to the best knowledge of the police, had only before been involved in petty juvenile trouble but never suspected of having been involved in any serious crime until now.

"This might," suggested DS Bright, "account for the 'amateur hour' mistakes that plagued the getaway."

DCI Grey looked at DS Bright as if he were trying to cover up his annoyance when he announced, "Well that obviously puts a different slant on things and while I still want you to keep all options on the table, we need to start taking a serious look into whether the Duncan family had any involvement in this business."

CHAPTER 5

Not long after Matt and Ronnie had left, Rob answered a phone call from Carol's parents, telling him that Matt had rung them to warn them about the media scrum and they were outside in the car and were about to come to the door but didn't want him to think it was the media. Rob loved Carol's parents and had always got on well with them, especially so after the deaths of his own parents but he didn't know if he could dredge up the required compassion they deserved from him, while he was wallowing in his own grief. When the doorbell rang, he was ready to let them in, while staying behind the door to avoid the cameras of the waiting press.

The next few minutes were spent in wordless hugs and tears until his father-in-law Jonathan, lacking the words of comfort he thought he should be able to offer, found his answer in the practicality of offering to make them all tea. The mutual expressions of sadness and provision of solace, filled their conversation for the next hour, along with the frustration of not having any clear answers as to what had really led to this terrible tragedy and who was responsible. Carol's mother Deborah, explained that their other daughter Joanna was going to be on the first possible flight home from India but conversation on both sides was half hearted, with all three of them being in a state of part disbelief and always on the verge of breaking down.

Assuring them that he had lots of support and didn't need to go back with them to stay at their home in Bristol, Rob was relieved when they agreed they should go home but would stay in constant contact and that he should call them at any stage should he need to. Rob knew that he should be able to offer more to his parents-in-law, who had just lost not only their daughter but also their beloved grandchildren but he was glad when he could close the door behind them, as they left with heads down in a futile attempt to avoid the media outside.

Rob had spent the hours since his parents-in-law had left, continuing to try to drown his sorrows with no success, because trying to remember his three loved ones in as much detail as possible became too painful. He would see-saw between recalling happier times and then struggle to wash away the pain of what that meant for him now from his mind. On a few occasions there had been a ring at his doorbell but after the second occasion of finding a member of the media there, he now simply ignored them, until he noticed after a while that they had stopped, either through frustration or because someone was stopping them. He didn't care why, just as long as they would leave him alone.

Rob finished the last of the whisky and was about to start the gin, when he realised that the last person to have touched this bottle would have been his darling Carol and, recognising that she would never do so again, he simply collapsed into a sobbing mess once more and fell into another fitful sleep.

He came to, with no idea of the time, a raging headache and a throat that required rehydrating with something other than spirits. He then became aware that the thing that had woken him was the doorbell and he was determined to ensure that when he answered the door this time, the bloody press would get the message that he really did not wish to be disturbed. He opened the door with a suddenness that made the person on the other side of the door take a step back and as that person was then grabbed by the lapels of his coat, he looked even more shocked.

"When will you heartless vultures realise that I do not want to be disturbed and the next one of you who disturbs me again will end up going over the hedge?"

"Mr. Price, I am sorry to impose at such a terrible time for you but I thought that at such a time as this, you might not feel like cooking and so I have brought you a meal that you can heat up to eat." Rob looked down at the person he was holding by the coat, to see a small man, of middle-eastern heritage, looking up at him with no small degree of concern on his face. Gradually, it dawned on him that this was Mr. Khalif, who ran their local shop but also as someone who had worked alongside Carol at the community foodbank every Wednesday and of whom his wife had spoken with real affection, as someone who was not only kind and thoughtful but also clever and funny. With this realisation Rob, guiltily released him from his grip immediately and mumbled an apology.

"No, no, Mr. Price, no apology necessary. I fully understand and I would not have disturbed you but I can only imagine how hard it must be to do the normal things of every day life hence the food. Please, when you have finished, just put the containers outside your door and I will take them away without disturbing you."

"That is very kind but….."

"No Mr. Price, this is not kindness. This is what friends do and your wife was a wonderful woman who I considered a real friend. Please know if there is anything I can do, just pick up the phone. I will leave you now but please be aware that while we can never know what you are suffering, when it gets really tough, know that there are many who share your pain and wish to help. I will go now."

Rob mumbled a thank you, took the proffered box of food and retreated into the house. In the kitchen he opened the box and was greeted with the most wonderful aromas that in normal circumstances would have had him tucking in immediately but he had no interest in food and placed the box by the front door. Fed up of having been in the same room all morning, he avoided the gin, grabbed a bottle of brandy and before going upstairs to the bedroom, put the box of untouched food outside the door.

Back at the station, the investigating team were having the sort of luck they rarely got this soon in an enquiry. "Sir, we have a number of people who have picked out the same two people from the mug shots, with varying levels of certainty but two of the witnesses in particular had been very positive. One, because they were just about to step onto the zebra crossing as the car narrowly missed him and he was staring at the occupants in the front seat in fury. However, the icing on the cake is that one of the witnesses is a delivery man, who recognised both faces from regular deliveries he has made to the same house. And guess which house that is. Yep, you've got it, the mansion owned by the Duncan family."

"That's excellent work Susie but we know how unreliable eye witnesses can be."

Disappointed that this news hadn't gained a more positive response from the DCI, Susie continued with, "Yes boss but something even better, even if we probably won't be able to use it in court, just take a look at this photo taken by our surveillance of the Duncan family at a family meal and celebration, the day after the robbery." The whole team joined their boss in turning to look at the screen at the end of the room, showing an image of a large gathering, raising a toast at a restaurant known to all present as "Duncans", the family eatery, owned by the biggest criminal family outside London.

"Well, I can spot all the usual suspects, if you'll pardon the pun, including Frankie Duncan the head of the family and his three not very pleasant sons but I fail to see how this is going to help, as they could simply claim they were celebrating the coming of age of their pet budgie or whatever."

"Well sir, you are nearer to the truth than you may think. Look at this and compare the two pictures." Next to the first image, another appeared on the screen of the four male members of the Duncan family, obviously enjoying a a group photo for the media, before teeing off in some golfing competition.

"You'll have to help me DS Bright."

"This second photo was taken for the local paper the day before the robbery, to help promote the Duncan Pro–Am charity golf tournament in which all four of the family played. If you take a closer look at their left hands and compare?"

Gradually as one, then another started nudging their colleagues and pointed out the difference, a smile spread over DS Bright's face, as the team began to acknowledge what this meant. Her balloon was slightly deflated by the response of her boss however.

"Very good DS Bright and I can see what you are getting at but this is not evidence. We know we need more than the fact the youngest Duncan is missing a signet ring in the golfing photo but is wearing one in the restaurant, so let's start tying up the loose ends and one of those has to be identifying the two people in the back of the vehicle."

Determined not to let the DCI's seeming indifference to her find get to her, DS Bright jumped in again. "We already know that from the photos we have shown to witnesses, it suggests that it was Duncan's second in command Peter Fitzpatrick sat in the passenger seat of the getaway vehicle and it looks as if the youngest of the Duncan clan Brad, was driving. Now this is a bit of a surprise because we have no intelligence that he has ever been involved in anything as serious as this before but that could well explain why this part of the operation, the driving, was such a mess. Again from the image we just saw on the screen I think we can take a pretty good guess that it is almost certainly the two other Duncan boys in the back of the vehicle but you are right boss, we are going to need more evidence." DS Bright added the last bit as a sop to her boss.

Waking early the next morning, as a head full of half- memories nagged at his sleep, Rob skipped the chore of showering and dressed in yesterday's clothes, before going down stairs to energise himself with coffee. While still feeling the desperate effects of the alcohol he had consumed and the lack of food and sleep, the coffee gave him the clarity to face what had to be done. Thinking about it now, simply reinforced the decision he had made in the middle of the night, when he had woken and sat up with a sudden realisation of the answer to the question that he kept asking himself, about how he would cope from now on. He had come to the conclusion that the answer was straightforward.

Rob wandered unthinkingly to the seat he had spent most of the last few days in and, staring at the blown up family photo he had been so reluctant to be involved in but which now hung on the wall opposite, he silently thanked the photographer for persuading them to go for the biggest copy available, as it enabled him to remember the details of his lovely girls, that he was ashamed to find slipping away from the grasp of his memory. His eyes then fell upon the unopened Valentine's gift on the mantelpiece but he could not bring himself to open it, fearing the feelings it might evoke.

He had no idea how long he had been sitting, there when the doorbell rang and he had to leave this oasis of memories, to let in Matt and Ronnie, receiving their hugs while noticing without emotion, that the box he had left out for Mr. Khalif had disappeared. His two friends were surprised but pleased to find that Rob was more than willing to sit down and start discussing the sort of funeral that he wanted for his three loved ones. Surely they thought, this meant that Rob had turned some sort of a corner and was now in the process of coming back into the here and now and not allowing himself to be dominated by wallowing in the past. Rob's acquiescence however, was more to do with him wanting to speed up this process, than any positive change in his demeanour, simply because once this was all over and people began to leave him alone, he had no intention of feeling anything.

Until then however, it was important that Carol and the girls had the send off they deserved and Carol's strong religious beliefs made much of the service easy to plan. Her Baptist church would ensure the whole occasion would be as joyous as any funeral could be and would ensure that there was an uplifting theme to the whole day, just as Carol would have wished for anyone else and that was the important thing here; her wishes not his.

Ronnie volunteered to be the liaison with the funeral company, once she had spoken to Carol's parents to include their wishes, to at least save Rob the emotional pain of continually having to discuss the death of his wife and children. Just then a ring of the doorbell saw Matt move from the lounge to answer the door to DCI Grey and DS Bright. The DCI apologised for disturbing them all, before addressing Rob.

"Mr. Price, we are sorry to disturb you but we wanted to check how you are and bring you up to speed with our investigation. We also have the belongings of the girls and your wife with us to return to you. This includes a list of all the items found at the scene, including the shopping your wife had bought that day but I am afraid we have had to throw away some of the perishable goods."

Rob was momentarily stunned, having not realised that of course this would happen but the idea of dealing with the belongings of his wife and children, that had actually been a part of them when they were killed, filled him with dread. He was brought back to the here and now as the DCI addressed him again.

"Mr. Price, I can also tell you that we have arrested four people in connection with the robbery and the hit and run and while nothing can ever be certain, we are confident that this will go to court."

Suddenly Rob felt sick and had to sit down quickly at the realisation that the cause of his despair and loss were actual, real, breathing, people and that they had been out there walking about, leading their lives, probably with no thought of the devastation they had caused.

"Where are they from? Who are they? What do they have to say about what happened?"

"All I can say Mr. Price, is that they are characters previously known to us and that they are not nice people."

"Surely you can give me some idea of who they are?"

"Seriously Mr. Price, not only can I not tell you any more than I already have but it really won't help you to dwell on this as it just cannot help."

"What do you mean dwell on this? What do you think is consuming my every waking and dreaming moment? How certain are you that you will get a conviction and how soon will it be?"

Susie Bright winced at the lack of compassion exhibited by her boss in his next reply to Mr. Price.

"Whoa. Now I know this must be eating you up Mr. Price but we have to take this one step at a time to ensure we have this case airtight. The reason I am telling you now, is because at some stage the media are going to get hold of this and I did not want you reading about it before I had warned you. Also, you must not believe all that you read in the papers and you will read an awful lot that will only make things feel worse than they already do."

Trying to retrieve the situation, Susie Bright stepped in. "Look, let's cross those bridges when we come to them. We will leave you in peace now but should you have any queries you already have my card and should you have any concerns you can ring me at any time, day or night."

"Absolutely," confirmed DCI Grey, "and on the way out we will leave the bags containing the belongings of your wife and children at the bottom of the stairs."

Rob stood to see them out and as he saw them off at the door, he noticed that a new box of food had appeared outside on his doorstep. He shut the door without touching the box.

As they walked down the path, DCI Grey stopped and stood in front of his DS. "Don't ever do that again sergeant. I will talk to people, including potential suspects, which is what Mr. Price still is, in any way I see fit. I certainly do not need you stepping in and molly coddling potential suspects who I am quite happy to see squirm."

"But Boss, he is more than likely an innocent man who has just been three times bereaved."

"Whether he is innocent or not is not for you to decide and if you have aspirations of getting on in this force, I suggest you toughen up and never question my methods again. Do you understand?"

"Yes Boss. I will be more careful in the future." DS Bright responded, more determined than ever not to turn out like her boss, if that was what was needed to get on in the police force.

Inside the house, Rob studiously ignored the bags of belongings the police had left and when Ronnie picked up the unopened Valentine's gift from the mantelpiece and asked Rob if he felt like opening it, he told her that he would only open it when his family's killers had been sent to prison. Both Matt and Ronnie tried to change his mind but being in no mood for conversation, as he wanted to take fully on board this new information the Police had given him and having agreed to see them tomorrow, he ushered Matt and Ronnie out of the door. Returning to his seat, he pulled the bottle of brandy from behind the curtain and poured himself a large drink to help him consider this new information.

CHAPTER 6

On returning to the station, Grey and Bright walked into the incident room and were immediately assailed by the two youngest members of the team, DC Johnny Hutchinson and DC Nazir Begum, who looked really pleased with themselves. The DCI told them to calm down and give whatever they had to his sergeant while he made a very important phone call. On hearing that the constables had some new information, DS Bright called all the other members of the team together and suggested to the now very nervous detective constables, that they should give their news to the whole team, knowing that however nervous they were now, this had to happen at some time and if the importance of their news matched their level of excitement, now was as good a time as any.

"Johnny you look very eager so you start please."

"Well Sarge, I went down to see the forensics team working on the car, as, to be honest, I have never really seen them at work before. They had finished their work in the car and were preparing to get it returned to its rightful owner. But a very kind forensic officer, said he would show me what they had done in the car. Because the car had been finished with, we sat in the front seats while he explained the fascinating processes they had been through. While I was sat there, I could smell something that I recognised but couldn't put my finger on it until I returned upstairs and having used the bathroom, I was checking myself in the mirror when it suddenly occurred to me when I had experienced the smell from the car before. It was the smell of very expensive hair gel that my girlfriend bought for me last Christmas. So expensive in fact, that I only wear it on special occasions. Now I knew it couldn't have belonged to the Forensics Officer for obvious reasons."

"You mean because he is a dead ringer for Kojak," shouted out the middle aged DS Willis, to which DS Pippa Jones asked, "Who's Kojak?" Not wanting to admit that she actually knew the answer, DS Bright interrupted, "Just think of the hairstyle of Matt Lucas the comedian Pippa. Get on with it please Johnny, where is this going?"

"Well it occurred to me, that maybe when they had the collision on the crossing, one of them might have bumped their head on the car interior."

"Yes, but even if we find traces of this hair gel and can prove that one of the Duncan's was wearing it, their counsel can claim that any number of people use that particular product."

Getting more excited as he continued, DC Hutchinson smiled as he answered. "Yes, but if their head made contact with the interior, so will have their hair. I rang the FO with my theory and they admitted that they had not tested the ceiling of the car interior other than for finger prints around the grab handle. When they did test, they did find a very slight smudge in the back seat behind the driver and when tested they came up with the DNA of one Alex H Duncan."

"Johnny, I could kiss you, but for now you'll have to make do with a well done."

A red faced DC Hutchinson sat down, trying really hard to hide the huge grin that began to spread across his face.

"Right DC Begum, can you top that?"

"Well Sarge, I might not be able to top it but I have information that will help our case."

"That's all we can ask for. Go Ahead."

"We have been wondering why the getaway vehicle was not torched to ensure that they didn't leave behind any forensics, which of course, thanks to Johnny, we have now found out that they did. Because, even though they wore the same sort of protective clothing we wear at a crime scene, including gloves, something like Johnny has described could, and hopefully has, caught them out."

"Go on."

"Well, our CCTV cameras happened to pick up a chauffeur driven Bentley driving away from the derelict industrial estate in the east of the city, a place I might add, that is notorious for the number of cars that are torched there and not the sort of place you would expect to see such a vehicle as a Bentley, let alone with a chauffeur driving. We think that maybe this was meant to be the place where they had planned for the getaway car to be torched and abandoned, with the Bentley available to take the Duncan boys on to Leicester race course where we know they were for the rest of the day. However, because of the collision during the bungled escape where they hit a concrete bollard and parked van, which we now know caused the fuel tank to rupture and limit the distance they could travel, we are guessing they had to divert south out of Blaby to the sports field where the helicopter picked them up.

We now have a parking steward at the race course, who says that the Duncans' helicopter was just about to land at the racecourse at approximately 2.45 pm., when suddenly it aborted its landing, pulled away and raced off. We are guessing again that the boys, realising they could not reach the rendezvous at the industrial estate, called their father who was en route to the racecourse and he had the helicopter go and pick them up. Underneath their protective clothing they will have worn their race clothes and so the whole family will have arrived together."

"That is great work Nazir. Now all we have to do is prove that your excellent theory actually happened but we are getting closer Team, I can feel it and I am sure that the DCI will be just as delighted and ready to congratulate you both when he gets off the phone." If there was a note of irony in her voice, DS Bright didn't really mind, as their team were more than used to receiving scant praise from the DCI, who liked to keep any praise that was going for himself. In fact, on hearing what DS Bright had to tell him when she brought him up to date, he barely acknowledged her before rushing back to his office where he slammed the door and made yet another phone call.

As is the case with all stories that become major headlines in the newspapers, interest in the robbery and the subsequent deaths of a mother and her two daughters quickly waned. While this had the advantage of no longer having to put up with being bothered by the reporters and photographers that had dogged his every move, in the first few days after the incident, it angered Rob that it seemed as if the death of his wife and daughters no longer mattered. Each day was a struggle just to get out of bed and get through the day. Matt and Ronnie spent as much time with him as they could but they had jobs to go to and when he was on his own they knew that Rob was drinking too much and hardly eating. He would occasionally peck at some of the food that his kind neighbour left outside his door every day but invariably Mr. Khalif would find the meals he provided, untouched. It seemed to his two closest friends, that Rob was merely surviving from day to day and that the only thing that was giving him the will to get up every morning, was the desire to have the perpetrators of his family's deaths punished, for making him go through the suffering that enveloped him.

Before that could happen however, they all had to get through the painful experience of a funeral. So it was that on a cold and wet March day, four weeks after their tragic deaths, the bodies of Carol, Holly and Penny Price were lying inside the three coffins at the front of a packed Whetstone Baptist Church. If you had asked Rob later that day what the funeral was like, he would not have been able to tell you, so unable to comprehend was he, that his wonderful girls were lying lifeless in those wooden boxes. He had been incapable of taking any significant part in the service and simply sat staring at the coffins or allowing others to steer him from place to place. It was left to Carol's sister Joanna, to lead the eulogies, supported by many others who wished to express their love for Rob's wife and daughters.

After the service and cremation, close friends and family went back to number 49, where Matt, Ronnie and Joanna hosted a wake, while Rob sat on his bed upstairs weeping. Gradually, people started to drift away, sympathetic to Rob's desire not to want to face the finality of the end of the funeral, being the end of the process of saying goodbye to his loved ones. When Carol's parents and sister came upstairs to say their own goodbyes, there was a mutual, wordless acknowledgement of what they had all lost. And as Matt and Ronnie waved them off, the parents, sister, grandparent and aunt of the three people who had been interred that day, looked up at the front bedroom window and saw the stooped outline of a sobbing man, sharing and understanding his pain and feeling of total despair.

Having washed up and cleared everything away, Matt and Ronnie tried without success to persuade Rob to come downstairs but having the empathy to realise his need to be left alone, they promised him that they would see him tomorrow and let themselves out of the house to return to their own home, where they knew they would go through the mourning they had promised themselves they would keep in check while in the presence of their friend.

Up in the room he used to share with his beloved Carol, Rob was partially in a daze, trying to come to terms with the fact that he had just been at the funeral of his beautiful wife and children, something he had never for one moment considered he would ever have to be involved in. There should have been birthdays, anniversaries and weddings for them all to share, that would now never happen. But he had girded himself for this. Realising he had to keep it together to enable him to get through this and then the trial and then, only then, when those murderous scum were behind bars, could he leave all this behind. Because all this, whatever this was, no longer mattered and once justice was served, as if it ever could be, then he would leave all this behind and be together again with Carol and his darling girls.

CHAPTER 7

Four months later, Matt and Ronnie felt strangely relieved when the case to prosecute the people who had been responsible for the deaths of Carol and their Godchildren came to court. They didn't know how much longer their friend Rob could go on as he had been. Drinking too much, hardly eating or sleeping and generally losing any interest in his appearance or hygiene. They hoped and prayed that when these thugs were sent down, Rob would be able to start building up his life again. They had sat with Rob and his parents-in-law as the prosecution outlined its case and called its witnesses. As the case wore on, they heard more and more about a crime family headed by a man called Francis 'Frankie' Duncan and that it was his second in command Pete Fitzpatrick, along with Duncan's three sons, Brad, Alex and Philip who were responsible for what had happened to Carol, Holly and Penny, during a botched getaway from a Building Society robbery. Rob had been totally focussed on every aspect and would crave reassurance at the end of each day from his friends that the case was going as it should. They were able to tell him truthfully, that from what they had heard so far, there seemed little doubt that the four men in the dock would be found guilty. The only fly in the ointment was the non-appearance of the two main eye witnesses, one of whom had actually committed suicide, increasing further the number of people who had become victims in this whole sorry saga.

The case for the defence had been going for just over a day and they immediately took a dislike to the smarmy QC who had been hired to represent the three young men and one middle aged man in the dock.

"Calling DC Jonathan Hutchinson," announced the Clerk of the court, who then swore in the Detective Constable, who waited nervously for the first question from the prosecuting council.

"Detective, I understand that you have been in your present role for just over a year?"

"Yes that is about right," a very nervous Johnny replied, rather grateful that the first question had been one he had answered without squeaking in fear.

"And in that time, how many major investigations have you been involved in?"

"Well, including this one, probably three."

"So would you say you are still very much learning?"

"Yes, I would and I expect I will continue learning for the rest of my career." Johnny began to relax at what he thought was quite a good answer.

"Let's hope so Detective, so you would agree that you are presently, relatively inexperienced?"

"Well I suppose so but…."

"A yes or a no is all I need."

"In that case, yes."

"And you might be more prone to making mistakes than perhaps some of your other more experienced colleagues?"

Feeling decidedly less confident with the direction this line of questioning was taking, Johnny muttered a measured, "Maybe, but if I have to deal with anything complicated, I always have a more senior detective to monitor me."

"Excellent practice and I am sure we are all very reassured to hear it. Now, let me turn to the occasion when you went into the forensic lab and asked to look at the getaway car, even though it had been signed off as having been finished with." In the gallery DS Bright groaned inwardly as she realised where this was going.

"Did you have a more senior officer monitoring you, when you actually sat in the vehicle and rather miraculously, when you asked the Forensics Officer to check the interior roof of the car, they magically found the DNA of my client?"

"I only sat in the front seat and the DNA was found in the back and the FO was with me at all times."

"So you say but how do we know that you hadn't by accident or design, brought the DNA of my client into the car?"

"At that stage I had never had any contact with your client or his DNA."

"Well, we only have your word for that and even if such cross contamination did occur by mistake rather than intent, it would hardly be that surprising, considering the lack of experience you have admitted. Can I ask you DC Hutchinson, were you fully suited, gloved and your shoes covered when you sat in the car?"

"Well no, but the forensic team had finished with the car by the time I sat inside." DS Bright groaned again, while trying to smile at Johnny, to try and give him back some of the confidence that was rapidly oozing from him.

"So, as far as you are concerned, any evidence found after the Forensic Team had officially finished their work should be considered inadmissible?"

"No that's not…."

"One last question before you step down DC Hutchinson. The clue that encouraged you to ask for the FO to check for DNA where you did, was that you had noticed the aroma of the hair product known as "Oribe Rock Hard Gel" Is that correct?"

"Yes it is."

"And am I correct in thinking that you received such a product as a gift last Christmas?"

"Well yes but I didn't…"

"Thank you DC Hutchinson. That will be all."

Feeling absolutely miserable, the young DC left the witness box believing that he had single handedly destroyed the case for the prosecution. In the gallery, Susie knew that their case had taken a huge blow but recognised that this was not the fault of her DC but that weasel of a lawyer in the pocket of the Duncan family who had twisted the truth to make a lie.

"Members of the jury, to sum up. The only real evidence the prosecution had to offer at the beginning of this trial was the identification of my clients by the many witnesses present on the day of this unfortunate incident. However, as the trial has gone on, of the two main witnesses, one has unfortunately died and sad as that is, one can only speculate whether feelings of guilt at being responsible for the incarceration of an innocent person……"

"Your honour I object."

"Sustained."

"Yes, apologies your Honour. In fact ladies and gentlemen, the main strength of the Prosecution case centred around the witnesses who supposedly identified my clients. I wonder if you also find it a strange coincidence therefore, that their second witness has also singularly failed to show up at court and again one has to surmise that this was the result of their uncertainty about who it actually was in the car, if they didn't have the fall back of another witness to support their own view and if they are uncertain, then ladies and gentlemen, how can you be expected to prosecute with any degree of certainty? It seems obvious to many I am sure, that the police have carried out a prolonged investigation of the Duncan family that amounts to harassment. Then, through sheer incompetence or, let us be generous, bad luck, when they could not find who was responsible for this unfortunate series of incidents, they decided to kill two birds with one stone; i.e. solve the crime and improve their statistics, while at the same time getting rid of a group of people they have an illogical obsession with, for no legitimate reason.

The following day was taken up with both sides summing up and then the jury were asked to go away and consider their verdict. Despite the fact that all the people he spoke to were convinced that the four men would be found guilty, Rob hardly slept that night. Curled up in what had become his chair of choice, facing the family photograph on the wall opposite, he eventually drank himself into a stupor. When Matt and Ronnie picked him up the next day to take him to court, he looked and smelled like some down and out, who should have been appearing in the dock rather than a respectable member of the teaching profession but he was in no mood to listen to any lectures and simply wanted to get to Leicester Crown Court and bring this part of his life to a close.

Once there, they sat in the waiting area not knowing whether an early return of the jury would be a good thing or a bad thing. Just after 2.00pm, it was announced that the jury were returning and all those involved should take their places. When the clerk of the court and the judge spoke, Rob was seemingly in some sort of trance, waiting only for when the foreman of the jury stood to announce the verdict that they had reached. When he announced 'not guilty' on all counts, Matt thought that Rob would erupt with anger but he simply slumped in his seat staring at his feet.

When all formalities were completed and they were leaving the courtroom, Rob excused himself, saying he had to use the bathroom and insisted he would be fine when Matt asked him if he would like him to go with him. Once inside the bathroom, Rob rushed into one of the cubicles where the pain, frustration and alcohol caused him to vomit violently. As he stood and turned to clean himself at the sink, the door opened and in walked the man who Rob had seen every day in court, wearing an ostentatious orchid on his lapel and who was the father of three of the men in the dock, Francis Duncan. He was accompanied by another man, who had been pointed out by DS Bright as one of Duncan's minders. Rob rushed at Duncan but was prevented from reaching his target by the minder who grabbed him and placed him in an armlock.

"It's OK Ernie. Let Mr Price go. He has, after all, lost his family and the police have not been able to catch those responsible. His frustration is understandable."

"You bastard! You should be ashamed of yourself, bringing up three thugs like that. You are a disgrace."

"I don't think I shall be taking too seriously, the insults of a man with vomit on his clothes and smelling of alcohol. However, I will make a concession on the basis that you are quite obviously upset and probably ashamed at your inability to protect your family."

Rob lunged at Duncan again but once more was restrained by the minder Ernie. This time however, Duncan told his minder to hold Rob up and he punched him hard in the stomach, so that Rob was painfully winded. He then lifted Rob's head by the hair and hit him twice across the face.

"Do you honestly think that someone like you can dare to try and attack me? You are a nothing. A Mr. Nobody, who cannot even imagine the lifestyle I lead and the power I wield. You are fortunate that my compassion for your situation means that you have not just suffered the fate that anyone who tries to harm me experiences. But do not ever attempt to harm me in any way whatsoever again, otherwise that will be the last thing you ever do. My family means everything to me and your failure to keep your own, makes you a nonentity in my eyes. Ernie, throw him down where he belongs." Pointing at the urinals as Ernie's target for Rob, he straightened his tie and orchid in the mirror and then walked out, with his minder, having carried out his command, trailing behind him.

When Rob eventually came out of the toilets he felt not just angry and totally humiliated but so very sad. It also made him more resigned than ever to go home and rid himself of his agony for good. DS Bright had been looking for Rob and when she saw him half staggering from the toilets she rushed to him, grabbing him by the arm and guiding him to her car through the back of the building.

"Come on, I am taking you home." Calling one of her colleagues to let Matt and Ronnie know that she would take Rob home, she helped him into her car and drove away from the waiting media. Parking on the drive of number 49, a look of "just you dare" from Bright to the scrabbling reporters who were waiting to get Rob's response to the verdict, ensured they stayed at the gate and she took Rob inside. Once there, she moved the bottle of whisky from the table next to Rob's now regular chair and made them both a cup of tea. After a long chat, where the DS tried to convince Rob that they would not be giving up, explaining that these crime families and gangs were not set up over night but over years and generations and so to bring them down would also take years and maybe generations. Bright promised she would be in touch and then made her way to the door, trying to avoid the sad sight of a seemingly totally broken man as she left and drove back to the station.

CHAPTER 8

Having decided that it was pointless carrying on hoping against hope any longer, Rob went into the kitchen and out of the toffee tin, took Carol's Benadryl tablets he had transferred from the medicine cabinet, where she had kept them for her severe hay fever. He had hoped that he would be doing this unthinkable thing, in the knowledge that those responsible for the death of Carol and his lovely daughters would now be getting their comeuppance. But like all aspects of his life in the last five months, fate had conspired against him and while the fury and desire for revenge had kept him going up until now, he no longer had the energy or desire to carry on for, what was it Bright said? "Could be years or generations." He could not carry on feeling like this for another day, let alone years.

Walking back into the lounge, he spotted the unopened gift still on the mantelpiece and recognising that he was never going to find justice for his family, he ripped off the paper to find a narrow jewellers' box which, when opened, revealed a beautiful gold locket and chain. The front of the locket had a highly detailed Welsh Dragon engraved on it but it was when he opened the locket that Rob's heart skipped a beat. Inside was a photo of his three lovely girls wearing Welsh rugby shirts and smiling back at him. Staring at this image longingly for some time, it was only on closing the locket that he noticed an inscription on the back which read,

"To the man we love more than anything in the world. So that what you love most will be always close to your heart."

The pain of seeing their photo and the words inscribed, were unbearable for him, and Rob, believing he had let them down following the court verdict, took the locket into the kitchen and threw it into the bin. Returning to the lounge, he had just finished pouring himself a large whisky when the doorbell rang. He tried to ignore it, assuming it was the press but it was persistent. Resignedly, he went to the door to tell any waiting reporter what he thought of them but found Mr. Khalif standing there with a box of ingredients.

"Mr. Khalif please go away, I do not want your food, lovely as it is, but if you leave it on the step I know where it is should I feel hungry."

"Mr. Price I am afraid this is not yet prepared but do not worry I will come in and cook it for you."

"You really are beginning to get on my nerves. Now go before I do something we will both regret." Mr. Khalif then did something that took Rob totally by surprise, as the small shopkeeper pushed him hard in the chest repeatedly, until he stumbled backwards into the lounge.

When Mr. Khalif spotted the tablets and the whisky he growled and then shouted at Rob to sit down and when he did not respond, Mr. Khalif simply shoved him down.

"You should be ashamed of yourself. Why are you giving up on your lovely family? You owe it to them to put things right. This is not the man who Mrs Price would talk to me about. This is not the man I have seen playing rugby for Blaby. Never the most skilful, the fastest or the strongest but always on the team because you never give up."

Rob had to accept that perhaps Mr. Khalif knew a little more about rugby than he had given him credit for but he knew nothing about how he was feeling now. As if reading his mind Mr Khalif shouted at him again with an anger that burned in its intensity and kept Rob quiet.

"Do you think that you are the only person who has ever suffered loss, or feels that what has happened to them represents the most burning of injustices? Everywhere you walk and look there is likely to be someone with something of what you are feeling now. You look at me and you see someone who I am not. You see a contented man, with a business of his own, making a success in a country he has escaped to in order to improve his life. But I am a shell. My whole life has been destroyed and I not only have to live with that but also with the guilt of what I have done."

"I don't understand."

"No, why should you? You have your own problems and I don't tell you this for pity but because I need you to see that it is possible to carry on. Before I came to this country, I was an opponent of the Government in Syria and because of that, I was captured and tortured a number of times. Then I found out that I was to be captured again but this time I was to be executed as an example to others. With my wife and children, I managed to escape but in trying to get across the border out of Syria, we were separated into different vehicles and mine was the only one that got away. I only found out an hour after we crossed the border and could do nothing about it. My wife and children are now held as captives in a prison for political prisoners, while I live a safe and comfortable life but also to my eternal shame, the life of the guilty. But what I have had to come to terms with for my own sanity, is that what we have to decide is, whether we are going to allow it to destroy us or make us stronger. There is really no choice, because if I am to save my family, then I will have to be stronger. Many succumb to the first feeling and who can blame them? But I have to carry on, in the hope that one day I can get my family back, while you Mr. Price, have one of the greatest reasons known to man to put right the terrible wrong that has been done to you. The loss of everything you love.

But even then many people will claim that they do not have it in their power to put this right. All the odds are stacked against them. Yes, exactly that. What can I do against a powerful and wealthy criminal, who even the police cannot catch? I am just an ordinary person. It is exactly because you are an ordinary person that you have an advantage over the police because their hands are tied by the law and the bureaucracy of their role in society. You, hopefully, will also not break the law but you do not have to be tied to it and certainly as an ordinary person you have freedoms that they do not enjoy."

Rob, who had been listening to what Mr. Khalif had to say in surprise and, he had to be honest, quite a bit of interest, had to now interrupt and bring Mr. Khalif out of his fantasy world.

"I am so sorry for what you have suffered Mr. Khalif but the rest of what you say is ridiculous. Even if I agreed with you, that as an ordinary person I have a little more leeway than the police, which I don't necessarily by the way, I have nowhere near the resources or personnel at my disposal that they have. I have let my family down. Right up until the moment they died, they were thinking of me and bought me a wonderful gift which I would have worn with pride once I had got them justice but I failed."

"Mr. Price, I do not understand."

"It's no longer of any importance. You need to go. There is something I am determined to do and even if you stop me today you will simply be putting off the inevitable."

"Mr. Rob, I will go but before I do, I want to ask you one question."

"Go ahead if this will get you to leave me in peace."

"Mr. Price, what if I were to tell you that I believe that there is a very real chance that you can have access to all the resources and personnel you would need, to carry out a credible investigation that would lead to the arrest of the Duncan family?"

"Well then…. But no. How could that possibly be?"

"Mr Price, I want you to go and have a shower and a shave and change into some clean clothes. When you come back down stairs, there will be a meal waiting for you. What can you lose other than putting off what you see as the inevitable, for a couple more hours?" Rob believed that he was in the presence of a fantasist but he had been good to him and if agreeing to what he had just asked would get Mr. Khalif to leave the house then he was right, he had nothing to lose and so he nodded, got up out of the chair and went upstairs to do as he was bid.

In the kitchen having prepared the food and put it on the hob to cook, Hassan Khalif started to tidy away and, as he was tipping the peelings from the vegetables he had prepared into the kitchen bin, he noticed something shining back at him.

Thirty minutes later Rob came back down to find a dish emitting the most wonderful aromas, sitting on the dining room table, with a glass of freshly squeezed orange juice next to it. Until he started eating, he had not realised how hungry he really was, with the result that he had soon finished what was on the plate and Mr Khalif wordlessly gave him a second helping, which he accepted without wanting to appear too grateful and encouraging this annoyingly persistent man. When he had finished, Mr. Khalif cleared everything away and placed the soiled plates and cutlery in the dishwasher.

"OK let's get it over with, so that you can be on your way. What were you going to tell me that would make me believe that it would be possible for me to get my revenge?"

"No Mr. Price, it is not revenge you will get but justice. I promise you that what I have to say to you will be very enlightening but I will not tell you now because you have had a long and tiring day. I will come back tomorrow at noon. You have eaten and now you must sleep and tomorrow when you are properly ready, I will explain to you how I believe we can solve your problem of gaining JUSTICE for your lovely ladies."

"But how do you know that I will not simply do what I had intended all along once you go through that door?" It seemed ridiculous the way they both skated around the subject of his intention to end his own life because Mr. Khalif quite obviously knew what his intentions were but even at the lowest point in someone's life, it seemed that the mores of a civilised society would not allow them to mention the actual words.

"Because Mr. Price, your wife and daughters loved you and you love them. I do not know which God you believe in, or what you think happens when we pass on from this life but if they are looking down on us, I believe that you would rather provide them with something to be proud of rather than something to pity and be ashamed of. Goodbye Mr. Price. I will see you tomorrow."

At that, Mr. Khalif left the room and after Rob heard the front door open and shut quietly, he poured himself a glass of whisky and gathered together all the Benadryl pills he had poured out onto the table and then sat there swirling the drink looking at the pills. He was still doing this thirty minutes later having been on the verge of picking up the pills on a number of occasions. At around midnight he shouted, "Sod it!" to no-one at all, placed the drink back down on the table with the pills, believing he could easily do what he had to do tomorrow and slowly climbed the stairs to bed, feeling incredibly tired, to the extent that he gave up undressing halfway through and simply got into bed as he was. He fell into a deep, but unfortunately not, a nightmare-free sleep, almost immediately.

On hearing the soft snores above him, Mr. Khalif crept out of the study where he had been watching to see if Rob Price would call his bluff and quietly let himself out of the front door.

The following morning, Rob woke at 10.00 am, the latest he had woken for as long as he could remember within the last few months and while he couldn't claim that the sleep was enjoyable because of the nightmares that filled it, it was certainly the most rest he had experienced since that fateful day. He shaved, showered and dressed, a routine that had become haphazard in its frequency of late and realised he actually felt like eating breakfast. While he still had every intention of carrying out his aim of ending it all, the talk with Mr. Khalif had allowed him the opportunity to get himself in order and face this, at least with a clear head. He would listen to what Mr. Khalif had to say, in the hope of placating him enough that he wouldn't bother him again while Rob carried out his plan. He also had to admit to himself that the rest and refreshment had made him feel better than he had for some time. Unfortunately, the hurricane of pain still continuously roiling around in his stomach, made carrying on impossible.

Determined to make full use of this extra time he had been granted by Mr. Khalif's intervention, he set to writing a letter that would have to serve as his will, leaving everything to Carol's sister Joanna. While addressing the envelope, the doorbell rang at 12.00 noon exactly and when he answered it, Mr. Khalif was standing there with a serious but excited look on his face. He told Rob to sit down; made them both their hot drink of choice, then began.

"Mr. Price, I know you understand how sorry I am for your loss. Not just because that is the polite thing to say but because through my working with your lovely wife, I came to realise what a special person she was and how close your family were. To want revenge after what you have been through is understandable but I cannot condone that. However, what I have to tell you will provide I believe, the opportunity to get justice. Even if my own Quran tells us that, *"If you take revenge only do so in proportion to the wrong done to you."* I prefer to follow the idea put forward by the Hindu, Mahatma Gandhi when he said, *"If we all take an eye for an eye then the whole world will be blind."* You have to decide if you want revenge for yourself or justice for your family. You cannot have both. One makes you as bad as the people who have done you harm, the other is a true tribute to the love you had for your wife and daughters."

"You have implied this already Mr. Khalif but I cannot see how David could slay Goliath in the real world whatever your faith."

"Mr. Price, what I have to tell you has the potential to be very successful but will fail on one very basic point which we may as well clear up now. I am sorry to bring this up but do you have the belongings of your wife and daughters from the day they were killed?"

Rob looked at him in disbelief, at this out of character lack of sensitivity and was about to suggest that this conversation should now end, when he remembered that Mr. Khalif had done nothing other than be supportive and helpful from the moment his world had fallen apart.

"Yes, they were returned to me some time ago and have lain untouched at the bottom of the stairs in evidence bags, ever since the police left them there because I have not got the courage to look at them. But if you think you could find some evidence there that will prove the Duncans killed my family, you are wrong, as they have been forensically tested to the 'nth' degree and I am not happy about having to touch the clothes they were wearing when they were killed."

"Mr. Price, if I am correct we will not have to touch their clothes, simply the belongings they were carrying."

"Well, the police said that it is all there apart from any perishable shopping bought on that day." A look of concern came over Mr. Khalif's face.

"Hopefully that should still be fine unless they threw away the bags those goods were actually carried in."

"I have absolutely no idea but if it will get rid of you, let's go and have a look." Both men went to the bottom of the stairs and, by agreement, picked up the evidence bags between them and took them through to the kitchen, where Rob stared at them for some time. They moved the bags containing his wife and children's clothing to one side then, again by agreement, Rob allowed Mr. Khalif to go through each bag, to search for what he had been reluctant to tell Rob he had been looking for.

There were items of household goods, some new pyjamas for the girls and bringing a silent gulp to Rob's throat, a packet of Jelly Babies. Having taken these out of the bags, Mr. Khalif then proceeded to search through the receipts at the bottom of each of the carrier bags. He looked more and more forlorn but Rob, growing less and less interested in what he deemed to be a fruitless exercise, was prepared to humour him, just to get him off his back. Finally Mr. Khalif asked if he could have permission to go through Carol's handbag and Rob reluctantly agreed but turned his back on the proceedings, to contemplate how long it would be before Mr. Khalif left and he could end all of this. The persistent shopkeeper searched methodically through the handbag, seemingly without success and then started to empty each of the compartments in Carol's purse. Suddenly he stopped and stared and a broad smile spread across his life-worn face.

"Mr. Price," he whispered slowly. "I have it."
Rob turned around, confused as to what Mr.Khalif could possibly have found that would allow him to attempt to achieve the justice for his family, that Mr. Khalif had promised. When he looked at what Mr.Khalif was holding between the thumb and forefinger of his right hand, he was not really that surprised at the disappointment he felt to find it was nothing more than a piece of paper.

"I don't understand." He said, resigned to the futility of the outcome of the bag search."

"Mr.Price, you have now got the choice of either giving up or, going after the Duncans and gaining the justice you thought was not possible." He then went on to explain to Rob the most incredible story, that actually increased his pain many times over, because of the potential this discovery would have had to change the lives of his family, were they not to have died on that fateful day.

"But Mr. Khalif, how can this possibly give me the opportunity to get back at the Duncans?"

"Mr. Price, on that awful day, I am grateful at least for the fact that I had the always immense pleasure of welcoming Mrs Price and your wonderful girls into my shop, as I did nearly every Saturday since we first met each other on our first day at the foodbank in Leicester. As always, we had a lovely conversation, with your charming girls delighting not just me but the other customers also. They made the same purchases they made every week. A Beano and a Phoenix Comic for each of the girls, and a bag of Jelly Babies for yourself, I believe."

Growing impatient and also not wanting these painful memories dragged back into his consciousness, Rob interrupted Mr Khalif. "Yes, but what has this to do with my revenge or, if you insist, justice?"

"Mr. Price, there was always one more purchase. Each week they would also buy a Lottery ticket."

"I have always said that this was a total waste of money and if you are now going to tell me I have now won some money, I really couldn't care less and I am happy for you to have it."

"Mr. Price this is no ordinary lottery ticket, the ticket your wife bought was a Euro Lottery ticket and whether you like it or not, I believe that this ticket proves that you are the winner of the biggest prize in its short history. The winner of this prize has not come forward and the Euro Lottery have been calling for whoever bought the ticket to come forward and claim their prize because the date for claiming runs out in three days time. Whether you want the money or not, I would not be allowed to benefit from your win as part of my contract as a seller of tickets. However, I am not convinced that you would want to hand me such a gift, when you know that the prize is 190 million Euros or £170 million."

Even in his present state of grief and his desire to get rid of Mr. Khalif so that he could get on with what he had been planning since he lost his family, Rob was totally taken aback by the huge sum of money on offer.

"Now that is a huge amount of money that I know you cannot imagine using to live a life of luxury without your family to share it with but just imagine Mr. Price, for just a few moments, the resources and man power and legal expertise you could have access to with money like that?"

And for more than just a few moments Rob did imagine.

"How...how do you know that that is the winning ticket?"

"Mr. Price, I have sold a ticket to your wife every week for nearly three years and she has always used the same numbers. When I heard that no-one had claimed the prize, I looked up the numbers as a matter of interest and then checked back to make certain it had been me who had sold the ticket. Mr. Price, you have it in your capability to use this money for real good and at the same time give yourself a reason to ensure that your family lives on and is never forgotten."

Rob was utterly flabbergasted and did not know what to think. Even if he had won this money, how could he, an ordinary teacher not blessed with great brains or physical ability, take on the Duncans? But did he have the right to give up this opportunity, as it was Carol and the children who had created it in the first place? Was it fate? Some sort of intervention to stop him ending his life? What? He needed time to think about this, as it could change everything or simply create even more problems in a life of problems he was trying to escape.

"Mr. Khalif, since I lost my girls you have been a true friend and I cannot begin to thank you for all you have done to try and get me back on level ground. You must appreciate that you have given me a huge amount to think about and I am not being rude, although I appreciate that that is all I have been to you over these last months, but I need you to leave now as I have much to consider."

Rob could see that this caused Mr. Khalif to look very concerned at this point and Rob had to reassure him that whatever he decided, he would tell Mr. Khalif in person tomorrow, to ease his worries that this might be another brush off, to enable him to carry out his original final plan. Mr. Khalif nodded slowly and thoughtfully and said he would return at 12 noon tomorrow. Rob stood, shook him firmly by the hand and saw him out.

He realised he had much to think about and for the first time since that day, he actually cooked himself a meal and after he had cleared away, again realising later that he hadn't done that in some time either, he sat down with a notepad and pen and began to think through the implications of what Mr. Khalif had just told him. He went to bed early, as he knew that tomorrow could be the most important day of his life, one way or the other and once again he slept deeply but this time without the nightmares. He woke with a start, not long after 6.00am and accepted that while he still had the pain and memories of that fateful day, the overriding feeling he had, was one of hope. That there was actually something positive he could do. During the night, whether it was a dream or an idea he had in a period of wakefulness, he had come upon a thought that might just give him the means to bring the Duncans to justice, with the realisation that he should at least give it a go, because the worst that could happen would be the same result as his alternative plan would have provided anyway. Surely, to perhaps lose his life trying, would be far better than taking his own life and not trying.

When Mr. Khalif arrived, punctual as usual, it was, he noticed with a smile, Rob who offered to make the drinks this time and he also noticed the absence of alcohol bottles or glasses. Rob had a number of questions. If he accepted the prize money could he do it anonymously? To which the answer was a definite 'yes'. He then questioned Mr. Khalif about his own life and how he came to be where he was today. When he had heard Mr. Khalif's own astonishing story, he told him that he had the beginnings of a plan but he would only be prepared to carry it out if Mr. Khalif firstly accepted a million pounds from his winnings, as a thank you for his support over the last few months and, that he became a part of the plan that Rob had come up with to gain revenge. But this was a deal breaker and the whole thing happened with Mr. Khalif, or not at all.

Mr. Khalif thought for a short while and said he would agree but he had some conditions of his own. Once Rob had collected his winnings he would lend, not give Mr. Khalif one million pounds and allow him a month to put his own business in order, to free him up for whatever Rob had in mind. Then at the end of the year, he would return the loan with interest and give him a year of his life to help find justice, not revenge, for the three girls. Rob told him the loan would have no end point and they both shook hands and much to Mr. Khalif's embarrassment and discomfort, hugged. Rob then said he had one more condition. Mr. Khalif raised his eyebrow warily but smiled when Rob said that from now on they called each other by their first names.

"Certainly Mr. Rob, that will be an honour. My name is Hassan."

Rolling his eyes with amusement at his new friend's polite insistence at retaining the word 'Mr' when addressing him, Rob shook his hand and replied, "I am very pleased to make your acquaintance Hassan. I hope you do not mind but I do not want to explain my idea here and now, as there is much still to think about but by the end of the month I hope to be ready to go."

They agreed to meet the following day to arrange to collect the lottery win and then would each spend what time was necessary, to put in place the mechanisms that would allow them to attempt something that was likely to be impossible but which would have made Carol and his girls so proud that they had at least tried.

CHAPTER 9

The next day, following a phone call from Hassan to the Lottery organisers, the two of them travelled to the headquarters of the Lottery in Hassan's car. Not wanting to raise interest in themselves by accepting the company's offer of a chauffeur-driven limousine, the whole business of collecting such a large sum of money was surprisingly easy as, of course, it was a money transfer rather than a cheque that completed the deal. After Rob had gone through the various different meetings the Lottery provided for financial management, for mental health etc., the meeting that did take the longest was the one to do with Public Relations, as the organisers were desperate for Rob to give up his demand for anonymity. However, it was the reason that potentially made him such a fantastic winner in terms of media appeal, that also forced even these hard-headed business people to sympathise sufficiently to realise that, while a father losing his family in such a traumatic manner would have sold many more tickets, even they could not bring themselves to keep on pushing the matter. Walking away from their headquarters as a multi-millionaire did not make him feel any different, as opposed to how other winners must feel he thought to himself but it did give him a feeling of relative peace, compared to even just a week ago, because now he had some purpose in his life, some significant reason to want to live.

Dropping him off at home, the two, now firm friends, agreed that they would meet up in a month's time, giving Rob the opportunity to start putting in place the foundations of his idea. They agreed that at the next meeting, Rob would lay out his thoughts and planning would begin in earnest. Before he drove away, Rob ensured that he had Hassan's bank details and as soon as he got home he began the process of transferring a million pounds into his account.

Rob's next task was to convince Matt and Ronnie that he was absolutely fine and the best way of doing this was in person. When he arrived at their door, having driven for the first time in months, they could see that although he had lost weight and looked sallow and worn out, there was a new excitement burning in his eyes and over the meal they insisted he stay for, he explained without telling them anything about

Mr. Khalif or the lottery win, that he was determined to see the Duncans pay for what they had done.

He went on to tell them that he would be going away for a few weeks, to help himself prepare for what was going to be a massive task but in a month's time they would meet again and he would lay out all that he had in his mind and in which they would hopefully also agree to be involved. They were about to say that of course they would but he warned them against saying anything they might regret agreeing to, until they found out exactly what it was they might be letting themselves in for.

"So, are we allowed to ask where you are going?"

"Well, to start with I am going to spend some time with Mick in the South of France."

"That's a brilliant idea," they both said in unison, because they both realised that Mick, the third of the three close friends from University who went on to share a house until Mick left teaching to follow another path, would be the ideal person, in the ideal location, to help get Rob back in shape both physically and mentally.

As he drove away from their house, he looked up to the night sky and said out loud, "Carol, this is for you and the girls," and for the first time since that awful day, he smiled to himself, as he imagined how they would have ribbed him for being so melodramatic.

Two days later Rob was on a flight from East Midlands airport to Le Puy airport in France, where he hired a car to drive himself the hour's journey to the Outdoor Pursuits centre that Mick owned in the Ardeche region, with its mountains, gorges and lakes providing the ideal natural resources for such a business.

Mick had been only too happy to agree over the phone to Rob staying with him for a couple of weeks, after first going through the sympathy process that Rob knew he would have to face with all their old friends from now on. But with Mick that was fine because he and Carol had become great friends from the moment Rob had introduced them, sharing the same sense of humour and outlook on life. Driving now through the wonderful French countryside that he knew Carol would have adored, he thought back to those days when himself, Matt and Mick had left University and all got teaching jobs in Leicester making it a no-brainer for them to share a house.

They had enjoyed four great years together, until one day Mick sat the two of them down and announced he was joining the Army. He loved teaching but he had always been the one amongst them who enjoyed the outdoor life and taking risks and while teaching adventurous activities at the County outdoor pursuits centre was great, it didn't provide the 'gulp inducing' adventure he wanted to experience while he was still young. Eighteen months later he took that desire a stage further and applied for, and eventually passed, the requirements to become a part of the SAS.

While he hadn't been able to tell Rob and Matt the details of what he had been involved in with this elite fighting group, they were able to pick up enough to know that there had been a number of hairy moments, providing Mick with exactly the things for which he had joined up.

Ten years later, Mick had reluctantly left the armed forces after a night parachute drop resulted in a twisted knee that he was told would make him ineligible for any missions in the future. Turning down the offer of a desk job, he decided to reluctantly leave life in the armed forces and used the money he had saved as a bachelor, to set up what had now become an extremely successful Adventure holiday business in the beautiful surroundings of the Dordogne.

The type of place and the person who ran it, were the two reasons why Rob had chosen to start the process of dealing with the Duncans here in France. As he turned into the centre owned by Mick, he smiled at the variety of activities going on above and around him, with zip wires, orienteering, bridge and raft building and there on the river, people learning to canoe. He had hardly parked up, when a grinning bundle of muscle came hurtling out of the reception building and Rob had barely cleared the car when he was grabbed in an all embracing hug that seemed to last forever, as Mick tried to make sure his tears had stopped before he was able to face his close friend.

"Mate, I cannot begin to tell you how devastated I was when I heard the news about Carol and the girls. I cannot believe that those scum bags have got away with this. Just give me ten minutes in a room with them and they will regret they ever messed with the people I love."

"Mick, let's not talk about this now. I just want to spend a few days sorting myself out and then I am happy for us to sit down and talk this through and in fact there is something I will need to ask you that will need you to have a serious think about."

"Ok. I'm intrigued. Come on, let's get you settled in and then I can tell you what a great success I have become."

That evening Rob found he was able to relax for the first time in months, as he and Mick sat on the balcony of his cabin overlooking the valley and with the sun setting, reminiscing about the fun they had shared at University and in the first few years of teaching. They parted at 11.00pm with an agreement to meet at 7.00am for a run before breakfast. An uninterrupted sleep saw Rob wake the following morning feeling fresh and ready to join Mick on a five mile run. This being the first exercise he had done for over six months and with Mick who was still SAS fit and whose knee was fine for what he termed "civilian activities," Rob finished the run in a state of near exhaustion but it was a feeling that gave him a sense that this was the start of him moving on with his life.

After showering and having breakfast, Rob spent the rest of the day joining in some of the activities with the different school groups, such as canoeing and orienteering, before finishing the day swimming in the river just before dinner. This became his regular routine for the next few days, as he gradually improved his fitness and the pallid look he had arrived with began to be replaced with a healthy looking tan. Along with the good food, by the Friday of the first week Rob was beginning to feel like his old self but always being aware of the ever present feeling of loss that remained in his gut.

Each evening Rob and Mick sat on his balcony and talked about everything other than that tragic day. But on the Friday evening, Rob felt ready to confront the topic he had so far avoided and Mick listened in silence and a growing feeling not just of loss but also a barely controlled anger. Once he had completed his tale, they both sat there in silence for some minutes, staring at the moonlight reflected off the lake, until Rob put down his glass of wine and told Mick he had a proposition for him. While he explained what he had in mind, he asked Mick not to say anything until he had finished and even then he didn't want an answer to his request, until just before he left in a week's time.

The first bombshell that Rob dropped as far as Mick was concerned, was that he was now a multi millionaire but before Mick could make any comment on this, Rob held up his hand and went through the charade of pretending to zip his mouth. Rob then explained to Mick how close he had come to ending it all and Mick realised that now really was the time to listen and not interrupt Rob opening up about his feelings for the first time since he had arrived. He heard how it had been a small Syrian shopkeeper who had brought Rob back to the land of the hopeful and made him realise that there was a chance with his newfound wealth, to avenge the deaths of Carol and the girls.

Rob went on to explain that he had given a great deal of thought about how he could achieve his aim of getting his revenge or bringing the Duncans to justice. He admitted that it was revenge he really wanted but in honour of the memory of his family, he might just have to settle for justice, as Mr. Khalif had put forward a powerful argument for so doing. Rob didn't want to expose his plan to Mick just yet but its success or failure would depend a great deal on whether Mick would be prepared to help.

"Yes," Mick said immediately but Rob told him he needed Mick to listen and think about what was needed before he agreed. Mick told him that there was no need to wait. He would be up for it anyway because of his feelings for Rob and Carol and the girls but in all honesty, while he loved what he was doing, he missed the excitement of being involved in something that involved a little more danger. Also, his business was now up and running and very successful, whether he was there or not. He had people he could leave in charge and as long as he could pop out to France every now and then to oversee things, he would be available for whatever Rob had in mind. Rob assured him that he could expect to be well paid for his services and although Mick implied that all he needed was bread and board, Rob explained that if this was to work, it had to be done on a very professional basis. He went on to explain that the other people he planned to have on board for his idea were Matt and Ronnie and Mr. Khalif and that he wanted them all to meet to discuss how they would move forward with his plan to find justice for his family. In the meantime, he would have a few tasks for Mick to carry out in preparation for that meeting.

Although Mick was adamant that he was definitely 'in', Rob insisted that he didn't want his answer until the day he left in a week's time, as what he was asking was not only a huge commitment but also potentially highly dangerous.

Over that next week, Rob slept, ate and exercised until he felt not only more like his old self but probably fitter than he had been since he had left University. Yet all the time he couldn't get rid of the feeling of emptiness whenever something reminded him of Carol, Holly or Penny and he began to accept that this was something that was never going to go away but that it was this emptiness that was actually giving him the reason and motivation to do something positive.

On the day of his flight back to the UK, as Mick helped Rob load his car, they hugged each other and before Rob could open his mouth, Mick spoke the words that would make the whole unlikely plan a little more feasible.

"Before you say anything the answer is yes and you couldn't stop me being involved, even if you tried. I will meet you at your house in just over a fortnight to finalise details with you and the others and you can lay out exactly what you have in mind. As far as the tasks you want me to carry out in the meantime, I should tell you I have already begun and it already looks good."

Having hugged his friend and whispered a "thank you," in his ear, Rob climbed into his hire car. He would never have questioned Mick's friendship, whether he had agreed to be involved or not, but his total commitment, without knowing the full details, made Rob realise how fortunate he was that, even though he had lost his family, he was not alone. Starting the engine, he waved through the open window as he set off on his journey back to Leicester and the next step in his plan.

Feeling more positive than he had done since that fateful day, walking through the front door of his house on his return gave him a jolt back to the reality of his situation, when he was greeted by the silence the house had been unaccustomed to and made worse by the mail that had been posted through his letterbox, addressed not just to him but Carol also. He went to the lounge and grabbed his old friend, the bottle of whisky but before he went through to the kitchen for a glass, he stopped himself. Realising that while he might have needed the whisky to get him through the early days of mourning, he now had a different and more potent answer to his despair. He put the bottle in a cupboard and went through the same processes that he and Carol would go through whenever they returned from holiday; unpacking, shopping for food and then preparing a good old British fry up, surprised by the comfort he felt from imagining that she was there in some way helping him.

While his meal was sizzling away in the pan, he rang Matt and Ronnie to tell them he was back and asked them if they could come over for a meal the following evening as he had some things he wanted to talk about. Wary of what these things might be but delighted that Rob sounded more like his old self, they readily agreed. Tired after his journey and also because of all the things that were spinning around in his head that would not settle until he had managed to start the process of putting his plans in place, Rob was in bed by 8.30 pm and slept more soundly in his bed than he had done for some time, with the comfort of knowing his life could still have some purpose.

The following day, rising early, as soon as he was fed and watered Rob went onto the internet to check on some issues he needed to have clarified, before the time came when he felt that estate agents would be open for business. He contacted all the ones he felt could offer him what he wanted and asked them to send him the details of his fairly specialised request and then spent the rest of the day researching and making notes concerning his plans for the future, until he realised that he ought to start preparing the meal for Matt and Ronnie if they were to avoid ringing for a takeaway.

At 7.00 pm the ring at the door signified that Matt and Ronnie had arrived. They were obviously surprised and delighted at how well he looked and that there was again, a light in his eyes that seemed to have been extinguished since the day his family were so cruelly taken from him. After catching up with each others' news, with an emphasis on how Mick was doing and how his business had taken off, his close friends, with a glass of wine each, waited for Rob to tell them why he had wanted to speak to them, suspecting that this was more than just an invite for a catch up. He explained to them, that first they would eat and then they could relax and chat. Impatient, but hungry and knowing that there was no point pushing their friend, they enjoyed a leisurely meal of sea bream, new potatoes and green vegetables followed by a fresh fruit salad, confirming to Matt and Ronnie, that Rob was at least now leading a more healthy lifestyle. They were also silently delighted that they spent much of the time reminiscing about Carol, Holly and Penny, something that Rob had studiously avoided in the previous months.

After the meal and having loaded the dishwasher, they sat in the lounge with their drinks and Rob took a deep breath and proceeded to put them in the picture. He started with the fantastic, in the true sense of the word, news of his lottery win and after their initial exclamations of shock, tempered by the realisation that they all would have swapped this for one more day with Carol and the girls, he went on to explain how this had made it possible for him to realise, that he now had the opportunity to get his revenge on the Duncans. He went on to tell them that that was one of the reasons why he had been to see Mick and he also laid out the role of Mr. Khalif in his plan. But while this would work without their involvement, he had an idea where, if they agreed, his plan would really take off. Either way he had a suggestion for them that he hoped would happen whether they wanted to be involved in the Duncan project or not.

When he had outlined how he wanted them involved, he told them that he did not want an answer now but would ask them to be ready with an answer when he had them all together with Mick and Mr. Khalif in a meeting to finally decide whether they were going to go ahead with the plan of bringing the Duncans to account. Matt and Ronnie both separately agreed that they were certainly intrigued by the initial idea that Rob had put forward but would need to hear more, before they could make a decision about getting involved in something as potentially life changing, as trying to bring down a crime family as powerful as the Duncans, however much they might desire to do so. Understanding their concerns fully, Rob told them that once he had a clearer idea himself about how he was going to implement his plans, they could all talk freely about their feelings. He suggested that this meeting should take place in two weeks time and that Mick and Mr. Khalif had already agreed that they would be there. Suddenly realising the lateness of the hour, the sound of the taxi horn was the signal for them all to get up and and say their goodbyes before Rob ushered them out of the door.

Rob went to bed that night feeling more positive yet again and actually looking forward at last, to something other than missing the most important things he had ever had in his life, as he contemplated putting everything in place ready for the big meeting in two weeks time.

The next morning, the post and emails presented him with a number of suggestions from the different Estate Agents he had contacted previously. Some were totally inappropriate but the ones he thought might suit, he googled and further whittled down the properties he wished to actually visit. Once that was done, he rang the estate agents associated with each of the properties that met his criteria and arranged viewings. This he did each day for the next four days and while there were one or two properties that had the potential to meet his needs, none of them fully matched his remit. All the estate agents he dealt with were, not surprisingly, extremely solicitous once they knew the amount of money he had told them he was prepared to pay for the right place but he had built up a particular rapport with one in particular, a Geoff Smethhurst of Bells estate agents, who he remembered fondly as someone he had played rugby against and with whom he had always got on well. He had the other advantage of not being as offensively pushy as some of the other members of his profession who Rob dealt with. Rob was sure that it was because Geoff took the time to chat to him about life in general and was not embarrassed to listen to him talk about his recent tragedy, that he had a real feeling for what it was that Rob wanted and so, when on the fifth day Geoff rang him to say a property had just come on the market that he felt might be the 'real deal', Rob arranged an appointment to view with more optimism than usual.

He had to wait for the following day and as he drove out into the Leicestershire countryside, he felt quite optimistic, a feeling that increased when he stopped outside the entrance gates of the property he was to view and saw the impressive gate posts topped by the most magnificent statues. The long, tree lined drive provided the time for his anticipation to increase, until he could see the building appear before him and he knew immediately this would be the place, whatever the condition of the interior. For before him stood a mock Gothic castle that had actually been built in the 1840's, nestling in, so the details read, 400 acres of land that include, a gate house, a gamekeeper's cottage, a lake and because it had been previously utilised as an equestrian centre, stables and well maintained lush meadows that would be ideal for converting into sports fields. As he climbed out of his car, Geoff ran up to greet him and ask him what his first impressions were but quickly realised by looking at Rob's face that he had been right to think that this could be the one. While the inside of the building was of less interest to Rob, as he had plans to make massive changes, he was pleasantly surprised at how suitable it would be already for what he had in mind.

Geoff then drove Rob around the property in his Estate Agent's ubiquitous Porsche, finalising in Rob's mind that this was the place he wanted and this was cemented when they drove up to the entrance gates, to admire the two rearing horses, one on each pillar protected by the wings of a huge statue of the mythical winged horse, Pegasus and Geoff agreed, rather dubiously that, yes it would be possible to attach a horn to the foreheads of each horse if one really felt the need to do so. Rob swallowed hard but could not bring himself to tell even Geoff, who he now regarded as a friend, that not only did he feel the need to do so but that he had once promised two very special little girls that should they ever win the lottery, one of the first things they would do would be to buy a castle and two unicorns.

Back at his own car, Rob left Geoff with a handshake and instructions to make an offer that would guarantee the purchase and drove home beginning to believe that perhaps finding the perfect property was the start of things falling into place. All he had to do now was persuade Mick, Hassan, Matt and Ronnie to fully come on board, once they knew what they were actually letting themselves in for.

CHAPTER 10

A week later, on the day when all the protagonists had agreed to meet, Rob was up early making sure that there was food ready to go in the oven when necessary, so as not to have any time wasted during what he hoped would be a long and full day. If it wasn't, then it would have meant that they had decided early on that his idea was a non-starter. Mick arrived with Matt and Ronnie who had picked him up from East Midlands airport and had had a good 'catch up,' on the forty minute drive to Rob's house. As they were all reacquainting themselves, a ring at the doorbell signified that it must be 10.00 am, the designated meeting time and therefore the time for Hassan to be his usual punctual self. Rob made the introductions as, although they had all seen each other at the funerals, there had been little appetite for socialising. Now, sat at the kitchen table, they looked at Rob expectantly and, not for the first time since he started to formulate his plan for gaining revenge for his family, Rob wondered whether what he was about to suggest was ridiculous and a fantasy, way beyond anything he was capable of. But then he realised, that in those expectant looks was also a love and concern for him that created the desire to do what was right for his girls and the frustration that justice was not something that had previously seemed possible. He had to do this.

Taking a deep breath he thanked them all for coming and told them that what he was about to tell them had to remain a secret, as the people they were after were violent and dangerous men and their very safety could be at risk should they decide to go ahead. For that reason if, after he had finished what he was about to say, anyone who wanted out could do so with no feelings of guilt or aspersions from the others. He then went on to explain how he had come to this point.

"As you know, after the day when Carol, Holly and Penny were so tragically killed, I was absolutely distraught and I think you know that at one point I had planned to end it all. The only thing that stopped me from doing so was the desire to see those responsible, answer for what they had done in a court of law but I had determined that once that was done I had no reason to live. After the court case, when those responsible were allowed to walk free, I was determined that this was the end of the line and the humiliation I experienced in the Court toilets that day convinced

me that the Duncans were untouchable. However, just as I was on the verge of carrying out my aim of finishing it all, I was stopped in my tracks by someone who I believe was sent to me by Carol, my own guardian-angel Hassan Khalif." The others looked at their new-found friend with warmth and respect, while he tried to avoid their eyes.
"He firstly made me realise that I had a duty not to give up on finding justice for the girls and then miraculously he gave me the means to attain that aim, by informing me of the lottery win which again I cannot explain, other than to believe that it was fate choosing to give me that immense good fortune for a reason. I will always be in your debt Hassan."

"Mr. Rob you must not keep thanking me, you have done much for me and before that your lovely family brightened my days when I myself had great sadness."

"You are a gentleman as always but I do wish you would call me just Rob. Anyway, while the lottery win would provide me with the opportunity, it was some way off from giving me a way of achieving the revenge, sorry Hassan, justice I so wanted. However, with a little bit of thought I have come up with an idea in which I would ideally like all of you to play a major part. After a great deal of soul searching, despite my desire for a quick result, I realised that the process of getting back at the Duncans cannot be something to rush. DS Bright once told me that such a criminal organisation takes years to build and therefore also takes years to destroy. I felt therefore that we also would need an organisation behind which we would be able to work while developing our strategy. This had to provide the facilities and expertise we might need to call on to achieve our aims. You see I do not want to bring the Duncans to heel just for what they did to me and mine. I want to destroy them in a way that sends a message to ordinary men and women, that there will always be some comeback for people who think that they are not only above the law but have absolutely no concern for society as a whole. I also wanted to ensure that I did something really useful with this money I had won, just as I know that Carol would have wanted some good to come out of all this. To achieve both ends therefore, I decided upon the following. Matt you and I used to talk into the night about how we would love to run our own school where we would appoint only teachers who really cared about their kids and where teachers put the emphasis on teaching the students rather than their subjects. We would rail against the privilege enjoyed by non-state schools where, because of their clientele and facilities, not the quality of their teaching, they would seem to have the answer to how education should work. Whereas we know that with similar opportunities, because of, not despite the comprehensive make up of the students, all schools could achieve just as well. This would also ensure that these students experienced in their school lives, not just a superior education but were also able to realise how in essence, they were all so very alike. Not to be pitied or looked down upon for their different lifestyles but able to be themselves in an environment of mutual respect. Why couldn't state schools benefit, just as schools of privilege do, in turning out students who go on to positions of responsibility and then being able to call upon each other whenever they needed a particular area of expertise? What if we were to set up a school where everyone could rely on the contacts they made there for the rest of their lives? I am not just talking about where government officials from the likes of Eton look after their own but where people from all walks of life, like shopworkers, plumbers and electricians, would have built relationships with lawyers and entrepreneurs and yes politicians and prime ministers. Matt, in my ideal world I would have you as Head of this school as you are the best educationalist I have ever met; someone who loves and cares about kids but has the ability to spot like-minded teachers, who also have a passion for getting children to share a passion in their particular subject. You would be paid the proper rate for the job as would all the staff and, if Ronnie agrees, you would live on site. In an ideal world I would like you, Ronnie, to be the bursar but I realise that would mean you giving up your present job. You would however be properly remunerated and you and Matt would basically run the school between you."

Having listened to what amounted to Rob laying out his utopian educational philosophy with growing interest for some time, Matt interrupted his best friend and asked him how he, as basically the owner of the school, would be involved?

"I would like to be involved in any discussions about the direction of the school but yours would always be the final decision. However, because I will need to be involved in the other part of my plan which would be the bringing down of the Duncan family, I would take on the role of the caretaker or premises officer as they are called these days, giving me reason to be on site. In truth, I would really be caretaker in name only and we would employ others to do the real work. In fact, I have already been in touch with my school who have been brilliant about giving me time off since the tragedy. They were really understanding when I told them I did not feel that I could go back and have accepted my resignation."

It was Ronnie's turn to interrupt, as she admitted that this all sounded very laudable and a brilliant way to make a good use of the lottery win but she couldn't see how this had anything to do with getting justice for Carol and her God-daughters.

"That then brings me nicely to Mick, who will also be on the ground staff but again that will be a front for the main work he will do, helping me get back at the Duncans. I have already asked Mick to get together a team of some of his ex-colleagues to help in this task. People who will be well paid, totally reliable and without a criminal record but with the skills I certainly do not possess that will be needed when mixing with the criminal fraternity."

While Matt was also interested in how they were going to deal with the Duncans, he had been ruminating over the fascinating potential of them setting up their own school.

"Just going back to what you were saying about the setting up of the school. Surely it would make more sense for you to be the Head of the school. I would be more than happy to serve under you if we eventually agree to go ahead with all this."

"That wouldn't work, first and foremost because I would never be any good at running a school, whereas you would be fantastic I know. Another reason is because I need to disappear, so that if Duncan puts two and two together and realises that I am the one who is after him, there is no connection to the school. It is for the same reason Hassan, that I will need to give you a significant proportion of my lottery winnings, so that you can be the actual frontman and sponsor for this school."

It was Mick who jumped in this time. "No offence Hassan but Rob, what is to stop Hassan from getting the money and just clearing off?"

"I fully understand your concern Mick because you do not yet know Hassan as well as I do. Firstly, if he wished to do such a thing I would let him because without him I would literally not be here today to even consider any of this. But more importantly, I trust him totally, as you will learn to do so when you have known him for even just a short time. Thirdly, if another reason is needed, a month ago I gave Hassan a gift of a million pounds for all he had done for me but he told me he would see it as a loan which he would pay back. That didn't ever concern me but yesterday he came around to see me and due to the financial acumen he obviously picked up in his past life, he was able to pay back the million pounds. This was because he has almost doubled that initial million in this short time and is using the profits to expand his own business, apparently using skills from his wife who appears to have been some sort of financial genius in their old country, thus enabling him to give his time to me. His ability to make money from money will be vital, because large as my lottery win is, it would eventually run out, as the school we are going to open is going to have the best of everything, with properly remunerated staff. On top of that, the operation to get revenge on the Duncans will also not be cheap, even though I expect to reclaim as much of the cost of everything we do as possible, back from the Duncans themselves. I have confidence that Hassan has the investment ability to keep us afloat."

Again, the more Matt was feeling excited about the idea of setting up their own school, the more questions he had. "You seemed to suggest earlier that the students of the school might somehow be involved in the retribution aspect of this plan. I am not at all happy about putting young people at risk and could not take on the role of Head if I thought that were the case."

"That is why I need you to be the Head and not me. You see, the other beauty of setting up a school is that it will help provide us with many of the facilities and resources we might need in our scheme to get the Duncans. The students are themselves potential resources because of their brains and the particular abilities they will possess between them. So you will have to be my moral conscience, preventing anything from happening that you feel would be too risky and I will always acknowledge your decision as the final one, accepting as I know I must, that my own personal stake in the bringing down of the Duncans could cause me to make decisions that might put others at risk.

There is much for you to mull over, so can I ask you all to go away and think about this before giving me your answers. However, you all have jobs and should we go ahead I would like to start at the beginning of the next school year in one year's time, which would give you time to resign from your present roles or get your affairs in order. During that time, we would also be putting in place, everything we will need to set up the school and to have an infrastructure that can catch the Duncans. To that end, tomorrow, while you are still deciding, I would like to take you to the property I have just bought in anticipation of this going ahead, whether that be without you but preferably with you. Should it be the latter, then it would also be the place where at least three of you would also live. Hassan, I think it would be strange for the sponsor to live at the school but we can discuss that. However, I would like you there tomorrow to have your input. If you have any questions, please can we save them until tomorrow because to be honest I am shattered?"

The following day, having all met at Rob's house just after 9.00 am, he drove them through the Leicestershire countryside to the property he was in the process of purchasing. Amazed with the magnificence of the entrance gate, they became even more impressed the nearer they got to the main building. When they climbed out of the car, Ronnie let out an audible, "Wow," which was repeated quite a few more times during the tour by one or more of them.

"The actual castle will be the central administrative hub of the school and obviously the accommodation for whoever happens to be Head." Rob suggested, while looking meaningfully at Matt and Ronnie. They smiled back non-committally.

"From the front of the school, back towards the entrance gates will be the playing fields, with the space to the right of the building being the sports facilities while to the left we will build the actual school with abundant spare space for further development year on year, as we hopefully attract more and more students. However, the specialist facilities will be in place from the very beginning and will be state of the art. There will be an area of the grounds given over to the business enterprises that Hassan will be setting up, including a very modern Greenhouse, the purpose of which will soon eventually become clear. Some of the students will be boarders, either through choice or, in the case of some of the more deprived students, through necessity and their accommodation will be overlooking the sports facilities. I have an architect ready to go but I want them to work in co-operation with the new Head to ensure the educational demands are all met and with Mick, who will ensure that security is as he would want it. I am happy for suggestions from all of you in terms of the building. For instance, because of the nature of the gang we are coming up against, Mick and I have discussed a number of extra security measures that should be put in place just in case. However, while we can make changes as we go along, I want to get this sorted quickly, as we need to be up and running in a year's time, when we will welcome our first cohort of students."

"Before Ronnie and I take this proposition seriously Rob, where are these students actually going to come from? We obviously can't take them from other schools."

"Ah Matt, good question. To start with, the local authority have, over the last few years, had the headache of trying to find places for the growing number of the children of migrants who have taken flight to this country both legally and illegally. I believe the local council would bite our hands off if we were to offer places at our school. Secondly, each year there are a large number of disillusioned kids who schools feel would be better off with a fresh start. I would like us to be that fresh start but only for those students who we will interview and who convince us they genuinely want to come here and make a real attempt to put their lives back on track with their education and not take advantage."

"I have no problem with that. You know my feelings about the way some schools get rid of their problem kids but that will of course create its own issues for us, in that we could be overloaded with kids who have been dragged down by a whole host of issues and we have always talked about the importance of having the whole ability and behaviour range to enable them all to learn from one another. We could be in danger of burying ourselves with students who take up all our time with excessive needs."

"Matt, I know that you are likely to be right but the migrants will not necessarily have to be a behavioural issue, even though they will have their own issues linked to suddenly finding themselves in a different country with a different culture. Plus of course they will still be suffering from any traumas related to what has happened to make them leave their home. But, and this is a big but, and one of the reasons why I have asked you to be Head, once we start getting the results and the reputation for excellence I am confident we will, someone is going to have to go out there and persuade the ordinary parents of ordinary children that this is the place they should send their children based on our outstanding teachers, fantastic pupil/teacher ratio and amazing facilities. Of course, if you do accept the job you will also have to oversee the building of the school and carry out your present full time job as well."

"Well, Ronnie and I have discussed this at some length already and we would like to accept the offer of the Headship if only to keep you on the straight and narrow but it depends upon you agreeing to me handing my notice in for the end of next term and you covering my salary until I officially take up the post in just over a years time. This will enable me to ensure that I can truly give the time necessary to set this school up properly."

"That's brilliant news. The only reason I didn't suggest that myself, was because I did not want to put you under the pressure of feeling you had to leave your present school and job which I know you love. In all honesty, I did not know how you would have found time to do all we've already mentioned and appoint staff, if you were still working." A delighted Rob then opened his boot and brought out a bottle of Champagne and four glasses.

"You old git, you knew we would agree didn't you?"

"No, I hoped but it's always good to be prepared." While they celebrated, the estate agent locked up the castle and had to leave because he had another appointment. Rob promised that he would close the

padlock on the gate when he left and the five of them sat on the grass enjoying what they guessed would be the last few hours of peace before life became really busy. It was Mick who held up his glass in time honoured fashion, to be joined by the others looking forward to their coming venture and there was an audible groan in response to his toast of "The A team."
Rob then spoke to each in turn in front of the other three to ensure they were all on the same page.

"So Matt, you will work with the architect and Mick to help design the perfect school with the added extras we will need to help us with the Duncan part of our scheme. You will also put into motion with Hassan and Ronnie, a bid for us to start our own school. Hassan and Ronnie, you will supervise the spending on the school and set up the relevant accounts. Hassan, I will transfer 100 million pounds into your account, so that any checks on your ability to sponsor the school will come back positive and you can also begin to use your 'magician like' skills with money, so that our initial fund can grow and sustain us in terms of running the school and carrying out our revenge, sorry, justice on the Duncans. Mick, you will continue building a team of people you can trust, who will be able to not only protect the school but lead the operations against the Duncans, while at the same time making sure that we have access to any specialised equipment we might need. I shall be looking into how we can actually get at the Duncans but I will also be available to help with any other aspects of your tasks that I can."

A little later, as they drove away from what was to become the new school, Rob stopped the car at the entrance gates and told them all that they would always have the final say over the building of the school etc. but he had two demands that he would not have refused. They looked at him in some puzzlement as he told them that firstly, he would like the school to be named The Castle of HOPE School. He explained that corny as it might sound, the name would serve the purpose of promoting one of the School's main tenets, that there should always be hope but also as a reminder that this school was in memory of Holly and Penny through the first two initials of their names and his promise that they would have a castle should they ever win the lottery. Secondly, and for the same reason, the two horses on the gate posts would be turned into unicorns to enable him to keep another promise he had made to his daughters but with the addition of an extra, larger unicorn to keep the two smaller ones safe wherever they might be. Odd as it might seem to anyone else, the others all accepted this as being a more than acceptable request and with that, they drove away from what was to become the centre of their lives for years to come.

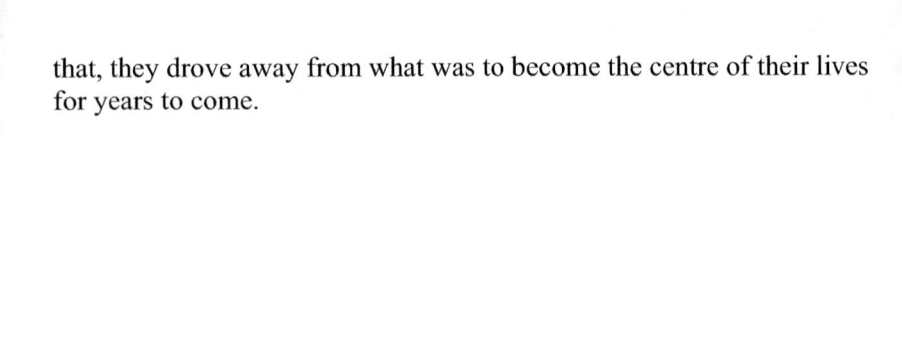

CHAPTER 11

August 2016

Having observed Galizia's success with quiet satisfaction, Rob leaned back in his seat in the front of the van and let out a breath that he realised he must have been holding throughout the proceedings he had just observed and also accepted that there was no turning back now. Knowing that there would be a little time before the next stage of the operation got under way, he picked up the magazine that had first helped provide him with the idea, that resulted in the operation they were now carrying out. He had to force himself to stay calm as, for the umpteenth time he read the introduction to the article about the man whose ego and arrogance had almost destroyed him and whom he loathed with a vengeance. Turning to the much thumbed page in the magazine "Leicestershire Today," he stared at the smiling face of a man in his fifties, standing in front of a very grand looking mansion, with the self- confident air of someone who wants you to know how successful he is. Immaculately but casually dressed, the most striking and jarring aspect of the whole picture was a flower that was far too big to be a button hole, attached to the lapel of his jacket, which frankly, beautiful as the flower was, looked ridiculous. Smirking in anticipation, as he often did when he looked at this subject of his loathing and struggling to rid the image from his mind of a peacock in human form, he once again read the article written by Judith Richardson, which accompanied the photo.

"This week's featured "Person About Town," is the rather controversial figure of Francis Duncan who, when I asked him to describe himself for you readers, listed, "Highly successful businessman, entrepreneur, philanthropist and world-renowned botanical expert" adding seemingly as an afterthought, "loving family man". Others have called him, "A violent head of a vicious and powerful crime family, who have been responsible for a whole raft of crimes including drugs, extortion and, it is alleged, murder and in regard to his botanical claims, 'a charlatan and desecrater of endangered species.' When I put this

contrasting view of his character to Mr. Duncan, rather than show anger he smiled the grimace of someone who had heard all this before and claimed that when you are as highly successful as he has become, you make a lot of very jealous enemies, who will do anything they can to undermine you in an attempt to destroy you. I refrained from suggesting that people such as Bill Gates and his family don't seem to suffer in that way but read that his forced smile and terse response to me was masking a seething anger at my having brought up these points. However, after years of refusing to provide an insight into his lifestyle, it was in fact Duncan himself, who contacted us about appearing in this article, to 'put the matter straight' because he feels that he receives a very unfair and bad press. So let us start by giving you a summary of the tour I was given of his palatial residence and estate.

Having driven up to an extremely imposing entrance gate, set into the middle of a twelve foot high fortified brick wall that surrounds the whole of his 500 acre estate, the wrought iron gates opened automatically, to reveal two security men standing just inside, who checked my credentials. Any thought of driving straight past them would have been tempered by the fact that ten metres into the grounds there was another, this time metal fence apparently electrified, which ran parallel to the outside wall ten metres inside the grounds, forming a second line of defence and begging the question, why was this really necessary? The gate in this fence did not open until the outside gate had closed and once again there were two security guards to check that I was who I said I was. Later in my tour around the grounds, I noticed that this ten metre area between fence and wall had a large number of Rottweilers patrolling different sections, that themselves were fenced off from the others. I would not have wanted to have somehow got trapped in that area and it occurred to me that for someone who claims to be so 'squeaky clean', this suggested that Mr. Duncan was concerned about being attacked by more than a snotty letter from some business rival or scientific competitor. But I get ahead of myself because firstly I should describe to you the luxurious living arrangements enjoyed by the Duncan family, which is made up of Francis, often known to his annoyance as 'Frankie', the patriarch and his three sons Brad, Alex and Philip."

Rob read that these boys were the apple of their father's eye, especially after their mother deserted them when they were only very young. The writer went on to describe the boys and their achievements, conveniently glossing over the many "*close scrapes that they had had with the police over the years as frequently reported in our sister publication, The Leicester Mercury."* She then went on at some length describing each room in the house, how it was decorated and which items of interest furnished each room. While the article was full of praise for the luxurious nature of the look of *"Duncan Towers, so named in an attempt to emulate a business hero of his and television reality star in the United States called Donald Trump, whose signature building and residence was called Trump Towers",* it would not be difficult to imagine the writer sniggering behind her notebook, at what she obviously considered to be ostentatious bling. It was when the writer was taken back outside however, that Rob became once again interested. Not because of the garages housing numerous sports cars or because of the polo ponies and stables that also graced the ground but rather it was when Duncan spoke about, but refused to show the writer his pride and joy, because this was the part of the article that really excited him.

"Francis Duncan really came to life when he explained to me that his real pride and joy were the orchids, that he had managed to produce in his purpose built bio-sphere, modelled on the biomes of the Eden Project in Cornwall, and situated at the far end of his property. He claims to have hundreds of examples of Paphiopedilum Rothschildianum, sometimes known as the' Gold of Kinabalu' or 'Rothschild's slipper', the most expensive and rare orchid in the world, growing in his grounds. This rare plant is a large, clear leafed orchid and is unique because it holds its petals almost horizontally, giving it a very distinctive appearance. Furthermore he claims to be the world's leading expert on this extraordinary flower and the only person outside of Malaysia who has been able to propagate and develop this unusual and much sought after orchid, other than those grown in the rain forests around Mount Kinabalu in northern Borneo. I should add here, that there is a great deal of distrust in the scientific world that this claim is true and if it were to be true, then what Duncan has claimed to have done is in fact illegal, as it is against the law of Malaysia to take plants or seeds of this plant out of the country. He swats away such claims as jealousy from inferior minds and that he collected the seeds many years ago before the flower was designated an endangered species by the Malaysian government, way before they were protected and became illegal to harvest. Those that are stolen and sold on the black market go for around $5000 or £3000 a plant. Duncan claims that he has no interest in selling orchids, as it is their beauty and the science of perfecting the growing conditions that interests him. Each flower can take up to 15 years to grow and he boasts that such is his mastery of their propagation that he has access to a

flower all year round, due to the temperature and environmentally controlled conditions of his bio-sphere. This of course allows him to indulge his rather bizarre habit of always appearing in public displaying one of these orchids on his lapel, even though they are demonstrably too wide to wear as a buttonhole. Such is his fanaticism with secrecy, that only he and one of his most trusted workers called Mateo, is allowed to even enter the Bio-sphere. Try as I might, I could not persuade Duncan to allow me to talk to 'Mateo' or indeed to see inside his, some have suggested 'mythical', bio-sphere and I could only see it from a distance. However, such is his anger at the slight he sees as being paid him every year, at the annual conference that is held concerning this orchid, when he is never invited to be one of the speakers, despite his self expressed expertise, he has taken matters into his own hands. This year's conference is due to be held on his estate, with all the delegates' expenses being paid for by him. But the thing that has really persuaded the scientific community to agree to this, is that he has promised to show them the orchids growing in his bio-shere and they have readily agreed if only to prove that he has been making baseless claims all this time. He, of course, has made it a stipulation of him being host, that he will be the key note speaker and he informs me that he expects to revel in all his glory as these 'so called world-renowned experts' have to eat the 'humble pie of their jealousy driven accusations', when he shows them that he has achieved something they could only dream of."

Rob's attention was drawn away from the magazine article once again as there was an increase in activity around the truck.

With Galizia disappearing into the distance on the back of Miss Harrison's motorbike, there was now a frenzy of activity at the back of the lorry. The high tensile steel wire that had been designed to trail behind the Javelin as it uncoiled from its container, especially devised to ensure its smooth travel through the air in the wake of the javelin, without affecting its journey, was now attached to the winding gear of the lorry. Mick and his men, then proceeded to build a small tower of climbing scaffolding, fixing a wooden platform to the top a few metres higher than the Javelin embedded in the faraway tree. Over this they draped the wire and then helped the 'Prof', as he was affectionately known, up onto the structure. (The 'Prof' was the nickname the pupils had given to Hassan, whose technical and scientific expertise they had frequently been exposed to in the various talks and lectures he had given at the school and a nickname in which he was secretly delighted.) Having steadied himself, the 'Prof' proceeded to flick a switch on the modem he held in front of him, causing the high tensile wire to rapidly tighten and provide tension between the lorry and the javelin which was stuck securely, fifteen metres up an oak tree that was situated 35 metres into the estate. Now, ready for the next phase of the operation, step forward, or more accurately roll forward Zippy, real name Zafir, so nicknamed because of his speed in his wheelchair and on the climbing wall. Chosen for this task because not only was he a talented weight lifter, who was one of the strongest in terms of body weight to strength ratio of the students in the school speed climbing team but also because he was one of the lightest. This was due in some part to the fact that he was naturally small but also because Zippy had lost both his legs due to a land mine, back in his native Afghanistan and was still receiving treatment, after which he could be fitted with prosthetics. Refusing help and hauling himself onto the bed of the truck from his wheelchair, Zippy grinned at Mick who was leading this operation and was now giving Zippy his last minute instructions. Nodding with excitement at the adventure ahead of him, Zippy using arms only, shot up the ladder that was part of the structure supporting this end of the wire. He gripped the handles of the mechanism that straddled the wire and with a second thicker wire being paid out from his backpack, he pushed off and began sliding silently on the downhill gradient, over the estate wall and across the ten metre compound where the Rottweilers were patrolling oblivious to what was happening above them, towards the javelin embedded in the tree 35 metres away. Applying the braking system as he approached the tree he stopped and scrambled onto the branch just above his head.

    He was really enjoying himself now, being able to use his climbing skills to move higher up the tree, where he fastened the wire that he had now removed from his back pack just as Mick had shown him in the practice sessions they had been through so many times back at the school. He now had to wait, while Mick at the truck end of the wire gradually tightened it until it was taut and safe for a return journey. Having completed his task, Zippy placed the zip wire handles over the newly-positioned wire and set off back to the truck. This had been great fun he thought to himself but as he got closer to the ten metre compound containing the dogs, he sensed himself slowing and then stopping, while hanging directly above the area that he definitely did not want to end up falling into. Watching all this from his vantage point at the top of the ladder supporting the wire at the truck, Mick used his walkie talkie to warn his two snipers situated in trees just outside the ground, that they might need to put a dart into any dogs in the compound beneath Zippy should he fall and then readied his rescue team. This would of course mean the end of this operation because although they were confident of rescuing Zippy, the drugged dogs would be a real give away to the security guards that something was amiss. That however, was the least of their worries should Zippy fall.

Up on the wire, Zippy was totally calm as he investigated why he had stopped. Realising he would need to take his hands of the handles and grab the wire, he knew he could not do this one hand at a time as the moment he took one hand off the handle he would tip into the compound. With a dynamic pull up on both handles Zippy let go of them on the upsurge and gripped the wire in his two gloved hands. Dangling precariously, he felt around the mechanism until his fingers came into contact with a build up of grease and tree debris that must have accumulated as the wire was being run out. This had now built up into a gungy mess that acted as a stopper on the mechanism. Cleaning this away with one hand while holding the wire with the other, Zippy then moved the mechanism back and forth a few times to ensure it could run smoothly, grabbed the handles and then finished the last part of his journey back to the truck. Mick grabbed him gratefully as he appeared over the wall of the estate and helped him return to his chair. "Well done laddy." Was all that Mick could get out before being further relieved when Zippy told him that the problem should not occur again because the grease on the wire that had been put there to enable the wire to run smoothly from the backpack on the outward journey, had now been cleaned off by his homeward ride.

Zippy and his chair were placed in the waiting van and he was driven back to school, his part of the operation a success but like Galizia, with absolutely no idea what had just been going on, other than it was one of the challenges that would gain him house points for his 'House'. The minibus that took Zippy back to school was the same minibus that had just delivered sixteen more of the schoolchildren to the truck, made up of eight of the Horticulture club with large backpacks and eight of the school cross-country team. The Horticulture club had spent a good deal of time in the previous few months researching the ideal growing conditions for specialist tropical plants and working with the 'Prof' back at the school, to prepare the specially built greenhouse for the arrival of some special guests. They had already been briefed and rehearsed what they had to do and lined up on the truck behind the 'Prof' and three of the ground staff led by Dave, who had rifles slung across their backs. The students smiled at this but appreciated the attempt by the school to make these challenges appear as realistic as possible but believing that there was absolutely no way ground staff would be allowed to carry a rifle let alone know how to use one.

As Mick tapped each in turn they placed their zip wire mechanism over the outgoing wire that Zippy had secured to the oak tree and set off silently across the compound to the tree where a ladder was set up by the school's ground staff for them to climb to the ground. Once they had all arrived at the base of the tree the 'Prof' led them at a jog until a large dome, made up of perspex prisms came into sight. They approached the bio-shere with caution, even though the 'Prof' knew it was usual for the building to be left unguarded at night because of the other security measures that were in place and Duncan's disbelief that anyone would dare try and steal some of his plants. Checking the building carefully, Dave waited for the 'Prof' to disable the security alarms with an electronic 'gizmo' he had come up with, before carefully picking the lock to gain entry to the biosphere. The sight that greeted them was, the 'Prof' would later admit, one of the most amazing sights he ever thought he would see in this country. Throughout the dome, there were numerous areas sectioned off, each with examples of the orchid often known as the 'Gold of Kinabalu', in varying degrees of development and each area with its own micro climate.

The students went to the area they had been designated by the 'Prof', where they took from their back pack, a thermometer which they used to check the temperature of that particular part of the dome. They then took out a specially designed temperature controlled transportation bag, into which they placed a plant, set the temperature gauge and handed to the runner allocated to them. Repeating the process so that the runner had two plants, the runner then set off back to the tree where two of the ground staff were waiting with one at the base of the tree and one up the tree. The bags containing the plants were then attached to the incoming zip wire where the slope and inertia carried them back to the team waiting outside the wall. When the runners arrived back at the biosphere after each trip, there were more plants packed ready for them to repeat the process of taking the plants back to the tree. Every now and again, spare packaging bags would also be brought back to the biosphere by the runners. These would also contain the plant Taraxacum Officinale more commonly known as the 'dandelion', that the gardening students replanted in the place of the Kinabalu orchids. This all went on in silence for almost two hours, only halted occasionally, when a security guard happened to take a stroll oblivious to what was actually going on and until there were no orchids left in the biosphere. With the last batch of orchids, both the gardeners and the runners shared them between themselves, while Dave and the 'Prof' remained for a few extra minutes to relock the dome and reset the alarms.

When all the students had returned safely to the truck, Dave disconnected the outgoing wire then clipped it to a device attached to his belt, before placing a small explosive device on the javelin and also on the loop of the connecting point to the oak tree that held the wire he would be travelling on back to the truck. Gripping the handles on his zip wire return, he set off back to join the rest of the team. As he travelled back, the disconnected javelin zip wire now attached to his hip was gradually being wound onto the motorised winding gear on his belt, preventing the wire from trailing across the ground and attracting the attention of the guard dogs. Once he was on the scaffolding back at the truck, he noticed that the students had already been driven away. Mick had a machine ready to wind in the remaining zip wire at the flick of a switch, which he did a split second after the two muffled mini explosions signalled that Dave had destroyed not only the wire connection to the oak tree but also the javelin, ensuring no evidence of their activities remained. They had already taken into account that as the remaining zip wire was being wound in, there would be some noise that would disturb the dogs as the wire was dragged across the compound fence. But by the time the Duncans' security guards arrived to see what was causing the dogs to get excited, the truck and all members of the operation had gone and were on their way back to the school. In his observation van, a contented smile spread across the face of a very relieved driver. Relief, because the start of the operation to bring the Duncans to justice had been a success but more importantly, it had been done with nobody coming to any harm.

CHAPTER 12

On the evening before the first official day of the World Conference on Rare and Exotic Plants, all the delegates were picked up in limousines from the most luxurious hotels in the Midlands, all paid for by Francis Duncan and transported to his mansion in the north of Leicestershire. They could not fail to be impressed by the magnificent entrance gate and tree lined drive that took them eventually to the imposing mansion set in vast and finely manicured grounds. They were all greeted with refreshments and shown to the large marquee erected for the purpose of the conference and in truth, to keep their prying eyes from having the opportunity to chance upon some of the less acceptable aspects of Duncan's activities should they have spent too much time in the actual house.

Duncan ensured they were all present before making his grand entrance, moving through the throng, stopping off at each small group to exchange pleasantries. He was fully aware all the time, of how they all stared in admiration at his trademark 'Gold of Kinabalu' orchid that he always wore in public but also of the undisguised loathing they had for him. This was his opportunity to 'show them'. Having been notified that the buffet was ready, he made his way to the small dais he had positioned with a microphone. A cough and a tapping of his glass with a pen brought the room to silence. He smiled and then scanned his captive audience before announcing.

"Please accept my warmest welcome to my modest little abode." He waited for, but barely received, the laughter he expected and so moved on quickly. "It is an honour for me to have so many world renowned botanists and environmental scientists here for these next few days, to discuss the topics close to all our hearts. We are all experts in one or more areas of this wonderful world of exotic and tropical plants." He couldn't fail to notice the sly looks some of the delegates shared, as if in some secret club from which they wanted him excluded. "Now, tomorrow you will all have the opportunity to see my own area of expertise, the propagation and nurturing of the Paphiopedilium Rothschildianum orchid. I hope you won't think it boastful of me to remind you that, I am in fact, the only person outside Malaysia to achieve this feat and certainly in such large numbers."

In order to kill off the muttering that met his last remark, he carried on to explain that the growing of the plants was done almost solely by himself, as the feeding, watering and temperature control were all regulated by computer and the system he had had installed. He implied that he had been responsible for devising this system but many of the experts in attendance were aware that, in fact, he had employed some of the top scientists in their field to devise a system which meant that he did not have to risk, what he considered to be 'unreliable minions' destroying his pride and joy. As he believed that only 'he' in the whole world had a real understanding of these wonderful plants, Mateo's part in the process being insignificant.

"Tomorrow I will open your eyes to what is possible but tonight you are my guests and you are here to enjoy yourself. So until then, please eat, drink and relax because the buffet is now open." Conversation started up again with many questioning whether, what they would see tomorrow would be the real thing, while others tried to buttonhole Duncan and persuade him to give them a sneak preview of his 'project' this evening. The most notable of these being the President of the association and his severest critic, Professor Charles Baxter. Duncan took great delight in the power he now held over these ingrates, who had belittled him for so long and he insisted that they would have to wait until tomorrow just like everyone else. Tired of their company, he retired to his office where he kept the quality whisky, while the delegates ate and drank their fill before being picked up by their cars and returned to their hotel at midnight. Right at the bottom end of the estate, parked up out of sight in a hollow of trees, interested spectators watched the last of the cars leave the estate and the gates swing shut, through night vision binoculars.

Early next morning, Duncan was up and about ensuring all the arrangements were in place to ensure that his moment of glory would have maximum effect. When the conference delegates arrived, they would receive light refreshments, before he would announce to them all that they would now be going to see the eighth wonder of the world – never one to diminish his own achievements- then they would all follow him in procession to the bio-sphere, where they would be amazed and compelled to acknowledge his true genius. As his detractors began to arrive, he refused to greet them personally, as they were of no significance to him, apart from the role they would be obligated to play in recognising his magnificent achievement and how much he had been maligned. On their part, the delegates were still uncertain, wanting him to fail just to crush his gigantic ego but also excited at the thought that all he said might be true and they would see row upon row of this wonderful example of nature's glory. Having personally provided the transport for all the delegates to be transported from their hotels, Duncan was fully aware when they had all arrived but was determined to leave them to wait a little longer, to raise the expectation levels. Just before he was ready to address the throng, he dispatched two of his more presentable body guards to go to the bio-sphere, to unlock it, turn off the alarms and be ready to act as 'meeters and greeters.' They would know better than to enter the dome, as he was the only one ever allowed to step across the threshold first, lest their ignorance caused them to alter the delicate atmospheric bubble he had so carefully created. With all the delegates mingling in the hallway at the front of the house, Duncan appeared at the top of the long winding stairway from where he felt his presence would most impress these people who had tried to belittle him over the years.

"Ladies and gentlemen, the time is now upon us for you to bear witness to, not only the most beautiful and awesome sight you will ever have seen, but also to a recognition of myself, as the only person in the world to have been able to propagate the Paphiopedilium Rothschildianum in such large numbers outside Malaysia. Following what I know will be a life changing experience for yourselves, we shall then return to the conference marquee where I shall take questions about my remarkable achievement. I feel the rest of the agenda will be something of an anti-climax after that but I shall make myself available for the rest of the day should you wish to congratulate me in person, or indeed in many cases, apologise for any slight you feel you might have inadvertently dealt me in the past."

There was a hubbub of angry mutterings as Duncan then descended the stairs like some Head of State and started to lead the way out of the door. As the delegates neared the bio-sphere, Duncan took delight in their murmurings of awe and appreciation of the sight they were encountering and he could hear some beginning to question each other's previous scepticism. Once at the entrance, Duncan waited until all were assembled and the greeters handed each delegate a protective suit, complete with hood, gloves and overshoes. While he knew that this was not totally necessary, as each plant was actually in its own individual compartment, he nonetheless thought it all added to the atmosphere of thoroughness and scientific exactitude that he wanted to create. When all were ready, he opened the door of the dome and stood back, allowing the delegates to demean themselves by pushing and shoving to be the first to see his prize creations. He struggled to keep the beatific smile from his face as he followed the last delegate into the building. He was ready to accept the showering of praise and worship that would surely be coming his way, from the very people who, for years had treated him as if he were some child who needed a pat on the head before being told to go away and play. While they were the adults who could be the only ones who really knew what they were doing. It was only then that he began to notice the giggling and suppressed anger and comments about wasting the time of such important people, as delegates started to push past him to leave the dome while ripping off their coveralls.

"Duncan you have gone too far with this charade. I have no idea what you had hoped to achieve with this ridiculous waste of time but you can be assured, that as President of a highly respected scientific organisation, I will ensure that you will never be involved in anything to do with the Rare and Exotic Plants Association ever again. And I expect transport to be provided for all of us to return to our hotel immediately. You shall be hearing from us about the compensation we expect you to provide for wasting our valuable time."

Duncan barely heard a word of what was being said because he was only now becoming aware of the devastation within the dome. As the true horror of what he saw hit him, he simply sat on the floor with his head in his hands and emitted a roar, inhuman in its volume and tone.

His body guards knew better than to try to talk with their boss but had the good sense to warn the staff back at the house that there would be a large number of unhappy people arriving there any minute now and that transport should be made available to them immediately, so that they were not around to further add to the humiliation of their boss when he eventually came too. They also realised that they did not want to be the ones dealing with him when he did recover and so Ernie, who had seen what his boss was capable of when unhappy, had the good sense to tell the people back at the house to send the three sons down to talk to their father.

With no interest at all in the orchids, the boys had planned a day of keeping out of the way until all these 'geeks' had left the grounds but on hearing what had happened, they rushed down to the dome, not so much out of love and concern for their father but because they recognised that what had happened also represented an attack upon them as a family. On reaching the dome, they found their father no longer on the floor where they were told he had been, but screaming and shouting at his body guards and looking angrier than they had ever seen him before, and that was saying something. He shoved past the boys as they tried to placate him and demanded that he saw everyone back at the house now. Once there, all his staff were gathered in the hallway and he erupted into a tirade of expletives, as he vowed that anyone found to be involved in his humiliation would be hunted down and dealt with. No-one was to leave the house until he and his sons had questioned all the staff. Only then, would his most trusted security staff begin an investigation into how this could possibly have happened. Brad, his youngest son, unwisely suggested getting in the police, the response to which was a slap to his face from his father and a roar, that translated into him not giving the 'plod' the pleasure or opportunity to look closely into his life. He also made it very clear to his personal assistant, Michelle, that none of this was to appear in the media and any editor or producer who might dare to do so, should have their name passed to Pete, his second-in-command, who would deter them from so doing, using whatever methods felt necessary. The boys and Duncan's secretary, were relieved when a timorous knock on the door took Duncan's attention away from them as he yelled for whoever it was to enter and into the room crept a small dark haired man in his thirties, who Duncan stared at impatiently.

"Well Mateo, my boys tell me that you could not have had anything to do with this debacle because you were still locked in the compound with the other gardeners when this all happened but if I find out…"

"Mr. Duncan, Sir, you know how much I loved looking after the orchids, I would never do anything such as this."

"Yes well there is now nothing for you to do and so you will go back to what you were doing before." Looking at his middle son Alex, he commanded him to send Mateo to one of their cannabis farm houses.

"I don't want his face around here reminding me of what I have lost."

"But Mr. Duncan Sir, you promised me that you would free me eventually because of my work with the orchids and now I cannot help you with the orchids I thought that…."

"Well you thought wrong. You still owe us a great deal of money for arranging for you to come to our country and believe me you will pay it off. Alex why is he still here?" This last command he shouted over his shoulder, as he stormed off to his office, demanding as he did so, that his sons should report back to him as soon as they had questioned all the staff and set the security guards to the task of searching the grounds and checking last night's security arrangements.

It did not take the boys long to ascertain that nobody on the staff knew anything about what had happened to the orchids, as their fear of the known consequences of crossing this family were well understood. The security guards could find nothing amiss concerning the grounds or the guard dogs and everything seemed to have been normal the night before. Hanging back so as not to have to be the first to deal with their dad again, they eventually worked up the courage to go and see him and explained that there was no sign of what had happened.

Beginning in a whisper but gradually increasing in volume as his anger could no longer be contained, the head of the Duncan family addressed his sons."This has to be a professional set up. There are three crime gangs with the resources and the desire to want to attack this family. Get our men out there and find out who is responsible because I promise you, that once I find out, there will not be a war there will be Armageddon. This is more than an attack on the family, this was my life's work, the one thing that was going to give me respectability and it has been ripped away from me. I won't have it, I won't have it!" he screeched and threw his whisky glass at the ornate mirror hanging opposite his desk. If Rob and the 'A' Team had been able to see, as the mirror shattered and glass cascaded to the floor, they might well have seen this as the first coincidentally, appropriate sign that the Duncans' feeling of invincibility had started to crack.

CHAPTER 13

The day after the the Duncans experienced their unprecedented humiliation, anyone visiting the school, whose personnel had been responsible for that humiliation, would not have noticed anything out of the ordinary. Lessons went on as normal and staff inside and outside the classrooms got quietly on with their work. What might have been noticed however, by someone particularly sensitive, was the jaunty step and satisfied smirks on the faces of the ground staff and premises officers, who had celebrated together the previous night, not so much the success of the operation but that they were now well and truly into the sort of thing that provided the danger and excitement they had so sorely missed since leaving the service. What had also delighted them, was the feedback from the camera they had set up in the Bio-dome to record the reaction of Duncan when he faced his humiliation and the hidden microphones that had also recorded the comments of the delegates as they left him in despair.

Equally satisfying was the video they had then downloaded onto the internet, allowing people around the world to see a man metaphorically explode with anger. It mattered not that once the Duncans' security staff saw the video, they would be able to locate the camera and destroy it because the angrier they could make Duncan, the more mistakes he would make and the more likely they were to catch him out. However, it was none of these things that brought Mick to meet with Rob and the others the following evening. After congratulating each other on a job well done, Mick explained how during the celebrations the previous evening, one of his men Phil, had been working on the inside as one of the waiters and he "had a couple of interesting pieces of information he thought we would like to know about." However, he actually came back this morning with something more than just information."

"What do you mean? We're intrigued."

Mick went to the door and Dave escorted in a small, swarthy man, looking very uncertain and frightened. "Guys, let me introduce you to Mateo, who Phil found hiding in his hired caterer's van when he went back to the Duncans' this morning, to help clear up. It turns out that Mateo here, was the sole worker responsible for looking after Frankie Duncan's orchids but has now been given the sack and told he would be working from now on, in one of the Duncan cannabis farms. He has been trying to escape for some time and this morning took his chance by hiding in Phil's van, only to be discovered when Phil got back to base. I hope you don't mind but I promised him that we might be able to take him on"

"Mr Mick, if I could intercede here. It would be of great benefit to me if Mateo could be employed within our Greenhouses to tend the orchids. His expertise and experience would be much valued." Hassan suggested.

Mateo looking more comfortable, made it clear that he would be delighted to help in any way he could if it took him out of the clutches of the Duncans. He also exclaimed how interested he was in Hassan's orchid programme and wanted to know what type they were. Hassan suggested that there would be time to explain all that but for now perhaps, it would be better for Mateo to rest and be settled in. Mateo's effusive gratitude was waved away as he left the room with Dave.

"Well done Mick, that really is a bonus and I will personally thank Phil but what were the interesting pieces of information that he also came up with?" Rob asked.

"Well firstly, it became apparent as Phil moved around the house, that there were lots of photographs of Duncan and the boys but none that included a mother of any kind whatsoever."

"Do we know anything about what happened to the mother? She is obviously no longer in their lives, as we have not seen her and she certainly was not there last night,"Ronnie asked.

"Well, I read that she had abandoned them but that is something we need to follow up. The other thing that Phil mentioned was that, also at the cocktail party the night before the supposed 'reveal', Duncan had many of his old and dearest friends present, including some well known criminals, presumably to show off and also as a bit of 'glad handing'."

"I suppose we should expect no less of someone with an ego like Duncan," Hassan offered.

"Yes, but amongst the delegates and his close friends etc., was someone who is an old friend of yours Rob and who Phil recognised from seeing you with him in a newspaper photograph during the court case. He managed to get a picture on his phone, which I have now got here on my phone. Have a look. I think you might be very interested, as I believe it explains a number of things we have never been able to understand."

Rob took Mick's phone and looked at the picture of a large group of people, obviously enjoying themselves but he didn't need anyone to point out who he was meant to spot because the person who seemed to be laughing most animatedly, was someone he definitely knew. This really does make things even more interesting Mick, tell Phil this is brilliant."

CHAPTER 14

Rob relaxed back into what had become his usual chair in the house he couldn't bring himself to leave because of the memories it retained of life as a family. Looking at the large picture of them all on the wall opposite, he sipped his glass of wine, basking in the feeling one gets when something you have planned goes far better than you could possibly have imagined. He thought back to that day seven years ago, when they had all accepted his idea for setting up the school and his plan to gain revenge on the Duncans. After viewing the property he had bought, he had dropped them all off and each had then got to work on the different tasks they had been allocated, to such a high degree of commitment and efficiency, that he now felt that even if he never brought the Duncans to book, he could look back with huge satisfaction on the success of the school in its own right. More important, he knew that if Carol was looking down now, she would have been so proud of what they had all achieved and, he had to admit, the fact that he had personally come so far, from such a low point. Thinking of how much he missed his two daughters made him literally ache. He knew that many people would think it a cheesy, superficial, nod to their memory that he had bought the castle with the horse statues at the entrance, that he had adapted to look like unicorns. Similarly, naming the school Castle of HOPE was a way of indicating to the students that their futures were now full of realistic opportunities. He had accepted also that by using the first two initials of his daughters' names would, he knew, have made him the subject of ridicule amongst many but to his great relief, not his close friends who were totally supportive and they were the ones whose opinion truly mattered.

At almost exactly the same time back at the school, Matt closed the door of his office, poured himself a drink from the bottle of Glenfiddich he kept in the bottom drawer of his filing cabinet and sat back in his chair with a satisfied sigh. Everyone had gone home, Ronnie was at her Zumba class for the evening and he loved this time when the school was silent and he could take the time to think. Looking back on the last seven years, he had to admit that when Rob had first come up with the suggestion of starting a school and getting revenge on the Duncans, he and Ronnie had gone along with it to give Rob something to focus on other than his grief. They both believed that the setting up of the school would be a fantastic opportunity, if it actually happened but of that they had been dubious and also believed that the revenge idea would soon blow over as being something impossible. Well, how wrong had they been? Here they were having given Duncan a 'bloody nose' and what a great feeling that was.

He thought back and realised that the first time he began to think they might actually have the ability to achieve their goals was when the school trip returned from the gymnastics competition in Syria. Actually of course, it all started before that, from when the school first opened with an initial intake of just 64 students in year 7, seven years ago, they were now up to 150 in each year group and with a post- 16 group of 170. The initial year group of 64 had grown to 110 by the time they sat their GCSEs two years ago, as the school's reputation grew and they started to pick up, not just those who left their original schools because they were unhappy but also students who saw the increased opportunities for success the school offered. Those first set of GCSE results had helped since then of course, with the School's burgeoning reputation being augmented in National league tables, however pointless Matt thought these were. There was an almost hundred per cent success rate also, for those students who left, either going into training, further education or work.

They had been able to give a number of University scholarships to students, some on the basis that when they had completed their studies they would return to the school and work for a minimum of two years in one of the many small business enterprises that Hassan had set up. Ah, Hassan! Thinking of that gentleman and that was the best way to describe him, reminded Matt again of that time four years ago, with the school having been up and running for three years, when one day, after ensuring that Hassan was otherwise engaged, Rob had asked Matt and Ronnie, along with Mick, if they could meet him at his house but that they should not mention that they were doing so to Hassan. Having developed real affection for Hassan, with the realisation of how much he had done to bring Rob literally back from the brink, Matt knew that like him, Ronnie and Mick felt uncomfortable meeting behind Hassan's back and made this clear to Rob when they arrived at his house together.

"I'm really pleased you feel like that because it shows me that you have found out what a magnificent human being he is already and it will make what I am about to suggest seem not such a ridiculous idea."

When they were all sitting with a drink, Rob had explained that he felt it only fair that he should explain something of Hassan's background before he had met him. They were not too surprised to learn that Hassan was a refugee from Syria but were taken aback to hear that he had also once been a much acclaimed and highly respected scientist, with much standing in Syrian society as a whole. His dissatisfaction with what was happening in his country however, resulted in him becoming a severe critic of the government and in particular its association with Hezbollah, considered widely to be a terrorist organisation. Eventually he had to urgently escape the country when it was made known to him that he was to be captured and executed that very night, to prevent him from inciting the growing anti-government feelings. He and his family were separated as they were attempting to cross the border into Lebanon, where he had hoped to find contacts who would get him to Israel. He had to hide in the boot of a car, to be spirited away to safety by sympathisers, while his wife and two children were captured and returned to Damascus. That is where they are now, held in a guarded camp for the families of people who opposed President Bashar al-Assad's regime and where they live in terrible conditions and have to undertake political indoctrination in fear for their lives. Eventually, he made his way to England but his family is still in Syria and he hasn't seen them for nearly six years.

"That is so sad and makes the altruism of his efforts to help you all the more admirable, when he would have every right to simply concentrate on his own problems."

"I couldn't agree more Ronnie but I have been wracking my brain and I have an idea that I would like to put to you all that could be beneficial to us and at the same time help Hassan."

"Why does this sound like something I am going to feel we need to do but would be stupid to get involved in?" Matt remembered saying at the time.

"It has worried me for some time that we are planning to take on a highly organised and professional crime organisation but apart from Mick and the lads, we have no real experience of planning and putting into practice an operation of the scale that is going to be needed. So I thought we should perhaps have a 'dummy run', by setting ourselves a task with a definite goal to achieve at the end of it and what better goal could we have than bringing Hassan's family to join him in England?"

The others just sat looking at him silently. It was Mick who spoke first, with a big smile on his face. "Well, that would certainly get my lads back in the saddle but you do realise what you are asking? Taking on one of the most highly organised and blood thirsty and, many would argue, terrorist, organisations in the world will not be easy by any means."

"I know and that is why I don't wish to let Hassan know what we're attempting, in case it all goes wrong and he has his hopes raised and then dashed again."

"But we're talking people's lives being at risk here you know and while taking on a highly organised criminal gang is scary enough, taking on a political regime is bonkers, if you don't mind me saying?"

"Matt, you are spot on of course, which is why we need to make sure we get this dead right. To start with, I think that there are two things we need to put in motion. Mick, I would like you to sit down with your men and come up with a plan that has more than a chance of working."

"Got it."

"Ronnie, I think that you are the person best placed to get Hassan to tell you everything you can find out about his family, without giving him any clue that your interest is anything other than one would expect from a caring friend."

"When you say I am best placed, are you basically suggesting that I am a nosey so and so?"

"Well I was thinking more of the close relationship you have developed with him but yes you are a nosey so and so also."

"Fair enough." Ronnie agreed.

"Guys, this is something I feel I owe Hassan, so while I see this as an opportunity for us to evaluate if we have the ability to take on the Duncans, I really hope we can get this done for his sake."

Suddenly the phone rang, interrupting Matt's train of thought and as he answered it, wary that it might be some parent with a complaint or problem, he visibly relaxed to hear the voice of Pete King his Head of Maths, who just wanted to let him know that they had been able to appoint an excellent young teacher that day from the six candidates who had come to be interviewed for a position created by the school's burgeoning numbers. After a little bit of general chit chat, Matt congratulated his Head of Department on being able to make such a good appointment and wished him goodnight. As he settled back down, he contemplated how lucky the school was in having so many excellent staff but he was under no illusions however, knowing that they had a huge advantage in being able to have such a low teacher/pupil ratio, helping to attract the best teachers, a number of whom he and Rob had worked with in their careers and some who they had once taught and had then become teachers themselves. They knew these teachers to be good people and were able to offer attractive salaries and way-above-average free time in the school day, for their preparation and marking and with access to the very best, state-of-the-art facilities in all areas.

Much of the early success with the troubled students they had taken on board, was down to a mentor system of qualified teachers being available to take on awkward and disillusioned students who needed time out from their timetabled classes. Not to be punished but to receive one to one tuition, where they could go "off piste" in terms of how the teachers built the trust and relationships needed, for the students to be ready to go back into their normal classrooms. In most schools this was not possible because of the lack of finance but all teachers knew that you could never treat all children the same. From the very start, it was not only the teachers but the students who had it drummed into them every day, that good teaching and learning is down to relationships. Without good relationships, you would never succeed in life and it was because of the quality of the staff that he and Rob had appointed, that this was the aspect of which he was most proud. There were many examples but because of recent events, he was reminded of Galizia and Zippy who had been such stars in ensuring that Operation Orchid was a success. Here were two children whose whole lives had been totally disrupted for reasons beyond their own control but who were now flourishing, both academically and socially, due in no small part to the school.

Zafir, or Zippy as he was affectionately known, had lost both his legs when a landmine went off when he left the track he was walking along, to retrieve a runaway football back home in Kandahar, while on the way to school one morning. His life hanging by a thread, the fact that his father was an interpreter for the United Nations enabled the whole family to come to the UK where, after extensive surgery and a number of further operations, Zafir was into his second year at the school. A naturally outgoing and cheerful personality, who had become popular with staff and students alike, he had found a particular talent for indoor rock climbing, making an advantage of the prodigious strength he was developing in his upper body from using a wheelchair, plus his natural agility. He had won a number of indoor climbing competitions and was ranked in the top three for his age group in the whole country.

He had been one of their real success stories for sure, as in fairness had been Galizia, who had been trafficked with her parents from Lithuania, living the life literally of a slave, while working on a farm in Scotland. Her parents managing to escape when they realised that the gang that had enslaved them were on the verge of grooming Galizia as a sex worker. The family had been brought down to England and was now living in hiding but in continual fear of being hunted down by the gang who had trafficked them and who did not look kindly on losing their workers. Galizia had found it difficult to fit into her new school at first but she was a quick learner, not only in her studies but also in various sports, excelling specifically in the javelin. The excellent relationship she had built with her PE teacher, Miss Harrison, had seen her blossom not just socially but to the extent that she was a strong candidate to win the English Schools Athletics championship in her event this summer.

Thinking of Helen Harrison reminded Matt of what he had been contemplating when the phone had rung. About a week after they had broken up from their meeting about potentially rescuing Hassan's wife Amira, Mick called a meeting of all of them, other than Hassan again, for obvious reasons and laid before them the plan he and his men had come up with.

"This is going to be much more difficult than we first thought and I have some good news and some bad. Firstly, the good. I have a friend in the CIA who is based undercover in Syria and he has informed me that Hassan's wife Amira and the two children, Ibrahim and Jamal, are secured in a stockade from which it would be impossible for us to carry out an extraction without potentially killing or injuring other innocent people. Also, we would then have the problem of trying to get out of Damascus, which is full of government troops."

"Apart from you having a contact there, this doesn't sound like the 'good news'." Matt suggested.

"I am coming to that. Every day the two children are taken off in a bus with the other children of political prisoners and driven to a school outside the city, where they receive Islamic teaching and political indoctrination. This could well be the opportunity to grab the children."

"What about the mother?"

"That is the bad news. I cannot see how we can get at Mrs Khalif without there being collateral damage and I am fully aware that you do not want that."

"So what are you saying?"

"What I am saying is, that we might be able to get the children out but the mother would be impossible."

"We can't leave her behind."

"Rob, I know how you feel but sometimes you have to cut your losses and there might be an opportunity later for us to get her out, when we haven't got to worry about the safety of the children also." When they voted on whether to go ahead, it was with a heavy heart that Rob agreed that it was the only way forward. Rescuing Hassan's children from that life was essential and he had to put aside his desire to be the great saviour until Mrs Khalif could be saved safely later on. If, of course, she was still alive at that stage.

Mick explained that the biggest problem would be getting into the country and out again, especially as on the way out, they would have two frightened children with them. He proposed that as a cover, they should arrange a school trip to a country close to Syria like Turkey, enabling him and his men to act as members of staff, while the school party would also provide the cover for the two extra children who could be hidden with the others on the way out.

"Will they have their passports?" was Ronnie's typically practical question.

"It is unlikely, which is why I propose driving from England which could take two or three days by coach but we could make that part of the itinerary for the trip. This would also make it much easier to smuggle the children out. Passport control at an airport is much more difficult to get around than borders and ferry terminals."

"This doesn't sound very plausible to me. Surely they are all very difficult to circumnavigate?" Matt's concern for his schoolchildren was now giving him second thoughts and while Mick would never do anything to intentionally put them in danger, he was much lower on the 'risk averse' scale, to the point of falling off the bottom, than his old housemate.

"We will need some luck but it can be done. Another advantage in our favour is the fact that Syria is experiencing horrendous bush fires across the country and so there is chaos everywhere. The corrupt government is practically bankrupt and so is having to bring in water helicopters from anywhere they can, to help fight the fires, ensuring that there are lots of people from charitable organisations moving in and out of the country, who would not normally be there, making it easier for us to explain our presence."

"Well that might help, but let's hold on a minute. If it all goes wrong, we could be putting our pupils and staff at risk."

"Matt, I want to limit the chances of that happening as much as you do. So if it all goes pear-shaped the students and staff will deny all knowledge of myself and my men and we will admit to having forced you at gun point, against your will to harbour us."

"But what will happen to you then?"

"Don't worry about us. We'll find a way to escape later, when you are safely back in England."

"This all seems a bit James Bond to me."

"Well Ronnie, if anyone has any better suggestions I am happy to go along with them but if we're going to get those poor kids back to their dad and out of that hell hole, then this is the best we've got."

"Oh I wasn't suggesting that 'being a bit James Bond' was a bad thing. I find it all quite exciting."

Matt frowned at his wife before suggesting, "Shouldn't we find out first of all if Hassan would agree to all this?"

"It would be unfair to ask Hassan because he would be torn between having his children with him and his wife being left behind."

"I agree, it has to be her decision but how can we find out what Mrs Khalif would think?" Ronnie looked around the room at the others as she asked this essential question.

"Let me see if my contact can get to her and find out what she feels." It was agreed that while Mick attempted to contact Mrs Khalif through his CIA friend, the others would look into whether such a school trip could actually work.

It was nearly two weeks before it was of any value meeting again, as they had all been waiting for a reply from Mick's CIA friend. Meeting at Rob's house so as not to pique the suspicions of Hassan, Mick reported back.

"My friend, who shall remain nameless, has managed to get a message to Mrs Khalif some time ago but as you can imagine she is in a very precarious situation and was only able to reply yesterday, through a trusted third party, who delivers food to the compound where she and her children are being held. She is apparently overjoyed, firstly to hear that Hassan is safe and also at the idea that her children could be taken away from the nightmare they are living and be able to join their father in safety. She insisted that we are not to think twice about her. She will cope she says, if it means her family are safe. We are just to let her know if there is anything she can do to be of assistance and she will do it. Until such time she will pray to Allah for her children's rescue."

"Well we have the go ahead and there is no way we can not go ahead now that we have raised Amira's hopes of having her children saved. Now all we need is a plan."

"Actually Rob, I think we have the beginnings of an idea that would at least get us into Turkey legitimately but then it would be down to Mick."

"What are you suggesting Ronnie?"

"Well I have been looking at the websites for companies that organise school trips and there is a very reputable company that Matt has used before, who are looking for schools to take their gymnastic teams to Turkey, to compete in what is ostensibly an international competition but is in fact a way of building relations with schools and countries across the globe."

"Actually, that has the potential to be ideal because my boys will easily be able to pass themselves off as gymnastic coaches for the team and I have an idea how the activity also has the added advantage of helping us smuggle the children out among the other kids." Mick added.

Despite his desire to go, it was decided that Matt needed to stay and run the school and be available should any emergency arise. Rob who had been a PE teacher and Ronnie, plus the female PE teacher Helen Harrison, who ran the gymnastics team, would go as staff, along with three of Mick's men Phil, 'Little' John and Mac, plus Mick himself. It was felt only fair that the basic skeleton of what they were hoping to do should be explained to the young PE teacher, Helen Harrison, so that she had the option of pulling out, but on hearing the explanation behind the reason for the trip her reply of, "Just try stopping me," meant that all systems were go.

It was almost two months later that a party of eighteen members of the school gymnastic squad, plus their 'teachers' boarded the coach that was to take them on, what they saw as a mini adventure but which the staff were concerned was going to be too much of a real adventure. During that two months, the gymnastics team had increased their training to an extra evening a week and were amused at the fact that some of the ground staff were now helping with the coaching. Their initial amusement turned to amazement when they realised that these men they had seen tending the grounds, were really quite skilled, especially in the strength based activities. They had a good deal of fun trying to beat them in some of the fitness exercises Miss Harrison regularly set to improve their strength and flexibility. The ground staff always won the activities such as rope climbing using arms only but had to admit defeat whenever any flexibility tests were involved.

Very early in the sessions Mick noticed that one of the youngest girls was getting closer and closer to beating his men on the arms only rope climb and on talking to Helen, he found out that while she was a fantastic gymnast, she was an even better rock climber, who was absolutely fearless. Mick asked Helen if he could work with the girl, whose name was Daisy, on some slightly different skills during the session. Giving her permission, she and the rest of the gymnasts soon got used to seeing Daisy sitting behind Mick astride one of the vaulting boxes and at a signal from him she would stand, put one foot on his shoulders and launch herself up and forward to grab a bar suspended about three metres from the ground. Each attempt would be timed and Mick and some of the other ground staff would give her tips on what she was doing. The pupils were told it was something to help Daisy with her rock climbing training. Daisy didn't question it, as she just loved doing anything that had an element of risk.

It had been decided since the last meeting that it would be a wise, extra precaution to not use a hired driver to drive the coach but to have yet another of Mick's men, Dougie, who was a fully qualified heavy goods and passenger vehicle driver, to be at the steering wheel. While his military skills could prove more than useful, his ability to drive a coach with twenty five passengers and tow a storage truck with all their gymnastic equipment was essential. When Miss Harrison began organising the loading of the gymnastic equipment, she was taken aback to find that three vaulting boxes were already in situ. When she questioned Mick about their presence and the fact that those types of boxes had gone out of fashion years ago, to be replaced by much lighter and more mobile vaulting tables, he asked her if she had ever seen the film The Wooden Horse. When she informed him that she had not, he suggested that she should stream it on her phone during the long bus journey and then she would understand.

Inside the storage container that was being towed, were also some pieces of equipment that would not normally be found among the usual gymnastic paraphernalia, including some items developed by Hassan's Research and Development department, that Mick had asked them to produce to help make the gymnastic training safer for the pupils but which Mick actually thought might come in handy on another aspect of the trip. Mick had been warned by the boffins in the research lab, that while they were happy with what they had produced, whether they would work in practice was another thing altogether. They felt that without more time to test them, they could not guarantee them working and they had repeatedly tried to make this clear to the ever optimistic Mick.

CHAPTER 15

The staff had nervous energy and fear of failure to fill their waking hours on the seemingly interminable journey. The pupils on the other hand, had no such distraction but were oblivious to the length of time the journey was taking, as being away from school with their mates and the potential this had for fun was a special treat as far as they were concerned.

The trip had been planned so that there would be time to spend a day in Paris, Munich and Salzburg to help break up the long journey but the pupils and staff were relieved when, after five days of travelling, they booked into their hotel in Ankara in Turkey and were able to start preparing for the real reason they had come.

Matt could remember sitting in exactly the same seat he was sitting in now and being so relieved when he had received the phone call from Ronnie, to say that they had arrived safely and that the students, as he would have expected, were being a credit to themselves and the school.

While Matt was proud of the part the school had played in encouraging the children in their sporting and academic achievements, he thought that perhaps the greatest gift that the school had given these young people was self-confidence, something the children at Independent schools always seemed to have in abundance and which he and Rob were determined would be a quality their pupils would acquire alongside humility. It just so happened that they were also highly successful in sport, the expressive arts and could compete with any school in most areas of the usual extra curricular activities, including many activities more often only associated with the supposed top Independent fee paying schools.

Much of this he credited to the input Mick and his team had employed to evolve the activities running at the school. Until the operation against the Duncans began, it had seemed sensible that only two of Mick's team would be based at the school, while the others continued to work at the outdoor activities centre in the Ardeche, rotating every three months. However, their responsibilities included not only some ground duties and security but also it had been decided that all pupils should take part in either some self-defence or Tai Chi classes that were run before and after school and at lunchtime by Mick's team. To help motivate the pupils, the staff had also agreed to take part, which helped build relationships with the students, who were able to see their teachers in a different light, in an environment away from the classroom, where they were as vulnerable as the students themselves. The young people took great delight in seeing their teachers thrown through the air, or screaming for mercy, while competing against each other in the self defence classes. While others were surprised at the large number of staff who took up the Tai Chi option, as well as the self-defence, which helped ensure that those pupils who chose Tai Chi would not be ridiculed for choosing a supposedly easy option. Soon however, the Tai Chi classes gained more and more of the pupils and staff, who recognised the physical benefits in terms of both core strength and relaxation but also as excellent preparation for those who were now taking the self-defence seriously. Matt had to admit to himself that this included himself and Rob, who often entertained the others with their titanic battles to outdo the other. But also students like Charlie, who had already excelled herself by being in the British Cycling High Performance unit, due to her BMX ability and who, since working with Mick and his team for a couple of years, had also just been selected for the Great Britain Taekwondo team.

The confidence that all the students gained, from their improved sense of being able to control and protect their own body, was apparent in many other aspects of their lives and had led to another suggestion of Mick's, that had become extremely popular with the students. Mick had suggested setting the pupils challenges, at first in the grounds of the school and then gradually further and further afield. Called 'Spirit of Adventure Tasks', the challenges were usually carried out in groups with a mixed age range, to enable the older students to help the younger and the latter to learn from the former. Often these challenges would involve search and find missions, where an item or a member of Mick's team would be the target; or covert surveillance operations, where they had to report back on the movements of a pre-warned member of staff and sometimes plant something on that member of staff or retrieve something from them. These would have house points as prizes, which would be incentive enough but had the added excitement of sometimes being carried out at night. Matt knew that the children's safety was always the highest priority, with each group having a designated adult observer, but he was also keen to ensure that the tasks were not overtly martial in format, aware as he was, of how easily influenced young minds can be.

While he fully understood the need for him to remain at the school while the operation to try and rescue Hassan's family was underway, he nevertheless felt uneasy putting Ronnie and all the kids in a situation of potential danger. Mick's plan to accept full responsibility should they get caught, allowing the school to deny any knowledge of the escapade and claim to be an unwilling cover for these men who had 'kidnapped' them would, he had to admit, have a good chance of success because who would believe that a bunch of teachers and school kids would be involved? But if people believed Mick because they thought that the alternative of a school being involved in such a situation was too preposterous, then it probably was preposterous and why on earth had he let them go?

He did know why however. Hassan had become a good friend over the last few years but more than that, he had literally saved his best friend's life and had done more than anyone to drive the school to become a success. He was extremely modest but when Matt had googled Hassan's life before he had become 'persona non grata' in his country, for criticising the harsh political regime, he had, along with his wife, been a part of something of a 'super couple'. They were both obviously extremely intelligent and Hassan had made a name for himself as one of the top scientists in the world and a prolific inventor. His reputation ensured that the British government were only too happy to grant such an able person asylum in this country but were then disappointed that he had vowed never to work again for any government because of the limitations on freedom of ideas that government would impose, having already escaped one regime, albeit a totalitarian one.

In the short time the school had been running, Hassan had set up state-of-the-art laboratories and workshops in the school grounds but separate from the school, where his research and development ideas were not only providing jobs for students but also producing items that could be sold commercially, again for the benefit of the school. He would also regularly give one-off lectures to the students who adored his 'outside the box' thinking and quirky teaching style, making it inevitable that they harnessed him with the nickname of 'the Prof'. What Matt was most surprised with however, was Hassan's ability to continually improve the school's bank balance, not just from the commercial sales of his inventions but from his ability with investments on the stock market. Hassan had claimed that this was something he had learned from his wife, who was known as some kind of financial 'whizz-kid' back in Syria, where she also had at first been happy to work for the government and bring much needed finance into the country, until she realised that this money was not being used for the good of the people but was in fact going into the pockets of those in power. It had been a real setback therefore, when they found out that while rescuing Hassan's children was a possibility, getting Amira out would not be possible. Matt remembered now, how he felt when he got the phone call from Ronnie on the night before the children were about to be rescued and how that changed everything.

Mick had planned for the extraction of Hassan's two children to take place the day after the gymnastics competition, in two days time, so that they did not have to keep the two children hidden for too long before returning home, but a phone call that night from his contact in Syria caused there to be a dramatic change to all their plans. Apparently, the military wing of Hezbollah were determined to send a message to the many people who were opposed to the political regime they supported in Syria and so were going to parade the families of political activists in Lebanon and broadcast the family members denouncing their activist relatives across the Middle East on live TV. Hassan's wife and children were going to be taken from Syria to Lebanon on the day of the gymnastic competition. When Mick told Rob and Ronnie the news they were horrified.

"All the effort we have put in and the hope we have built up, for nothing," raged Rob.

"Actually this could be to our benefit," replied the ever optimistic Mick. "But we will have to tweak our plans slightly."

"How can it be to our benefit?" Rob asked forlornly.

"Well, now we are going to be able to try and get Hassan's wife as well as the kids." When he explained what he had planned, Rob was even more worried.

"I do need to ask Helen to lend me Daisy however."

"Hang on a minute Mick, I can't risk a child's life in something so dangerous."

"You are going to have to trust me here Rob. We always plan so that the level of risk is minimised as much as possible."

"Yes, but there is still risk. I promised Matt that I would never put our pupils in any danger."

"If this is to work we need that little girl because me and my men are far too big to achieve what she can. Rob, this is the only way I know for this to succeed."

"OK, but I am really worried about this and we have to let her know what she is letting herself in for and give her the choice. I dread to think what her parents would think of this."

Ronnie felt now was the time to support Mick and make the decision easier for Rob. "Rob let me go with them and I will pull the plug if I think it necessary, whatever Mick thinks. Also, through spending time with Hassan, I know what Amira and the children look like and while I might not be any help in the operation, I can at least look after Daisy and the Khalifs when we get them."

"Oh great! Matt is going to love me when we get back. If we get back. Putting not only his pupils but his wife in mortal danger."

"He doesn't need to know all the details, does he?"

Daisy was thrilled at the idea of the adventure that was being suggested to her, especially when she was told about the specialised item of clothing she would be wearing and so that night, while the other children slept, Daisy joined Mick and the other four ground staff, plus Ronnie and waved goodbye to Miss Harrison and a worried looking Rob.

They travelled with Mick, Ronnie and Daisy in a hired car under the pretext of a family travelling to explore the historic sites of the Middle East. While the four members of Mick's team drove a truck filled with the equipment transferred from the school storage container and a number of dirt track motorbikes his men had purchased and given a special service earlier in the day. Their cover was that they were travelling to Syria to help fight the bush fires that were tearing across Syria, under the auspices of being trained fire fighters themselves. Both vehicles crossed the border uneventfully from Turkey into Syria at different points, leaving it until the next morning so as not to raise too much suspicion. Driving on to Damascus, they met up with Mick's contact at an old, remote farm. After a few hours sleep, three of Mick's men left with the car and two of the bikes to prepare for their part in the upcoming operation. Mick in the meantime, arranged with his contact for a message to be passed to Amira Khalif, warning her to be ready and of the small part that she would have to play in ensuring the success of the operation.

Not knowing what time the soldiers of Hezbollah would be moving the family, Mick, Ronnie and Daisy had been sitting drinking fresh orange juice at a pavement café, from just after first light. From their vantage point they had a clear view, allowing them to see the closed gate that entered and exited the stockade where the political prisoners were being kept. Daisy kept looking around self consciously to see if anyone was looking at her and even worse laughing. She had initially been excited about wearing the special suit designed to help in the operation but when that morning Mick had produced what looked like one of the shell suits that she had seen people used to wear in the eighties, from magazines they had studied as part of the modern history of Britain module at school, she was less than impressed. But when Mick had explained how this suit could save her life, she thought it was worth the embarrassment. Now, as she looked around, she realised that she actually fitted right in, as many of the locals also seemed to be wearing actual shell suits from the eighties.

At approximately 8.15am the gates were swung open and a flat bed truck carrying half a dozen armed men with a machine gun fixed on the truck bed, was followed out of the compound by a rumbling, old, rickety bus that Mick hoped was full of political prisoners including the Khalifs. His hopes were confirmed when he spotted a hand against one of the windows with just three fingers protruding , the sign that Mick had passed on to Mrs Khalif to confirm she on the bus. Mick was further reassured by the fact that the bus was the same as the one described to him as the one that took the children to school each day, which meant much of the old plan could remain in place.

"OK, we're on."

"Yes!" exclaimed an excited Daisy.

"Oh shit," exclaimed a less excited but highly strung Ronnie. "You will look after her won't you Mick?" she added as she watched him and Daisy set off to collect the dirt bike upon which he and Daisy would follow the bus.

"With my life," he called back to her over his shoulder, which didn't really make her feel any better as she paid the bill and then went to drive their truck to the rendezvous, where hopefully everyone, including the Hassan family, would meet up later that day.

Mick kept his distance behind the bus as it headed out of the city and was pleased to see that the bus itself was at least a good 100 metres behind the armed truck. Any attempt to speak with Daisy while they were travelling was drowned out not just by the sound of the bike but by the constant drone of helicopters that were constantly flying overhead, either to or from the bush fires that were plaguing Syria. Knowing he had the speed to catch the bus any time he wished, Mick stopped the bike and handed Daisy a headset and microphone, that would allow them to converse while travelling. Having shown her how to use it, he set off again after the bus, knowing that nothing was going to happen until they were well away from the built up area of Damascus and its surrounds. Once they were out in the barren countryside, Mick decided it was time to run through once again with Daisy what it was she would have to do. Their original intelligence, that the children's school bus always carried one armed guard on board truck suggested that the political prisoners' bus would be similarly guarded. However, the knowledge that the bus would be escorted by an armed escort in a separate truck had thwarted the original plan of simply stopping the bus with force and extracting the Khalif family. The escort would see the bus being stopped by him and his men and would have quickly come back to the bus, with the potential for injury and death and no guarantee that it was only the opposition who suffered. If the bus were to seem to stop of its own accord however, then the escort would not notice immediately and drive on, increasing the distance between them and the bus and reducing the danger of them being able to shoot. Hopefully by the time the escort realised that anything was amiss, the Khalifs would have been removed to safety and the escort could be dealt with, without fear of anyone innocent being injured by any shooting that might take place.

    Gradually the road they were on became almost empty of traffic as they drove deeper into the countryside and Mick asked Daisy if she was ready to go. With her simply putting a thumbs up in front of his face, Mick began to accelerate until his front wheel was almost touching the battered bumper of the bus and he concentrated on maintaining the same speed as the bus. The driver of the bus would perhaps have wondered where the bike had disappeared to from his mirror but would hopefully just think he was in the blind spot behind the bus and not be concerned. With the prearranged nod from Mick, Daisy carefully stood on her seat and with the speed developed in practice on the vaulting horse, back in Leicestershire, she barely hesitated before stepping onto Mick's shoulders and with a straightening of her leg, launched herself up and forward until she was able to grip the rear luggage rack. Steadily she began to crawl over the rack and its contents towards the window vent in the roof, between the front and back roof racks.

    In the bus, Amira Khalif who had previously opened the roof window vent the few inches possible and had been standing in the aisle for some minutes, blocking the driver's rear view mirror which would have shown Daisy climbing onto the bus, started making her way to the front of the bus. Once level with the driver, she complained to him that she was not feeling well and needed him to stop. He told her this was not an ambulance and threw her a plastic bag, telling her that if she did not sit down, he would beat her with the rather large stick he had threatened them all with, when they had first got on the bus.

    This small diversion gave Daisy the time she needed to reach the vent and with the hydraulic device she had been given by Mick, she removed the whole of the skylight and lowered herself into the bus. As she did so, she contemplated how disappointed she was that she hadn't been able to make use of the safety suit she was wearing that had been given to her in case she should fall off the bus while it was moving.

Inside the bus, the other passengers became aware that something was happening just before the window in the roof was popped out, as the sound of the helicopters flying overhead increased substantially. Seeing a very small white girl drop into their midst, further shocked them to silence, as they watched her put her finger to her lips and make her way to the front of the bus.

Once there, she tapped Mrs Khalif on the shoulder and ignored the surprise and then disappointment on the face of Mr. Khalif's wife, as she turned around expecting to see some large muscle bound rescuer. Her surprise however, was nothing to that of the driver when Daisy spoke the lines she had so carefully learned over the last few weeks.

"I think you should do as the nice lady asked and stop." For when he glanced around to threaten the person who dared to question his authority, he saw a very small, white, European looking girl and certainly no-one who he had personally seen onto his bus when they left the compound back in Damascus. Daisy shrugged her lack of understanding when he screamed at her in Syrian, "Who are you? What are you doing on my bus?" before slamming on the brakes and bringing the bus to a sudden stop.

Behind the bus Mick had dropped back in readiness for when it came to a halt and the moment it did, he accelerated to stop level with the door of the bus, ready to deal with the driver. Watching what was happening inside, he realised he needn't have worried. He looked on as the driver, a big, burly, moustachioed, brute of a man, raised a large stick to strike Mrs Khalif and Daisy but before he needed to react to help them, Daisy had pushed herself in front of Mrs Khalif and hit her left shoulder with her right hand, just as the stick was on the way down to strike her. Immediately there was a loud pop and the suit that had been designed to inflate into a ball that covered Daisy totally, from the top of her head to the end of her toes, to protect her should she fall off the roof of the moving bus, now served the purpose of protecting her from the stick that made contact on the oversized rubber ball like structure and rebounded to strike the driver on the head, laying him out cold, to the delighted cheers of the occupants of the bus. Making a mental note to inform the boffins back at the school how effective their invention had been, Mick pressed the button on the outside of the bus that opened the doors in an emergency and waited for Daisy to press the deflate button on the suit, as she was blocking the passage way of all the occupants of the bus trying to get off. Mrs Khalif called her children to her and along with all the other travellers on the bus looked towards the escort truck in fear of what would happen now.

Even though the truck was almost two hundred metres away, they could all see that it had stopped and was in the process of turning around to investigate what had occurred with the bus. Half-way through its three point turn on the narrow road, the occupants of the truck all seemed to look up in unison, as a water helicopter descended from above them and suddenly released close to 2000 gallons of water, causing some of the escort to literally drown, while others were severely injured by the force of such a gigantic rush of water driving them into the ground and against rocks and trees. The helicopter then rose and banked away, before heading towards the bus, where it landed close by. Mick looked up as the pilot's window slid open and Jimmy shouted out, "Taxi for Mr. Michael Thompson."

Hassan's wife was at first at a loss for words but when they came they came in a torrent of tear soaked gratitude and hugs.

"There will be time for that later. We are not yet safe. Quickly, let's get your children on the helicopter as we are still not out of the woods."

Mrs Khalif looked around, bemused by the lack of trees. As they made their way to the helicopter, Mick realised that while a number of the political prisoners stayed by the bus, afraid of what might happen if they tried to escape, more than a dozen were following them to the helicopter.

"Shit I hadn't thought of that. Mrs Khalif we can't take everyone."

"We cannot leave them here. It would be wrong"

"We can fit them in the helicopter but once we are in Turkey we have no way of protecting them."

"They will be happy to just get out of this once great country and throw themselves on the mercy of the Turks who are no friends of the Syrian government."

"So be it." They were all loaded onto the helicopter until there was just Mick and Daisy who were left. "You were pretty remarkable do you know that?"

"Thank you but can we get on the helicopter so that I can take off this ridiculous looking suit?" Laughing, he picked her up and threw her into the helicopter which started to lift off the ground the moment he placed his foot on the landing strut of the helicopter. Jimmy flew towards Turkey, relying on there being some time before anyone noticed the disappearance of the bus or the helicopter that they had requisitioned earlier that morning, using the rather hastily cobbled together credentials supplied by Mick's CIA contact. So delighted were the Syrian authorities to have anyone prepared to help them with their operation to fight the bush fires ravaging their country, that no-one looked too closely at Jimmy and Mac's accreditation. Even if they had, it was doubtful that they would have spotted anything amiss with the names of the two volunteers as Tom Thomas the mountain rescue helicopter pilot and the eponymous hero Sam Jones otherwise known as Fireman Sam, signed in as being volunteers from Pontypandy, the beautiful Welsh village of Rob Lee's imagination.

Flying low over the Turkish/Syrian border, so as not to be picked up by radar, Jimmy frightened the sheep and goats as he remained dangerously close to the ground over the desolate countryside, that took Jimmy to a lake surrounded on three sides by mountains, where he brought the chopper down out of site from any road. A little while later, Ronnie pulled up in the truck that she had driven back from Damascus and while she introduced herself to Mrs Khalif and her children, Mick and his men emptied their wallets and pockets of any money they had to give to the rest of the occupants of the bus who had come with them and who were, as Mrs Khalif translated, so very grateful for being rescued. Feeling guilty but knowing there was nothing more they could do to help, Ronnie ushered Hassan's family and the men, along with Daisy, into the truck and set off for Ankara.

CHAPTER 16

Back at the hotel, Miss Harrison had taken a victorious gymnastics team for a McDonald's, to celebrate their achievement before they would have to leave the following day. Rob sat nervously in reception, drinking coffee after coffee and consequently making more and more visits to the toilet. He would never forgive himself if anyone had got harmed in what he now thought was an impossible task. Jumping to his feet as he heard the sound of a truck pulling up outside the hotel, he had his heart in his mouth as the occupants of the truck stepped down and he counted them off one by one, with growing relief in the knowledge that all who had gone, had also returned. He was especially delighted to see that Daisy was unharmed and in fact seemed elated with the experience she had been involved in. But it was the appearance of the petite and exhausted looking woman, hugging two small children to her that gave Rob the biggest cause for excitement, as this was the realisation of the success of the first part of the mission.

The following day, as the bus set off for the long journey back to the UK, it was explained to the pupils, that the extra three members of the party were friends who were being given a lift back to Britain. The pupils smiled and waved a welcome and then returned to their phones and discussions of who fancied who. A few miles before they reached the Turkish border, Dougie stopped the coach on the side of the road for the occupants to stretch their legs while Mick and his men took Mrs Khalif and her children to the tow truck having already explained what to expect.

If the school pupils noticed that the three newcomers were not actually present when the coach passed through the Turkish/Bulgaria border, they certainly did not mention it. A half an hour after crossing the border, Dougie stopped the coach again and the Khalif family returned to the comfort of the coach. This became a well rehearsed routine with each border crossing but as they approached the crossing from Slovenia to Austria, the coach found itself in a much longer queue than they had experienced at earlier border crossings. While the coach was stationary in the long line of transport being checked to cross, Mick got off the coach and wandered forward to see what the hold up was, noticing the length of wait was being caused by the fact that the border control guards were not just opening up containers but checking through the contents carefully also. Going back to the truck he explained the potential problem to the other staff and explained to Helen how they were going to deal with it.

While Mick and his men unloaded the three very heavy vaulting boxes from the tow truck, Helen explained to the pupils that they were going to put on their vaulting display for occupants of the waiting vehicles. Mick and his men placed the boxes very carefully on the ground along with landing mats, near the crossing point and was about to be questioned about what he was doing by the border guards, when the pupils marched to their starting positions and began running and vaulting in a well trained, formation routine. People in the waiting queue of vehicles started to clap and cheer, while the border guards began to smile at this break in their usually, very tedious day. When the coach reached the point where it was the next but one to go through the border checks, the routine was brought to a halt to the loud applause of all who were watching and the Border control guards began the business of processing all the documentation and making a superficial check of the coach and trailer, as Mick and his men were loading the equipment back on the trailer. The guards laughed with the staff and the pupils and slapped Mick on the back, while one actually hand-walked beside the coach as it crept closer to the border. Once there, they were waved across with a cheer and a wave and continued their journey towards the UK.

A few miles past the border the coach stopped again and Mick and his men opened the tow truck and lifted off a couple of layers on each of the vaulting boxes within which lay one of the Khalif family, in the specially prepared storage space. Frightened still, but relieved, the three refugees were pleased to get back on the coach, their mother reassuring them that for each time they went through this process, they were one step closer to safety and their father. Coming off the ferry on arrival to the UK, the sense of relief was palpable amongst all the adults as Hassan's family climbed back into the coach for the last time, a few miles outside Dover. The pupils were unaware that anything out of the ordinary had occurred, as they played their games, listened to their music and organised their social lives either on social media or even sometimes by chatting to each other.

As the coach drove through the school gates after the long drive, the parents of the pupils were waiting to collect their children, along with Matt in his role as Headmaster but more relevantly as far as he was concerned, as a highly nervous, concerned husband and co-conspirator. Also in attendance was a surprised Hassan, having been asked by Matt, who had been thoroughly updated on everything that had happened on the trip by Ronnie, in their numerous phone calls, if he could come and take a register of the travellers as they climbed off the coach. This he was happy to do, as other staff were apparently unavailable but he thought it was a trifle unnecessary, as surely the staff on the coach would have known if anyone was missing. But Matt had convinced him that this was usual procedure and necessary in the smooth running of education in England.

Standing at the entrance to the bus with the customary clipboard, Hassan dutifully ticked off the staff as they climbed wearily down the steps and gave their names so that he did not have to look up to acknowledge them. The pupils followed next and came at such a pace in their excitement to greet their parents that he had no time to look up from his task and as the name was given he would find it on the sheet, add his tick and thank them with his customary politeness. Coming to the end of his list, he was surprised to still hear footsteps descending the steps and turned the page to see if any names appeared on the other side of the sheet and as he did so he heard the name 'Amira Khalif' and his greeting caught in his throat as he dared not look up to have his dream broken. Then the excited screams of 'Abee', the Syrian word for father, made him drop his clipboard and then fall to his knees sobbing in utter disbelief as he looked up and saw for the first time in six years, the people who meant more to him than life itself, moving towards him to envelop him in hugs he thought he would never again experience.

It was a couple of days later that Rob had been summoned to Matt's Headmaster's office, like some recalcitrant schoolboy but he realised it was more serious than that. He knew he had let Matt down by getting the pupils involved in something so potentially dangerous. Ronnie had filled Matt in on the details of the trip but while he was delighted at the success of the mission to get Hassan his family back, he was livid that Rob had broken his word.

"Rob, if we are to carry on with this plan of ours and I emphasise 'ours' not yours, I now know that I cannot rely on you to be honest with me, if it stops you achieving your still overriding aim of gaining revenge. No, don't interrupt. I have laughed at the idea when you have suggested it in the past, that I am your moral conscience, but from now on, whenever anything happens that involves the students, I will have the final say because you simply cannot be trusted to be objective when you weigh up the risks of danger, compared to you achieving your final goal. Either you agree to that or this all stops now."

"Matt, I am so sorry. You are right and I know I was in the wrong. And when I say you are right, I mean also that you have to have the final say because I know that my obsession could spoil everything."

At that moment there was a knock on the door and Matt shouted an impatient, 'Come in.' The door opened and Hassan entered the room. He picked up on the atmosphere that seemed to shroud the office and asked if he should come back another time but Matt stood and hugged him and told him how pleased he was for him, having not wanted to intrude on the day his family had been returned to him.

"I do not know where to begin to thank you and the others for what you have done for me. My life is made, I could never be happier. We have already had meetings with the Foreign Office, who have been very positive about a quick resolution to us all being allowed to settle as British citizens. My contacts in Syria have told me that the government and Hezbollah have fallen out, with each blaming the other over the escape of my family and they are at a loss as to who might have carried out the extraction. Please know that I will always be in your debt and I do not want to pry but I hope that any disagreement between you was not caused by what you have done for myself and my family. Because what you have done is the most marvellous thing anyone could do for another human being. But I will leave you to your conversation and say once again, thank you." At that he closed the door and Matt looked at Rob.

"He is of course correct but I still insist you must never take such risks with the pupils again."

"Matt, he is right but so are you and I will learn to live within those parameters."

CHAPTER 17

Following Operation Orchid, Rob was keen to find out if the police had been called to investigate the theft of Francis Duncan's orchids and so popped into the police station, having made an appointment under the pretence of talking to DCI Grey. He hoped to not only find out if the orchid theft had been reported but also to use it as an opportunity to push himself beneath the police radar, so to speak. After the court case, Rob had initially done all he could to ignore the concern shown by the Leicestershire police, most notably DS Bright, but of late he realised how much he had come to rely on them, not just as conduits of information but as friends who offered real comfort. Now however, he really could do without them looking too closely at his activities, if he was going to be able to put his plans into action without their knowledge and interference. While waiting in the reception area, Rob's attention was diverted to reading the posters on the noticeboards. Depressingly, he saw that one, asking for information regarding a hit and run in Blaby on the date of Saturday 14th February, had lost the drawing pin from one of its corners and was starting to curl away from the board, as if to signal a lost and forgotten cause. While at the same time, a bigger and glossier poster advertising an auction of the proceeds of crime to take place in a couple of month's time, simply reinforced his belief that criminals seemed to have access to a never ending supply of money and how difficult his chosen task was going to be, if he hadn't realised already.

He was not surprised or disappointed when, instead of DCI Grey, it was DS Bright who appeared. He felt that DCI Grey never really invested in the case of his family's death and certainly not to the extent of the DS, who went above and beyond to keep Rob up to date with their enquiries and to offer genuine comfort and support. As DS Bright approached, they both greeted each other and shook hands like the friends they had become. The Detective Sergeant brought him up to date with the little progress they had made with the investigation of the hit and run and had to admit that in fact, while they knew the Duncans will have likely been up to all sorts, there had been no dealings with them for some time now. Relieved that at least he would not have the police looking into his affairs too closely and that the orchid theft had obviously not been reported, Rob spent the next fifteen minutes convincing Bright that he was now in a much better place and ready to move on and the police were no longer to think it necessary to keep checking up on him. He would always be grateful for all they had done and would always consider the DS as a friend but he needed to look forward now, not back. DS Bright said that she understood and they parted with a promise of meeting up for a drink sometime. As Rob walked away, Bright stared after him with a faraway look in her eyes. "What is it Susie? That's a very sceptical look on your face."

Susie Bright turned to see the desk sergeant smiling at her. "Yeah, sorry Sarge. I was miles away, wondering why I have this funny feeling I might have just been manipulated."

CHAPTER 18

Although it had been over seven years since Rob had taken Matt, Ronnie, Hassan and Mick to see for the first time, the property that was to become Castle of HOPE School, Rob was delighted with what they had been able to achieve. The school was going from strength to strength but it had been the recent success of Operation Orchid that gave him a real sense that the other side of the plan, the bringing down of the Duncans, actually had a chance of succeeding. A slight chance admittedly but a chance nevertheless. What they had done was a mere bee sting in terms of the effect it had in the overall scheme of things but it was a bee sting that Duncan would be irritated by for an awfully long time and Rob had every intention of prodding and irritating that sting, as often as he could.

In the months leading up to that first operation, there had been weekly meetings with all four of his friends who, with the welcome addition of Hassan's wife Amira, still called themselves "the A Team", with tongues firmly in cheeks. Having had their first success, today they were meeting to discuss the next step in their plan. Once they were all settled in Matt's office, Ronnie assertively interrupted the general chit chat.

"Look you lot, Amira and I have been talking and we feel pretty pissed off that we have not been able to be involved in any of the exciting stuff you boys have been playing at, as usual. We have mentioned before, how useful it might be for us to try and find out a little more about what happened to Duncan's wife. Well, why you don't leave it to Amira and me to look into what we can find out about Mrs Duncan."

"There is no way we could have got to where we are now with the school or the operation against Duncan without the financial advantages you keep giving us with your brilliant investments and financial wheeler dealing." Seeing that Ronnie was about to argue Rob continued, "But I take your point and finding out if we can get any advantage from knowing about Mrs Duncan makes good sense, so yes, I think that would be a good move." Ronnie and Amira smiled rather knowingly at each other, while at the same time pumping fists.

"Now that we have that sorted," it was Mick who addressed the topic that had given them all some concern before, "I realise that the reason you wanted to carry out Operation Orchid is because you wanted to hit Duncan where it would really hurt but if we intend to really get to him, we need to affect his 'business' operations and I cannot see how we are going to do that without knowing what they intend to do from day to day."

"The problem we have there is, that as Mr. Rob has already told us, one of the reasons that the police have never been able to trap him is that they have not been able to bug his house or places of work because he regularly has them swept for surveillance devices, whenever they are empty."

Nodding her agreement, Ronnie added, "There is also no way we can safely get someone on the inside and in a position of trust, in such a short time, even if we could find someone foolhardy enough to risk it. Is that right Mick?"

"Unfortunately it is and the drones we have used to good effect in Operation Orchid, just won't be able to provide the audio we will need to really have an idea of what the Duncans are up to because of the height they have to maintain if they are not to be spotted. Also, we don't want to overuse those because if we do, they are going to get noticed sooner or later."

"You are all right, and that's something I've given a great deal of thought to and I believe I might have the answer to that little problem courtesy of our good friend DS Bright, which I will explain to you in more depth when I have thought through the details. But to make this work, I need us to come up with a crime to entice the three Duncan boys to commit, that they will not be able to resist carrying out. And before you say it Matt, I recognise that this has to be a crime that is victimless or at least in terms of honest members of the public and again the police have been very helpful in this matter, even if they don't actually realise it. The problem is I have been racking my brains but have not been able to come up with a suitable crime to tempt them."

"Yes, well you've never been that bright. After all you come from a country in the back of beyond where you spent all your time coming up with words that have no vowels in them."

"Very amusing Matt. As you are so ready to criticise I assume that you have a whole raft of brilliant ideas."

"Not off hand, no but I do have access to over seven hundred brains who might."

"Actually, that is a very good idea but are you sure that doesn't impinge on your principle that our students should never be asked to do anything illegal?"

"Just leave this with me."

And so it was that the very next day, having spoken to Ravina the head of Psychology and Brian the head of Computer Studies, the whole of the Sixth form attended their daily assembly to be told that their next extended essay assignment for their compulsory General Studies subject, would involve them working in groups of four and across a number of different subject areas. Obviously they would have their work marked and graded as usual but to add some economic realism to the task, the winners would be given a thousand pounds to spend on something that would benefit the whole sixth form and they would be the ones to choose what that would be.

As the excited students left the assembly hall, they were all given a flier with their task laid out and the names of the students they had been allocated to work with. They were a trifle disturbed to find that the make up of these teams were almost entirely of students from different subject specialisms to themselves and usually people they had rarely worked with before. Despite not wanting to appear too impressed by the prospect of being in competition with their friends and the opportunity to win a prize of one thousand pounds, groups of students were gathered together, excitedly reading the handout they were given on leaving the Assembly Hall, which read as follows,

'HOW TO CATCH A CROOK'

'Police forces across the country, waste huge sums of money that they do not possess, trying to get people accused of crimes or who have outstanding fines, to actually turn up to court or pay those fines. The criminals however, do all they can to avoid this and are difficult to track down. A successful strategy used by some forces in the past, involves sending out letters to the named individuals with outstanding arrest warrants or fines, often around Christmas time, which tell them they have won some money or prizes based on their last known address or National Insurance number. The money and prizes are not of such a value that the criminal might think is too good to be true but be attractive enough to tempt them, during the financial pressure of the festive period. All they have to do is turn up at a given location on a certain day and they can collect their winnings. Unbelievably, large numbers do turn up, with the police waiting to bring them to book for their misdeeds. However, we would like you to think outside the box, because we want you to come up

with an idea that won't attract your normal run of the mill, low level criminal to a specified location but the wealthier criminal who, while not being super rich, is too well off to be attracted by prizes and money that they can easily get their hands on. Once you have come up with an idea, you must then produce the paper work and anything else that might be needed to convince the intended victims that this is something they should take up. In order to make your focus more specific, the target group is male and in their twenties. The students who come up with the solution with the most chance of success will win our prize which, unlike the one offered to the criminals, really is genuine.'

Over the next two weeks, the students gave varying amounts of their time to the challenge, as was always the case with assignments set. What became apparent was that some of the students least expected to show any real effort were the ones who gave this some real thought. Perhaps this was because the topic was depressingly so close to home, in terms of the sort of people normally targeted by the police in such an operation and family members they could think of, who would be likely to fall for this. When the deadline had come and gone, there were over forty entries posted in the box on the desk in reception and unlike his experience in other schools, Matt found that none of them were what might be loosely termed "spoiled papers." This was not so much he thought, because they were wary of occurring his wrath but more likely because the gimlet eyed Mrs. Johnson, his secretary, was the one delegated to police the entry box outside the Head's office and she petrified even him.

The judging was carried out by himself, Ravina and Brian, plus the teacher in charge of Extended Essays, Miss Harrison. Having weeded out those that involved suggestions like pole dancing, a weekend away with the likes of the Pussycat Dolls/ One Direction or being offered a starting place in their team of choice in the next FA cup final, they eventually selected the top three that would be announced in assembly the following day. These were; in third place; a chance to drive with a top racing driver in an F3 car at Donnington Park race track; in second place, a pro-am clay pigeon shooting competition, where you shot in teams of four with the other three team members being celebrities. However, the winner was, 'an opportunity to be able to play with your favourite football team against a team of celebrities for charity'. This being organised off season, as part of the easier pre-season warm up games.

Matt had already taken the best ten ideas around to Rob's house the evening before, when they had sat down to discuss which, if any would be worth trying with the Duncan boys. A smile came over Rob's face when he read the idea that had achieved second place. "Perfect," he whispered, as he showed his friend the one he had selected.

"I don't think that will work Rob. This is not high profile enough for the Duncan boys and you have said yourself this needs to involve a crime where at least a million pounds is accumulated if it is to achieve the ends we want."

"If we were to take the idea just as it is you'd be right but if we make a few slight adjustments, by combining the idea that achieved second place with third and first place in the competition, I think we will have a goer. What is it apart from themselves that the Duncan brothers are really passionate about?"

"Well apart from robbing, stealing and thuggery, that would have to be flash powerful cars and supporting Leicester City."

"Exactly. Now before we plan this in more depth, I think it only fair that tomorrow when you announce the winners, you tell the students that due to the quality of entrants they will now have three thousand pounds to spend and the groups who came first, second and third will decide how it is to be spent." This was perhaps why the governors who happened to be visiting the school next morning were slightly taken aback by what might have caused the whooping and yelling that they heard as they walked past the Assembly Hall.

That same evening Rob and Matt sat down to try and put their plan into action, courtesy of the sixth form "brains trust" and Rob laid out to Matt what he had in mind.

"OK, now firstly I happen to know that the department who deals with the retrieval of the proceeds of crime, has regular sales to auction off items taken from criminals, that have not been claimed by members of the public. This is seen as part of the punishment meted out to said criminals and also a way of making them pay something back into society, even if it is against their will, and in almost two months time, they plan to auction off three Ferraris. If we could persuade the Duncans that they might like to hijack these three cars when they are being transported to the Auction in Birmingham, then my plan to have inside knowledge of all future Duncan dealings could come to fruition."

"Firstly, how are we going to persuade them to do this and secondly, surely we will be putting the life of anyone involved in the housing or transport of these cars in serious danger and you agreed that not putting innocent members of the public in danger, has always been something we have had as sacrosanct."

"The first bit about getting the Duncan boys to take the bait needs a little more thought I admit. As for the transport, that will be one person driving a car transporter and I will be that person, with our SAS boys hidden close by to ensure that nothing too drastic happens to me."

"What? You must be crazy! You've never been involved in anything like this before."

"No, not crazy, just determined to increase the pace of getting revenge for my girls now that we are under way. I know it has been necessary to take time to set things up properly but they have had too long to enjoy a freedom they shouldn't have. On top of that, I cannot keep expecting others to take risks on my behalf if I am not prepared to do the same."

"But that is why we have Mick's team. People who actually know what they are doing and have the skills to carry out such tasks."

"You have to understand Matt, I need to feel as if I am actually contributing more than just the money I happened to be lucky enough to win in the lottery." Matt nodded in recognition and understanding, of Rob's need to play a practical role in getting revenge for what had happened to his family.

"OK. Now if you could get the Head of Psychology, Ravina, and the Head of IT, Brian, to come and see me, I will start the ball rolling in terms of getting the Duncans to go for this."

The following day, while the sixth form were coming up with wilder and wilder ideas about how the three thousand pounds could be spent, Rob was sitting in Matt's office, explaining to Ravina and Brian what he needed, as well as providing the background information they might find useful on the Duncan brothers. They left his cottage with the excitement of having a real life project to get their teeth into, that would offset the tedium of the marking that they would also have to complete that day.

CHAPTER 19

A week later in the Duncan mansion, Brad was idly going through the Leicester Mercury that was delivered daily and which his father made the boys read every day, insisting that you could pick up all sorts of little pieces of information that could be useful for future jobs. Three pages in, there was a full page advert about a Proceeds of Crime auction being organised by Leicestershire Police Force in a few weeks time. But what really hit him in the eye was the photo of three top of the range 599 GTO Ferraris that would be for sale, along with many other items of value. "Wow, have you seen this?" he called to his brothers who were both cheating at pool in the billiard room. "For once the Mercury has got something in it that is worth taking a look at." He showed them the advert on entering the room. "Now would I like one of those. Why don't we go along and bid for them?"

"Because, my dear brother, we might get outbid and anyway why would we buy them when we could have them for nothing?" Was his eldest brother, Phil's response.

While his brother Phil was looking at the advert that Brad had shown him, Alex started scrolling through his phone for something he had spotted in the celebrity news section earlier that day. "Ah. Found it!" He exclaimed and showed his phone to the other two, on which they read a piece that was advertising a charity celeb-am driving experience at Donnington Park race track, where people with top of the range cars would pay to allow a Leicester City player to drive them around the track.

"Imagine if we were to turn up with our own Ferraris. We would have the pick of the players," Alex purred.

Unbeknown to the three brothers, competition for the players was the least of their worries because their particular Leicester Mercury was the only one anywhere in the county that advertised the proceeds of crime auction in a full page advert and it was only the phones of people in their house who received the news story about the 'driving celeb-am'. The entry details etc. were in fact controlled by Brian's IT department who also produced the Sale of Crime Proceeds advert, which had been inserted in the Duncan's paper by one of Mick's team when the delivery boy left his bag of papers at the entrance to another long driveway near where the

Duncans lived. The whole process was made easier by the fact that their name and address was clearly written on the tops of the Financial Times, Leicester Mercury and various magazines that the Duncans had delivered, ensuring that putting the insert in the correct paper was not an issue.

Fred Tuttle wished his wife a good day and climbed into his car to drive to the depot that he had been driving to for work for the past twenty seven years, not realising that within that usually monotonous routine, today would stand out as one of the more interesting and rewarding. Arriving at the home of Cobbs Transport a quarter of an hour later, Fred popped his head into the office, come porta-cabin and said his customary hello to Doris, who had been at the firm even longer than he had himself. Having exchanged the usual pleasantries, he then moved through to the second porta-cabin next door, which housed the drivers' rest room and pigeon holes, from where they received their tasks for the day. Grabbing his own named clip board with relevant jobs, keys and job authorisation attached, Fred noted he would be driving the newest of the car transporters, which normally signified that his cargo today would be something special and made his way to it with an air of 'all being right with the world'.

Having read the instructions for the first job, he set off away from the city to the Police storage facility out to the north of the county, with the radio turned to Radio 2 now that Chris Evans' show had mercifully finished and settled back to enjoy the relaxing drive through the Leicestershire countryside. After about ten minutes on a straight but narrow piece of country lane, he could see ahead of him what looked like a stationary vehicle. Getting closer still, he slowed as he recognised what was apparently a broken down car with a young woman standing next to the open bonnet scratching her head. With no way past but also because he would never leave a motorist stranded, Fred stopped his vehicle and got down from the cab to see if he could help. He was slightly taken aback when the young lady, who just happened to be called Ronnie and who was wearing a blonde wig, called him Fred and told him that he had nothing to fear but he was going to have to sit in her car while some of her friends just borrowed his truck which would be returned to him as good as new.

Shocked, and on the verge of objecting to this ridiculous waste of time, Fred suddenly became aware of four rather intimidating individuals in balaclavas surrounding him. One of these intimidating looking individuals tried to reassure him that he would come to no harm and in fact would be financially better off once all this was over. However, he would have to hand over his Cobb company overalls. Having no desire to test the speaker's promise of personal safety, Fred allowed himself to be guided into the car where he sat in the middle of the back seat with two of the balaclava clad figures either side of him and another sat in the passenger seat while the young lady prepared to drive them away.

Meanwhile the fourth figure, having donned the overalls Fred had been encouraged to take off, climbed into the cab of the transporter.

As the car drove away and disappeared into the distance, Rob made himself familiar with the paperwork he would need at the police storage facility. Taking a deep breath and concentrating on the instructions he had been given the day before by Dougie, in how to drive such a vehicle, Rob set off towards the police storage facility in the north of the county. The journey was pretty straightforward but as Rob approached the police facility, he started to feel the nerves one would expect of someone not used to breaking the law. Again however, once the paperwork was checked and accepted and there had been the expected banter about the unfairness of criminals owning such cars and what a shame it was that the police could not be allowed to keep them on the basis of "finders, keepers," it did not take long for the three Ferraris and two 4x4's that were also to be auctioned, to be loaded. Remembering to sign Fred Tuttle on the receipt, Rob breathed a sigh of relief as he drove out of the compound, now not quite so full of dodgy vehicles and accepted the fact that he would not make a very successful criminal.

From that moment Rob was nervously aware of all the traffic around him, wondering if any of them carried members of the Duncan gang. He reached, drove along, and then left the motorway towards Birmingham and began to realise what a long shot this was but also how naïve he had been to believe he could out think and then outwit people who made a living out of being devious. Having left the motorway and with only a few miles to go through quieter and quieter roads as he neared the auction rooms, Rob breathed a sigh of acceptance and, if he were to be honest relief, at the conclusion that their little trap had not come off. Just then, he became aware of the flashing lights of a police car overtaking him and signalling for him to pull over. His pulse quickened as he tried to work out how the police had cottoned on so quickly and he saw a layby just ahead that he pulled into. Beginning to panic with how he was going to explain to the police what he had been up to, his emotions became totally chaotic, as they bounced between fear and elation once he recognised the three policemen emerging from their car as no other than the three Duncan brothers. Rob wound down his window and in as calm a voice as he could muster he asked, "Sorry Officers, was I doing something wrong?"

"Would you mind just stepping down from the cab please Sir?"

"Certainly, yes. Always happy to oblige the boys in blue." Rob, with legs seemingly made of jelly, somehow managed to reach the floor without melting into a glutinous mess composed mainly of sweat.

"Sir, could I see your mobile phone please?" As Rob handed over the phone that had been given to him by Brian in the IT department especially for this purpose, Rob began to protest his innocence at any suggestion that he had been using his phone while driving, when the phone was taken from him, dropped on the floor and stamped upon while at the same time one of the other 'Officers' punched him with unbelievable force in the stomach. Bending over double and with the rising panic of not being able to actually take in any air to offset his discomfort, he became aware of a presence also bending to speak in his ear.

"Now Mr Tuttle, we really don't want to have to hurt you any more, so you need to listen. Do you understand?" Unable to speak, Rob simply nodded his head.

"Good lad. Now we are going to take your vehicle while you will sit on the verge. In about ten minutes time the two roadblocks at either end of this lane will disappear and at some time after that cars will start driving by and you will be able to flag one down to come to your rescue. So you will be perfectly safe, unless of course you later try to give any accurate description of what we happen to look like, in which case we will come and ensure that you are never able to drive anything other than a mobility scooter again. Do you understand?"

Not needing to act petrified Rob once again nodded his head and while one of the 'officers' climbed into the cab and started the engine, the other two got back in their Police car and both vehicles drove off. As soon as they were out of sight, Rob was surrounded by four of Mick's men, all smiling broadly.

"Couldn't have gone any better," laughed Mick patting Rob on the back, thus providing the release of the last barrier to him throwing up all over his own boots.

Meanwhile, a bemused Fred Tuttle was driven to within a street of where he worked and allowed out with a cheery wave goodbye. When he later explained to the Police what had happened to him, he didn't mention the pleasant chat he had had about football with his lovely abductors or the large amount of money he was given in a brown envelope for his trouble.

The Duncan brothers meanwhile, having driven to an old disused farm with a number of very large hay barns, placed the police car and transporter under cover and with the help of five of their gang who were already waiting there, proceeded to arrange for the three Ferraris to be placed on three different varieties of transport, covered with tarpaulins and driven off to separate destinations where they would be hidden until they could receive a makeover. The police car and the truck were forensically cleaned, on top of the precautions that the boys had already taken when actually travelling in both vehicles on the way to the rendezvous, having learned their lesson from the last time they had been arrested seven years earlier. They then changed into civilian clothes and gave the police uniforms to one of the men to be 'got rid of' in one of the many furnaces they had access to. Then high fiving their success, they drove home, leaving the police car, truck and two 4x4's to be found, perhaps by the police but hopefully by some scallys who would infect the vehicles with their own forensic detritus, thereby further muddying the waters for any investigators.

Returning to Duncan Towers they went through the routine they had come to live for. Sitting at the large desk in his office, with four glasses of the very best Irish whisky in front of him, was their father. Having explained how the hijack had gone, they now waited for either the disdain of their father pouring three of the whiskies into his own glass, which would result in them turning and leaving the room in shame because they had failed or, as was the case now, their father standing with a big grin on his face and all raising their glasses and toasting in unison, "Harold."

In Matt's office back at the school, Rob sat down in the armchair opposite the Headmaster and his closest friend and began to explain as he promised he would, the reasoning behind getting the Duncan brothers to hijack the Ferraris. "Matt you remember what a low ebb I was at, after the Duncans were acquitted. Well I know you were aware that I was also close to ending my life because I just could see no point in carrying on. DS Bright drove me back to the house to provide me with some protection from the media both outside the court and back at the house. Once inside, she made me a drink and I needed to know if she was certain that it was the Duncans who had carried out the hit and run. She said she was positive. But I really needed proof because if there was the possibility of someone else in the frame then I wanted to know, so that I could stay around in the hope of seeing them brought to justice. If it was the Duncans however, I knew it was time to call it a day because they were seemingly untouchable and I had every intention of ending my life that night if that were the case, something I obviously did not tell DS Bright."

"Yes, we were really worried about you but DS Bright insisted on taking you home."

"Well I am so pleased she did because it is what she told me then that gave me the idea for being able to always know what the Duncans were up to. She seemed to think to herself for sometime before making a decision and took out her phone and told me that she was going to show me something that if it got out, could get her the sack. I immediately promised my discretion and she proceeded to show me two photos on her phone. One was of the Duncan clan at a pro-am golf tournament the day before the tragedy and the second was of them again a few days after the hit and run, celebrating in their own restaurant. In each photo they have the same pose, with their arms around each others' shoulders. Bright asked me if I could see anything noticeable when comparing the photos and to be honest I couldn't see anything of significance. She then pointed to the ring fingers of the Duncans in the first photo and then asked me to compare them with the ones in the second. Well straight away I noticed that whereas in the first photo the father and the two oldest boys had a rather gaudy, identical signet ring on their finger, the youngest boy Brad, did not but in the second photo all four had the same ring."

"So what? I don't see the significance of that."

"No and neither did I, until DS Bright explained. Apparently the founder of the family crime organisation was Frankie Duncan's father, Harold, who wore a very similar ring to the ones in the photo. When his son Frankie carried out his first big job, Harold presented him with his own identical ring. When Harold passed away, Duncan had the original fake stone replaced with a real emerald as his fortunes increased. It then became tradition that as each of his sons carried out their first big job, they too would receive such a ring. The first job that Brad was involved in as far as the police are concerned, was the bank robbery that resulted in the hit and run and the fact that the first time he was seen wearing that ring was a few days after the robbery suggesting, because no other major crime had occurred in that week, he was involved."

"Wow, what a bloody family but I still don't understand what that has to do with us getting the Duncans to carry out another crime, in this case the theft of the Ferraris?"

"Well, it wasn't until you and I were talking about how we could possibly get any reliable intelligence on what the Duncans were planning, that I remembered the photo and and an idea occurred to me that became more appealing after I talked to 'the Prof'. Remember we couldn't work out how we could bug the conversations of the Duncans because they had their house and offices regularly swept for electronic bugging devices?" Matt nodded, uncertain where this was going.

"Well apparently, another little tradition the 'fantastic four' have, is that after every job of significance, they have a toast to the Patriarch Harold, then all their 'Harold' rings are taken to the same jeweller in Birmingham, from whence they bought the rings originally and a small "H" is inscribed on the outside of the ring to signify how successful they have been. A bit like fighter pilots having German planes stencilled on the side of their own plane when they shot them down in WW2. If they stick to form, I reckon that some time soon they will have their Harold rings inscribed to commemorate the theft of the Ferraris. I have someone watching the jewellers and the Duncan house to see when their rings are delivered for inscription. The moment they are, there is a team led by Mick ready to break in and place a tiny solar charged electronic device under the emerald of each ring, that will enable us to listen in on any of their conversations at all times."

"Again, wow. But are you certain this will work?"

"Well 'the Prof.' seems to think so and also that the sweeping for listening devices would not pick up the emissions from the ring, unless the ring is specifically targeted by the people doing the sweeping, which is highly unlikely."

"I have to admit though Rob, that I'm slightly upset that while we have achieved one of our major aims, which is brilliant, we have still allowed the Duncans to get their hands on three very sought after motors."

"Oh don't worry about that Matt. I think it is important that just as we teach our students that you get nothing without honest toil, the Duncans are about to learn the same lesson."

CHAPTER 20

The Ferrarris, travelling under covered tarpaulins in different directions, all eventually ended up at a supposedly legitimate vehicle scrap yard, owned by the Duncans. This also housed a car body workshop, where cars could receive what might euphemistically be called a "makeover" but was in reality a place where vehicles that had been stolen, were cut and shunted or, where vehicles designated to be used in crime, could be prepared. The three Ferraris were placed out of sight and work began on getting rid of any markings that could identify the cars as the ones stolen from the Transporter. Once that was done, the three red Ferraris received a complete respray; one in gold; one in silver; and the other in Azzurro blue and new number plates that were registered at the DVLA through someone working there, who also owed huge sums of money to a bookmakers owned by the Duncans. The work took the best part of two weeks and when it was completed, Dougie, who had been observing everything while working in his newly acquired job as a forklift operator in the scrap yard, reported back to Mick that tonight was the night to carry out the next stage of their plan.

  The following day the Duncan brothers were having a 'lie in' when their father burst into each of their rooms and demanded they meet him downstairs at once. Realising that he was in the foulest of moods, they responded more quickly than their hangovers suggested they wanted to and met in their father's study, looking at each other nonplussed but not daring to say anything for fear of incurring the wrath of their father, who seemed about to explode. "Do not say a word. This morning, while you were lying in your pits, we received this by courier." He pointed at a DVD he was holding in his hand. "Perhaps you should have a look and then we will discuss how it is, that someone is setting out to ensure that my family is being humiliated." He placed the DVD in the machine on his desk and then turned on the massive TV screen he had on the wall. He watched the boys as they watched the screen. They frowned as they saw appear on screen, three metal cubes about a metre square, one gold, one silver and the other blue. The camera lingered on the cubes of metal for a good thirty seconds with the boys staring with baffled looks at the images they were watching and when one of the boys tried to ask what they were looking at, their father barked for them to be quiet and watch. Then rather strangely, until they realised that the film was actually being run backwards, they saw a forklift truck appear with one, then the other two of the metal cubes, reverse away from them to the car crusher which seemed to regurgitate the cubes onto the prongs of the forklift. They then saw mangled metal, metamorphose into a gold, then silver then Azzurro blue coloured Ferrari which then reversed out of the car crusher. "Noooo!" squealed Brad, as the first to realise what he was actually seeing but by the time all three Ferraris were lined up in front of the crusher there could be no doubt for the other two either.

"Who would dare do this? Where were the night watchmen? This can't have happened," choked out Alex.

"Oh, it happened surely enough. I have had Tom go around to the scrapyard this morning and the workers apparently arrived to find the nightwatchmen trussed up like turkeys and locked in one of the containers. They will be dealt with but apparently they saw nothing as they were taken from behind by what seems to be a very professional outfit. Now, I need you to look back to the beginning of the DVD which is really the end of the operation and tell me what else you notice apart from those obscene lumps of metal."

Having returned to the start of the DVD they had to look closely but suddenly they all three realised that on top of each cube of what was once their cars, was a thin vase, with a single flower sticking out of the top. None of them dared ask their father if it was what they thought it was but they didn't need to, because he exploded, "Yes, they are "Gold of Kinabalu" orchids and almost certainly some of the ones stolen from my biosphere." The boys ducked as items from their father's desk started to fly around the room. "I want whoever did this found and I can assure you they are going to wish they had never been born once I find them and find them I will. Who would dare do this to us? Don't they realise that we are the Duncans?" he screamed.

CHAPTER 21

After seeing the photograph that Phil had provided of the person at the cocktail party, who stood out like a sore thumb as someone known to them, Rob asked Mick to arrange for that person to be put under surveillance. What emerged was more than interesting, in terms of the proximity this person seemed to have, to what could only be described as, 'dodgy dealing', especially when it was connected to a member of the police force, whose association with these "dodgy deals" was most definitely part of what made them dodgy. It soon became apparent to those involved in the surveillance, that during the working day, if DCI Grey was involved in legitimate police work he always had a colleague with him but when he went out on his own, he was usually involved with people he perhaps should not have been, as they all seemed to be associated with the Duncan family and their relationship seemed to be more than friendly. However, there were a number of anomalies, as every now and again, Grey would visit people in their homes who were certainly not criminals and seemed to be just like every day members of the public. When Rob was given a list of these people that Grey visited, he was also at a loss as to what connection they could have to Grey, as it was clear they were not part of any investigation he was involved in. This was of course the same Grey who had initially been so understanding when Carol and the girls were killed but who, it seemed to Rob at the time, had been determined to find Rob himself responsible for the whole incident in some way or another.

Rob took the names to Brian the Head of IT and asked him if he could do a bit of research when he had a minute. What Brian came back with by email, almost within an hour of having been given these names, was something Rob had not considered. Thinking back then to the court case that resulted in the Duncans escaping punishment for what they had done to his family, a chilling thought made him re-evaluate what he was going to do next, in relation to bringing the Duncans to account.

Rob had found out after the trial, from one of the jurors who felt so embarrassed by the verdict, having herself voted "guilty" and despite knowing she could be in serious trouble for revealing such information, that the jury had voted 7 – 5 to acquit the Duncan brothers. This had always troubled him because it seemed to him and to those who had a less personal involvement in the case, that the evidence was strongly pointing to a conviction. The news that DCI Grey had been visiting individuals without a colleague and that these individuals, he had been informed by Brian, had apparently just been called to be part of the jury in a case in which two of the Duncans' henchmen were on trial, suggested to Rob that maybe something had happened at the trial of the Duncan brothers seven years ago that caused seven people to vote against what seemed to be the obvious conclusion. Having been given a list of the jurors who had officiated at the original trial from his sympathetic juror, Rob felt he needed to talk to each one of them, even though it was probably illegal. He also realised however, that the moment any of them recognised him, which they were bound to, considering the fact that he had stared into their faces for much of the three week trial, they were unlikely to open the door to him, let alone speak to him. Who did he know with the gravitas and diplomacy to carry out this task for him?

So it was that evening, he sat in Matt and Ronnie's kitchen and after confirming how much they were enjoying their life helping to run a very successful school, he explained that he suspected that DCI Grey might have somehow got some of the jury to vote for the Duncans at the trial. They were to a certain extent disbelieving but accepted that Rob was no longer just driven by anger but a cold logic, powered by the need for justice and so heard him out without interrupting. When he got to the bit where he asked Matt if he were prepared to go and talk to the jury members, Matt was torn between thinking that it was probably a waste of time but also the desire to do something practical towards the process of gaining the justice he felt Rob, but more importantly Carol and the girls, deserved. Yes, he had been successful in setting up the school but he envied Mick and the others getting their hands dirty in pursuit of the Duncans. Not that he felt he had the skills needed to do what they did but this was something he could at least do and so he agreed.

Taking the list of names, he felt it would be a good idea to firstly question the five who had voted for a conviction, to ascertain whether or not they had picked up on anything untoward in the jury room and where better to start amongst that group, than the foreman of the jury himself, William Hardcastle. With too much to occupy him at school during the day, Matt left it to the following evening before he began his task and, wanting to catch the jurors unawares, he turned up at the address provided by Brian in IT, at seven pm that evening. When the door was opened a little after his first ring on the doorbell, it was by a smart looking man with thinning grey hair, who was probably in his sixties but whose eyes suggested the mind of someone younger. When Matt explained who he was and why he was there, rather than have to spend ages explaining himself, Hardcastle immediately invited him in with a confidence no doubt developed as the owner of a successful manufacturing business, now retired.

Entering the lounge, Hardcastle introduced Matt to his wife, who offered to provide tea or coffee and was soon back with a drink for all three of them and some lemon drizzle cake on a plate for Matt, explaining that they had just eaten . He tried to allay any apprehensions the Hardcastles might have about his visit, by explaining that he was a friend of Mr. Price and that he and some other friends were in the process of getting him to come to terms with what had happened to his family and that understanding how the jury reached the decision they did, was a vital part of that. He was careful not to suggest that he thought anybody had done anything wrong or that the jury had made a mistake. He was therefore taken aback when Hardcastle said how ashamed he was of that verdict and his role in reaching it. He explained that as the foreman who felt strongly that the Duncans were guilty as sin, he should have been able to persuade the other jurors to vote the correct way but even jurors who early on were strongly in favour of convicting, had changed their mind at the very end.

"Now I am not trying to suggest anything dubious occurred but at any stage did anyone try to influence your decision?"

"Absolutely not but I think that if anyone were to ask any of the other jurors, they would have realised that I was not the sort of person to change my mind and so anybody so-minded, perhaps would not have even bothered to try with me. However, I must admit that I did wonder whether anyone had been influenced by some of the other jurors speaking out of turn, away from the rest of us."

Having found out what he needed to know, Matt stayed long enough to be polite and then got up to leave. As he saw him out, Hardcastle asked him to apologise to Mr. Price for him and wished Matt luck with his other visits. The next two jurors Matt saw that evening also said that no-one had tried to influence them, although they were less welcoming and were only prepared to talk to him on the doorstep. It was too late to disturb anyone else that evening and so slightly dispirited, he went home with a plan to get back out tomorrow evening.

The two jurors he saw next, who had also voted for a conviction had a different story to tell however, as both of them had received visitors who basically had threatened them should the vote go the other way but because they were both without any family, they felt that any threats were less successful than if they had had family. They had of course passed on these visits to the very nice Detective in charge of the case, who had promised both of them he would give it his personal attention. 'I bet he did,' thought Matt as he said his goodbyes, with a feeling of growing scepticism about the veracity of DCI Grey. Tomorrow was a Saturday and Matt was determined to get as many of the jurors seen as possible.

Starting as soon as he thought that people would be up and about on a Saturday, Matt was expecting the jurors he would see today to be more defensive, as they had been the ones who had voted against a conviction and would likely be wary of speaking to someone who was a friend of Rob. He was not wrong, with the first two slamming the door in his face without further comment. A couple of others were only slightly less dismissive, speaking briefly on the doorstep to deny that any pressure had been put on them but looking very uncomfortable throughout the conversation and glancing furtively over his shoulder to the street, as they were talking and closing the door as soon as they could. As he walked away, he had the clear impression that something had occurred, despite protestations to the contrary.

The next visit was to Colonel Sutherington who, when he answered the door, fulfilled all the prejudices one might have when thinking of the archetypal old British colonel, even down to a bristling moustache that he constantly twirled at the ends. He had no hesitation in inviting Matt in to the house, seemingly confident in his belief that he would never do anything wrong and if he had an opinion it was quite definitely correct. 'Oh yes,' he had received a visit from a couple of likely lads but he had sent them off with a flea in their ear and a parting shout of disappointment that we 'no longer had national service'.

"So," Matt asked, "do you mind me asking you why you had changed your mind about conviction, right towards the end of the trial, being by all accounts adamant that the Duncans were guilty throughout the early part of the trial?"

"Well, as his friend you should know better than most, that once I found out about the sort of person Mr. Price really was, it became apparent he was up to his neck in the whole business."

With rising alarm Matt replied, "What do you mean?"

"Come on, if you really are his friend then you must know."

"Know what?"

"Well that excellent DCI Grey came to see me a few days before the summing up, to warn me about people who might try to threaten me to change my opinion. I told him about the louts who had visited and he was really impressed with how I had got rid of them and told me that even if they were right about who was really guilty, that wasn't how our justice system worked. I asked him what he meant and he told me that he shouldn't say anything but he knew that I could be trusted. He then told me that Mr. Price had been investigated for fraud and that the whole robbery and hit and run were all part of an elaborate scam he had going."

"I can assure you Colonel, that Rob is an ordinary teacher with a very ordinary lifestyle."

"Well, I know all about these lowlifes. You read about them every day in the Daily Mail and maybe he has pulled the wool over your eyes. My own dear wife was the victim of a scam herself some years back and the shame of it led to her dying of a broken heart." Realising he was not going to change the colonel's mind but having got what he had come for, Matt thanked the colonel for his time and left.

He was now feeling that they were getting somewhere and this was confirmed on his next visit to Gladys Williams, who confirmed that she had not had anyone threaten her but that she could not possibly convict, once she found out from that nice DCI Grey what sort of person that Mr. Price was. She appeared reluctant to disclose what had been told to her in the strictest confidence but, as he accepted another piece of her Victoria sponge, she obviously saw him as someone who could be trusted and recounted what she had been told. Mr. Price had apparently been a wife beater, who had abused his wife for years and that the hit and run was almost certainly something he had set up himself. Looking suitably shocked, Matt thanked Ms. Williams for her honesty and he left as soon as he could get away. As he got back in his car, he was seething that someone in a position of power like Grey, could have done this to his friends and he was more determined than ever to ensure they received the justice they deserved and that now included DCI Grey.

That night he and Ronnie provided a meal as they met with the Khalifs, Rob and Mick. While they ate, Matt reported back what he had found out. There was mutual agreement that Grey should now be added to the Duncans, as someone who deserved his comeuppance, in relation to the part he had to play in what had happened to Carol, Holly and Penny. They discussed a number of scenarios late into the night but it was Matt who, determined to play a bigger role than just provide a cover for all the cloak and dagger work, came up with a plan that would not only see Grey get his just deserts but also put another brick in the wall of the operation to unnerve the Duncans, before the final 'coup de grace.'

There were going to be two elements in the operation against Grey. The second element would be to try and get him caught red-handed breaking the law and the first part was the collection of evidence that would back up his own conviction and start to lay doubt on some of the cases he had been involved with in the past, most notably the one that resulted in the death of Carol, Holly and Penny. Mick had already suggested an idea for getting Grey caught red-handed but it relied upon split second timing and for the first time since it had been put in place, some intelligence, courtesy of the audio surveillance they were now able to carry out on all four of the Duncans, via their signet rings.

"Ok, from our surveillance we know that Grey has visited three of the jurors who are going to be officiating at the next trial, concerning some of Duncan's gang. What are the chances that he will go to see some or even all the rest of the jurors, to try to get them to affect their decisions, especially when they get closer to the end of the trial?" Mick asked.

"Pretty good I would say. Mick can you get listening devices into each of the remaining juror's homes, in case Grey goes to visit them?"

"I think that might be too difficult Rob but I think I have a better idea. What if we can get a microphone situated on Grey's person, just as we did with the signet rings for the Duncans? We can then pick up anything he says that might be of use to us."

"Is that possible? I mean, I don't think he even wears a signet ring and it would have to be something he has on him at all times?"

"You're right, we won't be able to repeat the signet ring idea but I know what you mean, leave that to me. Oh Rob, by the way, part of this plan involves you not shaving until it is completed."

"Is that a joke?"

"No, I'm afraid not."

"Not a lot of people know this, but hair on a man's chin is four times thicker than that on his head and men and women have the same amount of facial hair," Matt offered.

"You can go off people you know" Amira pointedly exclaimed while looking at Matt with a pout.

They all smiled but Rob started to laugh and explained to the others that he now felt that maybe things were getting back to "some sort of normal", as that was the first "not many people know this but…." That Matt had uttered since the day of the tragedy.

"Count yourself lucky you don't have to live with him, because I get this all the time," Ronnie retorted.

CHAPTER 22

When Rob had originally asked Mike to get involved and pull together a team, one of his criteria had been that those employed should have no criminal record and Mick had stuck to that but it did not mean he felt that he could not bring someone in for a one off job, especially if he was the one doing the employment and paying and not Rob. So it was that two days later Grey was returning to the station after purchasing his usual pastry from Greggs, just around the corner. As he stepped into the side road he had to cross, while biting into his sausage roll, he collided with a cyclist and was only saved from falling on top of the overturned rider by a passer-by grabbing him and keeping him upright. He thanked his saviour and held back a curse for the "bloody cyclists" who were nothing but a nuisance on the roads but accepting reluctantly, that in this case the cyclist had probably been totally blameless. Realising this, Grey ensured that the cyclist was OK and apologised through gritted teeth.

He had totally forgotten his saviour, who was walking on in the direction he had been travelling before and so would not have seen him offloading his police warrant card to a chap in paint spattered overalls. This 'chap' then climbed into his van, where a tiny microphone was inserted in the wallet of the warrant card by the Prof, who then passed it via the paint spattered driver to an elderly lady walking by. She then just caught up with Grey as he was leaving the scene of his altercation, to ask him if he had dropped his wallet. This time he was genuinely grateful for this act of help but was quite surprised that it had fallen from his breast pocket where he thought it was very safe, as to lose your warrant card was a serious breach of conduct within the police. Deciding that to pick up his fallen sausage roll would not be a good look; Grey accepted that he would be better off returning to the station and grabbing some of their healthier but less tasty offerings.

Later that day, Mick paid 'Fingers' O'Reilly, notorious Midlands pickpocket, the £200 for "assisting" DS Grey after his accident and took his mum and dad out for a meal for their part as cyclist and retriever of wallet in the escapade. Most of that meal was spent with them putting forward, more and more outrageous operations that they would happily be involved in.

Rob was delighted to hear about the success of the operation and while he knew any information garnered by this method would probably not be allowed to be used in a court of law, it would at least, perhaps serve to get the authorities to look closely at what Grey got up to. Stage one underway, it was time now to put in place the second and more risky part of their plan.

At their meeting following Matt's news about DS Grey's manipulation of jurors, Mick had reminded Rob about something that Dougie had said after the rather pleasing crushing of the three Ferraris. Previous to the Ferrari crushing, Dougie had been working as a fork lift truck driver at the breaker's yard that also acted as a front for the fully equipped 'cut and shunt' garage, owned by the Duncans. While working there, Dougie had become aware that every now and again, luxury cars would be brought in and after a short stay, would be taken out again. He found out from some of the other more talkative workers, that these cars had their registration plates and VIN numbers changed and then were sold abroad for large sums of money. With no other details, Rob tasked those members of his team who had been brought in to take it in turns to listen to the returns from the audio surveillance, to listen out specifically for any conversation concerning luxury cars.

After about a week, a picture was able to be put together concerning the Duncans' luxury car operation. It appeared that cars were stolen to order, mostly by young people who were happy to receive cash in hand but who had no idea who was behind the payment. They would drive the car to a meeting place, often a service station off one of the motorways, where they would swap the car for either cash or drugs, dependent on their need. The car was then loaded onto the back of a lorry or trailer and covered with a tarpaulin, before being driven to one of a number of places around the county, including old farm buildings and units on industrial estates, where there was very secure space for the cars.

When the time was right, the car would be taken to Duncan's breaker's yard 'come car makeover shop', where it would have its VIN number and registration changed and invariably a respray, before being returned to its secure storage. When they had about twelve cars ready to go, they were driven to a container depot where usually two cars would be stored in one of six 40ft containers, which were then taken to the port storage area to await loading onto the requisite ship. At the time of loading, customs officials would sometimes be asked by their supervisor to look inside the containers to ascertain that they contained what it said on the transport docket but it was always arranged that the loading was carried out on the night when the two security guards, who were in the pay of the Duncans, were on duty. Should the supervisor want to check or any other problem should arise, the container lorry drivers would ring a number they had all been given, immediately. That would result in DCI Grey arriving, to use his position to convince anyone who might be too nosy, that this was part of a police investigation and the container was being tracked. This had never had to happen because the two customs officials employed by the Duncans were very keen to keep the very generous payments they received for, 'not' doing their job.

It seemed that the Duncans were very proud of this particular operation, as it brought in huge returns for very little effort. The only disappointing thing as far as Rob was concerned however, was that the people running this operation were usually some of the Duncans' more trusted lieutenants and not the Duncans themselves. Therefore, it would not be possible to have them arrested while carrying out this crime but if his plan was successful, it would give them another bloody nose and hopefully sort out DCI Grey at the same time. But there was a lot that could go wrong and it was a very big 'if'. It became apparent that the next shipment of cars was planned for ten days time, with the containers carrying the cars having to be driven into the loading area two days before that and this was when the customs officers would sign them off. Rob and his team felt that this should give them ample time to put their next part of the plan into action.

As the week wore on, they managed to work out where the majority of cars were being stored and after some reconnaissance, they decided which of those cars would suit their needs best. During that time also, DCI Grey had been busy visiting three more of the jurors who were meant to be officiating at the trial involving the Duncan gang. From the conversations picked up from the microphone in his warrant card wallet, they were able to put together a compilation of audio that clearly proved that DCI Grey was trying to persuade the jurors to vote in a particular way.

On Monday afternoon, Rob rang DS Bright on her mobile. She had previously told him to ring her at any time if he felt the need to talk. She had kindly offered this service above and beyond what she was required to do, when it became obvious to her that Rob could be at risk of causing himself harm due to his loss and the subsequent unfairness of the verdict. Until now Rob had not taken advantage of that offer and so Bright felt that this must be important and offered to come and see him immediately but he asked her if she could come tomorrow evening, as he didn't feel up to visitors today. He felt guilty about leading on the one person who had been genuinely helpful throughout the enquiry over the death of his family but he assuaged his guilt through the knowledge that Bright would eventually gain much from the meeting with Rob, even if it might not seem so immediately. Everything was in place now but Tuesday night would be the riskiest part of the operation.

When Tuesday came along, the students at the school noticed that there seemed to be a severe shortage of ground staff and premises officers and were amused to watch their teachers having to carry out many of the tasks previously carried out by the support staff in order for lessons and indeed the whole school to run smoothly. Two of those staff, Jim MacDonald, known as Mac and Phil Clements, who had been the insider at the Duncan party, had much earlier that morning, before most people were up and about, quietly made their way to the Freight Terminal. Once on site and having climbed up the side of three containers, they were now ensconced in an empty container that had a window, through which they could see the very spot where the containers would be randomly checked by the customs officers. They set up their cameras and video equipment, laid out their bedrolls and settled in with their food and drink supplies, to wait for the action that would take place that night.

The previous night, Dougie Jennings and Billy Davis, who also would not be on ground staff duty the following day, killed the sound of the motocross bike they were riding and let it coast onto the track leading to an old abandoned farm, that nonetheless had extremely new and effective security fencing around one of the barns. It took little time for Billy to deactivate the alarm system and open the gates to the compound and barn, inside of which was a car shaped tarpaulin which when removed, revealed a Range Rover Sport. Again it was Billy, using the skills he had learned as a boy from his dad but which he had only up to now used in the service of his country, who gained entry to the car. Barely ten minutes after they had entered the compound, Billy was following Dougie in the now 'twice stolen' car, back towards the lock up on the outskirts of Leicester, that they had hired for the purpose of storing the car until it was needed the following day. Before leaving the compound however, Dougie found time to leave a small gift in exactly the middle of the space that the car had sat.

Tuesday came wet and breezy and at the breaker's yard belonging to the Duncans, six container lorries arrived throughout the day and each container was loaded with two of the cars that also pulled into the yard at designated times that day. The first sign of a problem came, when the men sent to pick up the Range Rover found it missing and in its place, a vase containing some sort of flower. It was Ernie who had the unenviable job of ringing Frankie Duncan and informing him that they were one car light. Duncan's fury was to be expected and he surmised out loud that it would be some young tearaways who would regret getting involved with the Duncan family once he found out who they were, which he would be bound to do, considering all his contacts. Ernie replied that young tearaways were unlikely to have been able to bypass the security system and they must have some front, because they left a flower in a vase where the car had been. Ernie started to feel uncomfortable as silence on the other end of the line seemed to create a physical presence where he stood.

"What did you just say?"

"There was a flower in a vase where the car had stood."

"Describe the flower." When Ernie called across the pick-up driver to come on the phone and describe what the flower looked like, his rather misguided attempt to find the discovery of a flower quite amusing, soon turned into a stuttering apology and the claim that while he knew very little about flowers and plants he was pretty sure that this was an orchid that had been left. On the other end of the phone, the stream of expletives did not just cause the pick-up driver to hurriedly hand the phone back to Ernie but in Duncan Towers, also caused the three brothers to come running into their father's study to find out what had happened. They looked on in trepidation, as their father called someone on the other end of the phone a moron, before slamming it down with such venom the cradle broke and he hurled the whole instrument across the room, forcing Alex to have to jump suddenly out of the way.

"Dad what's happened?" asked Philip.

"One of the cars that was meant to be part of our shipment has been stolen," Duncan wailed, without a hint of irony,

That won't stop the shipment going ahead though will it?"

"No Brad you idiot, of course not but when the pick-up driver went to collect the car, not only had it gone but one of my orchids was left in its place. Someone is attacking this family and taking the mick and you three have done nothing about it."

"Dad, we have had all our informants and those guys we've got undercover in all the obvious gangs, looking out for anything that might give us an answer but there is nothing. People think we are being paranoid," offered Philip, which was more a reflection of his own thoughts than anything he had heard from anyone else.

"Paranoid! My whole life's work is taken from me and then flaunted in my face, at the same time that someone has the temerity to mess with our operations. Believe you me, this is not paranoia, someone is actually out to get us and the sophistication of their operation seems to suggest this has to be someone big. Extend the search to all the major gangs in the country not just the Midlands. I want this sorted. No one messes with the Duncans."

"Do we carry on with tonight's consignment?" Alex asked querulously.

"Of course we bloody do. This gang, whoever they may be, are simply trying to annoy us for some reason but they don't have the b***s to halt our operations and there is no way they can know what we are doing tonight. Now get off your fat backsides and find me who is out to mess with us. Well what are you waiting for?"

Back in the listening room at the school, Jonathan, who was on duty while all this took place, could barely stop himself laughing, as he listened in on this encounter and made a copy to cheer up the rest of the guys but especially Rob.

CHAPTER 23

At 3.00 pm that afternoon, Dean Smithers and Wayne Pearson had just finished a few games of pool and a couple of pints in their local Conservative club and with three hours before their shift at the freight terminal, were about to go their separate ways, when a van stopped alongside them on their route to home on the same estate. The driver wound down his window and asked them if they knew where Jacksons the builder's merchant was? As they both moved towards the driver's window to give him the benefit of their local knowledge, they did not become aware of the three men who came from behind the van and as the side door was slid open, grabbed them and threw them in. Once inside, their attempts to resist soon became obviously hopeless, as they were trussed like turkeys and had hoods placed over their heads. Thirty minutes later, having been calmed down and been reassured that if they did what they were told they would come to no harm, a claim they believed more with hope than commitment, they listened very carefully to their instructions. Minutes later, the HR department at the Container terminal, received the news and offered the requisite sympathy to the information that Dean and Wayne had been involved in a road traffic accident and would be unable to come into work that night but would hopefully be OK for tomorrow. HR accepted this news readily enough because Dean and Wayne never missed a shift. In fact, on some occasions they would turn up even when obviously under the weather. HR of course, did not realise that this was through fear of upsetting the Duncans rather than any sense of commitment. Both men having made the telephone call were now even more petrified, not just because of their present predicament but because of the likely aftershocks from their second employers, for not being on duty when a certain shipment needed to be checked.

    Later that evening when she could no longer put up with the tedium of the backlog of paperwork, Susie Bright left the police station and drove to Rob's house. Unable to park outside his house due to the number of cars in the road, she found a place some way from his house, when she spotted a space just in front of a rather expensive looking

Range Rover Sport, that even she, with no interest in cars, knew cost a small fortune. She smiled at how incongruous it looked in this ordinary street but thought, who was she to tell people what they should spend their money on. After an annoyingly long walk to Rob Price's house, she was quite shocked to see the state he was in when he opened the door to her knock. She tried not to show how surprised she was by the dishevelled state of his ill-fitting clothes, actually the work clothes he had borrowed from school groundsman "little" John Cropper and his unshaven face and messy hair. Telling him how nice it was to see him after all this time, she was ushered into the lounge, that looked in no better shape than he did, with used food cartons and drinks cans (courtesy of the sixth form common room), making the room look like some student house the morning after a party. "Wow he must still be in some state," she thought to herself as she looked around. When he had cleared a space for her and they had both sat down, she enquired how he was doing. Feeling guilty about the act he was putting on, especially in the face of Bright's genuine sympathy, Rob tried to sound disheartened and said he was struggling.

"Thank you for coming DS Bright and sorry for the mess."
"No problem and actually it is now DI Bright."
"That's brilliant news and well deserved."
"In many ways I wish it could have happened some other way, as it was my work on the Duncan case that led to the promotion, even though we didn't get them in the end."
"That certainly wasn't down to you and I'm genuinely pleased for you but the reason I asked for you to come and see me was that I was hoping maybe you would have some news that would cheer me up, as you can probably tell I am not doing very well."

She guiltily told him that they had nothing new but that the Duncans were bound to slip up at some stage. They then talked in general and she found out that he was no longer teaching but had a job at the school where his friend Matt was the Headteacher but that it was more of a sop really and he often didn't go in, which he felt truly guilty about. Bright sympathised and told him these things take time but was determined she would ring his friend Matt after she had left, so worried was she for his condition. With little left to say, she got up to leave and Rob told her how grateful he was for her visit and efforts, especially after that fool Grey had messed everything up.

"Does he still think that I had something to do with what happened to my family? And does he still boss you around?"

"Actually I shouldn't tell you this but DCI Grey is no longer a member of our team and he can't boss me around anymore anyway, because we're now both the same rank after he was demoted."

"He shouldn't even still be in the force. Was it his failure in our case that led to his fall from grace?"

"Well, that was part of it but there were other cases where evidence went missing and procedures were not followed. The suspicion that this was deliberate could not be proven but the only other reason for the lapses would have to be incompetence and so he will never lead another major investigation again. Please Mr. Price I have told you this because I think we owe you but this must go no further."

"No, of course. I appreciate you being so candid with me." Encouraging him to look after himself and to contact her should he need anything, she got up to leave, wished him well and promised to pop in to see him again. As she walked towards her car, she rang Matt and told him his friend needed some company. Matt seemed surprised by her call but promised that he would go around and see Rob immediately.

Just before she got to her car, she started to search in her bag for the keys. She was actually looking into her bag as she came level with the Range Rover Sport she had noted earlier and realised too late that the backdoor was suddenly opened and two men in balaclavas pushed her into the backseat and slammed the door. They then nonchalantly climbed into the two front seats and drove away. Struggling to get out she realised the doors had been centrally locked and as she attempted to get at the two men sat in the front she was confronted with a perspex partition separating front from back. A slither of hope came to her however, when she also noticed that some of the householders near where the car had been parked were watching them drive off, having obviously seen the incident. Hopefully they would contact the police but there was no guarantee and she began to seriously fear for her life.

"You have made a big mistake," she shouted at the men in the front. "I am a police officer and all the resources of the Leicestershire police will be put in motion the moment those householders contact them."

The men in the front ignored her but she noticed with disappointment that the passenger was now going through her bag and had already removed her phone. Bright could tell that they were going towards the motorway network and was busily trying to work out what to do next when, without turning around, the passenger held up a paper sign at the partition which read. TAKE THE LAPTOP FROM THE POCKET COMPARTMENT IN FRONT OF YOU AND OPEN. Glaring back at him and not wanting to submit to any of their demands, she was nevertheless intrigued by what all this was about and so, feigning reluctance, she did as requested. As she then looked up she noticed that the man sitting in the passenger seat was typing onto his phone and this then appeared on her screen.

PLEASE DO NOT BE ALARMED, YOU WILL NOT BE HARMED IN ANY WAY WHATSOEVER. IN A FEW MINUTES YOU WILL HAVE YOUR PHONE BACK TO USE AS YOU WISH, EVEN TO CALL YOUR COLLEAGUES BUT BEFORE THAT, WE WANT YOU TO LISTEN TO AN AUDIO AND WATCH A FEW SHORT VIDEO CLIPS. PLEASE USE THE EAR PHONES PROVIDED.

Bright felt a little less concerned because of what she had just read but was totally mystified as to what this could all be about. The two men, and she was certain they were men, despite not seeing their faces or hearing their voices, sat in the front were obviously keen not to provide any clues as to who they were. Feigning reluctance again, she placed the ear buds in her ears and listened to the audio and watched the video footage which were obviously not in 'sync'. The first surprise was that the object of the video footage was her old nemesis DCI, now DI Grey, who appeared to be visiting a number of people who she did not recognise. After disappearing into the different houses however, the video froze but the audio continued and it soon became apparent that Grey was actually trying to persuade these individuals, who from the conversation were quite obviously future jurors in a particular case, to vote against convicting the accused in that case.

Her absolute disgust for this totally illegal approach, quickly turned to rage when she became aware that the case he was trying to ensure the not guilty verdict, was one she had brought to court herself and involved members of the Duncan gang. Having finished watching and listening, she wanted to ask her captors many questions but also to try and explain to them that whatever their plan was, this could not be used as evidence in a court of law. As if reading her mind the passenger, having seen that she had removed the ear buds, brought up the next message on her screen.

WE REALISE THIS CANNOT BE USED AS EVIDENCE BUT WE HOPE IT WILL PROVIDE YOU WITH THE BASIS OF AN INVESTIGATION e.g. INTERVIEWING THE PEOPLE YOU HAVE JUST SEEN ON SCREEN, TO GAIN EVIDENCE FIRST HAND.

HOWEVER, WE HOPE TO BE ABLE TO PROVIDE YOU WITH FIRST HAND EVIDENCE THIS EVENING AND TO PROVE OUR GOOD FAITH I AM NOW GOING TO RETURN YOUR PHONE. PLEASE FEEL FREE TO CONTACT YOUR COLLEAGUES BUT IT IS LIKELY THAT AS THIS IS A STOLEN CAR, THE POLICE WILL ALREADY HAVE PICKED IT UP VIA THE MOTORWAY CAMERAS AND IF LINKED WITH THE DESCRIPTION PROVIDED BY THE WITNESSES OF YOUR ABDUCTION, WE WILL SOON HAVE A NUMBER OF YOUR COLLEAGUES JOINING US ANYWAY. THIS IS SOMETHING WE WISH TO ENCOURAGE.

He then slipped her phone through a slit in the Perspex screen, obviously provided for just that purpose and she immediately rang the station where she had herself put through to Chief Superintendent Andy Flowers, who she knew was designated Gold Commander for that day.

Explaining what had happened, she was reassured to know that her colleagues were already aware of her predicament and armed response units would be tracking her any time now. Assuring the commander that she was fine, they agreed to keep her line open.

Almost at the same time, just over forty miles away in Daventry, the six lorries carrying the containers that housed the stolen luxury cars pulled into the freight terminal and joined the line of similar lorries, calmly awaiting their turn, as the vehicles in front were checked and slowly moved through to the freight terminal itself. The six drivers were relaxed, having done this many times before, safe in the knowledge that their containers would receive only a cursory check from the two customs officials who were under the employ of their boss Duncan. As they got closer to the front of the queue however, Speedy, the lead driver started to frown. That definitely did not look like Wayne and Dean who were climbing in and out of lorries and containers. Speedy climbed down from his cab and pretended to stretch his legs as he walked down the line to ascertain if he had been correct. A closer inspection confirmed his worst fears and he walked quickly back and spoke to the other drivers before getting on his phone and ringing Frankie Duncan.

"Boss, we have a problem."

"What do you mean we have a problem? What's up?"

"Dean and Wayne are not here. There are two other customs officials carrying out the checks and we can't turn around as we are in a long line of lorries with no room to manoeuvre."

"Ok don't let those officials see inside your containers whatever you do. Stall them as much as you can. Grey will be with you as soon as I can get hold of him."

DI Grey was sitting in front of the TV with a takeaway on his lap, just about to watch Leicester City play the second leg of their FA cup match versus Arsenal. It promised to be a good game, with a two all draw from the first leg setting it up nicely. After it had finished, he planned to go and visit his girlfriend Gina and for these few hours at least, he could relax and forget about the pressure of juggling the demands of two different employers.

Unfortunately for him, the employer who paid him the most and of whom he was most in fear, chose that moment to ring him. When Duncan explained the situation, Grey quailed at what he was being asked to do and tried to suggest it was too dangerous for him to get involved in this, without the potential for it to blow up in his face.

"I couldn't give a s*** about your worries. You are paid a lot of money to be on call for just such an emergency and up until now you have not had to do anything to earn that money. I have a huge amount riding on this shipment and if this should go down the 'Swannee', all future shipments will have to stop. Get yourself down there now and sort this out."

At the freight terminal, the drivers working for Duncan were becoming more nervous the closer they were getting to the front of the queue. Up in their place of observation, Jim MacDonald and Phil Clements were getting more excited the closer the Duncan containers got to the two customs officials. Elsewhere around the depot, more of Mick's team were getting into place and being talked through what was happening over the earpieces and microphones they all carried on any operation.

In the stolen Range Rover, Bright saw the body language of the guys in the front seats become more urgent and when she looked back she could see and then hear the sounds of sirens that she knew so well. At least this would be over soon and she could find out what these two clowns were really about and then have a look into this new information on Grey. But she then saw come up on the computer screen,

YOU'D BETTER PUT ON YOUR SEAT BELT AND HOLD ON TO THE GRAB HANDLE.

She obstinately sat perfectly still and stared her determination not to comply, back into the driver's mirror. He shrugged his shoulders and then she saw the passenger type into his phone which came up on the screen as, YOUR CHOICE.

Moments later, the car seemed to take off and it was all she could do to remain on the seat. She looked back to see the police cars rapidly disappearing into the distance as the Range Rover accelerated at a speed she did not believe was possible. As the car over and undertook any other vehicles that might hold them up, Bright grabbed the seat belt and secured it before clasping the grab handle above the door with both hands. She looked into the driver's mirror and noticed the driver look up and back at her and she knew that it was only the balaclava from stopping her seeing a satisfied smirk on the driver's face.

Just as the first of Duncan's drivers thought he was going to have to abandon his lorry and make a run for it, DS Grey's Porsche came skidding to a halt in front of him and the customs officers who had just waved through the vehicle ahead looked up in surprise and some concern. Grey climbed out of his car very calmly and with a big smile on his face. He approached the two Customs officers and casually pulled out his warrant card, which he displayed to the now very alert officials.

"How can we help you Officer?"

"Detective Inspector actually and it is more a case of how I can help you gentlemen."

"Oh, and how might that be?"

"Well, I am here to stop you from making one of the biggest mistakes of your life, which might even cost you your jobs."

The more confident of the two officials, fed up with continually being told they were less important than the police when he knew that he and his colleagues probably caught more crooks each day than the boys in blue did in a month, asked warily, "And how might that be?"

"Well, you see, you have stumbled upon a very sensitive police operation which your colleagues Wayne and Dean were well aware of, but sworn to secrecy. Although I am really surprised that you have not been brought up to speed. Bosses eh! Somebody will be for the high jump. Now we need you to let these next six lorries go through without any checks or interruptions."

Up in their observation position, Mac and Phil who were listening and recording this, rang the passenger in the Range Rover and gave the message, "Probably about another 5 – 10 minutes. So get close and I will give you the nod when it's more like thirty seconds."

In the car, the passenger simply replied "Roger that," as the car left the motorway and started to drive at speed through the urban areas leading into Daventry. The passenger began typing again and Bright read,

WE ARE QUITE CAPABLE OF LOSING YOUR COLLEAGUES BUT WE ARE ABOUT TO DRIVE THROUGH A BUILT UP AREA. CAN WE SUGGEST THAT WE AND THE POLICE CARS KEEP TO THE SPEED LIMIT UNTIL WE GET TO OUR DESTINATION WITHOUT INTERRUPTION, WHICH WE PROMISE WILL BE IN LESS THAN TEN MINUTES. HOWEVER, IF YOU REPLACE YOUR EAR PHONES AND WATCH THE SCREEN YOU WILL NOW BE ABLE TO WATCH SOMETHING THAT IS HAPPENING LIVE AT THIS MOMENT AND WILL DEFINITELY BE OF INTEREST TO YOU.

More and more shocked but mostly intrigued, Bright spoke again to Gold Commander Andy Flowers and explained that she wanted the police cars to simply follow but that this should all come to an end soon. She noticed their car slow immediately and looking out of the back window, she saw the police cars that had been chasing them, close the gap completely until they were now simply following very closely. She also noticed that as they approached Daventry Freight Terminal, they simply seemed to be driving around in circles as if waiting for something. However, having now replaced the ear buds and having glanced at the screen of the laptop, something else was now grabbing her full attention.

The customs officers studied Grey carefully, as he seemed to be a genuine police officer but this all seemed a bit too fishy.
"We'll have to ring our supervisor to check that this is all ok."
"If you do that, then the undercover nature of this operation could all be lost, as we believe somebody in your hierarchy could be involved. Look, just take my word for it as I am obviously a genuine police officer."
"Yes but it seems a bit strange that you are here on your own. Surely you should at least have a colleague with you?"
Up in the observation container, Mac spoke to Billy in the 4x4 and told him to be ready any moment now. Phil however, had just spotted that the six drivers of the Duncan lorries were removing handguns from under their jackets and hiding them behind their backs as things seemed to be going 'pear shaped'. Mac spoke into his microphone and Mick who was hiding behind a shed near where this was all happening, got the message and quietly slipped around behind the drivers and told them not to turn

around but to look at their chests. Each of the drivers did as they were told and were terrified to see red dots and all were experienced enough with firearms to know that these were sniper sight laser guides.

"OK now quietly place your guns on the floor," Mick suggested. As they did so, in the observation container Phil repeated, 'Go Go Go' over his phone to Dougie and Billy in the Range Rover, while ensuring that, like his partner Mac, he kept the powerful laser pen light aiming at the chests of the now disarmed drivers down below. Mick, hearing the sound of approaching cars, melted back out of the way, to a place where he could watch that none of the drivers would be tempted to pick up their guns. They however, could not take their eyes off the laser beams seemingly attached to their chests, which they assumed were from sights actually attached to sniper rifles, rather than the actual laser pointers usually used by people delivering Power Point presentations. Grey, unaware of all this, conspiratorially put his arms around the two customs officers and turned them away from any watching drivers, then took from his pocket a brown paper bag, which he assured them, contained two thousand pounds which he was permitted to give to the officials in recognition of the disruption this police operation would cause them. At that very moment, the Range Rover drove right up behind Grey's Porsche, followed by five police cars and an armed response van full of fully armed officers. Dougie the driver, released the lock on Bright's door and she jumped out demanding to know what was happening, despite already having a pretty clear idea, having been watching it all unfold on the laptop she had been studying with growing rage and incredulity for the last ten minutes or so.

"Ah, DI Bright what are you doing here?" asked a rather flustered DI Grey.

"DI Grey shut it." Bright turned to the two officers nearest her and told them to take Grey into custody.

"How dare you? You have no right. You have always been jealous of me and I hold you responsible for the miscarriage of justice that saw me demoted. Officers take your hands off me. Can't you see that it is that jumped up, female, excuse for a real police officer, you should be arresting?"

Bright ignored him as she was about to tell the other officers to arrest the six container lorry drivers but found that the armed response officers had already spotted the guns on the floor and had the drivers lying prone with their hands over the backs of their heads, wittering something about ensuring that someone should tell the snipers to aim their guns away from them. Suddenly, remembering how she had actually got to the depot, DI Bright told a couple of the officers to also take into custody the two occupants of the car she had arrived in. But, when they all turned to the Range Rover, there was no-one there. At the sound of a revving engine, they all looked up to see a motocross bike disappearing along the middle of the railway tracks with a rider and pillion who seemed to be nonchalantly holding on with one hand and having a telephone conversation using the other. Along that track there was absolutely no hope of pursuit in a police car and by the time they got the force helicopter in the air, the two abductors of the DI would be long gone.

Bright was annoyed but couldn't help smiling to herself as, although she knew she had been used, it had all actually ended up pretty well. Delighted to find that the laptop was still where she had left it, she grabbed it out of the Range Rover, as she knew the story she would be telling her superiors was too fantastical for anyone to believe without the evidence of their own eyes and ears.

"You will regret this you jumped up example of the need to fulfil the female quota and taking the place of a real policeman," cried Grey, just before he was manhandled into a police car for the journey back to the station. Bright decided to cadge a lift back with another car, as she had no intention of spoiling what was going to be a potentially riveting chat with Grey, that she did not wish to put in jeopardy by having him say she had spoken to him without a solicitor present in the car. She then realised that her own car was still parked in Rob Price's street and that was something else she pondered over on the journey back to the station.

Back in Leicestershire, having received the all clear from Billy the pillion rider on the motocross bike, Phil and "little" John took Dean and Wayne back to where they had picked them up, untied them and told them they could clear off. The two crooked customs officers were relieved but worried about the Duncans and emboldened by the reasonable treatment they had received, they asked their two captors what they should do. Having little sympathy for these two who were, when all was said and done, crooks, Phil gave them his opinion.

"No good asking me mate. If you swim with sharks you have to expect to get bitten. Our advice to you would be to go to the police before they come looking for you. As for the Duncans, have you ever thought of living abroad?"

Wishing they had never heard of the Duncans, Dean and Wayne scuttled off, looking furtively around them whenever they heard a noise.

In the Duncan household, the boys were doing all they could to keep their father calm, as time went on and no news was coming through to them. At last they got a call from one of their policemen on the payroll, who told them that Grey had been arrested but didn't know anything else.

"Are we cursed or something? Brad, get that overpaid lawyer Willington-Smythe down there immediately and get him to make sure that Grey doesn't say anything to implicate us. After that, I want you to make sure that everyone is here for ten am tomorrow because we are being attacked and I want to know who is after us and also, who is providing them with information that allows them to target us so easily." As he spoke, Duncan absent-mindedly brushed his signet ring across his beard repetitively as was his custom when he was in deep thought, a noise the listeners back at Castle of HOPE School were getting used to and having great fun guessing at what might be causing it.

At the police station, Bright filled her superiors in on what had been going on and while they were always reluctant to accept that one of their own had gone bad, each of them had a reason to want to get Grey out of the police force, as it was people like him who gave the police, the vast majority of whom were excellent, a bad name. As she went to start her initial interview, something she was quite relishing, one of her officers told her that Grey's lawyer was here.

"Has he had his phone call yet?"

"No Ma'am."

"Then how on earth...? Hang on a minute, who is it?

"That slug Willington-Smythe Ma'am."

"So the Duncans' pet slimeball is here without Grey even getting a phone call. Interesting. Just keep him occupied for me for a few minutes would you? There is something I must do before I carry out the interview." She popped into the incident room and called over her trusted colleague DC Nazir Begum. "Do me a favour will you Naz? I want to know if anyone has rung out of the station to contact someone in the Charnwood area since we got back to the station with Grey. Not just the landlines, I want you to check the signals from mobile phones also."

When Bright entered the interview room with her colleague DS Kevin Willis, Grey held his hand up and announced, "Before we start I want to talk to you alone Bright, without your colleague or my lawyer present and with no tape running."

Willington-Smythe began to object but Grey told him to be quiet and Bright nodded to her colleague, who escorted the 'huffing' solicitor out of the room. When they had left, Bright sat down and asked Grey what was on his mind.

"Now you and I know that all you've got on me is circumstantial and that none of the people who were present today will ever testify against the person you think is running all this. You've always had a grudge against me but you are not clever enough to ever catch me out. You must know that you have only got to where you are because they have to fill certain quotas, while proper coppers like me get pushed to the side."

"Proper coppers. You are no better than the crooks we put away every day and who you will be sharing a great deal of time with in the near future. The sooner we get people like you out of the force the better we will all be."

"You are so naïve. There has to be give and take between the crooks, as you so quaintly put it and us, if we are going to have a quiet life."

"Difficult as it will be for you to get your head around but we are not here to have a quiet life, we are here to make the lives of the citizens of this country safe and yes, quiet."

"Anyway, you know you won't get any of this to stick, so let's stop this pretence and we can both get back to our jobs."

"You really believe you are going to get away with this don't you? Look, I shouldn't do this but I want to rid you of your delusions before you make an utter moron of yourself." Bright opened her laptop and, ensuring that she didn't choose anything that might later be used in court, she selected a video of Grey at the freight depot and turned the screen towards Grey.

He paled slightly but said, "That proves nothing."

Bright then pressed another button and the sound of Grey's voice could be heard loud and clear. He looked gobsmacked.

"Where did you get that? It's illegal you can't use that in court."

"Oh I think we can." Bright smiled, luxuriating in the fact that Grey had no idea that they also had footage of him trying to interfere with the jurors in an upcoming court case, as she called her colleague and Willington-Smythe back into the room. When his lawyer sat down, he whispered to Grey that he had better not have been making deals with Bright that could affect Mr. Duncan and Grey suddenly realised with a sinking feeling in his gut, that while he had not mentioned Duncan to DS Bright, it would soon look to his lawyer, very much as if he had done so.

CHAPTER 24

The following day from 9.00am onwards, a large number of what the Americans call 'muscle cars', started driving through the gates and pulling up outside Duncan Towers and an even larger number of men with actual muscle climbed out, none of them daring to be late for the unusual meeting of all of Duncan's most trusted employees. These were the people who carried out the jobs planned by him and his sons and the ones who had the most knowledge of how his operations actually worked. About thirty large and unsmiling employees stood around in the party room, where chairs had been set out in rows, ensuring that no-one would get the mistaken impression that this was going to be anything like a party. Some of the attendees spoke briefly with each other but most stayed in the groups they had arrived in, as all were aware that they were all in competition with each other for Duncan's favour and this was an intentional ploy on Duncan's part, to keep these feral members of society loyal and on their toes.

At 10.00 am the Duncan family entered the room and sat together at the front facing their employees who were some of the biggest thugs in the country but who were nonetheless nervous about how this was going to turn out. Duncan ignored the niceties of welcoming them and simply stared around the room so that each and every one of them felt they were being studied as a potential sacrifice. Finally, he spoke and when he did, they all had to strain forward to hear the words that he seemed to be forcing out through clenched teeth.

"You have been very lucky men to have been tied to my coat tails, while I have taken you on a journey that has seen you gain wealth and the trappings of wealth that you could never have dreamed of when you were growing up. Most of you would have been on the streets or in prison if you had not had the good fortune to be under my employ."

While many of them would have liked to deny what Duncan was saying, they knew that he was correct and they all sat stony faced, not wanting to show an emotion or reaction that might make him focus on them personally.

"We have together, become one of the most successful crime organisations that the Midlands has ever seen and steadily building a national reputation. And yet….." They all sat up suddenly as his voice rose at the same time as he rose from his chair and banged the table with his fist.

"And yet," he bellowed, "someone is trying to bring us down and what is more, someone in this room must know who it is and even worse, is helping them to achieve that end. And…." By now he was screaming at these, usually confident and terrifying men, now cowering in their seats. "And I will not have it. I will not. But what are the rest of you doing about it? Nothing, that is what. Not one of you has brought me any information that would help me find this person or persons, which begins to lead me to think that maybe you are all in on it and this is some kind of takeover." Duncan reached under his table and pulled out a sub-machine gun and pointed it at the men in front of him, all of whom now questioned their good sense, having handed their own weapons in when they entered the room. "If anyone fancies taking over, then please come out to the front now and we can discuss it." Nobody dared move until they all did in unison, as they dived to the floor when Duncan let go a rapid burst of gun fire over their heads, that destroyed the classical paintings that decorated the end wall. Even his sons, who knew exactly what he was going to do were petrified. As the plaster stopped falling and the echoes of the machine gun fire ebbed away, the men on the floor gradually started to regain their seats. They knew that this man was mad and capable of anything and each of them was determined not to be the one to set him off again.

"Right, I cannot imagine that anyone is going to own up to what has been going on and you seem to lack the determination to put your hearts and souls into finding out and so let me provide a little incentive that might help expedite matters. The first one of you who can bring me proof of who has been ripping me off and double crossing this family, will receive one million pounds." There was a noticeable hush then and they all started to eye each other suspiciously, even those who had arrived together and were supposedly friends. They knew only too well that even if they were not guilty, someone here would be only too willing to cobble together some evidence simply to gain the one million pounds, with no thought for the consequences for the poor sap who had been set up. They knew because they would do exactly the same given the chance. The silence was interrupted by a knock on the door, followed by the entry of Pete, Duncan's most trusted lieutenant, so trusted that he had been waiting outside the room in case anyone had tried to make a run for it, and apart from the sons, the only one who would have dared to interrupt the meeting.

"Boss, this delivery rider has just come with this package and he says that you would need it for your meeting."

"Bring him here immediately."

When the initially care-free delivery rider first entered the room and looked around, his smiling face took on a much more wary and gradually terrified look. When he noticed the machine gun lying on the table at the front, he thought his legs were going to melt.

"How did you know about this meeting and who sent you?"

The petrified, leather clad, motorbike delivery rider replied with difficulty, due to the dryness that now afflicted his mouth, that he just got given the orders from someone over the phone. He had no details but the office might. Realising that the delivery rider was unlikely to be involved or know who was, Duncan told Pete to get him out of there. The rider practically ran out of the room back to his bike.

The package was put on the table and Alex was directed to open it. When he did he revealed thirteen identically wrapped smaller packages about the size of a pack of butter but much lighter. Wary of the contents, Duncan directed his sons to give a package to thirteen of the men randomly throughout the hall and told them to unwrap their package, while he and his sons moved further back in the room. The men given the task of unwrapping the packages, found themselves deserted by their "friends" and slowly and sweatily started to undo the wrapping. One by one they held up, with a confused but relieved look on their face, a model car. It was only the Duncans and the few who had been involved in the bungled attempt to get twelve cars onto the container transport who recognised that the cars being held up were all models of the cars that they had failed to load yesterday evening but it was the thirteenth 'unwrapper' who received the biggest frowns as he pulled a very rare orchid from its special wrapping.

It was with huge relief that the motorbike rider got on his bike and as speedily as possible started to leave the grounds of Duncan Towers, quickening his getaway with even more alacrity as he heard the most terrible scream coming from the house. This was followed by what, if he had been watching a film, he would have thought sounded like machine gun fire, but having been inside the house and even though heard through the padded helmet he was wearing, he knew that this was no film.

The following day, catching a taxi into work, having not yet collected her car from outside Rob Price's house, Susie Bright carried out some basic paperwork before asking DC Nazir Begum if she would give her a lift to collect her car.

"Certainly Ma'am. Oh by the way, I carried out the telephone check you asked me to follow up on and there was only one phone call not on the system between the time DI Grey was brought in and his lawyer arrived."

"Really and who made that call?"

"It was the civilian crime analyst, Miss Bradshaw."

"Which one is she?"

"Oh you know the one. Really attractive, the one who Johnny has a crush on. But he's had his nose put out of joint because rumour is she has a thing going with DI Grey"

"Tell you what Naz, you go and have a coffee. There is something I need to do before we go and collect my car."

As DC Begum moved off towards the canteen, Susie Bright rang the HR Department and ten minutes later she was sat in one of the Human Resources offices with the head of department Ron Higgins, when there was a knock at the door. Told to enter, in walked the attractive civilian crime analyst.

"Take a seat Miss Bradshaw."

"Wow, that's a bit formal isn't it Ron. You usually call me Gina. Have I done something wrong?" The charming smile she offered her boss changed almost to a scowl when she also acknowledged the presence of DI Bright, who answered before the Head of HR had a chance.

"Miss Bradshaw, do you know Detective Inspector Grey?"

"Of course I do. I have dealings with all the detectives in the building," the analyst replied challengingly.

"Let's not be coy Miss Bradshaw, we both know that you know DI Grey a little more than just as a colleague. Am I correct?"

"So what if I do? We love each other. It's not against the rules is it?"

"No it is not. But ringing a known criminal to inform them that your 'boyfriend' had been brought into custody, is not only against the rules but also against the law." Susie knew she was out on a limb here because without actually checking Miss Bradshaw's phone records, she was simply taking a guess, admittedly an informed guess.

"Everyone knows that you are just jealous of Damien. It's because of you that he has been demoted. You're just a sour old cow and somebody has to stand up for him."

At this point Ron Higgins interrupted. "I think I have heard enough DI Bright. I can take it from here now and of course, as well as the instant dismissal, there will be criminal charges for Miss Bradshaw to answer."

"But that's not fair. Damien is a wonderful man and I was only doing what any right minded person in love would do."

Susie, taking no pleasure in seeing a young woman, who had been taken advantage of by an older man in a position of authority, shook her head, stood up and left the room.

Having hidden in the kitchen when he heard DI Bright ringing his doorbell the day after the container operation, Rob now watched through the parted upstairs curtains as she drove away from his street having picked up her car. He was happy to speak to her and deny all knowledge of what had happened to her but a few days grace would perhaps be a good idea. He had also arranged to have a strategy meeting with those people he now trusted most in the world and this was to take place at the school as, being a Saturday, there would be no students present. Going to the doorway hidden in the pantry, Rob pressed the button on the wall before taking the now exposed secret passageway that had been installed beneath his house by the same company who had provided similar at the school. This one led away from his house to one of a row of garages situated in the next street. Once inside the garage he climbed into his Mondeo and using his remote control, opened the garage door and drove off to the school. Once there he went straight to the Headmaster's office, which ridiculously still made him feel as if he had done something naughty and evoked feelings of minor panic, before walking in on Matt, Ronnie, Mike and the Khalifs who were in high spirits, discussing not only the success of last night's escapade but also the now fully realised fantasy, of Grey getting his comeuppance.

Welcoming Rob with a coffee, they sat down and became serious. Rob asked Amira to report back on how the financial situation was developing and in her understated way she described how investments were doing extremely well and even though large sums of money were now going out on student scholarships, internments and supporting businesses set up by their ex-students, they were in a healthier state now than when they first started.

"It seems the old saying is right," said Ronnie, "and money really does attract money but what Amira is too modest to mention is that we are also still developing and growing the school in terms of facilities and resources."

Amira, embarrassed to be the centre of attention, attempted to bring this element of the conversation to a close. "In answer to your unasked question Rob, we are in a very strong situation should we wish to increase our fight against the Duncans."

Obviously excited by their recent success, Ronnie jumped in again. "So Rob, are we now ready to carry out the final part of our plan?"

"No, I would really like to rub their noses in it by hitting them once again."

"Aren't we taking a risk by not hitting them while we have them rattled and perhaps being a trifle self-indulgent?"

Rob was pleased that he had friends like Ronnie there, to keep him on the straight and narrow and not be afraid to tell him how she saw it.

"Firstly, yes I do want to rattle them even more but what I have in mind will also help towards putting a spanner in their determination to make huge sums of money, from one of the disgusting scourges that these people bring to our streets."

"Are we talking about drugs here Mr. Rob? Because if we are, I believe that would be a very worthwhile undertaking but potentially very dangerous."

"Hassan, I wish you would just call me Rob. The answer is yes, but when I set out on this path, I was determined that I would do anything to destroy this family who had destroyed mine, whatever the consequences to myself. Now however, I have begun to realise that a by product of my revenge, OK search for justice, is that we do actually have the power to do some good for the communities we live in. Working within schools we know better than most the evil effect drugs have on our young people in particular, destroying their futures and any advantage we might have given them in our schools. I would love to try and do something about that."

They were all in agreement with this sentiment and spent the next few hours listening to, then refining, Rob's idea for attacking the Duncan's drug operation. Their monitoring of the Duncan family conversations, seemed to suggest that there were two distinct areas upon which they focussed. The setting up and development of cannabis farms throughout the county and the selling of the product of those farms and of even harder drugs on the streets, utilising a large army of young teenagers who would act as the 'go betweens'. It was agreed early on that the teenage 'go betweens' and the mostly illegal immigrants who worked at the cannabis farms should not be the ones to suffer in this operation to destroy the Duncan's drug empire but such a stipulation would make this a much more complicated situation to deal with.

Having asked the listeners to the audio coming back from the Duncans' hidden microphones, to make a note of as many of the addresses being used as cannabis factories, that the Duncans had developed around the county as they could, Rob was shocked when he realised how many of these farms were based in ordinary houses in ordinary streets. He knew from talking to Mateo in some depth that the houses were usually rented under false identities, rather than owned by the Duncans, who would always pay the rent in advance so that the house owner would have no reason to visit the house. Once they had the keys, the rooms would all be stripped to allow for a specialised heating and watering system to be put in place, in all but the down stairs front room that people walking by might be able to see into. That however, would be where the 'farmer' would sleep and live, in very warm, humid and uncomfortable conditions. The 'farmers' were invariably illegal immigrants who had come to Britain to find a better life and had been promised work on a farm or in a factory, having accepted that the £16,000 it cost to be brought into the country, they would have to pay off through their work.

After a short time working on a regular farm to which they had been allocated, certain ones amongst them would be selected and told that they could pay off their debt much more quickly if they were prepared to work in the cannabis farms. Their jobs would be to basically tend the plants until they were ready for harvest and to ensure that no-one became suspicious of what was going on in the house. Once ensconced in the house, the 'farmers' soon learned that it would be very unlikely that they would ever be allowed to leave. Fear of the Duncans and also of going to the police, as they were illegal immigrants, meant that freedom was impossible and that they were basically modern day slaves. It wasn't difficult to decide that the plan Rob and his team came up with, had to ensure the destruction of the businesses but had to also ensure that these largely innocent people tending the plants, did not suffer.

Having been set their latest "Spirit of Adventure" task, the members of the Drama club were paired up and sent out on their challenges, for which they could potentially receive house points that would greatly improve their chances of winning the final prize of a day trip to Alton Towers. They were in five pairs and each one was allocated one of the premises staff who would, as far as they were concerned, simply act as their driver but was in actual fact also acting as their body guard and who was wired up to hear anything picked up by the hidden mics secreted in the clothing of the students. The students had been set their challenge and told that the houses they were going to would have one occupant who would not speak very good English and who they had to persuade to let them into their house, using their improvisation acting skills. Once inside, they had to carry out a task they had been set, surreptitiously. It had been agreed that they would all follow the same basic idea and then use their wits to complete the task.

Sophie and James were determined to ensure that it would be their House that would come out on top in the house championship and in this task specifically. Having already earned ten points for the realistic nature of the fake wound they had applied to James' head using theatre makeup, Sophie rapped firmly on the front door of No.35 Tennyson Avenue in the south east of the city. Eventually the door was opened by a swarthy looking man of thin build and a wispy beard who frowned at them. Sophie quickly apologised and explained that her friend had had an accident earlier in the street and was now beginning to feel faint and could she possibly get her friend a cup of water and let him sit down for a minute. The man tried to object in broken English but as James seemed to collapse into Sophie's arms he relented and told them to sit James on the only chair in what was a very sparse lounge and not go anywhere else while he got a glass of water.

Back in his car, Tommy their minder listened to all that was going on with a certain amount of admiration for their skills and confidence but also with a wary ear for any potential problems. Inside the house, the moment the occupier had left the room to fetch the glass of water, pulling the door to behind him, so that the two teenagers would not be able to see the plant feeding equipment piled up in the kitchen. Sophie and James took the containers from the inside pockets of their coats and sprinkled the contents behind the radiator and what would be behind the door when the kitchen door was opened again. Returning with the glass of water, the man was relieved when the boy seemed to recover somewhat and the two teenagers thanked him profusely and left the house to carry on their way. Pleased that he had been able to do someone a good turn and in all honesty because it helped to break up the boredom of the day, Besnik returned to watching Bargain Hunt not noticing the hundreds of Red Spider mites scurrying from where they had been tipped and heading towards the heat and humidity of the rooms where the cannabis plants were being grown and where a potential feast awaited them. Hassan, or The Prof as the students liked to call him, had chosen these particular insects because the effect they had on the plants would be very similar to a lack of nutrition, a common problem with such plants and it was likely that the remedy the 'farmers' would try to use for the first few days would be an upping of nutrients and by the time their mistake was realised, the plants would be devastated.

As they climbed back in the car, Tommy listened to the students' obvious pleasure at how well their deception had gone, as he set off for their next destination where the process would be repeated. At the end of the day, when the minders reported back to Rob, he was delighted to hear that only five of the houses had turned away their teenage visitors and three had caught the teenagers in the act of deploying insects. But in all three instances the minders had got into the house and told the teenagers to return to the car while they persuaded and in one case threatened, the 'farmer' to leave the insects to do their work and that as soon as it became apparent that they were destroying the plants, they would be removed and given a job on a proper farm with the promise of freedom and never having to deal with the Duncans or their thugs again.

    A few days later when it was felt that the insects would have been well into their feasts, each of the "farmers" was visited by one of Mick's team and offered the same deal i.e. They would be given fairly-paid jobs on the farm that Rob had set up years previously, to provide fresh vegetables for the school and local foodbanks. Dubious of whether they could trust these rather well muscled 'Ora', the Albanian equivalent of the British 'Fairy Godmother', their reluctance was offset by the opportunity this offered to escape the clutches and debts of the Duncans. The 'farmers' were also worried about what they should do with the mobile phones that they had been given, which they had only been allowed to use for texting their bosses. Apparently they were usually left to their own devices and simply had to text in every other day to confirm that everything was fine. Having received advice from Hassan that it would only take three days for the insects to destroy the cannabis plants, Mick told them to keep in contact with their boss for four more days, pretending all was well, then destroy their phones and they would be given new ones to use as they wished.

    Four days later, Mick and his men visited each of the houses that had been used to grow the cannabis and checked that the plants had truly been destroyed. They were shocked at the destruction these little insects had caused and felt slightly guilty spraying the rooms with an insecticide that the 'Prof' had assured them would get rid of the insects in just under an hour. During that hour, the men sat out in their cars and then returned and placed the carefully protected item they had brought with them, just inside the front door, which they then locked and left.

CHAPTER 25

Following the meeting that took place the day after Duncan had found his orchids missing; Amira and Ronnie had sat in their office contemplating how they should go about finding out the whereabouts of Mrs Duncan. Amira picked up the phone and as she started to scroll though her contacts, she explained that sometimes the most obvious answer is staring us in the face. Finding the number she had recently added to her phone, in case she had had to ring it while pretending to be the police, in order to create enough panic for Phil to be able to make his escape from Duncan's the evening before the Orchid theft, should the need arise, she rang the Duncan house.

"Good morning, this is the Duncan residence how can I help you?"
"Oh hello there. Could I please speak to Mrs Duncan."
"Who is speaking please?"
" Oh I am an old school friend who is arranging a reunion and I was hoping Mrs Duncan would be able to attend."
"I am afraid that Mrs Duncan no longer lives at this address."
"Oh, could you tell me where I could get hold of her please?"
"I'm sorry but I cannot help you. Goodbye."

With that terse ending to the conversation Amira looked at Ronnie. "Curiouser and curiouser. Lets do a bit of research on the internet and see what we can both come up with."

"Good idea. I will concentrate on newspaper reports and you concentrate on social media and any other likely areas and we will come together after lunch and see what we have found out." As she said this, Ronnie was already typing on her keyboard.

Ronnie munched on her homemade samosas while Amira gobbled a cheese and pickle sandwich. "You British have such great food," mumbled Amira as Ronnie shook her head, not so much at the absurdity of their respective meals but at her friend's rapid acclimatisation to everything British.

"So, what have you found?" Amira continued.

"Well, there are lots of stories and photos of the Duncans together at charity events and at international flower competitions, right up until about 1998 when suddenly there is no more mention or photographic evidence of Mrs Duncan still being around. Her first name was Lily by the way."

"Yes, I've picked that up also. Likewise she appears in minutes of meetings for the Women's' Institute, the foodbank she set up and a local nursery she also set up until around about the same time. I have checked, and there is no sign that her death was recorded. She just seems to have disappeared."

"This seems too much of a coincidence when we know what Duncan is capable of. Do you think she might be dead?" Ronnie asked, looking at Amira with a worried look on her face.

"Well what do you think?"

"We need to start looking a little deeper."

"Ok so how do we go about that?"

"I've given it some thought and I think the best bet would be for us to try and talk to some of the older serving staff who might have been employed by the Duncans around that time. But we will have to do it away from Duncan Towers, where they might feel freer to talk."

"That could be a good start and in fact there is no time like the present." The two women left the school in Ronnie's car and drove to park near the entrance to Duncan's estate, having discussed the approach they would take on the way over. They watched as cars drove in and out of the gaudily ornamented gates, concentrating on those exiting, ignoring the large four by four "muscle cars" that seemed to dominate the arrivals and suggested drivers who were young and male and with too much money and too little sense. Frustrated at not seeing anything that matched what they had expected to see, they agreed to take it in turns over the next few days, alternating between early morning and late afternoon to catch either cleaning or serving staff. After only two days they talked again and compared notes about what they had seen and agreed that the most likely candidates were an old Fiat Punto and a fairly new Ford Fiesta which they thought would be the type of vehicle a cleaner or low paid house worker would drive.

"You do realise that we are reacting with the same prejudices that we would be criticising our husbands for if they had just had that conversation?" questioned Ronnie.

"Yes, but they don't need to know that do they?"

The following morning, they were waiting outside the Duncan estate, when the Fiat Punto driven by a small middle aged female they had both spotted previously as a likely candidate, left the estate after what they assumed had been her morning cleaning shift, at around 10.00am. They followed the car until it drove to the small town of Shepshed and parked in the Asda car park. Following her into the shop, they saw the woman pick up only a few items before paying for them. Then buying herself a coffee and a cake, she found a seat in the shop's café. Buying herself a coffee, Ronnie was passing the table where the subject of their observation was sitting and pretended to stumble then sit down abruptly, opposite the startled woman. Apologising and feigning feeling faint, she asked if the lady would mind if she just sat there for a few moments before finding a table of her own.

"Don't be silly you must stay where you are and get yourself right 'me duck.' Do you need me to find you some medical help?"

"No, no I am just being silly. It happens sometimes when I get too warm."

"Oh I know what you mean." The two fell into an easy conversation, with Ronnie offering up her name as Hannah and in return finding out that she was talking to Jean who gave Ronnie, or Hannah as she now was, the opening she wanted by asking her if she had a job and Hannah told her about her role as a teaching assistant.

"Oh that must be nice, working with the young ones?"

"It has its moments. And do you work?"

"Oh yes, but nothing as interesting as your job I'm afraid. I've just come away from my job as a cleaner."

"Would that be in an office block?"

"Oh no, I work for a family who live in a big mansion out in Charnwood."

"That must be nice?"

"Well the place is nice but it's full of men and not very nice men at that. Although they do leave the likes of me alone thankfully."

"Isn't there a lady of the house to keep all that testosterone in line?"

"No, the wife of the owner, Mr. Duncan, left before I got there. I don't know what happened to Mrs Duncan and I have been there for three years. In fact the only woman who lives there all the time is the housekeeper Mrs Patterson and she's been there forever and takes no nonsense. Her husband also used to work for the family but he died some years ago now and so the job is her life really. But she is no fan of the men in the house either I can tell you. In fact after she has cooked the lunch each day, she goes off in her flash car and takes her frustrations out by swimming a ridiculous number of lengths in the town swimming pool."

"Sounds like a formidable woman. So what sort of 'flash car' are we talking about here?"

"Oh she has a BMW coupe."

Realising she now had the next piece of the puzzle to chase up, Ronnie thanked Jean for letting her sit and before getting up to leave, asked her if she could get her another drink to repay her kindness.

"No bless you. I now have the pleasure of going back to clean my own house."

Once back in the car with Amira, Ronnie told her what she had learned. She explained to Amira that they would have to go through the same process the following day but that this time Amira would have to bring her swimming costume.

"Why me?"

"Well, I think that you need the exercise and I also tossed a coin and you lost, by the way, we might not be cut out for this Cagney and Lacey detective lark as our prejudices have already resulted in us guessing wrongly about the type of car we should be looking out for."

The following day, having been waiting for almost an hour outside the Duncan residence, Ronnie watched as an electric blue BMW coupe pulled out of the drive and headed towards Loughborough. On the way, she used her hands free phone to inform Amira, who was sitting reading a magazine in the leisure centre café. "Ok its time for you to don your mermaid costume."

Grabbing her bag and moving towards the changing room, Amira blew a raspberry down the phone then added, "As my dear grandmother would so succinctly put it, 'May your goats fall in your cooking fire.' Wish me luck." Ronnie smiled to herself and continued to follow Mrs Patterson to the leisure centre and once there, watched her as she entered the building. Ronnie texted Amira to inform her that Mrs Patterson had just arrived. Parking her car, she entered the building herself and found a suitable table in the viewing area and sat down pretending to read a book, while actually watching the pool area. While waiting for Amira to enter the pool, Ronnie began to think of Carol and how much she missed her. She wiped away a tear from her eye and told herself to pull herself together, as she realised how ironic it was that the person she now thought of as her best friend had become so because of the loss of Carol. Fate had a warped way of playing tricks she thought but she had come to see Amira as someone more than a work colleague. Yes, they shared an office but they also shared so much more than that. They had a real bond not least because they had a similar sense of humour and also, Ronnie liked to think, similar principles. Ronnie knew that she was quite an intelligent person but she was in awe at the level of sophistication that Amira's brain worked at. Ronnie had little understanding of the conversations that Amira had in phone calls with people around the world about investments, share portfolios etc. and she seemed to be buying and selling commodities on a regular basis. Whether she understood the dealings or not, she certainly understood the results, which saw the funds of the school increase exponentially, allowing for the school to expand and grow into the dream they all shared.

Amira noticed the lady who had just walked though the doors into one of the cubicles while she was stood by the washroom mirrors in the changing room, adjusting her swimming hat. Anyone watching her would have been surprised at how long this simple process seemed to take and then how quickly it was suddenly completed when Amira set off for the entrance to the poolside, following closely behind another lady who, despite being no youngster, looked in excellent physical condition.

Mrs Patterson climbed into the pool in lane four allocated to experienced swimmers and with well practised movements, cleaned her goggles with her own spit, transferred them to her head and pushed off in a leisurely warm-up crawl stroke, which she alternated at the end of each length with breast stroke. Amira climbed in behind her and giving her a fifteen metre start, set off in pursuit, maintaining the distance until Mrs Patterson obviously felt warmed up sufficiently to concentrate just on crawl and began to increase her pace. Amira liked to think that she was quite a good swimmer herself but had not been exercising regularly of late and was soon finding it difficult to keep up. Luckily, after ten lengths Mrs Patterson stopped at the end to recover her breath and Amira realised that while she would also like to have taken a breather she needed to plough on in order to get in front of Duncan's housekeeper. This she achieved and was grateful when she looked back that her quarry had set off behind her but using the slower breast stroke, allowing the front crawl Amira was employing to keep her ahead without having to exert herself too much. Nonetheless, she was breathing heavily now and decided that she would have to stop soon. Slowing imperceptibly over the next length, as she turned she realised that Mrs Patterson was into a steady rhythm and in a world of her own, totally unaware of how close she was getting to the swimmer in front until suddenly she swam right into Amira who had stopped abruptly. The housekeeper stood and spluttered an apology, while noticing that the small Asian woman she had swum into was holding the lane rope to stay afloat and looked in some discomfort.

"Oh please don't apologise. I came to a halt with cramp and you couldn't avoid me."

"It happens to me all the time. Are you sure that you are all right?

"I'll be fine thank you. I think I have done enough for today anyway."

"Well if you are sure?" and returning her goggles from her forehead to her eyes, she set off while Amira swam to the side, climbed out and walked to the changing room affecting a limp to suggest the after effects of cramp. As she passed the viewing area, she poked her tongue out at Ronnie who was holding her nose and with her arm waving above her head, mimicking someone who was drowning. Amira had finished dressing and was drying her hair when Mrs Patterson came back into the changing room. She smiled at her and apologised again and insisted on Mrs Patterson joining her in the café when she was ready, for a coffee. Almost 15 minutes later, they were sitting together with a cake and coffee, each discussing the benefits of swimming for exercise, when Mrs Patterson mentioned that it gave her a much needed break from the mundane tasks of the day.

"Oh what do you do?"

"For my sins, I am the housekeeper for a family who live in a very large house in Charnwood."

"That sounds interesting. Are they nice people to work for?"

"Not really no. Not since the lady of the house left."

"Oh I am sorry to hear that. What are their names, are they famous?"

"Not famous as such but you might well have heard of them as they are often in the papers. Their name is Duncan."

"The lady of the house you were speaking about wouldn't happen to be Lily Duncan would it?"

"Yes. A lovely lady. Do you know her?

"Well I did. We were at school together but she had a different surname then. We used to be good friends but once she got married we lost touch."

With a sigh Mrs Patterson said, "Yes, I can imagine that."

"What do you mean?"

"Oh Mr Duncan likes things his own way and didn't like Lily having a life of her own."

"I'm sorry to hear that but what a coincidence. I would love to catch up with her again, could you give her my number?"

"Oh she left, well it must be just over twenty years ago now. Just wasn't there one morning. There was a rumour that she had run off with another man but while I could understand her wanting to get away from that husband of hers, she would never have left her sons as they meant everything to her."

Amira began to feel the despair of another dead end. "That's a real shame. So you have no idea how I could get in contact with her?"

"No, but if she is still around and if anyone knew where she was it would be the old butler, Mr. Robinson, who was really close to her. He was distraught when she disappeared. It was a good job he was there though because apart from their mother, he was the only one who could actually control the boys and he was far more of a father figure to them than their own father was. We all think that that was why Mr. Duncan got rid of him, jealous of the influence he had over the boys and annoyed at his close friendship with Lily." Seeing Amira's questioning look, Mrs Patterson added, "Oh not like that. He was in his late seventies."

Trying not to sound too eager and literally holding her breath. "Do you have an address for him?"

"Actually I do, as we still exchange Christmas cards. When I get back I'll text the address to you. I'd love to know how she is getting on myself. As I say, she was a lovely lady."

Deciding that Mrs Patterson was a lovely lady also, Amira determined that whatever happened she was going to make swimming a regular occurrence and that to do it with someone as nice as Mrs Patterson would be an added bonus. Making sure they exchanged numbers after a little more chatting, they both got up to go their separate ways.

Back in their office, Amira was discussing with Ronnie how the next stage of their search should continue, when a ping on her phone alerted her to the texted address that her new found friend had sent her.

With the Sat Nav set for Brighton and the address that Mrs Patterson had given Amira as the location of Robinson, the Duncans' old butler, Ronnie drove as Amira explained what she was thinking. It was a week after the swimming session and they had decided to turn up unannounced and determined not to return home until they had the answer they wanted.

"I am sure that she must be dead. From everything we have heard she was a devoted mother. Surely she would not have just run off with another man and not kept in contact with her sons?"

"We don't know for certain that she hasn't been in contact."

"No, but you would think that Mrs Patterson would have heard something and in all the audio we have picked up from the boys' conversations, not once have they mentioned their mother which seems strange don't you think?"

"Well, yes I do but we can't jump to conclusions."

"I know. But if we can prove that Duncan killed his wife, our whole plan to have him put away would become so much easier."

"Maybe but neither of us really wants this to be true do we, otherwise we are literally hoping that someone has been murdered?"

"Fair point," Amira agreed, feeling slightly guilty and suitably chastised."

It was midday before they pulled up outside a well positioned bungalow overlooking the sea on the outskirts of Brighton. As they walked up the path of the well-maintained garden, they went over between them the approach they were going to take with Mr. Robinson.

Having rung the doorbell, it took some time before the door was opened by a smiling gentleman, immaculately dressed in a cardigan that covered a plain light blue shirt and club tie that pointed down at finely creased navy trousers and highly buffed black loafers. The man himself, despite his age, stood erect with warm intelligent eyes staring at them from under his neatly combed silver grey hair.

"Well this is a pleasant surprise. I rarely get visitors and certainly not any as delightful as ladies such as yourselves. How can I help you?"

Slightly taken aback but suitably charmed by their welcome, Ronnie held out her hand, introduced them both by name and having previously agreed that the best approach would be the direct approach, asked. "Are you the Arthur Robinson who used to work for Francis Duncan in Leicestershire?" Both ladies noticed his face cloud over and the smile disappeared as he said, "I have no wish to carry on with this conversation and would appreciate it if you would leave." Before he could close the door Amira stepped forward and tried to reassure him.

"I can assure you we are not here to cause you any trouble."

"No? Which paper are you with?"

"We are not journalists Mr. Robinson, we are people who have suffered at the hands of Mr Duncan and we just want to ask you a couple of questions."

"I am sorry that you have suffered in any way but I can assure you that I had no part in Mr. Duncan's business interests."

Just as he was about to shut the door again he was stopped in his tracks when Amira continued with, "Maybe not but if you are unable to help us now we are convinced that his three sons are going to have their lives destroyed for ever." He looked at them for some time before making up his mind with a sigh and standing back while ushering them into his home.

Agitated as he felt, his upbringing and training made it natural for him to offer them refreshments and after the long journey they gratefully took him up on his offer of coffee and cake. While they tucked into their refreshments, Mr. Robinson made it quite clear that he had no intention of saying anything derogatory about his past employers but wanted to know what they had meant about potential problems for the sons. Between them, Ronnie and Amira explained honestly, that they had a good deal of intelligence that Mr. Duncan was an evil man who had caused much misery including to a close friend of theirs. They declined to go into details but they knew how much he thought of the sons and if things carried on as they were doing then they would end up in an early grave or prison if their father was allowed to continue his wicked influence.

"I have always feared this might be the outcome since I had my employment terminated and in fact that was one of the main reasons why I was told to leave."

"How was that if you don't mind me asking?" Ronnie managed to mumble between mouthfuls of a delicious carrot cake.

"Well once their mother was no longer around, the boys would have run wild but for some reason they and I had a really close relationship as you suggested and Mr Duncan didn't like the fact that I was turning them against the type of lifestyle he had envisaged for them, by encouraging them to follow their real interests. All three of the boys were talented in their own individual ways and performed brilliantly at school. On top of their natural academic intelligence, Brad was very artistic both on the stage and in the art room; Alex was almost the opposite, having a real passion for science and wishing to be an engineer when he grew up, while Phillip was an excellent sportsman who represented Leicestershire in a number of activities and was a national finalist in swimming. They would have excelled at university but Mr. Duncan was resolute in his desire for them to leave school at sixteen and work with him. It really is such a waste."

"Have you spoken to the boys since?"

"It was made clear to me that the pension I rely on to survive would be cut off should I try to contact them but even more concerning for me were the threats that were aimed at my family should I try to see or talk to the boys and I knew enough about Mr. Duncan to take those threats seriously. So you see, not only do I know very little about Mr Duncan's business, I daren't speak up even if I did."

"Mr. Robinson we understand totally but we also know how close you were to the boys' mother and we believe that Mr Duncan murdered her. We don't expect you to do anything other than tell us if you know whether this is the case. After that we would do the rest."

A look of amazement spread across the old man's face and he stood looking at the view of the sea before slowly turning and assuring them, "Thankfully, you are totally way off mark with that idea, unless this is something that has happened this morning because I spoke to Mrs Duncan on the telephone only last night."

The girls looked at each other, mixing the feeling of delight that Lily Duncan had not been murdered, with the disappointment that another avenue to get Duncan his just desserts looked to have been closed off. "Are you sure?"

"Oh yes, we are in constant contact, as we have so much in common in terms of not being able to speak to anyone else about our lives in that house and of course, a joint interest in the welfare of the three boys. I try to keep her up to date with any news I pick up from the media and I have a friend who still works at the 'Towers', who gives me updates."

Amira and Ronnie looked guiltily at their shoes, embarrassed at their staying quiet about having met Mrs. Patterson, Mr. Robinson's 'friend still working at the Towers.'

Luckily the old butler seemed not to notice as he continued, "Mrs Duncan and I feel so helpless in trying to stop the boys throwing their lives away. We don't know what to do and in all honesty, that is the only reason I let you in. The implication that you might be able to help them." He looked at them hopefully.

"We'll definitely come to that in a minute but if Mrs Duncan still feels so much for the boys why has she made no effort to contact them or see them?"

"If you truly know the sort of man Mr. Duncan is, you wouldn't ask that question. I won't go into detail but suffice to say the threats he has made against me are nothing compared to those Mrs Duncan has hanging over her. She did make every effort to contact the boys and I have evidence of that upstairs but Mr. Duncan never let the boys know."

"Would it be possible for us to see this evidence do you think, as it might help us to help the boys?"

"I don't suppose it could do any harm as long as you don't let any of this get back to Mr. Duncan. But you haven't yet told me how you mean to help them." Ronnie tried to explain without going into too much detail that they intended to bring down Duncan's empire. But when she included the fact that the boys would have to serve any jail terms that might result from a prosecution, Mr. Robinson looked aghast.

"I understand that the boys have done some terrible things and I would do anything to prevent them from throwing their lives away any further but I could never agree to provide you with information that would lead to them spending time in prison. I cannot argue that their actions might deserve it but those actions have been guided by their father, just as a puppet is manipulated by the puppeteer." Refusing also to provide the girls with an address for Mrs Duncan, it became apparent to them that they would gain nothing more from staying any longer. They thanked the old butler for his time and left him with a contact number should he change his mind. He apologised and assured them that would not be the case but wished them well, in what he saw, as their futile hopes of bringing down Duncan.

"That man needs to be stopped before his evil influence destroys even more lives."

Back in the car, the girls looked at each other and Ronnie said resignedly, "Well we tried but we didn't achieve much did we?"

"Well at least we know that Lily Duncan is still alive and we can cross out the idea of having Duncan put away for anything he did to her. Let's get back home and break the news to the others."

When they eventually got back to Leicester and recounted the results of their investigations, it was agreed that Mrs Duncan being alive was a good thing that also unfortunately prevented them from getting Duncan prosecuted for her disappearance. But even if she could be found, it appeared that she would be likely to take the butler's view of not wanting to provide evidence that would lead to the incarceration of her sons. Once again it seemed as if Frankie Duncan led a charmed life, that would guarantee he would never have to suffer the punishment he so deserved.

CHAPTER 26

Mick and his team had spent a couple of weeks observing the operation the Duncans ran for the importation and distribution of hard drugs and had surreptitiously photographed the youngsters who were used to deliver the drugs, given to them from the cars of the main dealers. These cars would continually drive to different spots in the city and county and collect the money back from the youngsters who had carried out the individual deals. This they did on the back of bicycles, enabling them to use back alleys and avoid being caught by the police. In conversation with Rob, they decided that they had to find a way of targeting the youngsters in a way that would get them out of this environment and away from the main dealers, to get them off the street. Mick contacted some more of his old mates to ensure he had enough people to track all the youngsters involved in the drug provision and by following them for a few days, they were able to find out who they were and build up a picture of them as individuals. Combined with the information that the IT department had been able to glean from their social media profiles etc. they came up with a plan of action that they thought would lure the teenagers away from the Duncans but if they were to keep them away, they would have to ensure that the Duncans' drug operation was destroyed completely, so there was nothing to go back to should they be tempted. Now, if they could also make these kids realise that the people who worked for the Duncans were not people who you should look up to, all the better.

With everything in place a few weeks later, each of Mick's team who had been tracking a bike rider/drug courier, in the area where they operated, met the pupil from Castle of HOPE School who had been allocated to them and with the pupil's own bike in the back of their vehicles, drove to the area that they had been watching. It had already been explained to the pupils, who assumed that this was another of the 'Spirit of Adventure' House Points activities, what their task was to be and that their targets had been told to put up quite a bit of resistance, so they would have to be on their toes or even as Mick tried to humorously put it, "their pedals," which none of the kids found at all funny.

The students chosen for this assignment were all at least sixteen and just happened to be members of the school cycling squad, who were on the verge of becoming regional champions and these particular ones had been selected because they possessed a good deal of self confidence and indeed initiative.

Mick's man Tommy, and his allocated pupil Charlie, watched as their target Jason, a fair haired lad in blue tracky bottoms, a white tracksuit top and Nike trainers, rode nonchalantly up to a silver BMW parked on the edge of the New Parks estate. The passenger window came down and the passenger tapped fists with the lad on the bike, who then palmed a number of small packages which he placed in the side pocket of his jacket and then rode off to complete his first deal of the evening. With lots of time to spare, he pulled a couple of wheelies and sat up hands free to light a cigarette he took from behind his ear. As he did so, too late, he became aware of a presence at his side, another cyclist, who seemed to tap him on his jacket and then rode away on a weird looking mountain bike. With a mouthful of expletives aimed at the bike accelerating away, he suddenly realised that the rider who had just passed him was now smiling back at him and waving what looked like….., "S*** he's got the stash," he exclaimed out loud to no-one in particular. He immediately began to increase his speed and listing the things he would do to this 'cocky dude' the moment he caught him, except that he wasn't catching him.

Thinking to himself that he really ought to cut out those fags, he decided that this called for some real effort and looking up, he realised that the bike in front had now stopped and the rider was again looking back at him. 'Right you arrogant so and so, you really are for it now.' but just as he got within twenty metres of him, the rider set off again, turned down an alley and shot away. It was all Jason could do to keep him in sight, as various thoughts coursed through his brain. "Is he on a rocket or what? But I can't lose those drugs. I really can't, they'll kill me". But then he began to smile because the bike in front had slowed down and was now turning into an alley that would take him right into the shopping centre, that the council had laid out so that it was impossible to ride your bike there.

His grin grew even wider despite the pain from the 'stitch' he could feel worsening with every pedal rotation, as he arrived at the end of the alley and saw the boy in front halted at the top of a vicious looking run of steps leading into the shopping centre. "I've got you now. But why is he looking at me with that smirk on his face?" he thought to himself. As he looked, he noticed the boy start bouncing his bike up and down, until he actually bounced it up onto the top of the wall that supported the hand rail of the steps and then rode down this, while calling out a childish and irritating "Wheeee," during the descent. "How did he do that?" gulped a shocked Jason who, lacking the skill or the courage to even attempt the same route, bumped uncomfortably down the forty six steps (he counted and felt every one of them), towards the cyclist who seemed to be waiting for him, before setting off again out of the shopping complex and along a track that would take them to a large industrial estate just outside town. Jason knew he had to catch him quickly, as he was getting seriously tired, so he dragged what energy he had left into a surge of speed that saw him gaining on the cyclist who turned into a compound, that he knew would be a dead end with no other way out.'Now I've got you and you are going to regret giving me the run around'. The cyclist stopped suddenly in the middle of the car park of a small printing company and as Jason skidded through the gates in pursuit, he heard them shut behind him. Stopping, he was suddenly aware of two fairly ordinary looking men standing either side of him.

"Hey, what's going on? What do you think you are doing?"

"We would just like to have a word with you." Tommy replied in as calm and reassuring voice as he could.

"You are in so much deep sh**. You have no idea who you are messing with." As he was talking, he saw that the rider of the bike he had been chasing had pulled a wheelie and rode out of the compound blowing him a kiss as one of the men opened the gate and it was only then he realised that the now helmet-less rider, was in fact a girl.

"We know exactly who we are dealing with. Your name is Jason Guillespie and you are 14 years old and you sell drugs for the Duncan family."

Slightly taken aback but refusing to let these blokes see his confusion, he snarled back, "If you know that much, you will know that interfering with their operation means that you are dead men."

"Oh, we are not worried about low lifes like the Duncans who are just bullies and cowards but we are worried about you."

"Why are you worried about me? I was doing just fine until you and that stupid girl got involved today."

"Well the way you are going you will end up like most of the people who work for the Duncans, either in prison or living on the streets."

"You are joking. Their gang are all minted and drive the best cars and have a 'sick' life."

"That life lasts about nine months on average before they either get arrested or the Duncans get rid of them because they know too much."

"You don't know nothing and once they find out about you, you will be finished."

"Oh we'll take our chances but we have an offer for you."

"Oh here we go, I might have guessed. You are a rival gang and you want me to work for you."

"Actually no, we will give you the money you would have earned today if you come with us and listen to a proposition we have for you."

"And what happens when the Duncans find out what I have done? They are not just going to let it go. They will come and want to know what has happened to their drugs."

"We promise you that will not happen but what have you got to lose? We've got your drugs anyway and after you have finished with us you will still have all the money you would have made if your sales had gone ahead." Realising that what this bloke said actually made sense and that he needed to get the money back somehow, reluctantly he let the two men put his bike on the bike rack of their vehicle and climbed in the back, determined to go along with them until he could get the money he owed his main dealer and find a way out.

They drove out of the city to the edge of the county and what he knew to be a deserted leisure centre, that had closed fairly recently because the owner had become bankrupt. But when he was taken inside, he was surprised to see that it had been refurbished and in what was one of the meeting rooms there was food and drink and even more surprisingly, the majority of the other lads and girls he knew who acted as runners for the Duncans' drug business. Grabbing some of the food and a can, he joined a huddle of lads he knew well and found that all the others had been brought here in very similar circumstances to the way he had, with some variations on a theme. No sooner than they had started to plot what they should do next, a man in a blue suit walked in and stood in front of rows of chairs and called in a loud and clear voice for them to all please sit down. Refusing to move at first but with some friendly assistance from the men who had brought them here, they found that compliance was the easier option. Once seated, they looked at the speaker aggressively but in silence, as they wanted to know what he had to say for himself and work out how they could get the money that would keep them out of the Duncans' bad books. Many of them, like Jason, were waiting to hear what scam they were going to be told they had to be involved in now, in order to be allowed to leave. They all believed that it would not be long before these idiots would find out just who they were dealing with and get a rude awakening from the Duncans.

"Gentlemen and ladies, my name is Matt Carter and can I firstly apologise for the rather underhand way in which you were tricked into coming here today and thank you for your patience."

"We was promised the money we would have earned from our sales if we agreed to come along. Where is it?" shouted out a lad called Dale, to be joined by a chorus of voices agreeing with their spokesman, who had given them the confidence to show their displeasure while hiding behind the safety of not speaking out alone.

"You were promised that and you will receive it when you leave here and after I have finished talking to you in less than fifteen minutes time. Firstly however, I would like to show you a short film we have put together. The lights dimmed and the man moved to one side as images began to appear on the screen behind him. Their looks of disinterest very quickly changed to ones of shock, as they watched a montage of themselves going about the business of delivering drugs and money to addicts and dealers. Each one of them at some stage, shown in full close up, carrying out what would amount to a very likely conviction. They also heard audio of the Duncan family talking about them as a group of 'low life yobs' and even on two occasions giving the names of two of their group who had recently been arrested by the police, to a detective called Grey as a way of ensuring he concentrated his efforts on gangs other than the Duncans and also apparently to give this policeman some kudos with his police bosses. When the lights came back on, the man in the blue suit spoke again and told them that the rather damaging evidence they had just seen would never be used and in fact would be destroyed in a week's time."

"Yeah and what have we got to do in return?" shouted out Janine, whose short life had taught her that you got nothing for nothing, with others chorusing their approval of the question.

"I promise that you will not have to do anything either illegal or anything that you will find unpleasant." Just at that moment one of the men who had been on the front doors when they had arrived came in and whispered something in the speaker's ear. He nodded and smiled. Then he announced to the audience sitting watching, that they were about to have a slight interruption as some visitors had arrived. Just then the door swung open and in swaggered three of the 'minders' of the "bike drug deliverers". The bike rider/dealers looked at each other with self satisfied and expectant smirks as if to say, 'now these goons will find out what they are messing with.'

"Can I help you gentlemen?"

"Are you the bloke in charge of this shower of s**t?" growled a very large man known as Popeye," as he marched towards the man in the blue suit. As Popeye approached the front, Jason noticed the girl who had given him the run around on the bike earlier, step into Popeye's path and say, "I am sorry but this is a private meeting and you will have to wait until we have finished and can we also request you refrain from swearing as we are basically children."

"Oh dear," thought Jason as Popeye placed his hand on the girl's chest to push her away. Instead of flying backwards, the girl simply grabbed his wrist stepped to one side and bent his hand back towards his face. A scream of agony was emitted from the lips of the surprised thug as he sank to his knees and his two colleagues rushed forward to help him. Two of the innocuous looking blokes standing around the edge of the room, then stepped forward and simply by pinching, just with their thumb and forefingers, a nerve in the muscle between the interlopers' necks and shoulders, both of Popeye's colleagues fell to the floor with a cry of pain. A communal and audible intake of breath came from the audience and the man in the blue suit calmly announced to the visitors that as they had been told this was a private meeting, they should do as requested and leave now. As they stood up, it looked as if they would have another attempt at getting to the speaker but now all the other men standing around the outside moved forward in a slightly menacing manner.

"You haven't heard the last of this I can assure you. We will be back tomorrow and we will be tooled and numbered up. Nobody treats us like this and gets away with it." As the thugs left the room, there was some low level murmuring amongst the drug runners who were rather shocked by what they had just seen. They had always thought that Duncan and his men were untouchable.

" *Now, where were we before we were so rudely interrupted? Oh yes, what do we want from you? Well we want you to realise that you are far better than the "lowlife yobs"as I believe Mr. Duncan called you. To try and prove that to you we would like you to attend this youth club for the next week at around the times you would normally be dealing drugs and we will show you there is a better way. We promise you that every time you turn up during that week you will receive the same money you would have got for your illegal activities. After that, if you decide you want to continue, it will be purely voluntary, with no payment unless you do some work. As you leave this evening you will receive your money for today."*

"Even if we wanted to do what you say which we don't, when we get home there will be one of Duncan's men waiting for us," called out a now less aggressive but still confident, Dale."

"Don't worry about that, as each one of you has been allocated a minder. You won't see them and neither will you be bothered by any of Duncan's men."

A disbelieving voice from the back shouted out, "And what are you going to do when they come back tomorrow mob-handed?"

"You leave us to worry about that. Now, if there is nothing else, you may leave as long as you want no more to eat and if any of you need a lift, the guys around the back of the hall will sort you out. It's been an absolute pleasure." At that, the speaker moved from the front and started speaking to some of the teenagers who had acted as the bait for the dealers. The dealers themselves stood around in little groups talking about what had just occurred and all seemed to be in agreement that whatever happened, they would definitely be back tomorrow just to see what the Duncans would do to these weird people. They also agreed that when they received the inevitable visit from their main dealer, they would all use the same story about being kidnapped by a big gang of men. Jason in particular was all for this. At that, they all moved to the back of the hall and demanded their money and a lift back home with their bikes. That night, every single one of the young people waited in nervous anticipation for a knock on the door from their main dealer but it never happened.

Outside each of their houses at different times throughout the evening and night, Muscle cars would pull up and the drivers of the cars were persuaded that it was not a good idea to get out of their cars or come back, by fairly innocuous looking men who employed all sorts of different but effective methods to get their point across.

That night, the team listening in to the Duncan's conversation back at the mansion, reported back to Rob and Mick, the Khalifs and the Carters, that they had picked up a really interesting piece of information. They had heard that a very large shipment of hard drugs was coming into the country in a few days time, hidden amongst a delivery of baby food. The six of them looked at each other and smiled. The smiles grew wider when they were told that the Duncans had then started talking about what was happening with their drug runners and that is when the conversations had become quite heated. Apparently they had decided to teach these idiots, who were obviously trying to muscle in on their operation, a lesson they would never forget. They would turn up the following day in six cars, all carrying four of Duncan's thugs and all armed with machine guns. Let's see how they cope when they realise they are dealing with the big boys now, was apparently what they had said.

"What do think Mick? Do you think we should cut our losses?"

"Oh no chance, Rob. My lads have been waiting for a chance to get a little action and I have a plan that should show "the big boys" a thing or two and at the same time help our young drug runners see these thugs for what they really are. Bullies and cowards."

CHAPTER 27

The following day, Matt had to admit to himself, that the fact that all the drug runners had turned up at the youth centre, probably had more to do with them being picked up by their minders and the desire to see what would happen when Duncan's thugs came back, rather than being excited by what the youth club could offer. However, when they got there, they were taken aback by what had been laid on for them and also flummoxed as to how these people knew what they would be interested in. As well as the games machines and tables, including pool and snooker that were there, Johnno, who had ambitions to be a rap star found that there was a recording studio for his use, with Edgy the Radio Leicester rap star available to give tips and he was soon joined by a couple of the girls who fancied themselves as recording artists. Dan and Gary were asked if they would like to join in with some 5-a-side and although they both loved football they didn't want to look too keen and were on the verge of turning it down when they saw to their absolute shock, that Jamie Vardy and Rihad Mahrez were each on one of the teams playing.

Tommy asked Jason if he'd like to meet the girl who gave him the runaround yesterday. He was about to refuse but she suddenly appeared and dug him in the ribs with a brilliant smile and introduced herself as Charlie. Tommy explained that Charlie was the national U/16 BMX and Cyclo Cross champion, so he shouldn't feel too bad as no-one could keep up with her. She asked Jason if he'd like to have a go on the BMX track that was laid out at the back and he and a couple of others jumped at the chance when they saw the quality of bike they would be using. Each of them had the opportunity to have a go at their favourite interest, with the very best equipment or with some recognised expert. A couple of them chose to chill out and were waiting to see how long it would be before they would be stopped from having as much food and drink as they could get down them. The answer was that they were full before they could find out. Every now and again one or more of the 'drug runners' would look out of the window to see when the fun would start. It did look rather strange, as the car park was absolutely full apart from a long, narrow area leading from the gates to what they found out was the canoe store. At around 7.30pm, they all stopped what they were doing and rushed to the front windows as they heard the revving of powerful cars and the raucous pumping of Klaxon horns, announce the arrival of Duncan's crew. Six cars came through the gates and parked bumper to bumper in the space left in front of the canoe store. They all got out of and stood next to their cars and each one of them carried a machine gun of choice. The boys and girls inside looked at each other but instead of smirking at what was likely to happen, a number of them looked worried as they had come to quite like some of these people.

"Look, it might be an idea to just let us go back to them before anyone gets hurt," Dale suggested reluctantly. "You don't know what they are capable of."

"Don't worry guys none of us are going to get hurt," Tommy tried to assure them but he could see how doubtful they were.

As this was something way below anything the Duncans or any of their top lieutenants would sully their hands with, it was Bruce, otherwise known as Popeye - so named to reflect the results of all the time he spent in the gym - the supposed leader of the thugs from the day before who took the lead today. He bellowed aggressively that firstly, all the drug runners were to be sent out to them, then all the adults should come out and stand ready to take the beating they had brought upon themselves.

"If you do not do as we ask, we have these rather nasty weapons and we are only too happy to use them but I am sure it won't come to that."

Mick strolled very casually out of the front door and looked across at Popeye and smiled. "Have you ever seen Crocodile Dundee?" he asked. "I know the kids will probably be too young but you are of a similar vintage to me."

"What are you wittering on about? Just do as you're told or suffer the consequences."

Ignoring Popeye's reply, Mick continued, "Well in that film a yob not unlike yourself but better looking, pulled a flick knife on the character played by Paul Hogan, who then replied 'call that a knife' and proceeded to pull out the biggest bowie knife you have ever seen. It was really funny."

"What's that got to do with anything? I can assure you that we won't be using any little knives," Popeye replied and was pleased at the laughs that his reply evoked from his men.

"Well, in reply to your willingness to use your 'rather nasty weapons' I would just like to say, 'call those nasty weapons.'"

At that moment the automatic door of the canoe store began to roll up and all eyes stared in amazement as a Seventy Ton, Challenger 2 Tank began to rumble out. As it approached the first car, one of the thugs started to try and get into his beloved vehicle to try and move it but luckily thought better of it as the Tank mounted the car, rolled straight over the top of it and then started on the next one. If it hadn't been so potentially dangerous it would have been funny to watch, as a number of the thugs started firing at the tank until they realised that they were more likely to be hit by the ricochets than cause any harm to whoever was driving the tank. They were also slightly subdued as the gun turret of the tank began to swivel towards them. As the tank finished squashing the last car, it added insult to injury by reversing all the way back to the canoe store just to make sure.

There was absolute silence for what seemed like ages outside, while inside there were giggles and shouts of glee. Then Popeye turned to look at Mick with a look on his face that suggested that he was less than happy and he began to raise his gun and point it at Mick who very calmly nodded at Popeye and then looked down at his chest which he tapped with his finger. Popeye glanced down at his own chest and saw a red dot waving around the area of his heart.

"We've heard about your tricks before at the freight station, using laser beams to fool those chumps. Well, we are in a different class." As he spoke Mick tapped his head with his hand and Popeye saw the red dot move off his chest and he smiled an instant before a shot was fired and his baseball cap went flying from his head with a hole through the top.

"Now gentlemen, if you would all like to look down at your chests and anyone who thinks that the red beam they can see is a laser pen then that's fine by us but those who realise that it is the beam from the sniper sight of a SA80 high velocity sniper's rifle, should place your weapons on the floor and start walking back to the main road, where you can catch a number 47 bus into the city centre or treat yourselves to a taxi. Oh by the way, next time we won't be so lenient."

During that same day, customs officials at the port of Dover received an anonymous phone call to say that a shipment of baby food on the SS Canberra, actually contained a large amount of heroin, cocaine and ecstasy pills. Later that day, the container carrying the baby food was broken into by the customs officials on duty and they were delighted to find one of the biggest hauls of hard drugs to ever be seized in Britain. By late evening, the Duncans had been made fully aware of how their drug runners had been taken from them and the humiliation that had been meted out to his thugs at the youth club. Disbelief and outrage reached a level they had never felt before but things got worse when Pete slunk into the room and explained that all their cannabis farms had been destroyed and the farmers had disappeared.

"What? How could that have happened? Who is doing this to me?"

"Boss you are not going to like this but when we went into each of the houses we have used for growing the cannabis, there was only one plant still alive in each house."

"What are you talking about? Spit it out!"

"Well boss, in each house, there was a vase left just inside the front door with one of these in." Duncan looked at the beautiful orchid that Pete held in his overlarge hand and screamed so loudly that staff throughout the house found something to do as far away from their boss's office as they could.

"Frankie, you need to sit down because that is not all. This note was also left with the orchids." Pete nervously passed a laminated piece of card to his boss who grabbed it and read.

ON BEHALF OF THE RED SPIDER MITES WE WOULD LIKE TO THANK YOU FOR THEIR FEAST. THE WORKERS YOU HAD TENDING THE PLANTS WILL OBVIOUSLY NEED A NEW CAREER. TO ENABLE THEM TO SET THEMSELVES UP AND BECAUSE YOU SEEM TO HAVE FORGOTTEN TO PAY THEM, WE HAVE TAKEN THIRTY THOUSAND POUNDS FOR EACH OF THE 'FARMERS' FROM YOUR BANK ACCOUNT. THEY ARE VERY GRATEFUL AS THEY WERE UNDER THE IMPRESSION YOU MIGHT HAVE BEEN TAKING ADVANTAGE. CHEERS!

"Brad, ring the accountant now and see if this is true." A few minutes later, Brad had the unenviable task of telling his father that close to three quarters of a million pounds had been taken from one of their bank accounts.

His father virtually exploded in a shower of expletives and spittle and screamed for Brad to get the account shut down.

"I will not have this. They are making us look like mugs, whoever they are and they are destroying our business at the same time. No-one will want to do business with us and will see us as a liability. You three contact all our media contacts and make sure that none of this gets out." Alex, who had been looking at his phone much to his Dad's growing irritation, nervously pointed to his phone and gave his dad the news he didn't want to hear. "It's too late for that Dad, it's all over social media." Looking at the various headlines saw Duncan's rage grow until reading

"DRUGS IN BABY FOOD FIND MAKES DUMMIES OF BUNGLING CROOKS" was the last straw, which saw him hurling Alex's phone against the wall.

"What about this crew who have just humiliated us with the drug runners? Surely we know who they are?"

"Boss they don't seem to be anyone who we have ever come across before and whenever they attack us they disappear into thin air."

"Who are these people? Why haven't you found them? It surely can't be too hard to find out at least which gang is involved, as we have people on the inside of all of them, including the police."

"That's just it Dad, nobody knows anything, it's as if they are all working together," ventured Philip.

"That's it. Because we are so successful they are all ganging up on us. Treble the reward for information. I want these ba*****s found. The cheek of them using my beloved orchids to taunt me. They are going to regret this for the rest of their lives. For now we are going to have to forget the drugs and the selling of cars abroad. It is going to take some time to build those areas up again. I need you to really concentrate on the human trafficking and modern day slavery part of the organisation. It brings in huge sums of money and the area is growing all the time, so we now need to be the leaders in that field and we cannot be seen to have this scuppered also. Apart from the money it brings in, if we mess this up along with the other problems we have been having, we will be a laughing stock and no one will do business with us ever again. Boys, you will now ignore all other areas of business and concentrate solely on this. You will take it over yourselves and be totally hands on, as you are the only ones I truly trust. The other areas can be run by the lads until we find out who is having a go at us and also who is almost certainly feeding information to that gang, who for some reason seem to be targeting us specifically. I will take charge of that because I am not going to be treated like some 'no mark' and I will personally deal with the person responsible for not just destroying our business but stealing my life's work with the orchids. Now, until we find out who it is leaking information, we keep everything of importance between ourselves and everyone else will be on a need-to-know basis.

In the youth club, there was a hubble of excited chatter and laughing as the runners and the pupils from the Castle School discussed how brilliant it was to see what had just happened. A loud whistle shut them all up and they all sat down as requested, to listen once again to Matt who said he would only keep them for a short while.

"Today is the last day that we will use this facility. However, you are all welcome to come to the facility we usually use at a school not too far away. You will not however receive any payment but there will be opportunities to earn money in our schemes to help in the community. However, for those of you over 16, we are happy to find a place in our Post 16 classes, where we will provide the education and training in the career you have most interest in pursuing, as long as you show you have the necessary attributes. Those under sixteen, we would like you to go back to school or we will do everything we can to get you a place in our school if you would like that. Either way we will offer you the same opportunities when you reach the age of sixteen as we have your older friends. This education will be free and you will be supported financially but this can only happen with the agreement of your parents or carers who we will talk to in the next couple of weeks."

"What happened tonight was awesome but the Duncans won't just let it go. You are now marked men. What happens to us when they have killed you?"

"What you have to realise is that it doesn't matter how tough you think you are, there will always be someone bigger, stronger and harder. You might have noticed that the only one of us who has had to use any physical force was Charlie when that thug tried to push her away and you can hardly accuse her of being your typical tough guy. We do not believe in violence but if it is necessary we have the ability to protect ourselves and those around us and if need be we will answer fire with fire. But you never have to worry about that, you need to live and enjoy your lives. We would like you to understand the importance of why, while it is wrong to fight, sometimes you have to stand up and be counted for the greater good. If you decide to come to our school, you will see the inscription above the entrance of a famous quote that says, "All that is needed for the triumph of evil, is for good men to stand by and do nothing." The people we want to turn out from our school are ordinary citizens, who will strive to be the best they can be in whatever walk of life they choose and to try to be good citizens. If that is something you are happy to encompass then you are more than welcome to be a member of our school and we will do all we can to allow you to achieve success in your life. Over the next two weeks, we will visit you and your parents or carers to ascertain whether you wish to be involved. We really hope you do but please, if you do not and you think you might resort to crime, come and see us and we will do all we can to offer something else to help you."

When Matt left the stage, the youngsters began to mingle to discuss what had turned out to be a fascinating night. The drug runners were by now quite comfortable with the youngsters who obviously already attended this supposed, fantastic school. While they were interested, these youngsters' experience of school had not been positive and they were loathe to commit to a couple of years at least, of something they had always hated. It was Charlie who eventually grabbed all their attention, when she explained that her previous school, life had been very little different to their own and that she came from a far from privileged background, with absentee parents. She now, not only thoroughly enjoyed her school days but she had a future to look forward to, not just in sport, which she would never have even attempted if it hadn't been for the school, but with the grades she was now getting, she could choose to go to University if she so wished. Her friends, who were less academically inclined, had careers lined up in all sorts of jobs that they really had an interest in. As the hopefully "ex" drug runners left the room to be taken home by their allocated minder, who apparently would be guarding them for the next couple of days at least, in case the Duncans should try to bother them, their thoughts were filled with confusion and also, dare they dream, a glimmer of hope.

CHAPTER 28

Later that week Rob called his trusted group of friends together.

"I think we are in touching distance of what has always been our goal. It will take some time but the opportunity is about to arise for us to put the final nail in the coffin of the Duncan family. I know that you were all concerned that my determination to get to the Duncans, would be a search for revenge at whatever the cost. Hassan in particular came on board and from the beginning, tried to convince me of the importance that the best revenge would be bringing them to justice and the rest of you have always supported that approach. While I wasn't so sure at first, I now realise that if I am truly to ensure that the deaths of my girls were not totally in vain, I must see that justice is done. The actions we have carried out against the Duncans have driven them into a corner, resulting in them making a decision that could leave them open to being finished off once and for all."

"Rob you know how much Ronnie and I think about what happened to the girls and we would like to support you all the way but this has to be finished in a court of law, not with some massive act of violence."

"I hope and think that you will find that what I have in mind will perfectly fit the criteria you have laid down and to truly serve justice." He went on to explain how the Duncans had decided to concentrate their main efforts into the area of human trafficking and so this gave them the opportunity not only to stop their involvement in what was an horrendous activity but to deal with the three boys directly and in consequence, their father. Rob laid out the skeleton of an idea, with the encouragement to them all to go away and add flesh to those parts of his plan for which they had some expertise.

"I think he's losing it," Philip suddenly announced as he and his two brothers sat in the Jacuzzi, while planning how they were going to ensure that their next operation was not going to go in the same direction that all the recent ones had gone i.e. down the pan. Convinced that the house was bugged, they were sure that the recreation area of the house would be less likely to have recording devices and that the sound of the jacuzzi would make anything they said inaudible, should there be a bug anyway.

"I wouldn't let him hear you say that if I were you."

"Shut up the both of you, even if he were losing it, we have to make sure that what we do is a success and maybe then he will see that he can start giving us more and more responsibility."

"That's all very well and good but we all know that we are not like dad and we are not naturals at this stuff. Now, we have to take charge of the human trafficking and we have always said between ourselves how much we hate the devastation our operations cause to people's lives and this is one of the most inhumane"

"For goodness sake Brad, Dad would go apes*** if he could hear us now. Alex and I are older and have had longer to get used to these things. You know we are not going to be able to change to a more honest way of life until Dad is no longer around, which will be some time yet. So we've just got to get on with it. Alex, where are we on this?"

"I've been in contact with Wilhelm in Belgium and they have almost got a full cargo for us. The Romanian and Albanian workers are already accounted for and they are just waiting for the last few Syrian refugees to be persuaded that they are better off hitching a ride with us, than trying to make their own efforts to enter the country from "the jungle" in Calais. They will set off about midday Tuesday next week, with a full shipment of workers and they should arrive somewhere on the coast near Hull at about 3.00am Wednesday morning. They will then be driven by coach to the usual Travel Lodge, where rooms have been booked for them and where they will be lulled into thinking that this is the level of accommodation and treatment they can expect. That is where we will meet them and assess them."

"That sounds good. Brad you will select the ones suitable for the sex trade first, then I will choose the ones who look strong enough to be able to cope with the farm and construction work. Alex you will then have the dregs for the factory work, car cleaning and other jobs we need to fill. We will have muscle on hand but that is just a precaution as they should all still be fairly pliant, thinking that they are all going off to do legitimate jobs. However, just in case, we will have the enforcers with us but do not let them know what they are going to be doing until you are on the road, cos dad was right about doing everything on a need to know basis. We will all drive off in our different directions and deliver our van loads to the appropriate gang bosses, return the vans to the cut and shunt garage for a forensic clean and respray and be back in Leicester by Wednesday evening. If we get this right, we will be in a stronger position to suggest to dad that maybe he should start taking a bit more of a back seat but we will have to be pretty clever about not making him believe we think that he is past it and that it's time for the new generation to take over. Rather because we need the chance to show what we can do and not because we think he is over the hill."

With their own final bit of the jigsaw in place, Rob and Mick sat down to plan the last details of what was going to be a very elaborate operation, that would hopefully lead to the Duncans receiving their just desserts. The consequences of it going wrong however, did not bear thinking about. Part way through the meeting, there was a knock at the door and Mick got up to let Mateo into the room and explained to Rob that he had asked Mateo to join them and fill them in on his experience of being brought into the country by the Duncans. Mateo, who was now an invaluable member of the school ground staff, specialising in working with the plants in the greenhouse, most notably the orchids, explained that everything had seemed so promising at first, as he and the other illegals were treated really well on arrival in the country and on the journey to the Travelodge near Hornsea in Hull. They were well fed and were impressed with the rooms they had for their one night stay, before their interview with the Duncans the following morning, to be allocated jobs suited to their abilities. He did make the point that when he arrived in Hull and he and all the others were very tired, he had been slightly concerned by the number of men who seemed to be in attendance for security purposes. They and all the illegals had rooms on the fourth floor and were told that they must not leave their room until they went down for breakfast the following morning. Mateo had heard the next morning how strictly this was adhered to from some of his fellow travellers who had attempted to go out for a smoke in the night. There was a guard on each floor near the lifts and one placed in the stairwell. At first Mateo thought that this must have been to stop them running away but he found out later, when working with the family, that the men were there to act as guards for the three Duncan brothers, as Frankie Duncan was paranoid about someone trying to get at him through his family.

Rob and Mick asked Mateo a few more questions to make certain they had a full picture of how the operation worked at the hotel and then thanked him for his help as he left the room. When he had gone, Rob suggested to Mick that this was going to make it really difficult to carry out their plan without the danger of it all kicking off and a large number of people getting seriously hurt, literally in the cross fire. Mick agreed but told Rob he would think about it, as there was always a way and he would discuss it with his lads and with Hassan.

Later, when he did discuss it with his lads, Mac reminded him of a job they had done some years back, where they had to rescue the daughter of a multi-millionaire from the clutches of a kidnap gang in Brazil, without anyone knowing how it had been done. "

"Yes," said Mick, "that would be just the ticket, although very risky. I need to talk to the Prof but Mac, for once I think you might have actually said something useful."

"Up yours," was the wittiest reply Mac could think of.

CHAPTER 29

Ronnie rang the Travel Lodge mentioned by the Duncans during their jacuzzi chat, later that same day and after the phone was answered by a bright and cheerful receptionist, she replied with, "Hello, yes I would like to book eight rooms for some of our workers who are on a construction job in your area for Tuesday and Wednesday next week."

"We will be happy to do that but actually you are quite fortunate in that we are very busy on those two days."

"Nothing too raucous I hope, like a stag party? Our guys need a good night's sleep."

"Oh no Madam, these are tourists from the continent and they have taken almost a whole floor."

"Oh that's fine, we like our workers to mix with our European neighbours, as we do a lot of work on the continent and maybe they will have the chance of practising their language skills. We would be quite happy to have some rooms on the same floor as the tourist group."

"That is refreshing to hear Madam, as not all our locals are quite as welcoming. We can give you three rooms on the same floor as the tourists which will be the fourth floor and the rest will be on the sixth floor."

"Oh, have you not got anything on the fifth floor?"

"Sorry Madam, we have some other important guests who have booked the whole of that floor."

"Oh, how exciting. But that will be fine thank you." The rest of the conversation concerned the payment, which allowed Ronnie to ascertain which rooms Mick and his team would actually have and having an plan of the hotel and room layout emailed to her. She had also casually asked whether there were conference rooms available, as her workers might need to have a meeting space and was informed that there were two conference rooms but one had been already booked by the tourist group from Europe. Ronnie explained that she would get back to them if they decided to go ahead with a conference room booking.

The following Tuesday afternoon, a number of Jackson construction vehicles arrived at different times into the car park of the Travel Lodge in Hornsea near Hull and checked into the rooms previously booked by Ronnie. Unfortunately, although they were on the sixth floor they had to use the stairs, due to the fact that the lifts were being serviced because of a problem that had occurred just that morning. They were informed that the lifts would be back in operation by tea time, which actually was not news to them because the men servicing the lift happened to be part of Mick's team and would later be smuggled into the rooms booked for the Jackson construction workers, ready to help in the operation to be carried out that night. The majority of Mick's team, once they had climbed the stairs, entered their rooms and simply lay on the bed to get some sleep in the knowledge that they would not get much sleep that night. Mac and Tommy however, sat in the bar/restaurant having a leisurely meal and drinking until they saw the Duncan brothers arrive and check into their rooms on the fifth floor. Later, Mac and Tommy took the now fully working lift to their rooms but pushed the button for the fifth floor, rather than the sixth, where their rooms actually were. As the lift doors opened they were met by a very large man who explained very politely that this floor was privately booked. Mac apologised and explained that they must have pushed the wrong button then carried on up to the next floor.

At approximately 3.00am, a coach arrived and disgorged its passengers into reception where the Duncan brothers took charge of the checking in and thereby, when this was completed, ensured that they also now had control of all the passports. The tired travellers went straight to bed with instructions to have breakfast between eight and ten in the morning but to be ready to meet in Conference Room A at 10.15am if they wouldn't mind, where their employment and accommodation for the rest of their stay would be explained to them. Leaving their men to see the 'illegals' to their rooms, the three brothers left them to it and entered the lift to get back to bed as soon as they could.

The lift doors closed and they pressed the button for the fifth floor. On the fifth floor the security guard saw the lift begin to rise from reception. The moment the lift doors closed, unnoticed by the brothers, Mac, who was stationed with Tommy on top of the lift wearing breathing apparatus, flicked the switch which the Prof had assured him would override the lift instructions and continue past the fifth floor and a another second switch which resulted in all the oxygen being removed from the lift, causing the brothers to lose consciousness almost immediately. Mac and Tommy turned off the apparatus sucking the oxygen from the lift, removed the hatch at the top of the lift and dropping into the lift, they removed the room keys from the pockets of the three unconscious brothers and then lifted the brothers out onto the carpet of the sixth floor corridor, where Mick, Little John and Dougie were waiting. Closing the doors again, they pressed the button for the fifth floor where the

Duncans' security guard Pat, was waiting to receive his three bosses. As the doors opened, he was taken aback to see the unreal sight of two people who, because of their breathing apparatus and protective clothing looked very much like 'ghostbusters', pointing two very real-looking guns at his chest and gesturing him to raise his hands.

While Tommy frisked and disarmed Pat, Mac jammed the doors open with a fire extinguisher. Having removed his guns, Tommy turned Pat around and handcuffed him, before pushing him towards the room belonging to Brad Duncan, which Mac had by now opened and into which Pat was unceremoniously shoved. Once inside, his phone was taken from him, his legs were also fettered and gaffer tape was pulled across his mouth, before he was shoved into the shower cubicle, the door shut and the handle secured by plastic ties to the wardrobe door opposite just to prolong any escape attempt. Mac and Tommy then closed the door behind them and went back to the lift, where Tommy removed his breathing apparatus on the basis that the lift should by now have been re-oxygenated and they returned to the sixth floor. Mac also now discarded the breathing equipment, when he saw that Tommy had not suffered any ill effects.

In the meantime, Mick, Little John and Dougie had trussed up the brothers and as soon as they were joined by Tommy and Mac, the five of them carried the brothers to the entrance to the stairs and having checked that the security on the stairs was down guarding the fifth floor entrance, quietly carried the brothers up to the roof. Once there, they roped them up and belayed them down the side of the building to the ground, where Billy and Phil loaded them into one of the waiting Jackson Construction Company vans and drove them off. Looking at his watch, Mick was pleased that all this had been completed within an hour of the brothers first getting into the lift.

The following morning, with the 'illegals' all enjoying a leisurely breakfast in a comfort they had not expected, Pete and the rest of the Duncan gang were becoming more and more uneasy, as the three brothers had not yet appeared and their men were loathe to invite their wrath by disturbing them. Eventually however, the need to get on with the business of the day took precedence and Pete and Ernie went up to the fifth floor where they were slightly alarmed not to find Pat on guard but assumed he had fallen asleep somewhere and would be feeling the consequences of their displeasure when they found him later. They firstly tapped quietly on the doors of their bosses' rooms, increasing in intensity because of the lack of response, the knocking became more and more frantic until their panic reaching fever pitch, saw them kick the doors in. The subtlety of asking for spare keys from reception not occurring to either of them. The two empty rooms shocked them but it was finding the still trussed up Pat in the third room that really made them panic.

After a quick search, they debated who would be the one to ring Frankie Duncan and it was Pete who drew the short straw.

"Frank, I don't know how to tell you this but all three of your sons have gone missing and they have almost certainly been taken."

"How do you know they have not just popped out?"

"Because Pat, who was securing their corridor, was attacked and tied up by whoever is likely to have done this." There was silence on the other end of the phone but then the explosion came and Pete could barely make out what was being said between the expletives and screaming. Eventually, a reasonable level of decibels was achieved and he listened as Duncan gave his instructions.

"Check the whole place again, including all the rooms occupied or not, then get out of there as quickly as possible in case the place is being watched by the police. But don't come back here until I tell you the coast is clear."

"What about the illegals?"

"Leave them, and don't have any more contact with them, so there is no connection to you. We're going to have to cut our losses."

"But boss they are worth a fortune to us."

"Do you think I don't know that you numbskull? I couldn't care less while my boys are missing, that is the priority now. If we're being watched and are seen to have any connection to the 'illegals', we really will be in trouble. I will ring you at noon and we will see where we stand but get back to me if you find anything at all." An hour later, before the search was completed, Pete was forced to ring his boss again.

"Have you found them?"

"No Boss, we are still looking."

"I told you not to contact me until you had something to report. Get back to the search and do as you have been told."

"But Boss I think you need to know this."

"This had better be good Pete or I will feed you to my dogs."

"Boss, Ernie went out to see if the boys' car was still there."

"Yes, hurry up you imbecile and was it?"

"Yes Boss, it is but there is something on the windscreen."

"What do you....?"

"Boss there is an orchid on the windscreen." There followed a worrying silence and then Pete had to hold the phone from his ear as Duncan raged at him.

"Get back here now. This is not the police. I want everyone here. We need to sort this once and for all"

Rob took delicious delight in listening to the steady unravelling of Duncan and also took pleasure in the change that was occurring from the arrogant cruelty of his mocking tone back at the court just over seven years ago, to his loss of control now, under the present pressure of losing his boys. He realised that he was enjoying a childish satisfaction as he thought to himself, "Now, let's see how you like it."

CHAPTER 30

A little while later, the Duncan boys started to come around and while they all found it difficult to understand what had happened to them, they had no difficulty with the realisation that they were now trussed like turkeys and lying on a very hard floor, with the very loud sound of a very powerful engine throbbing in their ears. Alex was the first to realise that he was in trouble and that there was something over his mouth which, because his hands were tied behind his back, he tried to remove by dragging it across the floor of whatever vehicle he was in.

"If you don't want to have the most horrendous headache, I suggest you leave the oxygen mask on a little longer," a calm voice from above him suggested. Determined not to show any fear or accede to anything his kidnappers said, he continued to work to remove the mask.

"Please yourself," was the disinterested reaction. Having removed the mask that had simply been attached by elastic around his ears, he rolled onto his back and saw immediately that his two brothers were also parcelled up and lying next to him but more worrying was the sight of five balaclavered individuals sitting too nonchalantly for his comfort, around the edge of the extremely noisy vehicle that was transporting them to wherever.

Gradually his brothers started to come around also and both copied him in ignoring the advice about keeping the oxygen masks on. With their mouths free they began to demand answers and to issue threats along the lines of, "you guys do not know who you are messing with," and "only if you let us go now will you come out of this alive." This was much to the apparent amusement of the men in balaclavas, whose features they could not see but whose nudging and giggling at the list of things that was going to happen to them if they did not let the boys go, now caused the brothers even more cause for concern and increased the level of anger, especially when they did not reply.

Taking a different approach, Philip tried to ignore the horrendous headache that was developing and suggested to their captors that this could all be sorted out amicably and to the mutual satisfaction of all parties, as their father was a rich and powerful man who would not only reward them greatly if the boys were released but who would certainly be prepared to offer employment to men who were quite obviously possessed of the skills that would be highly prized, in the area of work their father dealt in. Again the response was not what Philip had hoped for and the three brothers spent the next few minutes seemingly ignoring the situation they were actually in and the growing throbbing in their heads while recounting a list of tortuous punishments the balaclavered men were going to have to suffer. The only response they received was one of the men replacing the oxygen masks on all three and simply saying, "That will help relieve the headache and perhaps also shut you up for a few minutes and stop you from giving us a headache." More from the discomfort of the worsening pain in their heads and the position they had been lying in for some time, the brothers lay quietly, trying not to show the fear they truly felt. After a while, they realised that their headaches were receding and with the growing confidence of feeling physically better and the idea that if they were going to be hurt it would have happened already, they began to harangue their captors once more.

"You know you will never get away with this don't you? Our father will already have a legion of the type of men you do not want to mess with, out looking for us and we have a contact in the Police road camera surveillance unit who will soon have you and your vehicle found and tracked."

Mick decided that now was the time to put the boys in the picture to a small extent. "Let me tell you three little charmers what is going to happen. You seem to take a great deal of enjoyment from aiding very vulnerable people to enter Britain with the promise of jobs only to find that they end up working as slaves in one of the many nefarious enterprises your disgusting family run, receiving no money and being in debt to you without ever being able to relinquish that debt. Well, we have decided that you should experience what that is like for the rest of your miserable lives, by putting you in the same situation."

"You must be stupid if you believe there is any way you could keep us in a situation like that. Our father would soon find us or we would simply escape. Our immigrants have no passport, are illegal and barely speak the language, otherwise they could get away easily."

"Yes that is why we are taking you abroad, so that you enjoy the full experience so to speak."

"You're having a laugh and must be as stupid as you look. You will never get us through customs even if our father does not find us first."

"Oh, we are not going through customs, you see we are presently flying at an altitude of approximately 30,000 feet to your new country of residence."

"You can't do that. In any case how will you get us through customs in any country? Do you think we will just walk through quietly?"

"Oh, again we have no intention of walking you through customs as you will be parachuting in."

"You are joking. There is no way you can make us jump out of a plane. For a start, none of us have ever parachuted before."

"Not a problem. You will be attached to one of us."

The growing hysteria created by a realisation that these guys were not joking, set the boys off with their threats again but when they got no response, other than for some of the men seemingly going to sleep, they started talking among themselves about the situation they were in and agreeing that their father would get them out of this. There was no way that they could be made to jump from the plane without their own co-operation and that was not going to happen. They were interrupted a little time later, by Mick starting to untie Phillip who, once released, took a swing at Mick, only to find his swinging arm twisted behind his back and him pinned with his nose pressed to the floor.

"Now we can do this the easy way or the hard way. Do you understand?" Not receiving a reply, Mick twisted the arm a little more and received a grunt of acquiescence from Philip.

"Good, now stand up." As he stood, Phillip saw one of the balaclavered men open the door on the side of the plane and felt a rush of cold air forcing him to grip the metal struts on the inside of the plane to steady himself. The man who had opened the door was helmeted and wearing a parachute and came towards Phillip with another parachute which he explained Phillip would need in case of emergencies.

"I have already told you that I am going nowhere near that doorway."

"OK, then you will be strapped to me without the back up of your own parachute but that is your choice."

The eldest Duncan boy laughed. "There is no way you will get me attached to you however many of you try."

"Oh if you don't do it voluntarily we won't force you to be attached to me, you will simply go out as you are, on your own."

"Now we know you are bluffing. I have realised that you must be the guys who have been giving the family trouble all this time but despite the trouble you have caused, you have never actually harmed anyone. I reckon you haven't got it in you." At that, two of the other men in balaclavas grabbed Phillip by the arms and took him to the open hatch on the side of the plane.

"This is your last chance. You either go with me or you go on your own and as you have refused a parachute, I wouldn't advise it."

"I've met loads of your sort before. Supposedly hard men who can't cut it when it comes to the really nasty stuff. Do your worst."

"Is that your last word?"

"Yeah, so what you gonna do now?" Growing in confidence at this opportunity to show who was really in control, Phillip winked at his two brothers who looked less certain about what was happening.

"Ok guys you heard the gentleman. He asked for it. Do your worst were his very words."

At that, the two men holding Phillip by the arms stepped forward and threw him out of the plane.

"Wait, noooooo…" Alex and Brad screamed in shock but were immediately rolled onto their front with their noses pinned to the floor and told to be quiet or they would go the same way. A little later Alex was untied and without any argument, put on the proffered parachute and nervously allowed himself to be attached to one of the captors who was helmeted and wearing a parachute. They both walked awkwardly to the door and after some last minute instruction, they shuffled out. Some time later Brad, in total shock at the thought of what had happened to his big brother, went through the same process as Alex and he too, although terrified, allowed himself to be attached to one of the captors and shuffled out of the door. While taking your first parachute jump is meant to be an exhilarating experience, neither Alex nor Brad took any pleasure from their jump whatsoever, thinking only of what had happened to their big brother and fearing for what these lunatics might do to them if they were prepared to throw a man out of an aeroplane.

The brothers landed in different parts of Albania with varying degrees of discomfort but with equal amounts of relief. Along with their 'parachute buddy' who also doubled as their 'minder,' they were picked up by a truck a few minutes after landing and taken to the farm building within which they would be housed for the foreseeable future. The buildings that they were to be living in for some time, were similar, in that they were extremely secure, very basic and lacking in anything that could be considered a comfort. In fairness, at that moment they were simply pleased to be in one piece and even the hard bed with a coarse and filthy blanket did not prevent them from lying down and thanking their lucky stars that they were alive and that their dad would soon get them out of this nightmare. Brad and Alex kept waking with the sound of their brother's screams resounding in their heads. The thought of what had happened to him made them consider in absolute fear, the real danger they were in.

CHAPTER 31

Back in Leicestershire, their father was having his own nightmare. Who would have the audacity to not only try and destroy his empire but to kidnap his own sons? He needed to nip this in the bud or his whole reputation, let alone his business empire would be destroyed. When he found out who was doing this to him, woe betide them because they would never have imagined the pain and trauma he would cause them. In the meantime, he had set in motion strategies to firstly find his boys and he would deal with the repercussions later. Every one of his employees were talking to their contacts and offering threats and rewards in equal measure, in what turned out to be a futile attempt to gain any information about what had happened to the Duncan boys. After 24 hours of getting nowhere, Duncan called a war meeting of his most trusted lieutenants.

"Right, I want you all to put together a list of anyone we will have upset in any way, going back to when we first started operating."

"Boss, that is going to be a very long list," offered Pete.

"Can you think of any other way we can find out who is doing this? No, I thought not. So go and talk to the rest of the men and get me any names you can think of." A few hours later, they met again and started to compile what turned out to be an extremely extensive list of people who might have a grudge against the Duncans.

"OK, basically on this list we have rivals and other criminals who we might have upset and then there are what we can call civilians, who might have cause to hold a grudge because of some suffering we might have caused them in the past. The most likely cause of our problems are those on the first list, so we will start with them. If we get nowhere with that, we will look at the civilians." Duncan then divided the many names on the list between his trusted lieutenants and told them this was to take priority over all other matters and the moment anybody had anything remotely useful, they should get back to him. In the meantime, he was sure that he would be receiving some sort of ransom demand or a demand of some other nature, for the return of his boys.

As he spoke to his seated confidantes, he prowled the room and his wild staring eyes made them all feel like a herd of wildebeests being selected for the next meal. This ensured their total concentration but also their unwillingness to make themselves noticed by offering any ideas themselves. Pete, who Duncan had known the longest and believed correctly, that he was the most trusted of the men in the room and despite being fully aware of his boss's frequent loss of reality, had no such fear. He made the point that if these people wanted to kill the boys, there were many simpler ways of doing it and the highly professional extraction from the hotel, meant these people went to a great deal of trouble to kidnap the boys in one piece. "However, if we can get a lead on them before any demand is made, we will be in a better place to thwart them." Duncan suddenly brightened.

"Do you know, I think you are right. Yes, they must still be alive mustn't they and I will get them back one way or another?" Re-energised by this latest thought, Duncan sent his men off to find his boys, while he sat and ruminated about how he was going to recover from the set-backs that seemed to be coming at him repeatedly. What on earth had he done to deserve this bad luck?

Meanwhile, the causes of all his ill fortune were sitting in the Headmaster's study of the Castle of HOPE School, wallowing in the pleasure of their latest success and discussing their next moves. Matt waited until there was a moments silence in the excited reaction to Mick's report of the abduction of the Duncan boys, before trying to gain some reassurance that despite what sort of people they were, the Duncans were not going to be physically harmed. Arguing that that would make them as bad as the Duncans, Rob reminded him of their original meeting when the plan was first discussed.

It had been Hassan who had been given the role of getting into contact with the three different farms in Albania where the Duncan boys were to be housed. He had been given some good advice by Mateo, who knew not only suitable farms out in the countryside a long way from any urban areas but also trusted that the owners of the farms would be people who would not use excessive force. This was all the more impressive when he explained that he had chosen the particular farms that he had, because each one would have had a family member or friend who had previously been trafficked into the UK by gangs like the Duncans and had every reason to want to exact revenge. Hassan had convinced them however, that not only would these men receive their comeuppance but that their family member would be rescued and supported financially and legally. That was not to say however, that the Albanians could not make the Duncans' stay as uncomfortable as they felt necessary. They had discussed whether one of Mick's team should stay at each of the farms but in the end, once Hassan had visited the farms with Mateo and had spoken to the owners, it was felt that it would not be necessary.

CHAPTER 32

Having been left to sleep the night, the brothers awoke next morning to find that they were locked in the room they had slept in and that a note was propped up on the rough wooden table, which was standing against the wall opposite their bed. It read:

THIS WILL BE YOUR ACCOMMODATION FOR THE FORSEEABLE FUTURE. WE THOUGHT YOU MIGHT APPRECIATE EXPERIENCING CONDITIONS VERY SIMILAR TO THOSE YOU PROVIDE FOR THE MODERN DAY SLAVES YOU LEASE OUT TO THE MANY FARMS AND FACTORIES YOU HAVE DEALINGS WITH IN THE UK. YOUR MEALS WILL BE BROUGHT TO YOU THREE TIMES A DAY. YOU WILL SEE THAT YOU HAVE TWO BUCKETS, ONE YOU WILL USE AS A TOILET WHICH YOU WILL EMPTY EVERY MORNING AT 5.30 AM WHEN YOU WILL ALSO COLLECT YOUR WATER FOR WASHING FROM THE COMMUNAL TAP IN THE YARD USING THE OTHER BUCKET. WE SUGGEST YOU DO NOT MIX THEM UP. AT 6.00AM YOU WILL BE TAKEN TO WORK IN THE FIELDS, WHERE YOU WILL DO A TWELVE HOUR SHIFT. YOU WILL HAVE SUNDAY OFF BUT AS WITH YOUR OWN WORKERS/SLAVES, ALL FREE TIME WILL BE SPENT IN THIS ROOM. VERY FEW OF THE PEOPLE YOU ARE WORKING FOR SPEAK ENGLISH AND YOU OUGHT TO KNOW THAT THEY ARE RELATED TO PEOPLE YOU HAVE TRAFFICKED AS SLAVES IN THE PAST AND SO THEY ARE NOT VERY WELL DISPOSED TOWARDS YOU OR YOUR FAMILY. AT THE BEGINNING OF THIS NOTE WE MENTIONED THE FORSEEABLE FUTURE. YOU MIGHT BE WONDERING HOW LONG THAT MIGHT BE. IT WILL BE UNTIL YOUR FATHER PROVIDES US WITH THE INFORMATION WE ASK FOR, IN ORDER TO ALLOW YOU TO RETURN TO THE UK. YOU WILL ALMOST CERTAINLY IGNORE THIS NEXT BIT OF ADVICE BUT WE WOULD SUGGEST YOU DO NOT TRY TO ESCAPE OR UPSET YOUR HOSTS/EMPLOYERS, AS THEY ARE NOWHERE NEAR AS NICE AS WE HAVE BEEN TO YOU. WE SUGGEST YOU KEEP

YOUR HEAD DOWN AND USE THIS TIME TO REFLECT UPON WHY YOU ARE HERE.

    The boys' reaction to this was unsurprisingly similar, ranging from laughing out loud, to screwing it up and throwing it across the room. They were determined to show these people who was going to be boss until they were rescued and the idea that they would be doing physical work was laughable. The following morning at 5.30am, the boys were lying in their beds and refusing to rise when told they should do so. Across the different locations this was met with the same response which was a hosing down with freezing water. When they demanded a change of clothes, they were informed that their clothes would dry while they worked in the sun. Also, because they had got up late they had missed breakfast.

    The rest of the day, they toiled in the fields, admittedly with breaks for water until lunchtime. Perhaps toil was the wrong word to use, as the boys made very little effort to do what they were told but simply lazed around with a supercilious smirk on their faces. At lunch time, they queued with the other workers for their lunch, which was served off the back of a cart and having had no breakfast they were starving. When Brad arrived at the cart to be served his stew and bread, which he would have to admit smelt delicious, the foreman standing at the side of the truck asked the cook how much food he had been giving each worker. The cook answered in broken English, five spoonfuls and a piece of bread.

"Ok for each hour you did not work you will have one spoonful of stew taken away. As you did not do any work for the six hours this morning, you will lose the five spoonfuls of stew and for the sixth hour you will lose the bread."

    Alex was treated similarly and as can be imagined, the reaction of the Duncan boys to this news was not good but their attempts to grab some food off the foreman, was met with them being grabbed by a number of the men and dragged away to receive enough of a beating for them to realise that this wasn't going to be as easy to defy as they had first thought. Refusing to learn their lesson, the boys did little if any work in the afternoon, thereby receiving no evening meal and so they returned to their rooms in the evening where hunger and the heat of the day made them collapse onto their beds exhausted. Sometime later, each of them were taken from their room into another room, totally empty apart from a chair placed in front of a tripod upon which was a video camera. They were informed that they had five minutes to record a message that would be sent to their father and although it would be edited for any mention of names or places, they could say exactly what they wished. Not sure whether to believe them or not, the boys nonetheless decided that it was worth a go, if only to get a break from the boredom of their room.

    A week had gone by since his sons' disappearance and Duncan was more and more taking his frustration out on the men who worked for him, to the extent that they did all they could to avoid being anywhere near him at any time, using the truthful excuse that they were out trying to find leads on where the boys were. Each lead they turned up came to nothing and it became more and more apparent to them, that whoever had taken the boys and been carrying out this campaign to undermine the Duncan organisation, were not any of the usual suspects and in fact must be a new gang on the block and a very well organised and powerful gang at that.

    What worried them most was that it seemed likely that this gang could not be local but probably from London or even abroad. There were mutterings amongst the men that maybe they should get out while they still could, as Duncan's powers were definitely on the decline and if a war was to break out because this new gang wanted to take over the Duncan territory, perhaps they would be better off changing horses and see if they could get a ride with the other team. This was all discussed in twos and threes, between the guys who were close, for fear of anything getting back to Pete or Duncan himself, which added up to basically the same thing.

    Duncan spent much of his own time in his office and his usual immaculate appearance was every day being replaced by a relaxation of his standards, as his waking days were spent agitating over what was happening to him and his family and making phone calls to ascertain who was responsible. Whenever he managed to achieve some moment of calm, he would be thrown even deeper into his immense store of anger and frustration, by the picture on the wall opposite, of him standing amongst his once prized orchids when they were at full bloom. He found it difficult to come to terms with whether it was the loss of his boys or the orchids that gave him most pain. As he contemplated this, there was a knock at the door and without waiting for a reply, Pete brought in the post as he did every day, with them both hoping, since the boys' disappearance, for some ransom demand. Today however, his second in command threw the letters down on the desk and held up a package.

    "Boss, I think this is it."

Duncan jumped to his feet and virtually snatched the package from Pete. "Why, what makes you think that?"

"Look at the post mark." Duncan grabbed the package and sucked in his breath as he saw that the package had been posted in Kinabalu, Malaysia, the home of his beloved orchids. He ripped it open to find a DVD, which he immediately gave to Pete to play on his massive TV screen. There was no introduction but the first few scenes made him gasp with relief and cry out, "He's alive," and then his heart seemed to tighten as he fully appreciated what he was watching. On the screen were people working in the fields in hot and unpleasant conditions on what seemed like some massive farm. Unmistakably however, he could see that among those workers was his son Alex, looking dishevelled and exhausted but more worryingly, also totally subdued and on closer inspection bruised. After a few minutes, the scenes changed to his son sitting in a different room and talking to the camera. Despite how he looked, Alex seemed in good spirits shouting abuse at whoever was doing the filming and making threats about what would happen to his captors when his father found them very soon. Duncan was elated then, when the same sequence was repeated with his youngest son Brad as the subject of the video. Next, they both spoke directly to him, each in his own way, saying that they knew he would get them out of this mess and that they would soon build up the organisation to be bigger and better than ever before.

At different points in the recording, what they were saying was obviously bleeped out and their mouths pixelated. Duncan guessed that this was to ensure that it would stop anyone from ascertaining what was being said because they were probably trying to tell him where they actually were. Despite his elation at seeing that his two youngest sons were still alive, he felt uneasy about having to wait for Phillip to appear and this uneasiness turned to a real fear, when the two boys disappeared and words appeared in their place which he read with growing anger and disbelief.

DUNCAN AS YOU CAN SEE WE HAVE YOUR BOYS AND

THEY ARE WORKING HARD ON SOME OF OUR

AGRICULTURAL PROJECTS. WE THOUGHT IT WOULD BE

CHARACTER BUILDING FOR THEM TO UNDERGO

SIMILAR EXPERIENCES TO THOSE IMMIGRANTS YOU

AND THEY HAVE BROUGHT IN TO THE UK TO ACT AS SLAVE LABOUR FOR YOU, INCLUDING THE AMOUNT OF FREEDOM THEY HAVE, THE AMOUNT OF WORK THEY HAVE TO DO IF THEY WISH TO EAT AND A SIMILAR LEVEL OF COMFORT ALL ROUND. THEY WILL BE DOING THIS FOR UP TO ONE YEAR FROM THE TIME THEY WERE TAKEN. THEY WILL BE RELEASED ONLY WHEN YOU PROVIDE US WITH THE FORENSIC AND FINANCIAL EVIDENCE OF THE CRIMINAL ACTIVITIES WE HAVE LISTED BELOW THAT WILL ENABLE THE POLICE TO PROSECUTE THEM FOR THE CRIMES THEY HAVE COMMITTED. DETAILS OF HOW YOU CAN GET THAT TO US WILL BE PROVIDED LATER AS YOU WILL NEED TIME TO GET IT ALL TOGETHER. SHOULD YOU FAIL TO PROVIDE US WITH THE INFORMATION WE REQUIRE ANY TIME BEFORE THE YEAR IS UP THEN THEY WILL BE KILLED AND BURIED, IN THE VERY FIELDS IN WHICH THEY WILL BE WORKING UNTIL THAT TIME. YOU HAVE A CHOICE OF THEM SPENDING TIME IN PRISON FOR THE CRIMES THEY HAVE COMMITTED OR A YEAR OF VERY HARD LABOUR AND THEN YOU WILL NEVER SEE THEM

AGAIN. I THINK WE HAVE ALREADY DEMONSTRATED TO YOU THAT WE ARE QUITE CAPABLE OF CARRYING OUT WHAT WE SAY WE WILL DO. YOU WILL RECEIVE REGULAR UPDATES ON YOUR SONS' PROGRESS BUT UNTIL THEN HERE IS A LIST OF SOME OF THE CRIMES YOUR BOYS HAVE COMMITTED, FOR WHICH WE DEMAND GENUINE EVIDENCE. WE DO NOT REQUIRE EVIDENCE IMPLICATING YOURSELF IF YOU DO NOT WISH TO SHARE THE PUNISHMENTS OF YOUR SONS.

1. Evidence related to your people smuggling operation
2. Evidence related to your exporting of stolen cars abroad.
3. Evidence related to the bank robbery carried out on 14th February 2009 and the death of three people during the getaway.
4. Evidence related to the ripping out of cash machines from the premises of Co-op shops by mechanical diggers in the Midlands.
5. Evidence related to the selling of drugs across County borders throughout the Midlands and the North.

THANKING YOU IN ANTICIPATION OF YOUR CO-OPERATION.

Pete and Duncan stared at each other aghast at the idea that someone could have so much knowledge about their operations.

"There has to be someone amongst our men who is passing this information on," Duncan suggested.

"So why couldn't they just get the evidence without going through this pantomime?"

"Apart from you, me and the boys, no-one would have access to the level of documentation they are demanding. I want that b****** caught because they will be able to lead us to who is doing this. As if I would ever allow my boys to go to prison." Suddenly, Duncan realised that the video had come to an end. "But there must be some mistake. Where's Phil? Why isn't he on the video?"

"Boss, you know how hotheaded Phil is. He probably refused to go through with the charade."

"Yes. Yes, you must be right. That is the most logical explanation. He wouldn't have given them the satisfaction of letting them force him to belittle himself." As he said this, Frankie Duncan experienced a feeling he hadn't felt since his father Harold had beaten him with his belt for being weak, when he was a child and his pet rabbit had died. One of abject fear. He would get the recording analysed over and over for any clues that might be in the recording. He had to know.

Listening to a recording of this information in Matt's study, Rob looked at the others in the room with a worried look.

"I think we have gone too far in asking for so much information. We should have just asked for the evidence concerning the robbery and then subsequent deaths of my girls." Hassan could understand the fact that Rob had really only ever wanted to get revenge for his family and while he sympathised totally, he knew that such a revenge would not give Rob any of the moral comfort he needed but that real justice might just provide the solace he had been looking for since their deaths.

"Mr. Rob if we only demanded information for the robbery and getaway hit and run, the Duncans would have a good idea who would be behind this vendetta and would put all their efforts into stopping you. But it would not only be you who would suffer, as there are many people involved, not to mention the school and its students. This way we do not give them any clue as to where the problem is coming from and we create the freedom we need to complete our plan."

"But you heard him, they have no intention of providing the evidence we need."

Amira, in support of her husband, reminded Rob that this had always been a long term plan and that Duncan would be likely to change his mind after he had received a few more recordings of the degradations his sons were suffering and could not fail to be affected by the dissemblance of confidence and physical appearance that would almost certainly affect his sons when they appeared on screen.

"We know that even when, and notice I don't say if, he agrees to hand over the evidence, he will try and pull something to ensure we either don't actually get the evidence or to make it worthless. In the meantime, the bonus is that Duncan is so caught up with finding his boys and the people who have them, that his other criminal enterprises have fallen by the wayside and our intelligence is that any power he might have once enjoyed amongst the criminal fraternity in this country, is very quickly waning."

Rob not only understood all that his friends were saying to him but also fully agreed. However, he just wished that the nagging ache he always felt in his belly would eventually go and he knew that would never happen until he saw the Duncans get their just rewards As the others got up to leave, Ronnie put her hand on his shoulder but the reassurance of the squeeze she gave him, as the others left the room, could not prevent him from burying his face in his hands and weeping, as he came to the realisation once again, that it was only this desire to get his own back that was really keeping him going.

CHAPTER 33

It was Pete who formulated the strategy to concentrate their efforts in finding whoever was behind their travails, by focussing on all the people involved in the five different cases that the kidnappers had demanded evidence for. He knew this would be a massive undertaking as, in all honesty, their crimes had affected thousands. Surely, he thought to himself, it has to be someone who has a vested interest in one of the five areas of evidence that had been requested. But to start somewhere, he got the more intelligent of Duncan's lieutenants in a room and allocated each of them, one of the five criminal ventures listed by the kidnappers and told them to make a list of people affected by their allocated case in order of priority i.e. Those who would have most reason to hold a grudge as a result of being affected by their particular 'case''. Descending to those who would have been affected least. They were then told to not spare the resources and work their way down the lists with any uncertainties being run past him. Surely they were bound to get there eventually? In the meantime, he confirmed with his police contacts that they had no knowledge of any of what had been going on. As part of that process, he applied for a visiting order to HMP, Welford Road, Leicester to have a word with someone who, although now off the scene, had proved previously to be very useful.

  Two days later Pete was sitting in an orange plastic chair screwed to the floor in front of a low table in the visiting room of HMP Leicester and looked around him at the surroundings that were not exactly unfamiliar to him, although in fairness he had in the past been sitting on the other side of the table. Presently, only the visitors were seated but a buzzer and the air pressure release of a door at the side of the room admitted the men who were presently residing in this august facility and who were only too pleased to receive this slight respite from the drudgery and boredom of their day to day lives. Pete only looked up when ex-Detective Chief Inspector Grey sat down with a resigned slouch, not wishing to see this particular visitor, but not enough to refuse the chance to leave his cell.

  "So, DI Grey, how are you doing?"

  "Oh, absolutely fantastic thank you for asking. I'm thinking of requesting to stay on after my sentence is up."

"Well, unfortunately that will be some time yet, so in the meantime I thought you might like to earn yourself some money for when you do eventually get back outside."

"From what I hear, your boss and his family are struggling at the moment and might have a problem getting hold of any money."

"Don't believe all you hear, we are simply keeping a low profile at present, while we sort out a small local difficulty."

"If you say so. So how can I help you with that, considering my present living arrangements?"

"Well you are probably in one of the best places for the type of gossip we are interested in and of course you do still have some friends on the force."

"You reckon? Most of those dropped me like a hot potato, not wanting to be found guilty by association, while ex-coppers are not particularly popular in here as you well know. All I can say is, that even those associated with the top firms are a little intrigued and quite concerned about how effective this new outfit seem to be."

"Nothing we can't handle. If you hear anything, you know we will make it worth your while but there is something else you can do for us." Pete gave Grey a quick synopsis of the things that had been happening to the Duncans, without mentioning the abduction of the boys.

"Can you think of anyone who we have had dealings with, who might be trying to get revenge on us but also have the capability of doing so?"

"Wow, someone really has got it in for you guys. Well, I can think of loads of people who would want to but there aren't many who are capable, or would have the bottle to attempt it."

"Well, give it some thought but one of the cases you were heavily involved in was the bank robbery and the hit and run. The husband was pretty cut up by the death of his wife and kids and also attempted to have a go at Frankie at the Court when the boys were on trial. Could he be involved in this?"

"No, he was just a teacher, a nobody who was so distraught towards the end of the court case that he could barely keep it together and at one stage we thought he might top himself. Of course that 'hearts-and-flowers waste-of-space and promoted way beyond her abilities' DS Bright, did all she could to support him, while someone like me who did real policing got treated as if my years on the force counted for nothing."

Pete thought it better not to mention the fact that Grey could hardly be considered an example of what the police force should aim to be if he were to keep him on side.

"Besides, to carry out the sort of activities that you have told me about, someone has to have the sort of resources that he could not possibly access." Pete tended to agree and while he would not make Price a priority just now, he knew you should never underestimate the absolute need for vengeance when someone threatens everything you hold dear, let alone takes it away completely. You only had to look at his boss. No, he wouldn't dismiss Price out of hand just yet.

It was two weeks later that the second DVD was delivered to Duncan's house. Two weeks in which his men had failed to turn up any clear leads as to who was carrying out the vendetta against him. Again it was he and Pete who sat and watched the recording of his sons, working separately in fields that could be anywhere in the world, although they were quite obviously somewhere very hot as their skin was blistered by the sun. They looked haggard and drawn from the physical effort they were exerting, in order to ensure that they received the food and comforts such as a daily shower, which they had very soon realised they needed if they were to survive. Duncan's heart seemed to compress at the sight of the suffering his sons were going through and his fists clenched in automatic response to anything that questioned that he was anything other than all powerful. But again it was the lack of any footage of his eldest son Phillip that gave him most cause for concern. Why was he, not included in the video? He had to hang on to the more than believable hope that it was because Phil was refusing to co-operate.

However, it was the recording of the boys talking to camera that really affected him. While the two boys were still able to put on a show of bravado in front of their captors, it was quite obviously just that, an act to try to convince their captors that they could not be broken. It was Brad however, who truly showed how he felt by breaking down in tears and begging his father to get him out of there. He sobbed that they had already proved they were more than capable of killing him and he didn't know how much longer he could put up with all this. Duncan's mind whirred at the terrifying reasons as to how the kidnappers had been able to prove to Brad that they were capable of killing him but that was because, what he hadn't seen and heard was Brad recounting how Phillip had been thrown from the aeroplane, as that had been carefully edited out by some of Hassan's technical team, when they had received the recording back in England. Never had Frankie Duncan felt so helpless. The recording ended with each of the boys being manhandled by large balaclavered men out of the room and his youngest son shouting through his sobs for his dad to get him out of there. The action was then replaced with the following written notice:

> ELEVEN MONTHS LEFT BUT WE ARE IN NO RUSH, AS THERE IS A COMFORTING SENSE OF KARMA WATCHING YOUR BOYS BEING TREATED JUST LIKE YOU HAVE TREATED HUNDREDS OF THE IMMIGRANTS YOU HAVE SMUGGLED INTO THE COUNTRY OVER THE YEARS. YOU CAN HOWEVER LET US KNOW WHEN YOU ARE READY TO PROVIDE THE EVIDENCE WE HAVE REQUESTED BY FLYING YOUR RIDICULOUS FLAG IN THE GROUNDS OF YOUR HOUSE AT HALF MAST.

Whereas normally, such an ultimatum would have sent Duncan into a fit of apoplectic rage, he simply stared at the screen as the full extent of his opponents' capabilities came home to him.

"Pete, I will give you one more week and if you have come up with nothing at the end of that week, I am going to flush these people out myself. They really don't know who they are messing with."

Pete took his courage in his hands and suggested to Duncan that maybe they should call the kidnapper's bluff and see how far they were prepared to go at the end of the year. Duncan looked at him open mouthed, before asking him if he were really suggesting that he should risk his boys' lives.

"Boss, we don't know that they won't simply let them go at the end of the year if they don't get what they want."

"But what if they don't? You are suggesting that I condemn my own sons to death. You have been with me from the very beginning Pete but never think I will put anyone before my boys. I suggest you get out of here and make more of an effort to find who is doing this."

"OK, you're the boss." As Pete left the room, Duncan followed him to the door with his eyes burning with the anger of an unthinkable suspicion, as if he were trying to see into his trusted lieutenants very soul. Surely it couldn't be Pete but there was no-one else who had such intricate knowledge of his business and who was now unable to track down his tormentors. Duncan dismissed the idea but the worm of doubt kept creeping back to the outskirts of his thoughts, seemingly trying to wriggle into his deepest fear.

Pete, for his part, had known Frankie Duncan long enough to know that while he was concerned about his sons, it was more what their kidnapping represented that had caused him the most anguish. If his own sons could be kidnapped, what did that say about his position as an infallible crime lord? He was beginning to suspect that Duncan was seriously losing it and knew what the consequences would be for him if everything went pear-shaped. He would not wait around for that to happen but before he gave up on, what had turned into a very lucrative career choice, he wanted to ensure that all possibilities as to who the likely kidnappers were, had been checked. Having looked into all the major 'usual suspects' in fine detail and come up with nothing, perhaps it was time to look at those whose lives had been affected by the Duncan family and their operations but, who on the surface seemed unlikely to pose any threat.

He called in the men he most trusted to be thorough and allocated each of them a person of interest, however insignificant their dealings with the Duncans might have been or, however unlikely they would seem to be, in relation to having the ability to carry out the operation that had been waged against the Duncans.

Although it was coincidence that he left himself with the bloke Price, whose family had been wiped out in the bank robbery getaway all those years ago, he had always felt uneasy about the incident and knew that if it had been him, he could not have taken the consequences of what had happened as quietly as Price seemed to have done. Yes, they were different people but surely Price would have reacted in some way or other, even after being given the message by Duncan in the toilets of the courtroom, when the verdict had come through?

As the rest of his lieutenants went off to check the various victims of the Duncan operation, Pete rang though to Michelle, Duncan's personal assistant and asked her to get him any details she could about Price. Twenty minutes later, she rang him back with his home address and place of work. Pete then went into the kitchen where some of the men were lounging until given a job to do and selecting Pat as the best of a not-very-intelligent bunch, he told him to go and stake out Price's home and to stay there until he would be relieved at midnight, when he should report in before getting some rest prior to doing the same thing at 8.00am the following day. After Pat had left, Pete rang The Castle of HOPE School and asked to speak to the Headmaster. As the head was busy, Pete explained in a more refined English accent than was his custom, that he was a reporter for a well known national magazine group and would like to do a feature on the school and its burgeoning reputation, for which the school would be well remunerated, as well as receiving a great deal of positive publicity. The very nice secretary told him she would pass on his message and that Mr. Carter would get back to him soon. When Sheila Johnson the secretary passed on the message to Matt, they both agreed that this particular journalist was worth a closer look and Sheila had to admit that she had already made some enquiries and that this particular journalist did not actually exist. Matt thanked Sheila and told her to set up an interview in the next few days. He then called Rob into his office.

"It looks like someone is taking an interest in us and I suspect that means that what they really want to know is, whether you are the person causing them all the grief they have been having."

"Well, we guessed that this might happen at some stage. I think you should go ahead with the interview and we might find we can learn more from him than he does from us. In the meantime, I shall take great care to play my part as the defeated widower, who is barely able to hold down a job as caretaker in a school."

That evening when he returned home, Rob took note of two cars parked up near his house that weren't normally there. A couple of hours later, he heard the starting of a car engine and looked out of his window to see one of those cars being waved off by his neighbour three doors away, Mrs Goggins. Rob had already decided that the car remaining was the most likely candidate to be there for his dubious benefit, because of the tinted windows and expensive paint job of a 4x4, more suited to the streets of Mayfair than his little street.

Two days later, Pete, dressed in what he considered to be the attire suited to a respectable journalist of a national magazine, arrived for his meeting with the Headmaster of The Castle of HOPE School. The very nice secretary showed him into the office of Mr. Carter, the Headteacher, who suggested they should chat while he gave him a tour of the school and then they could return to his office for any remaining questions he might have. Pete on his best behaviour and using his best BBC voice didn't want to spend any more time here than he had to but agreed, with a forced willingness as a means to an end. Although expecting to be bored rigid, Pete was pleasantly surprised and impressed with what he saw and what seemed to be a million miles away from his own, admittedly fairly sporadic, school experience. Back at Matt's office, Pete was able to truthfully tell the Headmaster how impressed he was with what he had seen and when asked by said Headmaster where any article about the school might appear, he thought that he waffled quite convincingly about well known publications who would vie for the rights to the article and he would ensure that it was not just the magazine that paid him the most who he would choose but the one he felt would project the school and his article in the most positive light.

However, until such time as he had been paid, so positive was Mr. Fitzpatrick, that he wanted to give the Head a cheque of a thousand pounds as a gesture of good will. Pete could see that this was just what the Head had wanted to hear but also expected it to make him more receptive to his next request. "I wonder if, to gain a full flavour of the school, I could perhaps get a view from some of the pupils and someone on the non-teaching staff, preferably the caretaker, who would have a good overall view of the whole school from a non-academic standpoint." Mr. Carter was more than happy to take Mr. Fitzpatrick to meet Rob Price, the caretaker or Premises Officer as they were now known but warned him that while he was excellent at his job, he was quite a reserved and nervous fellow since an incident in his life some years ago and needed to be treated with compassion and patience. Pete was able to keep a straight face when he assured the Head that compassion was his middle name and he was also happy to agree to the Head's suggestion that he could chat to some of the sixth form students during lunchtime.

The Head found Rob in his office, checking off a delivery of cleaning products and told him to return Mr. Fitzpatrick to his office when they had finished their conversation.

"Good of you to find time to see me Mr. Price as I am sure you must be very busy."

"Oh, that's fine, I am always happy to help out the Head as he has been very good to me."

"He doesn't take advantage of his authority over the real workers then?" joked Pete.

"Oh no, on the contrary, he is an excellent boss who does a fantastic job at this wonderful school."

"Do you mind telling me how you got the job?"

"Well actually, I used to be a teacher myself but had something of a breakdown a number of years ago now, after quite a traumatic incident in my life and Mr. Carter sort of picked me up out of the hole I was in and has helped me to recover ever since by giving me this job."

"Wow, I hadn't realised. Do you mind telling me what happened to you?" Rob continued to promote the body language and demeanour of the beaten down loser but quietly seethed at being in the presence of someone who could have been partly responsible for the loss of his family and struggled to control the urge to extract some form of revenge. He held himself in check however, knowing that by playing the long game he would achieve more than some satisfying but short-lived moment of violence against this thug.

"I'm afraid it is still too raw for me to talk about it."

Pete said that he understood perfectly and asked a few more what he thought might be pertinent questions but felt he already had what he wanted and so after another fifteen minutes or so, Rob returned him to the Headmaster's office and shook Mr. Fitzpatrick by the hand as he left him. The Head then took him to have a surprisingly, very good lunch with some of the sixth form students, who were to return him to the Head's secretary when they had finished. Matt had apologised to his visitor that he had other business to deal with but not to hesitate if there was anything else he needed, to contact him via his secretary. Pete thanked him for his time and after his lunch with the students he was duly returned to the Secretary's office, where he gave his thanks and said his goodbyes.

Later, when Matt asked the sixth form students how they had got on with Mr. Fitzpatrick, they were their usual non-committed selves but reported that he seemed more interested in Mr. Price the caretaker than what they did or thought and he wore too much aftershave. As for Pete, when he returned to Duncan Towers and joined the rest of the lieutenants for the now daily feedback meeting, he explained that he was now pretty certain that Price was not the person they were looking for and while some of the others were still researching their targets, they also felt pretty despondent about the chances of identifying the person behind the attack on their 'firm'.

Duncan looked around at his most trusted men with a look of disgust and told them that he had come up with an idea that would enable him to confirm whether their targets were responsible or not and at the same time find out for certain who was truly responsible for this mess.

"OK, I have had enough of leaving this to you lot and sitting on my hands while someone out there is destroying the business I have built up over the years and taken away my family." Duncan was pacing around his office while his lieutenants sat around with their customary practice of not daring to meet his eye, in case they became the subject of his wrath. Even Pete, who had been his right hand man from the beginning when they used to rob village shops in their teens but had always appreciated the precarious position he was in with such an unstable personality, felt it best to not raise his head above the parapet.

"We are going to set a trap and find out who is doing this once and for all. I am going to contact them and tell them I have had enough and that I am prepared to provide them with the evidence they have asked for. We will then follow the trail of the package we give them to the source of our troubles and catch who is doing this."

Ernie, realising that there could soon be a leadership vacancy, as Pete's failure to find who was behind the attacks on the family was causing him to be less and less popular with his boss, said he thought that this was a great idea but what if they lost track of the package and these people got the evidence anyway. Duncan turned to him and immediately he knew he had made a mistake by speaking up.

"Do you really think I would be stupid enough to actually put any real evidence in this package? No wonder we have got nowhere up to now."

Realising he had to reassert his position before others began to fancy their chances, Pete suggested, "Boss, if we are going to do this, then it will take all the manpower we have and probably some extra muscle. Also if they demand the information electronically, we will need to have some serious brain power to track any IT element."

"Yes Pete, you're right but everything is at stake here and I am prepared to put all my resources into this." It did not escape Pete, or some of the other men sitting around that Duncan had talked about his resources and not theirs and more and more, there was a feeling that they needed to have a get out plan of their own, should this all go wrong.

This conversation was of course reported to Rob and the others when Matt welcomed them all into his office the next morning for their daily update.

"Well, we expected something of the sort, especially after the school had our visit from Mr. Fitzpatrick who has probably come to the conclusion that they have nothing to fear from the pathetic old school caretaker."

"I'll accept 'pathetic' but less of the 'old', thank you very much," Rob exclaimed as he poured himself a coffee and joined the others, who had been discussing the recent audio tapes when he walked in. He'd just completed his daily routine of signing out the school cleaners, just in case anyone was watching to see if he actually was the caretaker he claimed to be.

"So, has anyone got an idea how we should approach this next stage?" asked Ronnie, speaking with a chocolate biscuit waving around in her hand. "Because I have been talking to Hassan and I believe he has come up with a very pleasing idea." She smiled at the thought of what Hassan was about to suggest and then listened as he expressed those thoughts to the others.

"Thank you Mrs Veronica. It occurs to me that while it would be very simple to have the evidence supplied to us electronically, I think it would be more fun and, importantly, more annoying for Mr. Duncan, if we give him a bit of a runaround."

"Oh I'm all for annoying Duncan as much as is possible. So what does your devious brain have in mind Hassan? But once again, how many times have I asked you to call us by our first names without the honorific of Mr and Mrs?"

An hour later they all broke up, having been allocated their own tasks to carry out the next stage of their operation.

At Duncan Towers, Jean the cleaner couldn't understand why she had been asked to lower the flag that flew, rather ostentatiously she thought, above the walls of the enclosed property, to half mast. She certainly wasn't aware of anybody passing away. Unless of course something had happened to one of the horrible sons and if so good riddance to bad rubbish she thought and then chastised herself mildly for harbouring such uncharitable thoughts. Even if those thoughts she mused, would probably be echoed by anyone else who had had the misfortune to come across them and again she gave herself a mental slap on the wrist for being unkind. In truth, when they weren't around their father they could be quite nice but it seemed as if they had to put on some sort of act in a need to impress Mr. Duncan, who was no sort of role model. From what she had heard from other staff who had worked for the Duncans much longer than she had, the boys had been really lovely before their mother had left. She vowed to try and see their good side from now on if possible.

While this internal debate was occurring, Frankie Duncan had large numbers of his men surrounding the estate, looking out in the off chance they would catch someone taking an interest in the position of the flag half way down the pole. However, later in the day, after the flag had been lowered, a courier arrived at the gate house with an envelope for Mr. Duncan. So soon was it after the lowering of the flag, that the gatemen did not think it necessary to stop the courier for questioning about the letter's origin, much to the anger of Duncan and the gateman's discomfort at what punishment might befall him when it was realised what the envelope contained. On ripping open the envelope and reading the contents however, Duncan's anger dissipated and he called Pete into the room with an exultant look on his face.

"Yes! Pete we've got them. Not only have they fallen for it but they have asked for a method of delivery that puts them right into our hands." He read out the contents of the letter to his second in command.

WE ARE DELIGHTED THAT YOU HAVE AT LAST SEEN SENSE AND DECIDED TO PROVIDE US WITH WHAT WE HAVE ASKED OF YOU. THIS WILL TAKE PLACE AT BRADGATE PARK THE DAY AFTER TOMORROW, THURSDAY THE 12TH. YOU WILL ENTER THE PARK AT THE NEWTOWN LINFORD ENTRANCE AND WALK ALONG THE MAIN FOOTPATH FOR 7OO YARDS WHERE YOU WILL FIND A BENCH ON THE RIGHT HAND SIDE OF THE PATH, NEAR A LARGE OAK TREE AND WITH A GREEN BIN NEXT TO IT. SIT ON THE BENCH AT THE END NEAR TO THE BIN AND PLACE YOUR PACKAGE IN THE BIN AT 8.00AM. REMAIN FOR ANOTHER FIVE MINUTES AND THEN LEAVE THE WAY YOU CAME. DO NOT LOOK BACK OR BE TEMPTED TO RETURN. SHOULD ANYONE TRY TO PREVENT US FROM PICKING UP THE PACKAGE THE DEAL WILL BE OFF AND ONE OF YOUR SONS WILL

SUFFER THE CONSEQUENCES. ONCE WE HAVE CHECKED THE PACKAGE AND FOUND IT TO BE WHAT WE HAVE ASKED FOR, YOU HAVE OUR WORD THAT YOUR BOYS WILL BE KEPT SAFE AND RETURNED TO FACE JUSTICE WHEN THEIR YEAR IS UP. TO SHOW GOOD FAITH WE SHALL ALSO PROVIDE YOU WITH A VIDEO A WEEK LATER, OF YOUR BOYS RECEIVING SOME REWARDS FOR YOUR CO-OPERATION.

"They think they have been so clever up until now with their schemes but they can't get the better of me for long. They have fallen right into our trap. Right, we need to get everything in place. You and I will put the false package together so that it looks realistic at least from the outside. Get Jennings to install the best tracking device possible, in case we should by some chance lose sight of the package when it leaves the park. You go to Bradgate Park now and scope out the particular bench and the best place for our men to place themselves to be able to follow whoever picks up the package. Also, have vehicles at all the car parks to ensure we can follow whoever takes the package. Once we have their destination we will swoop but I want whoever picks up the package followed for a few days whatever happens, in case this all goes wrong. At least we will be able to then force any info' we need out of their courier. Also, I want all the main suspects we have been looking into, watched for 24hrs before and after this operation, to see if there is any unusual behaviour that will point to them being the one involved in this."

Pete, who was less sure than his boss seemed to be about their ability to outwit these people who always seemed to be one step ahead, tried to bring a sense of reality back to his boss.

"Frankie, this will take a huge amount of manpower and we will have to bring in extra help."

"Then do it. This is how we are going to show these people that we are not to be messed with. It will all be worth it. This is how I am going to get my power and reputation back and I don't care how much that takes because that means everything."

Pete tried to remind him that if this went wrong it could turn out badly for the boys.

"That is a risk worth taking. Of course I want them back but in reality their real importance here is that their kidnap is a reflection on my status and the true purpose of getting them back is to show that no-one messes with Francis Duncan and gets away with it."

So it was, that two days later, on a pleasant June morning at 7.30am, Pete pulled up in the South car park of Bradgate Park and as he went to pay what seemed a rather extortionate parking fee, ignored the other vehicles he recognised as belonging to his men, who should already have positioned themselves so that they had the nominated bench covered from every conceivable angle, either as rather muscle-bound joggers, unlikely looking dog walkers or simply concealed behind the myriad of bushes, trees and rocks. With the package under his arm, he strolled, in what he thought was a casual manner for approximately 10 minutes, until he arrived at the designated bench and sat down to pretend to read the copy of the Leicester Mercury he had bought for the purpose of having a reason to be there. Looking at his watch every few minutes until it was 8.00am and with a quick glance around, he placed the package in the bin, waited exactly five minutes, got up and returned to his car, once again ignoring the men positioned in the vicinity for the purpose of tracking whoever picked up the package.

Once back in his car, he surreptitiously put in place an earpiece that allowed him audio contact with all his men and with Duncan back at the house and drove out of the car park in case his car was being watched. Most of his men were maintaining radio silence until anything occurred as instructed but Ernie was hiding behind a boulder 200 yards from the bench, with high-powered binoculars trained on the bench, the bin, and the immediate area. He also had the task of providing a running commentary for Duncan and anyone else in the gang who did not have a line of sight.

"There's a couple approaching but…no they have walked straight by. A fit looking bird is jogging in that direction and when I say fit I don't.., ok, she has passed by also. Hang on, a dog walker has stopped by the bin. This could be it. Eugh! Dogs are disgusting; he's pissing up against the bottom of the bin but this could be a ruse, no the bloke is now walking away with his stupid mutt. Nobody close at the moment so… hang on. Wow, what's happening?"

"Yes, what is happening you moron?" shouted Pete.

"That's just ridiculous. The top half of the bin seems to be rotating and its increasing in speed." Other members of their gang started joining in so that there was a cacophony of voices creating an unintelligible gabble.

"No one else say a word other than Ernie," screamed Duncan back at the house, just before Pete was about to shout something similar.

"The top of the bin has detached itself and is now getting higher and higher. It's now flying towards the Folly that's on the hill they call Old John. It must be some sort of a drone."

Duncan screamed into the earpieces of his men to follow it whatever it took and anyone in the park watching would have witnessed the strange sight of at least a dozen grown men running from different places around the park and staring into the sky while following what looked like some sort of flying saucer. This became even more amusing as the running men, with their eyes on the sky, frequently and repeatedly tripped over the many obstacles that existed in the park. At both ends of the park, some of Duncan's men were in the process of driving out of the different car parks when, by some coincidence, articulated lorries chose that time to attempt to turn their vehicles around, by reversing into the entrance of the car parks, before eventually driving away after a great deal of manoeuvring.

While the very apologetic lorry drivers were arguing with the very irate men attempting to leave the car parks, the 'bin shaped' drone had disappeared over the walls of the park and flown into the grounds of a farmyard and then in through the open back doors of a DHL delivery truck that immediately set off in the direction of Anstey and the roundabout on the A46 that would lead to the motorway.

At Duncan Towers, an apoplectic Frankie Duncan was screaming over the earpieces to all his men that they had better find that bloody flying bin, when Pete interrupted him, to remind him of the tracking device they had inserted in the package. This went some way to mollify Duncan, who could not believe that whoever was causing him all these problems seemed to always be one step ahead but at least he would have them now.

As the DHL delivery van approached the roundabout that could take traffic onto the A46 leading to the M1, it pulled up in the middle lane next to an open back lorry in the inside lane indicating to take the slip road onto the aforementioned A46. Billy, who was sitting in the passenger seat of the delivery van, wound down his window and threw the package that he had checked but unsurprisingly found to be full of blank paper and a small tracking device, into the back of the lorry with a fine example of a very unusual orchid attached to the package. He then wound his window back up as Mac drove them across the roundabout in the direction of Castle of HOPE School, firstly ensuring he wasn't being followed and the lorry disappeared onto the major roadway leading south out of Leicestershire.

Going into the room next door to his office, Duncan demanded of Jennings his IT expert, what was the present position of the package and smiled to be told it was on the M1 heading south, confirming his suspicions that the person out to get him was from London. This information was passed on to all the men who were now in their cars and setting off in pursuit, receiving regular updates as to their position in relation to the tracking device as they closed in on their target. Meanwhile, having caught up with what they were rather surprised to find was an old builder's lorry, Duncan's men followed it to a builder's yard just outside Bedford and watched as two men climbed out of the cabin of the lorry and entered a portakabin, quite obviously without the package in their possession. A few minutes later they both exited the portakabin, locked it and while one got in an old Rover and drove out of the gate to wait, the other wrapped a chain around the two sections of gate before padlocking it and joining the Rover driver and disappearing towards the town.

One of Duncan's men followed them, even though there seemed to be no sign of the package on them, just in case, while the others waited until it started to get dark before breaking into the yard and the Portakabin, where they found nothing. Ernie forced the door of the lorry and still found nothing but on walking back to join the others, he looked over the side of the lorry and spotted something that stopped him in his tracks. Although not wanting to, for fear of what he thought he might find, Ernie climbed onto the back wheel to get into the back of the lorry, where he found what he knew would not be a positive end to their task. This he held up for the rest of his colleagues to see and like him, they paled at the potential consequences when their boss found out what had happened. Ernie realised that, although he didn't want to be the one to bear the bad news, if he had any real designs on moving up in the organisation, then he had to be the one to take on the burden of responsibility. He moved away from the others as he rang Duncan but the others were only too happy to be as far away as possible from the likely fallout of this phone call. After a few rings, Ernie began to think he was going to be able to get away with leaving an answer phone message but he physically stood up straighter as the phone was answered with a peremptory demand from Duncan as to what was happening?

"Ah, Boss, we've followed the package to just outside Bedford."

"Excellent. Who has it now? Who are these b******s?"

"Well, we have it now Boss."

"What do you mean you have it? I specifically told you to keep a low profile until you find out who has been targeting me. Have you got a name?"

Ernie was literally squirming on the spot as he replied.

"Well, no Boss. You see whoever picked up the package from the drone obviously threw it into the back of a lorry travelling south and the people driving the lorry don't even know it was there."

"How do you know, you fool? These are really clever operators who could very well be watching you this very minute, before checking if it was safe to pick up the package. If you have messed up this operation your life will not be worth living."

"Boss, Boss, I can assure you that our little trick was tumbled long ago."

"How do you know that?"

"Boss, rather than explain over the phone, I will send you a photo of the package as it is now and you will see what I mean." At that, Ernie rang off, feeling quite pleased with himself that he had managed to find a way of not actually having to tell his boss the worst part of the news. He then took a photo of the package lying on the floor and sent it to Duncan. In his office Frankie Duncan stared at his phone, waiting for the supposed proof that that imbecile Ernie was meant to be sending through, while at the same time silently planning the punishment Ernie would be facing if he had, as Duncan expected, messed this up.

As the image came through, Duncan slumped into his chair and looked in disbelief at the opened package they had so carefully prepared for the handover earlier that day but now with the tracking device taped to the outside along with....

"What is it Boss?" a very wary Pete asked as he watched this disintegration of his boss before his very eyes.

"Look for yourself." Pete took the phone from Duncan and barely noticed the opened packaging or the tracking device, as the picture he was looking at seemed to be dominated by a very fine example of a very exotic looking orchid.

A few days later, Duncan was back to raging and blaming all around him for the cock up of an operation with the dud packet of evidence. Driving his men on, to find out who was behind all this, when in fact they had exhausted all avenues and were simply going through the motions, at a loss as to where to go next. They were all present in Duncan's office when a parcel was delivered that, from the way it was wrapped and the typing on the address label, was recognised immediately by the men on the gate, as another DVD from whoever had taken the Duncan boys. It was quickly brought to the house, where Duncan told Pete to read the contents and load the enclosed DVD ready to play. Those sat around listening would have smiled at Pete putting on his best BBC voice that he seemed to be affecting more and more of late, if it had not been for their fear of Duncan reacting to their levity. As it was they listened with growing anxiety as Pete read out loud.

> MR. DUNCAN, IT SEEMS THAT YOU ARE INCAPABLE OF LEARNING YOUR LESSON. YOUR ATTEMPT AT TRYING TO TRICK US AND THEN FIND US WHEN YOU SHOULD HAVE BEEN PROVIDING US WITH THE EVIDENCE WE REQUIRE, SUGGESTS A WORRYING LACK OF INTELLIGENCE AND CONCERN FOR THE WELFARE OF YOUR SONS. YOU ALSO SEEM TO DOUBT THE VERACITY OF OUR PROMISES TO YOU. WATCH THE DVD WHILE REMEMBERING THAT YOU HAVE NO ONE BUT YOURSELF TO BLAME AND ALSO THAT THERE REMAIN ONLY TWO MONTHS BEFORE WE FULLY CARRY OUT THE PROMISE MADE IN OUR ORIGINAL CONTACT WITH YOU.

Shaking with fearful anticipation at being able to see his sons again but also with the nagging concern that he was also going to watch something he wouldn't like, Duncan nodded at Pete to press the play button. All eyes turned to the giant screen on the wall at right angles to his desk and watched as the camera scanned towards a barn situated in a desolate landscape, that looked to those watching as Mediterranean in terms of the sunlight and terrain. Duncan gasped and sat upright as his youngest son Brad appeared from the right of the screen, walking towards the barn. As he neared the barn three more figures appeared, walking behind him, one of whom was carrying a large tarpaulin over his shoulder while another was carrying a shotgun, which to Duncan's increasing alarm was pointed firmly at the back of his son. The camera stayed focused on the entrance to the barn that Brad had just entered with the three unidentifiable captors.

Time ticked silently as none of the men in the room wanted to be the first to ask what they were all thinking. Such a necessity was ended with the sound of what was unmistakably two shotgun retorts. Duncan stood and walked closer to the screen as if he would be able to look around the corner of the barn entrance and see what had happened. Finally he got the answer he had been dreading, as two of the men emerged dragging the tarpaulin, now wrapped around a large and, by the effort being used to move it, heavy object from out of the barn. As they and their load got closer to the invisible camera man, the tarpaulin could clearly be seen to have large red stains begin to emerge on the outer surface. The camera followed the men as they dragged the tarpaulin out of what looked like a farmyard to some rough ground where a grave shaped hole had been dug and into which the tarpaulin and it's contents were unceremoniously tossed. Duncan walked slowly backwards until the edge of his chair hit the backs of his legs, causing him to sink onto its seat, while all the time keeping his eyes fixed on the screen as if expecting at any moment to see his son climb out of the hole into which he had just been deposited.

"Who are these people and why have they been sent to haunt me?" he whispered. His men looked at each other, all with their own answer to his last question but none daring to share their thoughts.

Brad had been bending over weeding between rows of potatoes when farmer Bektashi prodded him. "We have pig to kill in big barn. You will help." Brad hated having to watch the slaughter of any of the animals, to the extent that he began to question his own immense meat-eating history but he was used to having to be the one who had to clean up after the grisly deed was carried out in preparation for some feast or other, that seemed to occur with amazing regularity in this country. As he moved towards the barn he turned to check, and yes Saban, the usual dispatcher of animals was following with his trusty shotgun and his close mates Zamir and Ardian. What he didn't notice was that their journey to the barn was being filmed and that, whenever he was facing the front, Saban had his gun pointing at his back, to be edited later by the cameraman. Once in the barn, with Brad unable to look, Saban shot the pig which had been made to stand on the tarpaulin. Having checked that the two shots had done their job, Zamir and Ardian wrapped the tarpaulin around the prostrate animal and dragged it out of the barn.

Brad knew from previous experience that it was his job to clear up any mess left behind and take any blood spattered straw out the back and burn it under the watchful eye of Saban. Later, when the camera had been turned off, Zamir and Ardian returned to the 'grave' of the pig and unrolled it out of the tarpaulin, before transferring it to a wagon and then pushed it to the spit where it would be prepared for the evening's feast.

CHAPTER 34

The Albanian sun was getting hotter each day and work started earlier, with a siesta during the hottest part of the day, so that work could continue in the less excessive heat of the late afternoon and evening. On their respective farms, the two youngest of the three Duncan boys had long ago accepted the situation and the routine, to the extent that they began to actually find some real satisfaction at what they achieved each day and also noticed how much healthier they felt and how much better they slept. Not that they had accepted their situation was a lost cause but the food was good and they even started to learn some of the language as their fellow workers seemed to accept them the more they did their bit to fit in.

Alex lay on his bunk sobbing to himself as he thought of his brother being thrown out of the aeroplane. Yes, of course they had done things in their lives that they shouldn't have but he hadn't deserved that. Alex had idolised his big brother and had tried to be like him in any way he could, even if Phil had always ridiculed him and had hated the fact he had had to look after Alex when he had wanted to be with his mates, without some snotty nosed hanger-on. What sort of people were these who could so casually end someone's life like that? But of course, he knew what sort of people they were. They were just like his father and, although he didn't like to admit it, just like he and his brothers were turning into. Phil was a hothead, he knew but to die like that was not right and he was fully aware that similar or worse could happen to him.

At first, he thought that these 'local yokels' would soon be a pushover but they seemed more than willing to hurt him and probably kill him should he step too far out of line. He was petrified in the knowledge that some of his fellow workers had had family members who had been encouraged to go to Britain for a good job, only to end up as modern day slaves. Some, most probably, in the clutches of his own family.

His early resistance had proved futile and he had now settled into a routine where, although the work was hard, he got fed surprisingly good food and was able to sleep and keep himself clean. He would bide his time and then get away from this hellhole. The sound of a bolt being drawn back on the other side of the door was the signal for him to be ready for breakfast and then work. He no longer had an escort to breakfast or to the fields, as there seemed no place to go or means to run away and his captors seemed quite confident that should he attempt to do so, they would take great pleasure in hunting him down and returning him to even more Spartan conditions than the ones he endured when he first arrived. When at first he had shown some resistance, this had simply resulted in the withdrawal of food or even the meagre comforts like a bed and a shower. Learning to accept his lot, at least at face value until he could escape, had made life bearable but he almost started to cry again when he compared this to his past lifestyle. But more and more, the thoughts that were creeping into his head were the realisation that, while he had been enjoying that lifestyle, he was also responsible for his family's modern day slaves suffering even more than he was now. At first, they had been fleeting memories that he quickly discarded but the long hours alone in his hut invited an introspection he didn't want to face but could not avoid.

    At breakfast, some of his fellow workers who came up from the local villages, were now at least nodding to him. He realised that his family's reputation would prevent them from ever being friends but they seemed to respect his work ethic and the soft fitness he had accrued in all those gym sessions over the years, had now been hardened into a level of fitness that made him one of the most productive workers there. It had in fact been the gym strength that allowed him to make his greatest progress with his fellow workers, when he had almost certainly saved one of the men from serious harm just a few days before.

    He and another worker he knew as Bujar were using long iron poles to dislodge large boulders from an area that the farmer wanted to develop for planting. Once they had dug around the boulders with the sharpened end of the pole, they would lever it up and create space for chains to be fixed around the boulder to be towed away by a tractor. Three other workers were doing the same to a particularly large boulder a few metres away, when a scream followed by shouting made Alex and Bujar look around to see one of the three had slipped into the hole left by the partially levered rock and the other two were struggling with their own iron poles to keep the rock from falling totally back into the hole and thereby crushing the worker. Alex ran across and jammed his pole under the rock, heaving with all his might to lift it off the man. As his workmate Bujar arrived and did the same, Alex released his grip with one arm and grabbed the stricken worker by the collar and dragged him out, milliseconds before the weight of the rock proved too much for the men and it fell back into the hole. Alex could see that the worker who had fallen in the hole had nothing more than a few cuts and abrasions but that worker also knew it could have been so much worse and even life-threatening. Just as Alex turned to go back to his own work, he was grabbed by the shoulder and turned around to be faced by the man he had saved and who clasped him by the hand, pulling him to his chest and muttering words repeatedly, which Alex realised would be Albanian for 'thank you'.

Back at his own work, a feeling came over him that he couldn't remember having since he had been a boy. A feeling of having done something for someone else, with no thought of reward. But there was a reward and that night when they had all showered and eaten their evening meal, Alex stood to return to his hut as was the routine, when the farm owner and his family placed bottles of beer on the table for all the workers and the farmer himself opened a bottle for Alex and patted him on the back. After a few beers, the workers began to sing and Alex luxuriated in an atmosphere he had rarely experienced, of a warmth of feeling and camaraderie that he could not explain to himself. The workers were then pointing at him and and signalling that he should now sing. He tried to indicate that he was no singer but they either could not understand him or couldn't care because they started a chant that only stopped when he began to sing one of the few songs he knew by heart, which was a hymn from his old primary school assemblies, at the end of which they all cheered and clapped. Soon after, the farmer indicated that it was time to clear away and Alex returned to his shack and as the bolt was pushed into place on the outside of the door he sat on his bed and contemplated the fact that he hadn't enjoyed an evening so much for many, many years. He understood that this could be a reaction to the comparative misery he had endured since he had been captured but he knew it was more than that and as he lay down and before going to sleep, he returned in his head to the contemplations about his life that had grown increasingly to dog his thoughts. Did he really like who he had become?

The next few days saw a continued thawing in the attitudes of the other workers towards him and a couple of them who he worked with regularly, began to share their snacks with him and started to try to teach him the language. Getting his captors and the workers to relax around him had been an initial plan to lull them into a sense of trusting him until he could escape. Now, however, the thought of escape did not really cross his mind, not seriously anyway. He had come to a realisation that this 'punishment' was probably the least that he deserved and it would only be for a few more months. But if he was honest with himself, this lifestyle had provided him with a stress free peace of mind he had not had since his mum had left them all those years ago.

On the Sunday, his day of rest, he was sitting outside his hut enjoying the shade from the midday sun when he saw a familiar figure striding towards him. Each month Mac, who he had been strapped to when he had to jump out of the aeroplane, came to receive feedback on how things were going. Alex always put on a front of couldn't care less but he looked forward to these moments, not just because it was a relief to talk to someone who he could understand and who could understand him, it was more than that. Mac spoke to him in a way that a father should talk to his son but in a way that his own father never had. He was understanding and gave Alex things to think about in terms of what society was actually about, without ever preaching. He put forward ideas that his own father would never have contemplated about how a society could only progress if the weaker members of that society were looked after by those with the abilities and resources to do so and other ideas that he would previously have called 'liberal codswallop', because he had always been in the section of society where he didn't have to worry about his own comfort. Mac asked if he could sit down and join him? Alex nodded and grunted affirmation.

"I understand you have done a good thing."

"I did only what I had to do."

"Maybe, but I'm not sure you would have done something so selfless a few months ago. We would like to reward you. You can request a gift within reason. Just tell me what you would like and as long as it is not a helicopter or any other means of escape then…"

Before he could finish the sentence Mac was interrupted by Alex.

"I would like a generator, a supply of diesel and a jackhammer for each attachment point on the generator."

"Well I have to admit that I wasn't expecting that. Do you want to explain why?"

"These people work harder than anyone I've ever known for little reward. What in Britain would be a simple task, is made harder here by the lack of the correct equipment. We would only need it for a short while to clear the field we are trying to develop."

It was not lost on Mac the use of the pronoun 'we' when talking about the work on the farm. Mac said he would look into it but as there was an element of altruism here, as well as Alex perhaps finding a way to make work easier for himself, was there something that he would like just for himself. Alex sat and thought for a moment then said. "I would like a phrase book that would allow me to learn the language."

"Well, you are full of surprises aren't you? I think we can manage that, even though I am fully aware that this could aid any escape plan you might have. But I will take the risk."

A couple of weeks later, a large transporter lorry arrived at the farm and the workers were told to stop the work they were doing and help unload a second hand generator along with diesel and jackhammers. The excitement this generated, matched the palpable feeling of goodwill towards Alex, who was more and more enjoying the warm glow of being made to feel a part of something good and worthwhile since the incident with the worker almost being crushed by a rock. A couple of days after the visit by Mac, he had found an Albanian/English phrase book on his bed when he returned from work and in the many spare hours he had to himself, he immersed himself in learning the language, much to the amusement of his fellow workers on whom he would practise what he had learned the night before.

There were still workers who were wary of him but he knew they had every right to despise him for the part he had played in enslaving their relatives and friends back in England. But he had become determined not only to create a good impression through his deeds but also through the words that he was determined to master, so he could explain and apologise in their own language. He would frequently lie awake at night wondering where this feeling of wanting to do the right thing had come from and he was coming to the conclusion that it had always been there but he had allowed it to be leached from the essence of who he really was, by his father who he increasingly saw in an unflattering light.

Having requested paper and pen from the farmer, he spent his evenings putting together the words he felt that he had to say to the men he worked with. And so it was one evening, after he had eaten, he stood up and much to the surprise of all assembled, banged his spoon on the table twice to ask for silence, which he received more from surprise than a desire to let him speak.

He was more nervous than he could ever remember being but this was something he had to do if he were to stand any chance of gaining any respect with these men he worked and lived with every day. He read from the sheet which was about the twentieth copy of his attempts to express what he had felt for some time. He had practised the unfamiliar words over and over until they became less unfamiliar but still he stumbled and still he ploughed on in the best of his newly learned Albanian. *"I am fully aware that you know about my life before I came here and that many of you, if not all of you, have good reason to hate me and want to do me harm. The first thing I want to say is thank you for not trying to exact revenge and leaving me to become fully aware of the lack of humility and humanity I have allowed to rule my life. If you had taken out your anger on me in any way I would have used that as an excuse to hate you and feel justified for my previous actions. Your own strength of character in allowing me to find out for myself how disgraceful my previous lifestyle was, embarrasses and shames me. All I can say is, that I am sorry and that I will do all that I can in my future life to put right the wrongs I have committed in my past life. Thank you for listening."*

The men who had been staring at him throughout his speech nodded and in silence continued to eat. He returned to his hut not having expected any applause or praise but feeling to his surprise, freer and more at ease with himself than he had done for as long as he could remember.

Over the next few days, while there was no big change in the atmosphere at work, Alex thought he could detect a further thawing in attitude, even from those who in the past had been openly hostile towards him. Small, but to him significant, things such as men coming to help him when he seemed to be struggling with a particularly awkward rock, sharing their water with him and, only three days after his little speech, being indicated to join the table of some of the workers at lunch, which until then had always been a solitary affair for him.

Every evening since he had been at the farm, half of the workers had to down tools and walk the 200 metres or so to the river that flowed through the village. Once there, they filled and manhandled, dozens of large barrels with the river water to be carried back to the fields on a trailer pulled by the tractor where, dealing with a couple of fields each evening, the other half of the men would water the land. While the work during the day was hard enough, this was metaphorically the straw that broke the camel's back and after this task, the men were only too glad to simply eat their meal then fall into bed. Over the months Alex had given this a great deal of thought and using the paper and pen he had been given, he drew a plan of how he thought the whole process could be made easier. With his faltering Albanian he asked to see the farm owner Mr. Dervishi after the evening meal and tried to explain what he had in mind. With his very poor Albanian and the farmer's faltering English, the concept of digging water channels from the river to the potato fields became a topic of discussion that was laborious in nature but positive in the manner in which it was received. Apparently, the farmer's father had had a similar idea although not as refined as the one Alex was suggesting, with sluice gates built in to control the flow of water. However, it had turned out that the digging of the water channels by hand would have been an almost impossible task, as the workers could not be spared from the fields to do the digging and was soon disregarded as not being possible. However, with the jackhammers, this could now be a real possibility.

Plans were put in place to attempt the digging of the channels when the harvest was over but when Mac visited a few weeks later and heard what Alex had suggested when in conversation about his progress with the farmer, he implied that he might be able to help. So it was that a week later, a big yellow digger was delivered to the farm having been hired for however long they needed it. Immediately, the farmer put Alex in charge of a team of four men to put the water channel project in place. Alex was delighted to have something to occupy his mind as well as his body. The men allocated to him were also enthusiastic for this to work, in the realisation that this could eradicate the need for the evening water collection that was so physically draining but also because Alex was a 'hands on' project manager who spent as much time on the tools as giving orders.

With two entry points for the river water into two major channels, these developed into a myriad of smaller channels that fed each field with large sluices where the river water would enter the system and then a series of smaller sluices to enable the targeted direction of the water once in the system. A couple of months later, with more and more of the workers voluntarily giving up some of their own time to help complete the task, the system was ready to be put into action and all that was needed was for the ground to be dug out between the two major sluice gates and the river. All the workers and the farmer's family were there to witness what would either be the answer to many of their prayers or a huge disappointment and a waste of labour over the previous two months. Alex was more anxious than any of them present because there was more than the success of being able to water the field at stake here. With everyone looking at him expectantly, he gave Edon the nod and the digger driver swung the arm of the digger towards the river bank and down, before gouging out a huge section of earth to just before the open sluice gate. He repeated the process to ensure the channel's entrance was below the level of the river and water followed the digger's box as it was dragged back to the previous stop point. It was now or never as Edon dug the digger's claw through the remaining bridge of earth, to break through to the channels that would feed the fields.

Alex didn't need to look to know that the water was now surging though to the fields beyond, like the release from a dam because he could hear the rushing water and the cheers of all the people standing there, not believing this could actually be possible. The farmer was the first to hug him and thank him but he was followed by seemingly everyone else there, who appreciated the significance of this to the farm and to their day to day work. Eventually, he was able to excuse himself with the need to go and open up the other entry point further along the river bank. He was hoping that he would also get the chance to sit down and weep because the need to do so was the overriding emotion he was feeling but they all insisted they wanted to watch this also and so it was only when he sat down on his bed later that night, that he could truly let go and he wept uncontrollably into his hands because he had never felt so happy or so wanted.

CHAPTER 35

If Alex had found the life of a farm worker hard, it had almost broken Brad, the youngest of the Duncan brothers who had never been into the physical activities and games his two elder brothers had thrived on. They had laughed at his attempts to play football or get involved in the boxing lessons their father had insisted upon. Especially Phil, who he loved but who could be cruel in his comments and in his over enthusiastic attempts to toughen him up. He suddenly stopped what he was doing and tried to come to terms with the full comprehension that his eldest brother was no longer alive and that here he was thinking badly of Phil, when he would give anything to hear him calling him names again. It wasn't bullying, he was just trying to help him become a man. What else could he have done when his father had been the role model, never accepting weakness or a desire to do anything other than what he had planned out for his three sons? He was destined to maintain the family business, even if Brad hated any association with the misery his family caused. But he realised that he was really no better than any of the other thugs who worked for the family firm because he just went along with it all. And now they had their own misery to endure, not just being, literally slaves but having Phil thrown from an aeroplane by the monsters who had captured them all. Who could do such a thing? And in thinking the question he looked around, as if someone close by, would be able to see his thoughts, because he was ashamed to admit that it was people like his father, who could and would do such a thing.

    A couple of months into his predicament, Brad had just about got used to the drudgery of the long hard days and the isolation, made worse by the fact that none of the other workers would barely acknowledge him, let alone speak to him. He had looked for ways to escape but without money and a phone and seemingly in the back of beyond, it seemed almost impossible. Once he had stolen the farm truck when all the rest of the workers were enjoying the daily siesta but such was the community spirit of the area, he was soon stopped by a roadblock of vehicles from other farms who had obviously been contacted to look out for him. Attempts to bribe or threaten anyone was laughed off and he was loathe to attempt an escape again without a fully formed plan because the beating he had suffered when he was unceremoniously returned to the farm after his last attempt, was not something he fancied repeating any time soon.

He would have to get hold of some money or a phone but at present that seemed a forlorn hope. The only bright part of his miserable life was Zerina, the farmer's daughter, and one of the most beautiful creatures he had ever seen. She was nothing like the plasticised, high maintenance girls he was used to. Devoid of make up and dressed very simply, she had a charm that he found difficult to understand. She would teach the village children each day, under the shade of a tree or throughout the winter in one of the barns. The children would arrive mostly by foot, being almost as excited to see their teacher as Brad was to see her. Perhaps it was her wonderful smile and obvious passion for what she was doing that attracted the children but Brad realised that it was more than that. They actually loved her because she quite obviously loved them. He'd had teachers like that but his dad had got him out of school as soon as he could. Having said that, he had never had teachers who looked like Zerina and any excuse he could find to carry out a task where he could watch her, he would take.

He got the impression that she was aware of his sly looks and sometimes she would look around suddenly to catch him staring and she would raise an eyebrow before returning to her task with a dismissive shake of the head. On the first occasion this had happened, Brad was petrified that she might have told her father and he would suffer the unpleasant consequences but it seemed that she didn't think him worthy of any such consideration as there were no consequences.

One day, when he had been mucking out the shed where they kept the few cows they maintained for milk and manure, he was able to observe the children and Zerina using large pieces of chalk to decorate small rocks that they had collected earlier. At the end of the day when clearing up, he found that one of the pieces of chalk had been left out by mistake. That evening, after his meal, he was normally allowed to do what he wanted for an hour or two before he was locked in his hut, such was their confidence that he couldn't escape. Taking the piece of chalk he had found, he walked to the barn where the children would have their lessons if the weather was not suitable to be outside and feeling an elation he had yearned for, he began to exercise the creative side of his nature that had been made to lie dormant for so long.

The next morning as Zerina walked from the farmhouse towards the teaching barn, she could see that the children, who had already arrived, were standing around the side of the barn in a state of true excitement. On reaching them she could see that they were laughing at the drawing of a large cartoon dinosaur poking its tongue out, seemingly at whoever was looking at it. She could not resist a smile but her overwhelming emotion was amazement at the quality of the drawing and bemusement as to how it had got there. On questioning the children she was none the wiser. The next day a similar sight greeted her as she approached the barn but the excitement seemed to be multiplied from the day before and on reaching the barn she could see why. There was a female with facial features remarkably similar to her own, being chased by a bull wearing a mortar board and gown and wielding a cane. The children were in paroxysms of laughter and while it was all she could do not to laugh out loud herself, she sternly told them to get inside and prepare for their lessons.

That evening Brad, having finished his evening meal, took his rapidly diminishing piece of chalk and made his way to the teaching barn, looking forward to what had become a huge part of his day. While he only allowed himself about an hour for the drawings, so as not to attract the attention of the men whose job it was to lock him up at night, it had immediately assumed a disproportionate occupancy of his mind, as the one thing that gave him any real pleasure in his captivity. He had decided to focus on drawings featuring a couple of the children each night while the chalk remained. He had barely begun when to his horror he heard footsteps behind him and as he turned the accusation, "So it is you who has been desecrating my lovely school."

Zerina looked at him with a look of disgust on her face but it wasn't that, or the surprise that this was the first English he had heard spoken for almost two months but rather the fear that he would be in for another beating that occupied his thoughts. Then he spotted that Zerina was starting to smile as she added, "For someone who is not a very nice person, you are a very talented artist." The opportunity to actually speak to someone who could understand him did not prevent him from stumbling over his reply now that he was face to face with the object that had filled his thoughts every waking hour of every day.

"I understand why you would think the first part of your statement to be true but the bit about me being a talented artist is highly exaggerated I think. But how is it that you speak such good English, I thought nobody here would understand me?"

"There are many here who can get by in English but have no desire to speak with someone like you, who has caused so much misery to our friends and families. Why would they?"

Brad looked down at his feet and tried to find some explanation to answer the accusation implicit in what Zerina had said but could not come up with anything that would be plausible, as he had for a long time thought the same.

"You obviously know a great deal about my background and I cannot say anything to put right what has happened in the past but I can assure you that I am suffering for it now."

"You think this is suffering? You have no idea. This life you have and your supposed suffering, is nowhere near to the same extent as the people you enslave in your own country but while you cannot put it right, you could start to make an effort to make up for what you have done."

"How can I do that over and above the work I do for your father."

"That is something you have no choice over so it does not count. Perhaps if you were to do something that was voluntary."

"Such as?"

"Well, I am very comfortable teaching the maths and science to the children but the arts subjects do not come naturally to me. Perhaps you could do some art with the children because, despite what you say, you do have a talent."

"Even if I wanted to, the only free time I have is on a Sunday when the children do not come to school."

"I could persuade my father to let you help me for an hour a day but you would have to make up the time lost elsewhere."

It didn't take Brad long to think this over, as the break from the monotony of work was encouragement enough but to be able to spend time with Zerina would have been all that was needed to sway his decision anyway. He didn't want to sound too eager however, so he nonchalantly put his head to one side as if he were contemplating the pros and cons before dragging out a, "Well I suppose I could manage that."

And so it was arranged that at 11.00am each day, he would make his way from the fields, to what was optimistically called the school room and encourage the children in basic artwork that he could just about recall from his own time at school. At first, all they wanted him to do was to produce more cartoons for them and were especially thrilled when he would do caricatures of them or their family members, some of whom worked on the farm. But gradually he began to see their desire to produce work of their own, as it dawned on them that they didn't have to be able to draw and that there were other materials other than paint and brushes with which they could create the ideas and emotions that took their fancy that day. So the art lessons developed into Biology lessons as they explored their natural surroundings for the materials that they thought would best suit their creative ideas on any particular day. These were the days that Brad loved best because unlike the pure painting and drawing sessions when Zerina would take the opportunity to prepare for her next lessons, on the days when they went looking for materials, she would join them to explain the scientific or geographical points of interest that might arise with each discovery. On these occasions Brad and Zerina would often be physically close, to the extent that he realised that not only did she look fantastic but she smelt of the soap and shampoo she used every day, a smell unlike any of the expensive perfumes so many of the girls he had known would dowse themselves in but one of the purity of the countryside and the Mediterranean air.

They would frequently end up laughing together at the antics of the children and Brad began to look forward to these moments more and more, even though he had to make up for the hour of work missed either before breakfast or in the evening. With pictures from books provided by Zerina, Brad helped produce the Mehndi henna patterns on the hands and arms of the children and make gifts for their parents as Eid approached. Zerina suggested that as quite a few of the children were from Christian families, they should put on a nativity play with all the children involved as part of their religious education and Brad felt elated by the freedom to use the creative side of his persona that for so long had been quashed and discouraged from being developed. It appeared also that more boys were starting to attend the school with the knowledge that there was a male present and Zerina asked him if he would do some PE activities more suited to the boys as she was limited in that area.

One morning, as Brad was washing the brushes and other equipment that they had been using that day, Zerina nudged him and pointed at a small boy called George. "You have a bit of a fan there you know."

"What do you mean? He is just helping me clear up."

"He follows you wherever you go and hangs on your every word." Brad realised after some thought, that he did seem to find George hanging around him much of the time. "He's obviously a boy of immaculate taste," he said to deflect the embarrassment he felt.

"Or perhaps," replied Zerina, "because he has no father he looks to you as some sort of role model."

"Oh, what happened to his father, don't tell me he's dead?"

"No he went to Britain with the promise of a job so that he could send back the money he was going to make but nobody has heard anything from him for nearly two years now," she answered with a meaningful glare. Brad was glad that it was time for him to get back to work, so that he could avoid where this difficult conversation was leading. Unfortunately, his brain did not want to leave the conversation however, and he spent the rest of the day turning it over in his mind until he felt thoroughly depressed.

The fact that none of the other men wanted anything to do with him and the backbreaking nature of the work would have broken him, if it hadn't been for the oasis of delight in every day when he could spend that time with Zerina and he had to grudgingly admit, the children, who he was growing more fond of by the day, especially George, who seemed to find excuses to be with him whenever he could, much to Brad's guilty pleasure.

It had been three months and more since his capture when, on one particular Sunday while Brad sat watching the blue waters of the Mediterranean glistening on the horizon, he suddenly became aware of a presence and looked up to see Mick, the man who had thrown his brother Philip from the aeroplane, standing over him.

"Can I join you?"

"It seems that you can do what the F*** you like but don't expect me to welcome you with open arms you murdering b*****d."

"I think I could accept that with some degree of understanding if it wasn't muttered by a member of the Duncan family. People in glass houses and so on."

"You didn't need to do that…"

"He wouldn't do as he was asked and he deserved everything that he got. Explain to me if you would, how seven years ago a mother and her two children deserved to be mown down and killed on a pedestrian crossing in Blaby?"

A memory he had tried to bury years ago seemed to reach down and squeeze his heart. How on earth did this gorilla know about that? "I don't know what you are talking about."

"You and I both know that you are fully aware of what I am talking about and I could list many other similar incidents that you would rather people did not know about I am sure, but that is not why I am here, so let's change the subject shall we?"

"Fair enough but I will never forgive you for what you did to my brother."

"Upset as I am not to have your approval, I will learn to live with it I am sure. Now the reason I am here is that while I get regular feedback on your, shall we say progress, from farmer Bektashi, we feel it is a good idea to visit you now and again to actually see how you are getting on."

"My living conditions are awful and I am treated like a sl…" Brad decided to change the wording of what he was going to say so as not to add further fuel to what was obviously burning inside this man he had to deal with, "I'm made to work ridiculously hard every waking hour but otherwise everything is hunky-dory."

"From what I know, your living conditions and certainly your food are far better than anything the equivalent poor sods enslaved by you and your family would experience. But it seems that you have turned a bit of a corner in that, not only are they pleased with your work, now that you have toughened up quite a bit but you seem to actually be doing something for reasons other than just your own personal reward."

"What's it to you?" replied Brad trying hard to maintain the image of the stroppy and self-confident gangster, when in fact he felt surprisingly pleased to have his efforts recognised.

"In all honesty, having met the lovely Zerina, farmer Bektashi's daughter, I am not totally convinced that your actions are not without an ulterior motive but I should warn you that should you try it on with his daughter, the punishment you would receive from us at the end of your incarceration will no longer be an issue for you because you will not be around for us to deal with. But that is a warning that hopefully is not needed because I am going to give you the benefit of the doubt and assume you are partially at least, a reformed character. So to ensure we treat you brothers equally, because you have made an effort to be unselfish in your actions we are going to offer you a gift of your choice, within reason of course."

"You have seen Alex. How is he? What has he done to deserve a gift and is he all right?"

"He is as well as can be expected and that is all I am prepared to say on the matter. Now, is there anything you would like?"

Brad thought before answering, even though there had been something he had wanted to try to do but lacked the resources to achieve it. "Does it have to be something material or can it be asking you to carry out a task for me?"

"Let me know what you have in mind and we will see if it is possible."

"There is a boy who attends school here called George Ahmetti. Two years ago his father went to Britain and it looks like he became employed by one of the slave gangs. I have no idea if it is one run by my family or someone else but either way I would like you to find him and bring him back. If you agree to do this I will give you the name of someone you can contact in England who will be able to find out where he is."

"That is some request and what makes you think that even if I could find him, we would be able to get him away?"

"I think you have already proven that your lot, whoever you are, are more than capable of dealing with whatever you might come up against."

"Even if we could do what you have asked, this is a more expensive gift in terms of cost and resources than we were expecting. Are you sure you wouldn't like something simpler and a little more to your personal benefit?"

"No, if it's not this then I want nothing else from you, as I never want to be personally beholden to you for anything, as that might spoil my pleasure when I eventually get even with you."

"Fair enough but what you have asked for will involve a massive undertaking and I cannot guarantee firstly, that we can do it, or secondly that we will."

"Then there is no more to be gained from this conversation."

Mick nodded, got up and returned in the direction of the farm house.

Over the following couple of months, Brad spent many an evening considering the conversation he had had with Mick and was annoyed to admit that in all his dealings with this very unassuming but deadly man, he had always come across as fair and respectful and much of what he said about Brad's own previous character hit very close to home. As for his request to find George's father, he held out no hope whatsoever. He had to admit that he had not only started to get used to his life on the farm but had also come to the awareness that he really enjoyed many aspects of this lifestyle. This could have been because the weather was getting warmer and the days longer as spring approached summer but he knew that a lot of it was to do with his daily contact with Zerina who seemed to now see him at least as a friend and no longer as someone to be despised or pitied. The thing that nagged at him most however, was the fact that none of the other workers would have anything to do with him and this made the working day so very tedious, being unable to join in the banter and back and forth that made the workplace acceptable the whole world over, whatever the nature of the job. He mentioned this to Zerina one day when the children were engrossed in a task, without the need for teacher input. She looked at him with eyebrows raised as if he was stupid to even have to ask.

"They all have someone who has been trafficked by you or your like. People they love and hold dear. My father was loathe to have you on the farm when first asked because he felt he could not guarantee your safety. His workers are good people and have only accepted your presence as a favour to my father. But be under no illusion, my father is only putting up with this because he is being well paid. He also has reason to hate you and want you harmed."

That night, Brad lay in his bed and thought about what Zerina had said and knew that she was right and that his life up until now, had resulted only in misery for others and certainly no real happiness for him. He promised himself then, that whatever happened to him, when this was all over and he finished what was likely to be a lengthy prison term, he would make sure that no one would have reason to ever hate him again.

A few days later, he mentioned to Zerina that she must be pleased that now summer was approaching the children would be able to learn at least in a warm environment.

"Ha, unfortunately we will always suffer one way or the other. While it is freezing in the winter, in the summer our teaching barn is too hot and we struggle to find shade for the whole class outside."

Brad had walked past a totally collapsed old barn each day as he walked from his hut to the communal dining area. He asked Zerina if her father would allow him the tools and nails to carry out a partial rebuild of a building, with open sides to offer shade and allow the breeze in.

"When would you carry out such a task?"

"I would do it in my spare time on a Sunday."

"You would do that for the children?"

'No', thought Brad, I would do it for you but replied, "No of course not, its just that I don't want to be burned to a frazzle when I am helping you in there."

"What is a frazzle?" she laughed but was privately delighted that Brad was showing the type of person she had recently suspected and hoped he was.

Finding it impossible to ignore any request from his only daughter, Farmer Bektashi agreed to what he thought would be a half-hearted attempt at building by the soft English gangster. And so it was, that the next Sunday, Brad started clearing the wood from the fallen barn and rescuing the least-damaged of the timber. He had only been working for about an hour, when he suddenly realised that George had somehow found out what was going on and was now helping him by copying everything Brad did. Smiling at his efforts to lift wood way too big and too heavy for him, Brad gave George a hammer and the task of removing the nails from the wood on the pile that was going to be used in the rebuilding. Apart from the difference in their respective tasks, George replicated Brad in everything he did, including his mannerisms, resting when he did, taking a drink when he did and sighing when he did. Unfortunately, he also swore when Brad got a splinter in his hand and uttered a word that young boys should not be aware of even if they could not understand the meaning.

    By mid afternoon, having carried on through the usual siesta time, Brad had to pretend to finish for the day to ensure that George went home, and allow Brad to do a few more hours. On the second Sunday, Brad was ready to start erecting the building and of course little George was waiting for him when he arrived at the prepared pile of wood. Having dug holes for the uprights, Brad would concrete the base of the posts, while George supported them so that they stayed vertical until Brad could put wooden battens in place to hold them in situ while the concrete dried. All the time, George would look up at Brad for approval and would generate the most wonderful smile when he received it, followed by a shouted repetition of the swear word he had heard and re-uttered the week before. With the uprights in place and with the concrete needing time to set, Brad sent a reluctant George home and sat in the warmth of the late spring sun, realising that he had rarely felt so at ease with himself and his life. If he could only forget the reason he was here.

    The following week was a special one in the local village calendar, as it was the celebration of an annual feast where all the surrounding villages would converge on the main town of the region to celebrate the Eid al-Fitr, the Muslim festival for "Breaking the fast". There had been some argument in the Bektashi household as someone had to stay and keep an eye on Brad if he were not to be locked in for the day and also look after farmer Bektashi's ailing mother. Zerina had volunteered but it was felt socially unacceptable to leave a young woman alone with a young man, especially one with the reputation that Brad had gained for himself. It was agreed eventually, that Zerina would stay to look after her grandmother while one of the farm hands Merghim, who was miserable at the best of times and had no desire to attend the feast where everyone else would be enjoying themselves, would stay also and keep an eye on Brad. It was also felt wise to take the only key to the only remaining pick up truck with them to the feast, so that Brad would not be able to steal the vehicle and escape, should he find a way of eluding Merghim.

Brad remained in bed listening to the revving of engines and the laughter and excited chatter of the family and their workers as they prepared to leave for the feast. Once they had disappeared, he went to the makeshift canteen where bread, cheese and ham had been left for him and once fed, began work on the schoolroom project. He was disappointed but realised he shouldn't be surprised, that George had put the more exciting prospect of the feast before the idea of working with Brad on the schoolhouse. Nonetheless, Brad had to keep swatting away the pin pricks of jealousy that kept entering his thoughts and chastising himself for being annoyed that the boy was not showing the affection for him he rather pathetically revelled in. He became even more irrationally irritated later, when Zerina brought a drink and chatted to Merghim who had been sitting under a tree, supposedly watching him but being asleep more than awake. Just then a commotion from three women crying and shouting, while carrying something in a blanket between them, made the three occupants of the farm turn in alarm towards the farm entrance, from where the noise emanated. The women carefully placed the bundle on the ground in front of Zerina and gabbled at her while frantically pulling at her clothes. Brad ran across to see that she was safe but was then aghast to see that lying on the sheet the women had been carrying, was George and he was whiter even than the sheet that had been used as a makeshift stretcher.

"What's happened to George? What are these women saying?"

"George has been feeling ill for some days but through the night this has got much worse and they think he is dying."

"Why haven't they taken him to a doctor?"

"Everyone is at the feast and there are no vehicles or anyone to drive him to hospital."

"Why haven't they called an ambulance?"

"They have no phone which is why they have come here but by the time an ambulance gets through the crowds in the town, it could be too late."

"Then let's get him in the truck and take him ourselves."

"We don't have the keys because Papa didn't trust you," she answered accusingly.

Realising that he could hardly blame farmer Bektashi, Brad grabbed George and ran to the truck, telling Zerina to tell his mother and one of the other women to sit in the back of the truck to support George, who he handed to them very carefully when they were in place.

"What are you going to do?" Zerina demanded as she grabbed his arm.

But Brad sat in the driver's seat ignoring the gun that Merghim was nervously pointing at him and smashed open the plastic covering around the steering wheel, to gain access to the wiring that he pulled out and proceeded to reconnect in a way that he had learned long ago when hot-wiring cars in his youth. As the engine roared into life, Zerina jumped in beside him and waved Merghim away, while telling Brad that she was coming with him.

"You don't trust me not to run away is that it?"
"No, it is that you have no idea where you are going and because you are stupid, you have not learned to speak the language that could help you."

She has a point thought Brad as he manoeuvred the truck out of the farm yard and onto the dirt track road that led to the major road system. Once under way, Zerina was amazed at how fast he could get the old truck to go and yet, while travelling so quickly he was also doing all he could to ensure the truck did not bump or sway around with the precious cargo they had in the back. The Town was about twenty miles away but as they entered the outskirts, it soon became apparent that the closer they got to the centre of the town where the hospital was, the roads were getting more and more clogged up by people walking to the feast. With the horn blaring making no noticeable difference, as others were also peeping their car horns in celebration, Brad realised they had to stop.

"Right we will have to go by foot," he shouted over his shoulder to Zerina, as he jumped out of the truck and ran around to the back. He grabbed George in his arms and as Zerina explained to George's mother and aunt that they would have to complete the journey on foot, they set off running. The revellers seemed oblivious and totally ignored the shouts of the odd group led by an attractive young woman and a rather dirty looking man, carrying a small child in the direction of the hospital but also the festival. Zerina realised that while in terms of distance it would be longer, a quicker route would be through the backstreets. Brad's arms were in agony at the exertion of running and carrying but he recognised that the muscles and endurance he had developed over his time in captivity, along with his determination not to let his little friend die, had provided him with some quality within himself he never knew he possessed.

At last, they reached the hospital and as they ran into reception, Zerina shouted for help and she was quickly joined by a couple of nurses who, after hearing a brief explanation from the mother, had Brad place George on a trolley and called for a porter, who rushed him off to a room where a doctor soon materialised. Brad could only look on and listen to the unintelligible back and forth between George's mother and the doctor. The curtains were drawn and Zerina came back out to him."

"How is he?"

"It looks bad but the doctor is examining him now."

"I really hope he is going to be ok."

"He has more of a chance now than he would have had if you had not acted so decisively. Thank you."

"It is ironic perhaps, that the only time in my life when some of the less admirable skills I have learned in that life, could actually do some good rather than harm and yet it could all be for nothing if the little man doesn't make it."

"You have done all you could."

"I am of no use here now. I think I should go back."

Brad could see her considering the implications of him going but finally coming to a conclusion, "Yes, you go. I should stay and support his family. Do you think you will be able to find your way back to the truck?"

"Yes I think so." He could feel her eyes looking into his as if trying to judge whether or not she could trust him.

"OK then you go. We can ask no more of you here," and she touched his hand with a look of gratitude and, he thought, a signal of permission to be free if that was what he wanted.

As Brad worked his way back in the direction of the truck and against the flow of the revellers moving towards the centre of town, he considered the fact that this was his chance to escape. He could drive to Tirana the capital city, as he had seen signs on the main road into the town, with the picture of an aeroplane and the name of what he assumed was the capital city on the gantries above the road. He could easily get hold of a mobile from some unsuspecting victim and contact his father to provide him with money and a ticket out of the hell he had been living. By the time he reached the truck and got the engine started again he had made up his mind and having driven out of the town to the major road leading one way to the capital city and the other towards the farm, he looked back towards where Zerina would be in the hospital and with the determination of a decision made, pulled out into the traffic.

Later that evening, Zerina's taxi dropped her off in front of the farm house and her mother and father, who had returned early from the feast when she had phoned them with news of what had happened to George, ran out to greet her with hugs and many questions. She burst into tears of relief at the sudden comfort of knowing that whatever happened, her parents were there to protect her but also at the sight of the old truck parked where it had been left that morning and signifying something far more than just the fact that Brad had not grabbed the opportunity to run away. Her parents told her that he was back at the farm when they retuned and that he had been working on the schoolhouse. She excused herself and went to Brad's hut and knocked and asked if it would be all right for her to come in. Brad shouted back a delighted, "Yes. How is George?"

She pulled back the bolt that locked him in and opened the door to find him standing at the door eagerly waiting for news.

"When I left he was in theatre, having an emergency operation for a burst appendix. It is touch and go but, if we hadn't got him to hospital so quickly he would definitely have died. I cannot thank you enough for your actions."

"But he is still in danger?"

"I am afraid so yes. We will know more in the morning after the operation."

"Thank you for letting me know." As tears of relief and fear began to come to his eyes he turned away and thanked Zerina for coming to tell him but he would like her to leave now. Rather than be offended, Zerina recognised the situation for what it was and as she closed and locked the door and acknowledged, that the feelings she had been finding confusing of late, had crystallised into something she had only rarely felt before. And were connected totally to this man who she knew she should loathe.

When he arrived at the canteen the following day, it was the first time that Brad had encountered some of his fellow workmates actually acknowledge him, even if it was only a nod. Farmer Bektashi even made the effort to come in and shake him by the hand and say in broken English. "Well done. Yesterday you do good thing."

Brad felt a surge of emotion and surprise, that such small actions could have such a huge effect on his feelings about himself and his situation. The work that day seemed to be so much more enjoyable, simply because he seemed after all this time to be accepted by the people he worked with, even if they were unable to express any of their thoughts through words. Despite this, the morning dragged until he was able to join Zerina at the schoolroom to find, much to his distress, that George was still under sedation and it was still touch and go whether or not he would survive. Zerina told him that that evening she was going to join some of the Christian families along with George's relatives at the village church, to pray for the little boy and she wondered whether Brad would like to also join them.

Insignificant as his association with religion had been since he was a small lad and his mother, who he could barely remember, would take him to the local Baptist church, Brad agreed immediately with the thought that if there was a chance of anything helping George, he was prepared to give it a go. So after the evening meal, he and Zerina walked into the village saying little, so focused were they on George's predicament and once in the church they sat separately and prayed in their own way to their own God. At first, Brad felt strange and uncomfortable but the longer he sat there staring at the crucified son of God filling the front of the church, a feeling of calm and deep serenity came over him. It seemed as if a film of his life was being played within his mind, not flashing before him as was supposed to happen when you were dying, but this film was seemingly playing at normal speed until those moments when he had been at his most happy and then the film appeared to slow down, allowing him to recognise what it really was that made him happy, usually featuring his mother, his brothers or the last few months but never, he realised, his father. In fact, this film of his life probably lasted less than half an hour but at the end of it, he looked up at at the cruciform image dominating his eyeline and vowed that if George came through his ordeal, he would change and would become the person he knew he could and should be.

    Strolling back with Zerina in the warm night summer air, Brad felt a tranquillity that he had rarely felt before. Yes, he was churning up inside about George's condition but for some reason he felt calmer about it and the presence of Zerina gladdened his heart beyond anything he had experienced before. They chatted about nothing in particular and she laughed at his attempts at humour and playfully admonished his clumsiness when he tripped over a loose stone. Just before they arrived back at the farm, she touched his shoulder to stop him and facing him said, "I know that you have done bad things in the past but you are a good person deep down and I thank God that your goodness has become a part of our lives here."

    With that, she softly kissed him on the cheek and ran off into the farmhouse. Brad stood there staring in total surprise and delight for some time, before floating back to his hut to enjoy a sleep filled with the dreams of possibility. When he arose to leave the hut the next morning, he realised that they had forgotten to lock his door and when he got to the canteen the other workers stood and clapped to his utter bemusement, until Zerina came out to tell him that George had woken up and that he would almost certainly recover totally.

"Perhaps, those prayers actually made a difference," Brad offered to cover his embarrassment.

"I am sure they did but perhaps what really gave George the strength and desire to come back to us was hearing the sound of his father's voice."

"I don't understand."

"Yesterday afternoon, your 'friend' Mick turned up with George's father and very soon after, George woke up."

"That is wonderful news on two counts."

"Yes," replied Zerina, "and it is the case I think, that you had something to do with his re-appearance."

"I can take no credit for solving a problem that I might very well have been responsible for creating."

"Yes in your past life you did things you should not but we all spend our lives trying to put right the wrongs we have committed and that is how we develop as human beings. You have done much to fill your ledger with 'ticks' since you have been here."

"I am afraid they will never outnumber the 'crosses' I have put in that ledger over the years but I suppose I have made a start." And in his mind, Brad took a metaphorical look up to the sky as if to acknowledge the debt he now needed to continue to repay for George's return to good health.

The following Sunday, now he no longer had to wait for his hut to be unbolted because, since that first day when he thought they had forgotten to lock him in, it seems that they now trusted him not to run. He rose earlier than usual with the intention of starting early and finishing the last bit of work on the Summer schoolhouse. He had been grafting away for some hours and the heat of the day was causing the perspiration to run off him in rivulets, when he heard a car pulling up in the farm yard. Out of it climbed a man he had never seen before and then to his utter joy he watched as George's mother climbed out of the car and the man reached into the back seat to bring out the small bundle of joy that was George.

They all came over to Brad who climbed down from the ladder to be smothered in hugs from the mother and at the same time he felt more hugs around his legs from George. The man stood back and watched all this with an uncertain look on his face and Brad in his delight at seeing George, suddenly realised that this man could very easily want to kill him and he felt he could hardly blame him. The mother stepped back and pulled George away and the two men faced each other. George's father moved towards Brad, looked him in the eye and put out his hand and simply said, "Thank you. I owe you my son's life."

At a loss as to what to say for some moments, Brad swallowed his shame and embarrassment and replied, "It is I who owe you an apology, which I know I can never fully pay back."

"You have done that and more. What happened to me was not down to you but people like you once were. Apparently you are not that man anymore and I know that my boy George is a fine judge of character and he cannot stop talking about you. If he likes you, then so do I."

Brad was touched by the magnanimity of what George's father must have found so difficult to say, knowing full well that he had every reason to hate him. His thoughts were interrupted by George's mother giving him a large cake and George himself, who was still physically subdued while his recovery continued but emotionally exploding, asking his father a question. He then repeated it to Brad, having translated it into English.

"George wants to know when the building will be finished?"

"Please tell him that I have just completed the finishing touches with the sign across the eaves being the final flourish."

They all looked up and the smile on George's face blossomed into a look of utter delight, as they all read the sign that read in Albanian and English, 'George's Schoolroom'.

After they had left, due to George needing his rest, Brad was able to sit under the shade of a beech tree and contemplate how the last few months had affected him and while he accepted that he could have done without the physical labour and being shunned by his fellow workers, he had rarely been happier than he felt now. He thought about how fantastic it must be for George's father to know that he was loved so much that he could bring his son out of a coma. That then morphed into a picture in his mind, of the reaction his own father would have had on his sons in a similar circumstance but the thought was too painful and he moved on to the miracle itself of George's dad being found and brought to his son's bedside. It must have been that b*****d Mick who had done it. The same bloke who had pushed his brother out of the plane. He could never forgive him that but he did know how much time, effort and resources, must have gone into the finding of George's father and then extracting him from what would almost certainly be pretty vicious gang masters.

That evening, he shared his cake with the other workers and Farmer Bektashi brought out bottles of wine and beer that he had augmented with those provided by George's father and it seemed that the acceptance granted by George's father, had encouraged the other workers to follow suit and Brad had the added bonus of finally being accepted by his work mates as someone who had more about him than they had first been led to believe. But the highlight of the evening was when Zerina came and sat with him, away from all the others and kissed him on his cheek and simply said, "Thank you."

For the first time in his life he, who had always been so confident with girls, started to blush and he mumbled something inane like, "It was nothing."

"No, it was something very special, not just in helping to save George but in saving his father also. I have known for some time what a good person you really are but now even the others are beginning to believe it."

"Do you really think I am a good person, because if I am honest, I can think of many reasons to contradict you?"

"For someone who was so brash and cocky when you first came here, you are remarkably naïve in reading people's feelings. Do you not know that I have strong feelings for you?"

Brad's hopes soared at the words he could only have dreamt about and in fact, had dreamt about.

"Why didn't you tell me? Surely you knew that I felt the same but never thought anything between us would ever be possible."

She looked at him with a sadness that made his heart clench.

"Nothing could ever happen between us, even if my parents would allow it, although my mother would be more easily persuaded than my father. Soon you will be leaving my country and from what I hear, you will be spending some time in prison. I cannot put my life on hold on the off chance that you might still feel the same about me in however many years to come."

Despite himself, he realised the sense of what she had said but could not give up. "Zerina, I have known many girls but I have never felt what I feel for you and I will never feel any different however long it takes. You are the most wonderful person I have ever met and the thought of spending the rest of my life with you would complete me."

"You should not say such things, as neither of us knows how we will feel after years of not seeing each other and developing into people who reflect the environment they will have lived in during that time apart."

Brad recognised that she was politely not referring directly to the effect prison might have on him and also that it was unfair for him to expect her to wait for him and miss out on the opportunities that life throws up while he was being infected by the miasma of influences a life in prison would ensure. But he also knew that if he was a better person now than when he arrived, much of that was down to her influence.

"You are right, I know but please do not give up on me. You must live your life to the full but I am going to do all I can to be there with you."

She looked at him sadly. "Even if I cannot hold you in my arms, I will always hold you in my heart. But for now we should simply enjoy what time we have together before you leave."

He smiled and nodded agreement, while his heart constricted at the thought of what his past life was going to see him miss out on. That night, he lay in bed, bereft with longing for what might have been but determined to do all in his power to never be in this position ever again.

CHAPTER 36

When their spell of captivity was up, the brothers left what had been their home for the last year with a heavy heart. This was something they could not have imagined when they woke up on that first morning, after being locked in their hut. Brad and Alex's sadness was lightened somewhat, when they were reunited but darkened again when they were placed in a container for their return trip to the UK. They were told that this was the final part of their punishment, to enable them to 'enjoy' the full trafficking experience. When they eventually climbed out of the container after two days of travel across the continent, they had both vowed that they would never put anyone through that horror again.

They were now sitting in a room with Mick and Ernie standing over them, having been told to wait. After a short time the door opened and to the utter shock of Alex and Brad, in through the door walked Phillip followed by Dougie. The three boys stared at each other in utter shock and then rushed into a group hug with Brad and Alex sobbing in delight and amazement. Phillip, embarrassed by all the fuss told his brothers to stop acting like little girls.

"But how is this possible?" asked Brad. "We saw you thrown out of the aeroplane and assumed you must have died."

"Yeah well these b******s obviously wanted you to think that, to help keep you in your place so that the same or similar did not happen to you."

"But how did you survive the fall?" Alex asked incredulously.

"Ask pigface here," Phillip answered angrily and nodded to Dougie, who explained by reminding Brad and Alex that back in the aeroplane, immediately after Phillip had been thrown through the door, their faces had been turned from the open door of the plane and pressed into the floor. But if they had been able to see what actually happened, then they would have seen Dougie immediately follow their brother out of the plane and in sky diving mode, hurtle through the sky towards Phillip's falling and screaming body, in a version of the practices the SAS regularly carried out, to ensure they could help a colleague who got into difficulty should their parachute not open. Dougie explained how, as he closed in on their brother, he prepared his harness and on contact, grabbed the falling body with one arm, while attaching Phillip to his harness with his free hand.

Unsurprisingly, there was no fighting from their brother, not because he was aware that this might affect the help he was receiving but because he had fainted. Dougie smiled at the eldest brother as he scowled at this part of the story and then continued. It was probably also not surprising that, as he came back to consciousness a thousand feet from the ground, he screamed and grabbed Dougie as tightly as he could, still apparently not gaining any of the enjoyment people usually remember from their first parachute jump. The actual landing was awkward but painless as their brother seemed by then to be quite keen to take on board the advice he was given, to avoid breaking his legs. "In fact your brother now seemed in no mood to argue with me about anything and as we came into land, did just as he was told.

Phillip did not enjoy hearing again the story of what had happened on that day. As Dougie took pleasure in reciting the story, Phillip thought back to how it had affected him. Once on the ground, Phillip lay sobbing for some time, before he was actually able to move or communicate. He had no time to wallow in his near death experience because shortly after Dougie had collected together his parachute, a truck arrived and he had his hands tied before being thrown in the back of the truck which was then driven off over the bumpy field, until the smoother surface of a tarmacked road saw the truck pick up speed.

Thinking back now over what had happened in the last year, it seemed much longer since the truck stopped at that Godforsaken farm in the middle of nowhere and he was thrown into a hut where he was locked in, so exhausted, that he dropped fully dressed, onto the bed that was more like a cot and fell into a deep but troubled sleep. A few times he would wake suddenly in the night in a cold sweat, as he could not get rid of that feeling of total fear, as his dreams kept returning to that moment when he was pushed out of the plane and thought he was going to die.

The following morning, when he knew he was unlikely to get any more sleep, he rose to see the note propped on the table opposite his bed that, unbeknown to him, his brothers had also had a copy to read in their own huts. 'If they think that is going to happen to me they have another thing coming,' he promised himself, before going to the door which he kicked and thumped while shouting "Let me out you b******s. You're going to regret this." After a few minutes of shouting, he was beginning to tire when a smile came over his face as he heard the bolt on his door being drawn back. 'I'll show these people who they are messing with,' he thought, before exclaiming. "About bloody t…" As the door swung open he was about to step out when he was hit by a jet of freezing water from a large hosepipe, that drove him back into his hut and sprawling on the floor. Dougie appeared at the door, gave him a pitying look and advised him. "If you behave like a heathen you will be treated like one. We'll try again tomorrow shall we?"

At that, he slammed the door and bolted it just before Phillip scrambled from the floor and ran at the door shouting and kicking once again. Having tired of that, he later tried a different approach and in a pitiful voice said he was hungry, which he was and that they needed to feed him. This quite obviously fell on deaf ears and he resorted to shouting, screaming and hitting walls repeatedly for most of the rest of the day, before collapsing in frustration and fatigue onto his bed. The next morning, Dougie opened the door to find a more subdued but seething Phillip waiting to be let out. Not being completely stupid however, he behaved himself as he was taken to get some food from a large hut that adjoined what he found out later to be a farm house. He pushed in front of a queue of men and began to grab the freshly cooked bread and cold cuts to sate the hunger that had been gnawing at him, not having eaten for almost two days. As he did so, a large hand clamped around his wrist forcing him to drop the food while its partner grabbed him by the shoulder lifted him off the ground and threw him out of the queue.

"How dare you touch me you…" but as he looked at who had just manhandled him, Phillip gulped at what could be described as the definition of the term 'man mountain' and decided that discretion was the better part of valour and sullenly joined the end of the queue. Later, as the men set off for the fields, Phillip refused to join them and so Dougie told him to return to his hut. On refusing to do so, Dougie hit him so hard in the solar plexus, that he was winded and buckled over, only to be caught by Dougie who then carried him to his hut. Once there, Dougie threw him on the bed and told a wheezing Phillip to listen carefully.

"You are a bully who has destroyed many lives. If you do not do as you are told, we will have no compunction in doing the same to you. This is your chance to prove that you can be a decent human being. Take it and you will benefit throughout the year before receiving your just rewards back in Britain. Abuse this chance you have been given and you will have a very difficult time. I am leaving today." On hearing this, Phillip began to forget the pain he was in and start to think that once Dougie was gone he would soon be back with his dad. But what he heard next gave him pause for thought. "However, before you get any ideas I should tell you that at least five of the men you will be working with, including the gentleman who took exception to you pushing in at the breakfast queue, have relatives who have been trafficked into modern slavery and know only too well about your past. If you think that I am a nasty b*****d, then just give them a reason to deal with you and you will realise what a pussycat I really am. Now you will be in this hut until tomorrow morning and you will not be fed because of your behaviour this morning but unlike the slaves you have working for you in Britain, you will have a chance to start again tomorrow morning."

"But that is not fair. I am starving, you cannot do this to me."

"Oh, grow up. I think you will find that I can and I have. The whole purpose of this, is to try to show you what it is like to live and be treated like a slave. But unlike your operation in England, here you will benefit from good behaviour. It is your choice. Now I will leave you and return in a couple of months to see how you are getting on."

As Dougie closed the door and left, the eldest Duncan boy muttered under his breath that there was no way he would be there in two weeks time, let alone two months. There is always someone who will take a bribe and he would be way too smart for these country bumpkins. Over the first few weeks of his captivity, Phillip Duncan tried everything he could to skive off the work he was asked to carry out but each time he did, he received an even harsher punishment than the one before. Stubborn as he was, he eventually realised that if he was to be in any fit state to organise an escape then he would, at least for the time being, toe the line and do as he was told. While he found the work absolutely back breaking, not having ever done any real physical work in his life before and finding out that working out in a comfy gym was nothing like the work that he was being asked to carry out here, he also realised that this was the best opportunity he would have to bribe one of the workers and get hold of a phone or the means to escape.

At first, the men he worked with seemed immune to the attempts he started to make to be friendly but gradually they made an effort with him, by coming to his aid when he was seemingly having difficulty with a particularly demanding task, or allowing him to sit with them at mealtimes, even though they made no attempt to include him in their conversations. And of course, that was the other problem. Hardly any of these 'morons' could speak English and so he realised that he would have to bide his time to build a relationship with one of the few English speakers. This task was made easier by the fact that for many of the jobs on the farm, the men worked in pairs and the farmer obviously thought it judicious to place him with Guzim, who could speak some English and could therefore explain to Phillip what had to be done during the working day. Guzim, despite his obvious dislike of his workmate, also saw it as an opportunity for him to improve his English and had ambitions to get a job working in the city, where such a skill would prove useful and not forever be grinding away on the land.

Picking up on Guzim's dream of a better life, Phillip constantly talked of the opportunities available to him if he could get a leg up and of course who better to give him a leg up than Phillip himself, who could promise him money and, if he wished, a job in England, where his father would be so grateful to him, that he would have a life he could only dream of. After over a month of dripping his ideas into the ears of a seemingly more and more enthusiastic Guzim and while they were working together trying to remove a tree from an area that the farmer had decided had the potential to be developed into more arable land, Phillip decided that the time was ripe to make his move.

"Guzim, if we are to get you the future you deserve then you and I need to get out of here."

"Why do I deserve better future?"

"You're obviously so much smarter than these other clowns we are working with. Why should you have to put up with working like a dog, when you have so much more to offer?"

"What would we do to get away?" Phillip's heart began to beat faster as he realised that his patience had paid off and he was going to find a way out of this mess.

"Can you get the keys to one of the vehicles?"

"Yes, that would be easy. We are allowed to borrow the vehicles outside work time if we need them."

"Then one night you borrow one of the vehicles and when everyone else is asleep, you come and unlock me from my hut and we drive towards the airport in Tirana. On the way, I will use your mobile phone and contact my father who will arrange for some of his Albanian contacts to meet us and get us out of this Godforsaken country and on to the luxurious life you will lead in England. By the time anyone realises we are missing, we will be safe and preparing to enjoy the next exciting part of our lives."

They arranged for their escape to take place on the following Sunday night, as everyone went to bed earlier on that night in preparation for work the next day and would be less alert after the high jinks of the weekend. Having made the arrangements, Phillip had to impatiently get through what had become his normal monotonous Sunday, as nobody bothered with him on the day when there was no work to be done and the only contact he had with anyone was at meal times, when he was still ignored. As he was locked in for the night as usual, he repeatedly sat on the edge of his bed, then paced back and forth across his small room, barely able to suppress the excitement of knowing he would soon be home and also planning how he would come back with some of his men and make these peasants who had made his life hell, suffer. At last he could hear the bolt being scraped back on the lock and the door was pushed open to reveal Guzim with his finger to his lips.

"Come," he whispered, "we must be quick." Phillip followed Guzim in a crouch as he ran soundlessly to the dirt road that ran around the back of the hut where he had been imprisoned all this time and led to the main road that would take him to freedom. Once in the truck that Guzim had chosen for their escape, they drove slowly to reduce the chance of being heard. Phillip told Guzim to pass him his phone so that he would be able to contact his father back in England as soon as they were on the main road. He needed the phone now, because he had no intention of Guzim being with him for very long and he wanted to make sure he had the phone so that he could take advantage of the first chance he had of getting rid of him. As they reached the end of the track that led onto the road, they had to come to a stop so that one of them could open the gate that blocked their exit. Phillip made the excuse that he needed to get through to his father as soon as possible, so Guzim should open the gate. As Guzim jumped down from the truck and went to the gate, Phillip grabbed his chance and slid across the bench seat into the driving seat and as Guzim unwittingly swung the gate open, Phillip put the truck into gear and pressed down hard on the accelerator, causing the truck to surge forward towards the main road.

The elation of freedom he experienced was suddenly quelled, as one of the large animal transportation trucks owned by the farm appeared in front of him blocking off his escape. Phillip turned his head to reverse back the way he came and find another exit, only to be dazzled by the headlights of another truck that had obviously been following them from when they had first set off but with its lights off. The eldest Duncan son screamed in frustration and hammered the steering wheel with his hands as he realised that all his hopes of escape had come to nothing. The door of the truck opened and he was dragged roughly from his seat and walked back towards the farmhouse before being thrown to the ground near some of the outbuildings. Seven of the farm labourers surrounded him and Guzim spat on the ground where he lay.

"You are an arrogant son of a bitch. Do you really think I would want to come and live the life that you crave and leave my family and friends? My sister was tricked into believing she would get a better life in your country but was lucky enough to escape before the fate her traffickers had planned could be carried out. She eventually came back to us after many tribulations. Most of these men here have family who have not been so lucky and we would all kill you now, if it were not for the fact that the men who captured you have promised us that they will bring back our family members if we keep you safe."

Phillip was terrified, but relaxed slightly with the news that they were to 'keep him safe'.

"But make no mistake, that does not mean that we are not free to punish you in any way we want." At a nod from Guzim the men surrounding Phillip began to kick and beat him while he writhed and squealed on the floor. They stopped at another signal from Guzim, just as he thought he could take no more.

"You call us morons, and clowns and treat us like shit. You, who treats people as animals to do your bidding. We will show you what shit really is." At that three of the men lifted off the cover to a large tank and they all gagged involuntarily as the foetid gases escaped from the farm's septic tank and to his screaming horror, four of the men grabbed Phillip by his limbs and threw him in. He closed his mouth just before he sank below the surface of the ordure but as the stinking contents enveloped him and entered every other orifice, his feet touched the bottom of the tank and he pushed himself up and almost sprang over the edge and out of the tank to lie blubbing on the hard ground, vomiting and then retching until the rasping burning in his throat overtook the discomfort of the clinging human waste. The men gave him a wide berth as they placed the cover back on the tank.

"We do not want to have to work with you tomorrow smelling like that. Get in the river and clean yourself fully, then we will lock you back in your hut. You should know that this kindness we show you is more than you deserve."

Still throbbing from the beating and sobbing at his humiliation, the Duncan boy crawled the twenty metres or so to the river bank and rolled into the shallows near the bank and scrubbed himself and his clothes which he painfully removed but at no stage did he feel clean and thought he never would. Any thoughts of anger and revenge were pushed down by the degradation of his situation and the need to get back to his hut, away from the pitying eyes of the farm labourers who he realised, despite their financial disadvantages, saw him as being the lowest form of mankind.

The following day, the lock on his door was drawn back as usual but he could not face leaving the hut and no-one came to make him do so.

He lay on his bed all day naked under the thin blanket, while his clothes lay damp in the corner of his room. He lay there in total despair at the acceptance that he would never be able to escape from this living hell and thought for the first time since he had been brought here, about what it meant and what it said about his life and himself as a person. He had truly been broken and only time would tell how he would rebuild himself.

While he remained surly and distant, Phillip had made the decision that he would be stupid to antagonise his captors any more. He also realised that trying to lull them into trusting him would also fail, now that he had played that card with such dire consequences. He decided to toe the line without ever over exerting himself and see out his time until his father got him out of here, as he surely would but he would never stop being alert to the possibility of making his own escape. As weeks turned into months, he began to accept and, although he would never admit it, even enjoy, the simplicity of his life and he even took pleasure in the effect his daily routine of working in the fields had upon his physical conditioning.

He was well fed, enjoying a variety of dishes cooked with fresh ingredients at which in the past, he would have turned his nose up if it had been offered him. The day off on Sunday became a real highlight, the value of its restfulness being accentuated by the hard work of the rest of the week. As the warm Spring evolved into the hot Summer, the farm workers and neighbours would have picnics down by the river, eating, singing, playing and bathing with their families and while Phillip did not join in with any of these activities, he sat some way away, basking in the warmth of the sun. He envied the simple pleasures that the others were enjoying and had, he realised, been denied him when he had been growing up.

On the really hot days he would swim in the river, the strong currents making even him, an excellent swimmer, have to really work to prevent himself being washed away. He got a huge sense of achievement being able to do something at which he excelled and he could enjoy it without worrying about having to come into contact with any of the others, of whom, he had found out, very few could actually swim and certainly none would venture from the shallow water near the river bank. Despite feeling something of a pariah at these occasions, he was inexplicably touched by the fact that, when the others started to eat, children from the different families would be sent to him with portions of food from their own picnics, which they would place next to him and then run off giggling. By making silly faces and bowing in an exaggerated manner in thanks to the children, they would linger and laugh with him a little longer each time and he would nod to their parents in a small concession of gratitude. Lying in his bed at night, he would think about these moments, chastising himself for gaining so much pleasure from such small gestures but looking forward to the Sundays more and more, with the emotional lifeline of human contact they offered.

It was on a particularly hot Sunday that he was lying under a tree, feeling too lethargic to even cool off in the water, when suddenly he became aware of shouting and screaming coming from the area where the families usually based themselves. Coming up on his elbows, he immediately saw the reason for the sounds of distress as one of the little girls, who had often brought him food, was being dragged by the current towards the middle of the river, where she would definitely be washed away. Her father was half running, lifting his knees to clear the water, then half swimming with a basic crawl stroke, limited in effectiveness by his thrashing straight arms and high head position causing his legs to drag. Reaching his daughter, he grabbed her with one arm and with the other grabbed the branch of a tree that was perpetually trapped near the middle of the river. It was obvious to Phillip that the danger was not over because the current was plucking at the little girl and it seemed unlikely the father would be able to hold on to her or the branch for much longer.

Fearing what would happen next, Phillip who was already standing downstream of the father and daughter, ran at an angle away from them into the river and started to swim towards the middle using a powerful crawl. As he turned to breathe upstream, he saw that the father could hold on no longer and the terrified little girl was bowling away on the ever increasing current.

With everything he had, Phillip drove his limbs faster and head down, until he intersected the line she was on and turned to look up as she crashed into his chest where he clutched her before turning onto his back and kicking for the shore. As he reached the shallows, a variety of hands took the little girl from him with shouts of hysteria and elation. One woman however was pulling at him frantically, which he could not understand until he realised it was the child's mother who didn't seem to be thanking him but frantically pointing back to the river where he saw the father, barely still hanging on to the tree branch and looking as if he would have to let go any moment soon. Exhausted, but realising the effect losing her father would have on the little girl, Phillip dragged himself to his feet and ran up beyond the level of the tree before entering the water again and began the slow agonising pull across the current towards the stricken father. As he neared the tree, he realised that the father was

Burim, the same giant of a man who had deposited him on his backside at his first mealtime and he groaned inwardly at the realisation that his task had just become even more difficult. With neither of them being able to speak the language of the other, Phillip found it impossible to explain to Burim what he needed him to do if he was to save him. To make matters worse, the panic that his situation had created resulted in the large Albanian letting go of the tree branch and clasping his huge arms around Phillip's shoulders, causing them both to sink below the surface. Unable to extricate himself from the potentially life ending clutches of this huge man, Phillip brought up his knee swiftly between Burim's legs, the resultof which caused him to immediately let go and bellow in pain as they both came to the surface. As he closed towards Burim again, Phillip kicked strongly with his legs to gain as much height as possible and punched Burim as hard as he could, knocking him unconscious before turning him on his back and kicking for the shore. Going under a number of times through the sheer effort of his exertions, at last they were both grabbed by the reaching arms of some of the other men who had waded out into the river as far as they dared. Once on the bank, Phillip flopped exhausted onto the grass where he drew huge gulps of air into his burning lungs. Eventually, he rolled onto his front and sat up to see that Burim had also recovered but was still struggling to breathe because he was being hugged tightly by both his daughter and wife.

  That evening while he was dozing outside his hut, still recovering but also enjoying the last of the evening sun, Phillip was startled to look up at the sound of footsteps and see the towering Burim standing over him, rubbing the fast developing bruise on his chin. Phillip's relief was palpable as the big man smiled and was joined by his wife and daughter and Guzim, who had obviously come along as a translator. The mother and the little girl hugged him while he sat unable to rise from his chair. Burim beamed and said something which Guzim translated as, "Burim says you have good punch for such a scrawny man."

  Extricating himself gently from the wife and daughter, Phillip told Guzim to pass on that he only saved Burim so that he could have the chance to hit him. Once translated, Burim laughed extremely loudly and put out his massive hand, which Phillip shook uncertainly but with a huge feeling of pride, that surprised him. Taking their leave, the mother and daughter kissed him and as they walked away Burim spoke a jumble of words before catching up with his family.

"What did he say?" Phillip asked the departing Guzim.

Guzim turned towards him. "Burim wants you to know that he will always be grateful to you for his own life but especially for that of little

Matilda. He say that when you first came here you smell of shit, now he believes you are starting to smell of lemons." Grinning as he walked away to catch up with the other three, Guzim did not see the huge smile that his last comments elicited from Phillip.

Suddenly, Phillip became aware of the others in the room looking at Dougie as he finished recounting his side of Phillip's story. He found it difficult to believe that all those memories of the last year had flashed through his mind in such a short time. He smiled inwardly at the surprise he felt, not for the first time, at the happiness he experienced in those last months of his captivity, when he became treated as one of the community and a feeling of acceptance and worth he had never felt before, had enveloped him. He was jolted back to the present by the sound of the door opening and two middle aged men entering the room. They sat at the desk that faced the window and indicated to the three brothers that they should sit in the three chairs facing the desk. The man sitting nearest the door then began to explain with a faint Welsh accent what was going to happen now.

CHAPTER 37

A Couple of Months Earlier

It was a Saturday, which would usually mean an early start to help prepare the Cricket square and other sports facilities that would normally be required for the weekly fixtures the students competed in at the school. But the school summer holidays meant that any work at the school could be completed in the normal working week. Having a leisurely breakfast, Rob suddenly realised that of late, not every waking thought had been about Duncan and how he had destroyed his life. He argued with himself about whether or not this was a good thing. Yes, it meant he was more relaxed, especially as his vendetta against Duncan was proceeding far better than he could ever have hoped. But what always nagged at him was the dread that forgetting about Duncan, even if only briefly, meant that he was forgetting about his girls and that filled him with horror and a gut clenching feeling of guilt. He repeated the vow to himself, that he would never forget them and would ensure that their legacy would be celebrated with the burgeoning reputation of the school.

While sitting in the kitchen they had once all inhabited and thinking about them and the days they had shared, he realised that it had been such a long time since he had been down to Grace Road to watch the Leicestershire Cricket team play, something he would sometimes do with the girls to give Carol a break and which they loved because of the treats they knew they would be given and the opportunity to play with the other kids in the outfield during breaks of play. Today they were playing Glamorgan in a three day game, which would add some extra bite to his conversations with Matt, who he thought he would ask to join him. Even as he was thinking these thoughts, his phone rang and he smiled at the coincidence of Matt contacting him.

"I was just thinking about you."

"Don't feel embarrassed, I am sure there are people all over the country who cannot get me out of their minds."

"Hopefully they all have access to some quality counselling. I was going to ring you and ask if you fancied going to the cricket today."

"Yeah definitely but can we make it this afternoon because the rest of the gang want us all to get together to discuss a development with the Duncans?"

"Oh, what's happened now?"

"Let's not talk about it over the phone. Can you meet in my office at 10.00am say and we'll discuss it then and go on to the cricket after?"

"Ok good idea and as it is basically Wales against England, the loser buys the drinks.

"Bring lots of money then. See you at ten."

As Rob approached Matt's office at 9.50, he was slightly surprised to hear a hubbub of conversation and checked his watch to find that he was early rather than late. As he walked in, the conversation stopped and there seemed to be an awkward silence as they all looked at him and Mick rather obviously seemed to fill the silence by asking Rob if he wanted a coffee, as he was about to pour himself another.

"Yes, you know how I like it. It looks as though you guys have been here some time, did I get the wrong time Matt?"

"No you are on time but there was something we wanted to discuss before you arrived."

"Really, now I am intrigued." Rob sat down and took his coffee from Mick who returned to his own seat. "So what is it you guys want to discuss that it is so important that you are willing to sit inside on such a lovely day?"

They all looked at Matt, who knew that what he was about to suggest would not go down at all well with Rob but it had to be said.

"Rob, for some time now we have all, at different times, been feeling uneasy about the direction that some of what we are doing has taken."

"How do you mean?" Rob asked warily.

"The whole idea of bringing down the Duncan Empire is one we support wholeheartedly but the growing area of concern for us, is the imbalance between what will eventually happen to Duncan as opposed to what will happen to his sons."

"Hang on a minute, you know that the original idea was to punish the boys for what happened to my girls and then for Duncan to suffer the collateral damage of having his own family taken away from him, just as I did mine." Rob was getting slightly agitated that what he had always dreamed of since that fateful day, was now being questioned.

"And that was what we all wanted to start with also. However, since the start with Operation Orchid, we have all I think, grown to realise that the boys are simply pawns in this whole business and the person who should suffer most should be Frankie Duncan himself."

"Pawns. They killed my girls. How..?"

"No, hear me out. It is apparent that for all his supposed claims of family being all important, he couldn't really give a hoot about his sons. Family is simply a symbol of the superiority he sees in his bloodline. He cares not a jot for the actual people who make up his family. He has made those boys into what they are today and we have seen from the way they have developed in Albania, that basically they are good people. You and I have always believed throughout our teaching careers that there is good in everyone and saw it as our job to find it and nurture it and that often involves giving people second and sometimes third chances and more. We think these boys deserve another chance and that we should concentrate our efforts on putting Duncan away for good."

"But those boys are the ones responsible for me losing my girls," Rob pleaded almost hysterically.

"You know we are not minimising the awfulness of that action but you know also, that if they had gone to court, they would have been done for causing death by careless driving and would likely to have received a sentence that ran in conjunction with their conviction for the robbery."

"You seem to be underplaying the fact that they robbed a building society and not to mention all the other crimes they have been involved in."

"No, we are not forgetting that but we know now it is the insidious effect that Duncan has on his sons that has led to them being who they are now. Haven't we always said that if you have a problem pupil in school, nine times out of ten you only have to look at their parents to find the reason?"

"So what are you saying? We should let the Duncan boys off scott free."

"Its hardly 'scott free' when we take into consideration the punishment they are going through in Albania, which is ten times the hardship they would have experienced in a British jail. But it's the fact that they seem to have turned their lives around that is making us feel most uneasy about what we are doing. Shouldn't we give them the chance to show that they are truly better people now? We can always hold the evidence we will have against them as a deterrent to any future misdemeanours and we will then be putting away the person who is truly most responsible for all the misery at the same time, Frankie Duncan."

Rob stood up from his seat slamming his mug of untouched coffee down on Matt's desk and looked around him. "And you all believe this is the way we should go?" They all nodded back at him. "Well sod you lot. Just as we are on the verge of achieving what I have dreamed of for over eight years, you want to pull the rug from under my feet. Well no! It's not happening. I won't have it and I am the one who finally decides what goes on here. That is the end of the matter," and with that he stormed out slamming the door behind him.

The others left in the room looked at each other sadly but not with any sense of real surprise because they understood that the dream that Rob spoke of had festered and grown within him since the day the girls were mown down.

Amira looked at her husband and touched his arm. He nodded and stood up. "Let me go after him." The others were relieved that someone other than themselves would try to find the right words to not just calm Rob down but more importantly, to comfort him. As he left the building, Hassan looked about and saw Rob sitting forlornly on the bench that looked across the school playing fields at the two smaller unicorns, being protected under the wings of the huge unicorn rearing proudly at the centre of the arch, rising over the gate posts either side of the entrance to the school. As he approached, he could see that Rob had been crying and asking if he could join him on the bench, he offered him a crisp white handkerchief, which Rob accepted wordlessly. The two men sat there silently for some time. Eventually, Hassan touched Rob gently on the arm and nodded at the gate.

"They would be so proud of everything you have achieved you know."

"But it won't bring them back will it?"

"No, it won't and neither will destroying the lives of boys who would likely be as innocent as your girls, if they had had a different father."

"But it just seems so unfair."

"It is unfair. But we don't change that by adding to the unfairness and punishing these boys for the sins of their father."

"But they need to pay. They are not children with no idea of the difference between right and wrong."

"Perhaps not but their boundaries have been warped by the influence their father has over them."

"So do you all think we should let them off?"

"They won't be let off. They have already suffered greatly this last year and we will monitor their future lives to ensure that the buds of goodness that have begun to emerge in Albania are maintained and the moment they stray out of line, we will possess the evidence to ensure they learn that they cannot escape justice. They will know that they are on a perpetual suspended sentence. You might remember Mr. Rob, that when I first came to see you after the terrible death of your family, we talked about the importance of seeking justice not revenge."

"Yes, I remember but I looked it up in your Quran where it says that you should gain revenge in direct proportion to the harm done to you."

"I think you know that you have read that totally out of context Mr. Rob but if you want quotes, I am a great admirer of someone a little more recent and who was not living in the context of what was acceptable in the seventh century when the Quran was written. Mahatma Gandhi said that, 'If we all take an eye for an eye, then the whole world will be blind.'"

"Hassan, you know that I owe you my life and if you tell me that I must do what you say then I will but it is not what I want."

"I know that. However, I cannot tell you what you must do. That has to be your decision and I know that whatever you decide we will all support you but it will grieve us deeply because we know that you will never sleep comfortably doing it your way because you are a good man and seeking revenge would not be the actions of that man. I will leave you to your thoughts and I will return to the others."

Rob watched and wished he could be half as good a man as the one walking away from him.

The 'A team', had been appraised of the conversation Hassan had had with Rob and sat gloomily discussing nothing in particular but unwilling to get up and leave, with the uncertainty of the next stage of their operation up in the air. When the door opened, they were relieved to see that Rob seemed calm and in control once more and even more relieved when he smiled at them and apologised for his outburst.

"You are some of the best friends a person could possibly have and without you I daren't think of where I would be now - although I think it was very sneaky sending Hassan to talk to me, knowing that it is impossible to refuse him anything. I desperately want revenge for my girls but I have always argued that the people least qualified to decide the fate of someone who has done something terrible to another human being, is anyone close to that human being. I know that you feel almost as strongly as I do about the loss of my girls but you are in a much better position to look at the situation objectively. So deep down, as much as it pains me to give up on my dream of revenge, I know that you are right to insist upon justice first and foremost. Tell me what you have in mind."

With only a relatively short time before the year would be up on the boys' captivity, which would lead to the provision of evidence for the police to carry out a prosecution, a way had to be found to collect enough evidence to convict Frankie Duncan as opposed to his sons, for whom they should have ample evidence courtesy of their father. Amira and Ronnie smiled at each other and put forward their idea that they felt would give them at least a chance of getting what they needed. With the agreement of the rest of the team, when the meeting broke up the two ladies stayed behind to begin the process of putting their plan into action.

The following day, with everyone having agreed upon their plan of action and being tasked with the different elements that would hopefully result in a positive outcome, Amira and Ronnie once again sat in their shared office. Preparing to make the phone call that would ultimately decide the success or failure of the whole plan, they were nervously reluctant because of the fear of being the one who tipped the fine balance onto the side of failure. They tossed a coin and as the loser of the time-old decision making mechanism, it was Ronnie who picked up her phone and rang the Brighton number. She was not surprised when a very wary sounding Arthur Robinson, immediately tried to assure her they had no more to discuss but relying on the courtesy and gentlemanly behaviour of the old butler on the other end, she was able to persuade him to listen to how the new proposition they were about to put forward, might well change his mind. Having listened to Ronnie with growing enthusiasm, the call was ended with him wishing them good luck and Ronnie excitedly waving an address based in Greece that she had just jotted down on a piece of paper. So far, so good. Now for the difficult bit.

The following Wednesday, a small, Asian lady and her taller companion dressed as the archetypal British tourists on a package tour to hotter climes, sat in Economy, sipping gin and tonics, while contemplating how their potential meeting in Greece, could lead to the fulfilment of their whole operation. With just their carry-on luggage, they were able to quickly navigate passport control and pick up the previously booked hire car, that would take them the short journey to the small village of Oropos, nestling in the hills near Piraeus on the Greek coast. Parking their hire car at their hotel, they dropped off their bags and freshened up. A short time later, they set out for their destination and after a few enquiries, were directed to a small but well maintained villa at the eastern edge of the village. Opening the gate and then moving through the neat and colourful garden, they looked at each other nervously because of the potential significance of this visit, before knocking on the door. It was opened by an attractive middle aged woman, dressed in a diaphanous kaftan and smiling as she greeted them with the words. "Ah you must be the ladies who the lovely Robinson told me to expect. Please come in."

CHAPTER 38

The boys had been brought to the courts from their three separate prisons and placed in separate cells so that they could not collude. But to the surprise of the boys themselves and the custody sergeant, both the defence and prosecution council gave their permission for them to be placed in a cell together. The pleasure and reaction to seeing each other again were put on hold, as DI Bright entered their cell with DC Smith to whom she introduced them. DI Bright was still coming to terms with the ease with which this had all fallen into her lap. Having received folders full of evidence relating to the Duncan boys' indiscretions, she was then contacted by Rob Price, who claimed that the Duncan boys had been in touch and were prepared to consider giving up their father should they be allowed to go free. How this had all come about was still a bit unclear to Susie Bright but she was not one to look a gift horse in the mouth, hence today's meeting.

"I understand that Mr. Price has explained to you that through much persuasion by him and the fact that two of you at least are now reformed characters apparently," she looked pointedly at Phillip who just sneered back at her, "we have no real interest in prosecuting you for the sins of the real culprit here, your father."

"So you are going to let us go then?"

"In truth, despite my better judgement, I have agreed to let you go under certain conditions but you would have to be prepared to give evidence against your father."

"You must be mad, we would never do that. Anyway he will get us out of this like he always does, don't you worry Missy."

"You really have not changed very much at all have you, Sonny?"

Realising that Phillip was having to stand up for their father on his own, Alex joined in. "Brad and I realise that what we have done in the past was wrong and we are prepared to accept the consequences of our actions but we aren't prepared to implicate our father, whatever his perceived wrongdoings."

"Mr. Price told me that he feared you might take that attitude. However, before you completely make your mind up, there is someone I would like you to meet." She nodded to DC Smith who called through the cell door that it should be opened. A few seconds after it swung back, a figure appeared at the door and walked slowly in, followed by a policeman they did not recognise, carrying a box that he deposited on the table in the room before leaving and pulling the door to behind him. The boys, as one, were slack-jawed in surprise as they recognised their old servant and much loved friend Robinson, who they had assumed was dead.

"Masters Bradley, Alex and Phillip, it is so good to see you again after all these years."

"But …how… we thought you were dead. Where have you been? What happened to you?"

"I have been living down in Brighton in a very nice bungalow I was able to afford on the money I had saved from my years working for your family. As to my supposed demise, your father made me agree to disappear and not contact you, with threats against me and my family."

"That's ridiculous, why would he do such a thing? These police have put you up to this haven't they? Why would you say such a thing about dad?"

"Firstly Phillip, in respect of believing your father, I am assuming that he told you I was dead. Well as you can see I am not. As to the why, he thought that I was a bad influence on you and that I was trying to make you 'soft' as he called it, by trying to keep you on the straight and narrow, just as your dear mother had asked me to do when she was forced to leave."

"What do you mean 'forced'? She left because she had an affair and ran off with another man."

"I can assure you that that is as far from the truth as it is possible to be but you don't have to take my word for it." Robinson looked at DI Bright, who again nodded to DC Smith, who again called to the duty sergeant to open the door. If they were surprised to see Robinson they were even more taken aback when they recognised the very smart and attractive lady standing at the door. It had been almost 20 years since they had last seen her but not a day had gone by when all three had not thought about her and they recognised her immediately. It was Phillip who went to her first, as he had always been so very close to her and as the eldest had spent more of his life in her presence. But just before he got to her he stopped and simply asked, "Mum why did you leave us?" echoing the troubled thoughts that were going through the minds of his two brothers.

Wiping tears from her eyes, she asked the boys to sit. "I never left you willingly. On the contrary, I was going to leave your father and take you with me."

"Do you really think we would want to live with your new fancy man?"

"There was no 'fancy man', that was a story your father made up to cover the true reason for me leaving."

"Mum, I don't understand."

"My beautiful boys. Myself and your father were falling out more and more about his, let's call them 'business dealings' and the way he was trying to turn you into clones of himself. You were lovely, intelligent, gentle boys but your father didn't want that. He had dreams of being head of a criminal dynasty and he saw me as a threat to that because you and I were so close and my influence was the opposite of what he wanted to achieve. Also I began to find out what kind of man he really was and some of the horrific things he had done to get where he was. I had been so naïve. Don't get me wrong, I knew he wasn't squeaky clean but there is a difference between sailing close to the wind and the violence and drugs and people trafficking I found out that your father was involved in. I told him that I wanted a divorce and that I would be taking you with me. He simply laughed in my face and informed me that he would gladly divorce me but that I would not have any access to you boys from then on. I tried to argue that no court in the land would let you stay with him rather than your mother. It was then he smirked and said that the courts would not be involved. I was to leave that night, alone."

"But why did you never try to see us again or contact us?"

"He told me that I had to go and live abroad and if I were ever to contact you boys again he would have you killed and I knew that by now he was spiteful and wicked enough to ensure, that if he couldn't have you, then no one would. I just couldn't take the risk and so I had to leave."

"Mum, what has happened to you? Dad has his faults but he would never do or say something like that." As Phillip pleaded his dismay of their mother, Alex and Brad looked at each other questioningly.

Robinson then coughed and asked if he might interject a moment.

"Boys, as much as I would never want to come between a son and his father, I have to tell you that what your mother says is correct and in respect of her trying to contact you, she sent you letters every week but your father would just throw them in the bin and in that box on the table are all those letters which I reclaimed from the rubbish bins without your father's knowledge." As he said this he stood and took from the box some of the letters and the boys recognised their mother's writing on the envelopes that were in three separate piles, each pile being addressed to one or the other of the boys. Quietly they opened some of them and began to read but soon realised that this was something they would want to do in private and at leisure and so reluctantly put them back.

"Mum, this only proves that you tried to keep in contact after running out on us but the rest of what you say cannot be true. Dad would never threaten to harm us, family is everything to him and if you hadn't had an affair none of this would have happened. You don't really care about us; you have your new family now."

"What do you mean? I live on my own and have never had any wish to have any family other than you boys."

DI Bright had listened uncomfortably to this heart-rending family tragedy and could see the uncertainty in the boys' faces. Contemplating what she should do, she stood up and started to slowly pace the room.

"I had hoped it would not come to this and I had promised your mother that I would only resort to this course of action if everything else failed."

"Please Detective Inspector, let me try once more."

"No, Mrs. Duncan, we are running out of time. I appreciate that you are trying to protect your sons but if we are to stop this trial then we have little time left and your sons need to be convinced of the real truth."

"What are you rabbiting on about? What sly underhand trick are you trying to pull on us now?" Again it was Philip who was dominating the boys' side of the conversation.

"You're right, it is a sly underhand trick but it is not being played on you but your father. Mrs Duncan I will leave you to explain to your boys what has actually happened since you arrived in the country."

"I think I need to start further back than that. Since being forced to walk away all those years ago, I have been living in Greece in a villa that belonged to your father and I and which he allowed me to use. Not through any generosity I should add but because it allowed him to keep an eye on what I was doing and ensure that I never tried to come back and see you. I have lived a quiet life but apart from missing you boys it has been a good life. I had no man to live with, as implied by your father. Oh, don't get me wrong, I have had the odd relationship over the years but I could never commit to any of them long term through fear what your father might do to anyone if they became too close. I had no need of a job as your father kept his word over providing me with an allowance but I volunteered at the local hospital and was popular in the village. The only thing I really wanted was the one thing I was denied by your father. Then some months ago, I had a couple of visitors who came to the villa and who, after their initial explanation of why they were there, stayed for three days. They explained to me what had happened to you and how far your father had sunk in terms of what he was prepared to do to achieve his dream of being head of a truly 'great' criminal dynasty. I was horrified at what had happened to you but these visitors explained to me that you had earned the right to a second chance but that they would need my help to ensure it would happen. I knew that deep down you were still the boys I had loved with all my heart, all those years ago and so I decided to risk everything and come to talk to you. I explained to them that there was a man in the village whose job it was to report back to your father about my every move but they assured me that they would deal with that. When they left, they informed me that they would contact me again when I was needed. I was dubious about whether these ordinary people could achieve what they were setting out to do but I began to dream that maybe they could help you, when, a few days later I was going around the wards in the hospital where I volunteered. I was amazed to see the man who I knew had been reporting back to your father about me, lying in one of the beds having apparently been involved in quite a nasty accident. He seemed to cower away from me at first but then to my huge surprise mumbled an apology to me and promised that he had now given up his previous employment with my ex-husband. While I could not condone what I guessed had been done to him, I began to believe that maybe these people could help you. Then a week ago a letter arrived at the village telling me it was time for me to come to England, with tickets for my flight included. I arrived yesterday and was met by the visitors to the villa who have been looking after me ever since. Last night they explained to me what I would have to do, in case you would not listen to my request for you to give evidence against your father, if you were to have any chance to escape going to prison.

    The opportunity to receive this 'chance' that Mrs Duncan alluded to, involved her sitting in a room with her ex-husband and talking to him. This had been arranged by the boys' lawyers who pre-warned, were ready to intervene the moment Duncan had seen his ex- wife walk into the court building. As he began to accost her, they suggested that it would be more seemly if any altercation between them was not witnessed by others and would be better held in a private room they could arrange for them, that was usually used for solicitors to talk with their clients. And so it was that an hour earlier, Duncan and his ex-wife had sat facing each other across a table, in a room on the first floor of the court building.

    "Before we play you a recording of your mother and father talking, I am firstly going to let you listen to a recording of your father in conversation with his second in command, Peter Fitzpatrick from some time back:

"Boss, we are going to have to send the evidence they are asking for if you don't want them to kill the boys. I know you don't want to send your sons to prison but at the moment it is better than the alternative we are being offered. We can perhaps do what we have done in the past and ensure that once the court case gets under way we get them found not guilty."

"Do you honestly think that this outfit we are up against now would let that happen?"

Reluctant to say it but feeling he should, Pete then mentioned the unmentionable, "The other alternative of course that they have suggested, is that you give yourself up, then the boys will be promised a reduced sentence."

"Are you insane? There is no way that I am going inside. The boys are young. If need be they can cope. To be honest, the more I think about it, the more I am concerned that any evidence I provide could link me to the crimes they have asked for evidence to convict the boys, so I will limit to the very basics, the stuff we give them, to ensure that I cannot be implicated."

"But Boss they have stipulated that if we don't give them exactly what they want then they will kill the boys anyway."

"So be it. Hopefully it won't come to that. Don't look at me like that. You know that I believe that family is everything but what that means in reality, is the family name is everything, the actual individuals within that family are not important. They are just representatives of that name."

"But you wouldn't want anything to happen to people you love."

"Pah, love, that is a concept not a reality. You and I are too big and ugly to believe in that. I say I love my boys and I do but that is because they are my family. I don't actually like them as individuals as they are weak and often stupid but they are only part of what makes a family great. It is not the individual members that make a family but what is achieved by the 'whole'."

"If you really believe that, why have we put so much effort in trying to find them over this last year?"

"Because don't you see, them being taken is a slight on my family's reputation. In all honesty, I was more angry about the loss of the orchids than the boys, because that was a direct attack on what they knew I loved most in my life and I will never forgive whoever took them and believe me they will suffer."

DI Bright stopped the tape there and explained that their mother did not want them to hear what they had just listened to and now gave them the choice of whether or not they wanted to hear the conversation between their parents? The already shocked boys silently looked at each other and nodded for the DI to carry on.

"You really don't have to you know?"

"No, we need to," whispered Brad.

DCI Bright pressed the 'play' button once more.

"What the hell do you think you are doing coming here now?"

"I couldn't let my boys go to court and not be there to support them.
I would have come the last time they were in court ten years ago but you assured me they were not going to be found guilty. How could you guarantee that by the way? Never mind, but I notice you are not offering such guarantees this time."

"Before we go any further stand up and lift up your blouse and take down your skirt. Don't worry, I have no interest in you like that but I do need to check that you are not wearing a wire. One can never be too careful." Lily Duncan did as she had been requested and felt nothing but loathing for the man who made her turn as he checked for any hidden audio devices. Having reassured himself he sat back down and once she had righted her clothing, she also sat.

"So are they going to get off this time?"

"It would seem very unlikely. The last time we were able to get to some of the witnesses and jurors but that has been impossible this time."

"So what I have heard about you losing it, is true then?"

"How dare you. Who told you that? Well, whoever it was will soon find out that I will be great again."

DI Bright had encouraged Mrs Duncan to get him angry and to play on his vanity, so that he would say more than he meant to. But after years of watching him turn into the monster he now was, she already knew the right buttons to push.

"So what's to stop me from telling the boys everything and getting them to reduce their sentences by giving you up?"

"They would never believe you. They are still devastated that you would leave them to take up with your lover, even if he didn't actually exist. Oh, by the way, I have since added a drop more fuel to the fire by telling them you now have a lovely little family of your own and have not given the boys another thought."

"You know that is not true. Did they not read the letters I have sent them every week?"

"No, it seems that the postal service around where we live is not what it was. I blame the government. However, going back to your question about speaking to the boys. Have you forgotten what I told you would happen, should you try to speak to them again?

"I couldn't care what happens to me, you have already made my life soulless but you would never do such a thing to your own sons."

"Would I not? It just goes to show how little you know me and that we could never have had any long term future together. If I thought that they would stop me achieving my goal I would get rid of them like that. Oh don't look so shocked, you have only yourself to blame. It was your benign influence that made them so soft and basically unsuitable for taking on the family name. So if anything, shall we say 'untoward', happens to them, it will be your fault in more ways than one."

"You disgust me and I am well rid of you. It sickens me the effect you are having on my lovely boys but I will never give up on them and while I will not risk their lives by contacting them now, I will be there, whatever happens, when they eventually realise what a lowlife you really are. And they surely will."

"Whatever. I think you credit them with far more intelligence than they actually possess. Now, when we leave this room you will go straight to the airport and get on the next available flight to that Godforsaken backwater in Greece and I never want to see or hear from you again, otherwise, as you know, it won't just be you who will suffer the consequences."

"Don't worry; I do not want to be in the same country as you, let alone the same room. You are so set on the idea that family is everything. Maybe it is to you but maybe it is love that is everything and one day the one will bite you because of a lack of the other."

"You talk utter rubbish. Now get out of here before you regret it."

CHAPTER 39

DI Bright turned off the tape and looked at the boys' mother and nodded in recognition of a difficult job well done. Recognising the effect of hearing their father talk about them in such an unfeeling way, Lily Duncan turned to the DI and whispered quietly, "Would it be possible for you to leave us alone together for a short while?"

"Well, it is a trifle irregular but I suppose all of this is." She ushered DC Smith from the room and left Mrs Duncan with her sons, who seemed totally shocked, having had everything they believed in taken away from them. In just under twenty minutes, Lily Duncan called DI Bright back into the room to talk with her and the boys, after which the detective rushed out to talk to the Prosecution lawyer.

An hour later, with everyone in place and the boys brought up from their original cells, it was time for the court case to begin.

As the boys appeared and entered the dock, Frankie Duncan was still coming to terms with the knowledge that Phil and Brad were actually alive and that the recording he had watched of Brad's supposed death and the lack of any recording of Phil had all been a hoax, designed to make him think that if he did not provide the evidence requested, all his boys would be killed. The anger he felt at being so cruelly and easily duped overwhelmed any feeling of utter joy he should now be feeling at the knowledge all his sons were still alive. All he could think of was how he was going to make the perpetrators of his pain and humiliation pay.

The confrontation with his ex-wife had disconcerted Duncan, having hardly given her any thought over these last twenty years or so but he was certain that a reminder of what would happen if she contacted the boys had persuaded her to get back to where she had come from. He was annoyed however, that the man he had on his payroll in Greece, had not contacted him to let him know she had taken a flight to England. He had been paid on a retainer all these years and had not done his job. When this case was over, he would have to send a message to Demetri that would remind all his other employees, what the consequences were of not doing their jobs properly. Seeing her again however, made him think what might have been, as she was still a very attractive woman and when they had first met she was a great deal of fun. But there was no way he could have her turning his boys into the people she wanted them to be, if he was to achieve his dream of having a crime dynasty that would be feared by everyone.

Duncan had been in court rooms before and was not interested in the seemingly interminable formalities that had to be gone through preceding the actual case itself. But from the moment he had taken his seat and allowed himself a lazy look around the court room, he had not been able to concentrate upon the proceedings at all but sat there seething at the sight of the man sitting opposite him on the other side of the gallery wearing one of HIS orchids. This had to be the person responsible for not just stealing his precious orchids but for all the problems that he had been experiencing over the last two years. It occurred to Duncan that he might have seen this person before but he could not for the life of him work out where. He certainly was not connected to any of the crime gangs that were established in England that he knew of.

As he kept staring in confusion at the man opposite, that person turned and looked straight at Duncan and to Duncan's mounting wrath, smiled at him, while bending to smell the orchid on his lapel. If this didn't confirm his suspicions, then what would? Barely able to contain himself, Duncan took out his phone and texted Pete to be ready for when the court broke and then to meet him in the foyer. He was contemplating whether he should call for more of his men just in case this person who had done him so much harm, was likely to have a support group of a large number of men, when suddenly something stirred in his memory. But no it can't be him. He was a nothing, totally insignificant. Was it possible that someone like that could have caused him so much pain? The more he looked, the more he became certain that the man sitting openly smiling at him, was the same loser who had confronted him in the toilets of this very court all those years ago, because his family had been wiped out in the bungled robbery escape. There is no way he could be the person behind all that had happened to Duncan but if he has access to my orchids then he will know who is responsible.

Frankie Duncan started to smile back at the man sitting opposite him, at the same time devising in his mind the world of pain he was going to deliver and he smiled even more as he realised that the answer to all his dilemmas was some loser, whose name he couldn't even remember and not some murky underworld figure who he should have any fear of. Oh, he was going to enjoy putting this no-mark in his place. Down in the court room, the boys kept looking up to the gallery for some semblance of reassurance from their father but he didn't seem interested in what was happening to them and was instead staring fixedly across the spectators' gallery.

Duncan's fascination with the man wearing the orchid was eventually interrupted by the clerk of the court calling for all those present to rise, and his honourable judge Lord Featherstone entered the court room.

"Your Honour, before we begin proceedings, my learned counsel for the defence and I, would like to approach the bench."

"This is going to be an awfully long trial I would imagine and I would rather not make it any longer than it needs to be but if you are both in agreement, then if you must, you must," the judge replied in frustration. The QC representing the three boys, Barrett-Jones, who had been an advocate for many years but had never experienced anything like he was about to be involved in and was more than apprehensive about making the upcoming suggestion to the judge, swallowed and explained to the judge that some new information had come to light and would it be possible for himself and the prosecution council to discuss it in his chambers.

"This is highly irregular at the very start of a major trial. Are you in agreement with this?" he directed his question towards the prosecutor, Sir Elwyn Stephens.

"Yes, my Lord I am."

Judge Featherstone banged his gavel and announced to the full courtroom, who were watching in fascination at what was happening at the front of the court, "Ladies and gentlemen, as often happens in such potentially complicated cases, the barristers for both sides wish to discuss a point of law before we begin and so there will be a short adjournment when you may leave the court room and an announcement will be made when we are ready to return. Clerk of the jury, will you please escort the ladies and gentlemen of the jury back to their jury room?"

A nod to the clerk of the court resulted in him announcing, "All rise." At which point the judge, followed by the Counsel for the defence and prosecution trailing behind, like two boys about to be dealt with by their headmaster, entered his chambers behind the bench.

Duncan was slightly confused as to what the hold up could possibly be about. He had tried all sorts of his usual tricks in trying to affect the outcome of the trial but he had been thwarted at every turn and he started to get even more worked up at the thought of who was probably behind his frustration. However, seeing the object of his anger rise from his seat in the gallery opposite and make for the exit of the courtroom he began to get excited. He was now about to have access to the person who, if he wasn't responsible for what had happened to him over the last few years, would at least know who was. Duncan slipped out of his seat and pushed past the other spectators, most of whom seemed to be happy to wait in their seats for the eventual start of the trial. Once outside, he could see that the man wearing one of his orchids had appeared on the other side of the gallery and was descending the staircase on that side, towards the ground floor. Duncan moved swiftly to the stairs on his side and not taking his eyes from the object of his chase, descended them two at a time. Pete had seen him from his position by one of the ornate pillars in the foyer and ran to meet his boss as he reached the bottom of the stairs. Duncan reached him just as he observed Rob push open the doors of the 'Gents', into which he disappeared.

"Boss, what's happened?"

"We are about to solve all our problems, Pete." Grabbing his henchman by the arm, he directed him towards the door where Rob had just disappeared, continuing their conversation on the way. "The person who is the key to all our problems has just gone into the 'Gents' but he won't be coming out on his own two feet."

"What do you want me to do to him boss?"

"Nothing, I want you and the boys to make sure we are not disturbed and I will take great pleasure in dealing with this myself."

"OK, but if you need us, just call out," Pete said as as he held the door for his boss and in closing it, positioned himself rather threateningly in front of the door while at the same time nodding across to Ernie and Pat.

"What took you so long? I thought you were never going to get here." Rob was leaning against a washbasin at the far end of the room. Duncan was slightly taken aback by the confidence of this man facing him but reminded himself who he was actually dealing with and how pathetic he had been the last time they met in this room.

"Oh, you must think you have been very clever but all that is about to end and I will soon get back all I had before and you will be nothing as you always have been."

"Is that right? And how long do you think it would take you to be in a position to grow these lovely orchids again for instance?" While saying this, Rob was gently stroking the flower on his lapel.

"Just for that alone you will never leave this room," and in a rage Frankie Duncan rushed at Rob who nimbly sidestepped him and as he came level, grabbed Duncan's arm, twisting it until he heard a crack, then used Duncan's momentum to hurl him face first into the wall upon which the urinals were situated, breaking Duncan's nose on contact and then watched him slide down the wall until he sat in the base of the urinals themselves. Rob enjoyed a deep feeling of satisfaction on two counts. One being able to give back to Duncan some of what he had received from him in this exact same place nine years ago and two, pride in being able to put into practice some of the self defence lessons he had been following at the School.

Duncan was literally stunned but was conscious enough to compute that this should not have happened. The last time they had met, this man Price had been putty in his hands. Come to that, surely Pete would have heard the commotion and checked that everything was ok. As if reading his thoughts, Price smiled at him.

"If you are waiting for some help from your goons, some of my friends have taken them away for a quiet chat, so it will just be you and me for now. Actually, it is the same friends who taught me how to do what I just did to you and any other bullies I might come across. It is odd isn't it, that in films, a fight like the one you just started would go on for ages but in real life of course, you are now in too much pain to attack again and also you are a coward and would only risk having a go if you had back up. But please, if you really want to, I would love to have the excuse to hurt you again."

"You have broken my arm and my nose you b*****d, I need an ambulance."

"Ah well, I think you might find that that is the very least of your worries. Up until now, we have merely been playing with you but now you are about to be totally destroyed. I have ruined your euphemistically called business and you are now going to suffer your greatest ignominy. You took away my family and now I am going to take away yours. This is not like some novel or film where the good guy suddenly comes to his senses and refuses to be as bad as the bad guy and lets him off, to allow his conscience be his punishment. You see, people told me that the pain of losing my family would get better, that the pain would gradually become less intense. But what people don't realise, is that the pain becomes less intense because you begin to forget what the subject of your loss looks like or sounds like and there are long periods of time when you suddenly realise that you haven't thought about them at all and that is the real agony, knowing that they have gradually slipped away from you. You would think that that would make me more, rather than less able to forgive and let bygones be bygones but you see, that is not what happens. I want to feel that pain so that I can conjure up their memories in an instant and not lie in bed at night unable to sleep because I feel that I have let them down, not just because I failed to keep them safe, but by actually unintentionally beginning to erase them from my memory, as if they were never actually there. So rather than do the decent thing and be the bigger man, I am determined to make you suffer in the same way."

"You are a weak man Price and a loser who has no family. I am a powerful and successful man whose family is still alive and who one day will be back with me. And from what I have just heard in the court, that day could be sooner than even I could have dreamed. You can enjoy this short period in the sun but in reality I have won again. You have not beaten me because you are a nothing, a Mr Average who could never truly harm a man like me. I will build my empire again, have my family back and you will still be a nothing."

"We will see about that. Oh, by the way. I am sure you remember having your bank account hacked to enable your ex-Cannabis Farm employees to be recompensed. It was a good idea to move your money to other accounts by the way but we have now found those accounts and have emptied them to enable us to pay restitution to your trafficked slaves and anyone else we can find to whom you have caused suffering."

The dark cloud that seemed to come over Duncan's features and the spluttering outrage he began to emit was interrupted, when at that moment Mick walked in, looked approvingly at the sight of Duncan sat in the contents of the urinals and said to Rob, "The court has just been called back into session. You ought to take your seat to see what the outcome of the adjournment is."

As they walked out of the toilets, Mick turned back to Duncan. "I will send in your friend Mr. Fitzpatrick to help you clear up your failure in the toilet-training department."

Duncan tried to make a threatening gesture with his arm but cried out in pain and looked down at the wet stain spreading across his trousers from the water in the urinal.

Having raged at his second in command for being useless, Duncan overcame the agony of his arm and had Pete give him his own overcoat to drape over the embarrassment of his wet crotch and made his way painfully to the court room. His arm could wait, while he found out what was happening to his sons. Sitting at the end of the row because the pain he was in precluded him from pushing to his original seat, Duncan looked up, then looked away immediately as Rob smiled at him and waved as if in greeting from the opposite gallery.

The clerk of the court once again announced the arrival of the judge and, after the usual formalities, Lord Featherstone addressed the court. "Ladies and gentlemen of the jury and anyone else with business in this court. Having spoken with both Counsels for the prosecution and the defence, information has come to my attention that has convinced me that this case cannot continue. The defendants should please stand."

The boys stood, not believing that this could actually be happening and joining hands listened as the judge announced, "You have been found to have no case to answer and you are hereby free to go without a stain on your character. Ladies and gentlemen of the jury, I thank you for your patience in this matter and you are also now free to go."

At that, the Clerk of the court announced 'all rise' as the judge stood, bowed slightly to the court and exited to his chambers. Duncan suddenly forgot the pain he was in and glared triumphantly across at Rob who, to Duncan's frustration and confusion, simply smiled back.

As everyone emerged from the court building onto the steps outside, Pete supported Duncan by his good arm and told him that a car would be around at any moment to take him to hospital.

"That's ok. I want to speak to the boys first when they come out and tell them I will join them for the celebrations when I have finished at the hospital and I'm also going to shove the sanctimonious claptrap back down the throat of that Welsh b*****d who will have to laugh on the other side of his face, now that I have my boys back. Take me over to where he is standing."

Reluctantly, because Price was standing with a large group that included the rather innocuous looking men who had given him and his own men a bit of a lesson in being a bodyguard earlier on, Pete guided Duncan over to where Rob and his friends were standing and much to Duncan's frustration were laughing and joking. "You see my boys are free and we will rebuild. People like you can never come out on top against people like me. You have had your little wins but ultimately I have triumphed and I can assure you that you will suffer for all you have done to me."

Rob gave him a look of utter disdain. "You once told me when I was at my lowest ebb and you had just taken advantage of that, before giving me a beating, that family was everything but you are wrong. It is love, whether it be that of your family or your friends that is everything. Friends are just as important as family and you have never really had any friends, just people too afraid to say no to you and now you have lost your family and your freedom, you will have nothing. Where you are going, there will also be some people who might have once pretended to be your friends but who, because of the way you have got to where you are, will be only too pleased to show you what they truly think of you."

"What are talking about, you can never be better than me. Yet more sanctimonious claptrap from a loser, which means nothing. You might think that you have destroyed my business but surely even someone as stupid as you can see I have got my boys back and we will be successful again?"

Duncan told Pete to help him up to his boys, who had just appeared at the top of the steps but was stopped in his tracks as he realised they were with his old butler, Robinson and even worse, their mother. How dare they all stare at him with that pitying look and he shouted, "Boys come here this instant," but looked on aghast as they turned from him and started to walk away. As he stood there watching them disappear together, he became aware that he was on his own in more ways than one, as he turned to see Pete scurrying away with his head down, as he passed DI Bright and a colleague, with three uniformed police officers approaching him on the steps. With a huge smile on her face, Susie Bright announced, "Mr Francis Duncan, you are under arrest for the following crimes, firstly……" Duncan didn't hear the rest, even though the DI continued with the list of charges through the howl of frustration that emerged from the crestfallen boss of the Duncan Empire. As one of the uniformed officers proceeded to place him in handcuffs, there was a further scream of pain, due to the policeman being totally unaware of Duncan's broken arm.

CHAPTER 40

It was a few days later that Rob, having previously found out where they were staying and having rung ahead first, drove up to the gates of Duncan Towers to find that the gates were wide open and there was not a security guard in sight. Driving up the long driveway, he thought back to the first time he had sat in a van outside this estate and waited to begin Operation Orchid. So much had happened since then. Had it all been worthwhile and had it improved anybody's life? He would like to think it had, not least all the people that had been trafficked by the Duncans but were now free. He hoped also, that he too had improved as a person. Certainly he hoped that the purpose of his visit today, would reinforce for him that his eventual actions, admittedly guided by his wonderful friends, would restore his faith in the idea that it is possible for everyone to show, that beneath everything, we are all basically good but sometimes we just need the opportunity to prove it.

Climbing the steps to the front door, his need to ring the bell was precluded by the door being opened by Lily Duncan, who smiled, before hugging him and telling him how grateful she was to him for saving her sons, firstly from prison but more importantly, from their father's clutches. She showed him into the lounge where the boys were sitting nervously awaiting his arrival. Mrs Duncan explained that all her ex-husband's men and all the staff, had cleared out the moment they had heard what had happened to their boss. Then to his surprise and delight, Arthur Robinson, whom Mrs Duncan explained had insisted on staying on to help, entered the room and asked if Rob would like any tea or coffee which he declined, before taking a seat facing the four of the Duncan family, who were sitting together on the giant sofa that dominated the room.

"Is this where you are going to live now?"

"No, we are here temporarily until we sort things out. None of us have any wish to stay here any longer than we have to but even if we wanted to, DI Bright has told us it is likely to be confiscated as part of the proceeds of crime order that has been served on my ex-husband. That of course, all depends upon whether he is found guilty but all the advice I have been given is that there will be nothing for the boys when all this is over. In all honesty, Mr. Price, we wouldn't want it anyway. We have all agreed that we have had a lucky escape and we know that we owe this to you and your extraordinary compassion and we would like to thank you."

Alex then stood and looked Rob in the eye, took a deep breath and began to say what he knew was going to be one of the hardest things he would ever have to do, but the other boys had agreed that it was necessary, if they were to move on. "Perhaps not for us but for you, this all began that day when we killed your wife and daughters. There is nothing we can say that will put that right and we have all been haunted by it ever since, as I know you have but probably a hundred times more."

Brad could see how upset his brother was becoming and pulled him quietly down to the sofa as he stood and continued the theme of what they had earlier agreed to say to Rob. "We have never intentionally hurt anyone and it is only in retrospect that we realise how naïve we have been, to kid ourselves that the business we were involved in with our father, was doing anything other than destroying lives. When we hit your family on that zebra crossing, it was never our intention. It was truly an accident but it became so much more when, immediately after, our sheer selfish fear for our own futures made us drive off. We can never apologise adequately for what we did but if it is any consolation at all, we have agreed that we will spend our futures trying to make up for our pasts."

Rob looked pointedly at Phillip. "Does that go for you too?"
The eldest of the Duncan boys shuffled with embarrassment in his seat, realising that this man, with every reason to hate them, saw him as the potential problem. "I am aware of what you must think of me, especially as I now know how the last year has affected my brothers, in contrast to the way I reacted. I am ashamed to say that as the oldest I am more like my father than anyone and it will take me longer to shake off the years of venom he will have dripped into me. But as the oldest, I also had longer to build a special bond with our mother and now knowing how she has been treated, I am determined to spend as much time with her as possible and try to make her proud."

Rob nodded and inwardly rejoiced in the decision he had made to listen to Matt and the others, about following what had once been his long-held belief in giving everyone more than one chance and that there was good in everyone. Even as he thought this, he tried to come to terms with the idea that this would mean that Duncan himself should be given those chances also but decided that was a moral maze he wasn't bright enough to compute on his own. The long silence that allowed him this thinking time, was in truth an opportunity for him to regain his composure, as he had been quite touched by what the boys had said and talking about the day his girls had died always made him choke up.

"This conversation was meant to be so very different a month ago and was meant to take place when I visited you in prison. But people far better than myself persuaded me, that following the way you turned your lives around while in captivity and the affect on you of the overbearing influence of your father, you should be given the chance to try and redeem yourselves. The second thing in your favour, was your decision to give evidence against your father which I know could not have been easy. But I am ashamed to say that, not only did he need preventing from creating further misery for so many people, I also needed someone to suffer for what had happened to my family. Further evidence of my own weaknesses, is the fact that we still have all the documents needed to put you away should you ever return to your old way of life. But I trust they will never be needed. On a more positive note, do you know how you intend to go on from here, without the financial support of your father?"

"I am going to return to Albania and I have already contacted farmer Bektashi who has agreed to take me on as a foreman on his farm. I also have some money put aside, not a lot but enough so that I can invest in some more up to date equipment that will aid my plans to make the farm a real success."

As Alex finished explaining his future Brad took over. "I too shall return to Albania, there is someone who I want to spend time with and I intend to help develop the facilities for the children and young people in the area." Being more aware of Alex's situation than perhaps Alex knew, Rob smiled and nodded approval before turning to look at Phillip but it was his mother who spoke. "Phillip wishes to come and live with me in Greece, away from the malign temptations of some of his old acquaintances and we will work together in the hospital where I already work."

Rob looked around at them all and felt some satisfaction that maybe more good had come out of this whole situation than he could ever have dreamed.

"On the basis of what you have said, I am truly delighted that you have such positive plans to move forward and I would like to help you. To that end I intend to give each of the four of you £100,000 to allow you to set yourselves up in your new lives." All four looked at him aghast at a generosity they did not feel they deserved. "There is however one small condition."

"After such generosity we would agree to almost anything."

"I need you to let me have your "Harold" rings for a few days, to have the 'H's" removed as a reminder of your past lives and one of which represents the day my family died."

All three boys were surprised that Rob even knew about the "Harold" rings but were more than happy to forget their past and it was Phillip who replied. "That is no problem but rather than put you out, we can arrange for the removal of the 'H's. You have our word."

"I really do trust you on this, to do as you say but it will provide me with some catharsis if I can be allowed to have this done." Rob did not wish the boys to know the true reason for him wanting to deal with the rings. Better that some things were left unsaid.

Having been given the three rings, Rob got up to leave and waved away the gratitude for something they could never have expected and certainly did not feel they deserved. "I just hope that you make a success of your lives and appreciate how lucky you are to have family to share it with."

Rob was met at the door by Arthur Robinson, who thanked him for rescuing this family and when asked what he would do now, he replied with a huge grin on his face, that he would be going to Greece to see out his days with Madam Duncan and Master Phillip.

CHAPTER 41

It was a beautiful summer's morning as Rob drove up to the gates of Castle of HOPE School, on the last day of the summer holidays. There were just a few tasks to complete to ensure that the school would be ready for a smooth start to a new academic year and all the promise that had to offer. As he drove in, he still found it strange not to see the large greenhouse in the corner of the grounds, where the Paphiopedilium Rothschildianum orchids had been tended. When Mateo had suggested that the orchids should be returned to Kinabalu as yet another attempt to right the wrongs created by Frankie Duncan, it had been an easy decision to agree. Once they were gone, there was no longer any need for the greenhouse and it had been taken down and sold some months ago.

Having parked his car, he thought, as there was no-one else around, that he would take advantage of the quiet and went to sit on his favourite bench that had the uninterrupted view of the entrance gate and its three unicorns. He was at peace with himself.

As he looked at the three statues, he hoped that if his girls were looking down on him, they would know that he had done all he could, to not only get justice for them but ensure their memory lived on through the legacy of the school, whose reputation reflected the work it was doing, to give young people a real chance in life. He hoped too, that they would look at him and see that he had become a better person and be grateful, as indeed he was, for the wonderful friends he had around him, who were responsible for all the good that had come out of that tragic day, nine years ago. He knew that if it wasn't for them stopping him from gaining revenge on the sons of Duncan, rather than Duncan himself, he would be no better than that man who epitomised real evil and what would that have made him?

So lost in thought was he, that he hadn't noticed that Hassan had arrived and had been standing looking in the same direction. They acknowledged each other and Hassan asked permission to join him. Nodding assent and smiling at the anachronisms of life, Rob reminded his friend. "Well, we seem to have been here before."

"Indeed we do."

"I can never thank you enough, not for the first time, for persuading me to see sense."

"Mr Rob, it is I who will always be in your debt."

"How on earth do you work that out?"

"You gave me something that I could never give you. You gave me back my family, something for which I will always be ready to pay you back with my life. But Mr. Rob, while I can never give you back your family, I think I can help you with their memory."

"What do you mean?"

As Rob asked the question, Hassan put his hand in his jacket pocket and pulled out a pristine folded handkerchief which he handed to Rob, with the request that he should open it up. When he did so, Rob gasped and stared unbelievingly at the locket that lay there, with the engraving of a Welsh dragon, that he had thrown in the bin, what seemed like a lifetime ago.

"But how....?"

"That does not matter. What does matter is that you fought and succeeded to get justice for your family. That locket deserves to be in only one place. Please allow me to place it around your neck."

Rob could not reply immediately as his throat constricted at being reminded of the fear of never seeing his family again, being diluted somewhat by what his friend had done for him. With the locket around his neck, he opened it to look at the photo inside and read once more the inscription.

"To the man we love more than anything in the world. So that what you love most will be always close to your heart."

With tears in his eyes, he turned to Hassan and clasped his hands in his own. "Nobody could have brought my family back to me but you did give me back my own life and the ability to ensure that my girls' lives have allowed others to excel above and beyond what might have been possible, both through the school and the freedom gained by so many, with the destruction of Duncan's empire."

They both looked up as a police car pulled up in front of the school and DI Bright climbed out and walked towards them. Hassan stood, bowed to the DI and gave his compliments, asking her to excuse him.

"You have some lovely friends," she offered, as she joined Rob on the bench.

"Yes, I know I am very fortunate but to what do I owe the pleasure of your visit Detective Inspector? Please don't tell me that Duncan has escaped?"

"Oh no. He is well and truly put away, probably for the rest of his life and between you and me, he is not enjoying it one little bit."

"I thought these crime lords were supposed to lead the life of luxury in jail."

"Don't believe everything you see on TV Mr. Price. Duncan has the added problem of having upset many of the people he is sharing his new residence with over the years and believe me, these are the sort of people who can hold a grudge. Add to that the fact he no longer has any financial back up to help feather his nest so to speak, means that he is in a very unpleasant place in more ways than one. You wouldn't by any chance know how all this eventually fell into our lap would you Mr. Price?"

"Me? I am just an ordinary school caretaker. How would someone like me have the skills or resources to do such a thing Detective Inspector?"

"I think you do a very good job of flying under the radar Mr. Price but as we have already agreed, you also have some very good friends and from the moment I met you, my own career has benefited greatly."

"I…"

"No need to say any more. But what I will say is that, whoever was responsible for bringing down Duncan's empire has done society a huge favour and it would be a shame if the skills they possess were not to be utilised again, whoever they may be."

"It all sounds a little far-fetched to me but would you really sanction the vigilante activities you are suggesting DI Bright?"

"Normally I would say no, because vigilantes are rarely much better than the people they are trying to bring down but in this instance, with the compassion that has been shown to Duncan's three sons, even if I wouldn't necessarily have agreed with it, it shows that the person or persons who were responsible for bringing Duncan down, actually have some scruples and principles that overrode any desire for vindictiveness."

"I guess we will never know Detective Inspector."

"Actually it is now Detective Chief Inspector but you are right, some of us will never know but that doesn't stop us hoping that maybe this isn't the end of the story."

"Congratulations DCI Bright, I am so pleased that 'you' are no longer under the radar and that your abilities have been recognised."

"Well, I have whoever was responsible for providing the evidence that brought down Duncan for that. Either way Mr Price I wish you a happy life and thank you."

"For what exactly?"

"Oh, I'll leave you to decide on that." The newly promoted DCI walked away to her car and waved, as the rest of the 'A Team' came out to join Rob, carrying picnic baskets and bottles. They waved back as she drove away from the school.

"What did the lovely DI want?" Ronnie asked as she started to lay out the picnic they had brought out.

"Actually the lovely DI is now a DCI."

"Wow, good for her, she deserves it. Up the sisterhood I say and at the same time 'up' ex- detective Grey. Is that what she came to tell you?"

"No, to be honest I think she came on a fishing expedition."

"Did she catch anything?"

"Actually I don't really know." As they tucked into the food the school cook had prepared, they sat in the midday sunshine, enjoying the feeling of mutual satisfaction of a job well done. Looking again at the unicorn statues on the entrance gate, Rob nodded to them and raised his glass. "Since I lost my girls I can honestly say that I have been truly blessed, to have had you as my friends and so I raise a toast to you all. To friends!"

They all joined the toast then Matt pointed at the gate and said, "It's funny you should say that but not a lot of people know the answer to this. What is the collective noun for more than two unicorns?"

To his delight none of them knew but when he told them, for the first time he could remember, nobody groaned. They all turned and raised their glasses towards the gate and toasted in unison.

"A blessing of Unicorns!"

Printed in Great Britain
by Amazon